KELCIE MURPHY
and the ACADEMY for the
UNBREAKABLE
ARTS

TOR BOOKS BY ERIKA LEWIS

Game of Shadows

ERIKA LEWIS

KELCIE MURPHY
and the ACADEMY for the
UNBREAKABLE
ARTS

STARSCAPE

A TOM DOHERTY ASSOCIATES BOOK • NEW YORK

This is a work of fiction. All of the characters, organizations, and events portrayed in this novel are either products of the author's imagination or are used fictitiously.

KELCIE MURPHY AND THE ACADEMY FOR THE UNBREAKABLE ARTS

A Starscape Book
Published by Tom Doherty Associates
120 Broadway
New York, NY 10271

www.tor-forge.com

Library of Congress Cataloging-in-Publication Data

Names: Lewis, Erika, 1968– author.
Title: Kelcie Murphy and the academy for the unbreakable arts / Erika Lewis.
Description: First Edition. | New York : Starscape, Tom Doherty Associates
    Book, 2022. | Series: The academy for the unbreakable arts ; 1
Identifiers: LCCN 2021039451 (print) | LCCN 2021039452 (ebook) |
    ISBN 9781250208262 (hardback) | ISBN 9781250208255 (ebook)
Subjects: GSAFD: Fantastic fiction.
Classification: LCC PS3612.E96455 K45 2022 (print) | LCC PS3612.E96455
    (ebook) | DDC 813/.6—dc23
LC record available at https://lccn.loc.gov/2021039451
LC ebook record available at https://lccn.loc.gov/2021039452

Our books may be purchased in bulk for promotional, educational, or
business use. Please contact your local bookseller or the Macmillan Corporate and
Premium Sales Department at 1-800-221-7945, extension 5442, or by email at
MacmillanSpecialMarkets@macmillan.com.

First Edition: 2022

Printed in the United States of America

0 9 8 7 6 5 4 3 2 1

For Timberlake.
I'll love you forever.

KELCIE MURPHY
and the ACADEMY for the
UNBREAKABLE
ARTS

No one was ever supposed to find her.

Her mother's magic and father's sacrifice made sure of that.

But they did.

And she's about to set the Otherworld on fire.

1

KIDNAPPED!

THERE WERE NO seismic quakes, horrendous storms, nothing suspicious at all to warn Kelcie Murphy that she was about to unleash the greatest evil the world has ever known. Only a field trip to the Boston Museum of Fine Arts.

She'd been suddenly moved back to Boston last week, to a group home as miserable as the last nine, and it was her first day at yet another new school.

The bus ride was filled with the usual awkward smiles. Kelcie did her best to remain invisible, choosing a seat in the very back, and slinking down, pretending like she was asleep.

A slimy spitball struck her nose.

The boys across the aisle laughed, waving at her, trying to get her attention.

"Hey . . . Red?" one of them called.

Kelcie wiped the spitball off with her sleeve, hoping they'd move on to someone who cared, but they didn't.

A wet straw poked her cheek. "Hey. I'm talking to you. What's your name?"

"Asher, you're so disgusting." A girl with brown pigtails and flower overalls in the seat in front of Kelcie glanced over her shoulder, rolling her eyes. From the smirk on her face, Kelcie could tell she didn't actually find him disgusting in the least. She spun around, smiling. "Your name's Kelcie, right? I was behind you when Mr. Katz took attendance."

Kelcie nodded. She pressed her sliding sunglasses up her nose, leaning the back of her head against the window, hoping the cool glass would ease the pounding in her skull. Kelcie's head hurt, all the time. A dull ache that never went away. Bright lights and stress made it exponentially worse. Before tests, her eyes always felt like they were going to pop out of their sockets. It was why she never did very well in school. The pain made it hard to concentrate on anything but wanting it to go away.

"Sinusitis," the first doctor had said.

"Vertigo," the next diagnosed.

The last doctor was a different kind. He told her it was all in her head. Basically, she was nuts. After that, Kelcie stopped complaining.

"I'm Jenna. This is Susan."

The blond girl next to Jenna saluted.

"I like your jean jacket. Looks vintage," Jenna said, sliding into a gasp. "And that necklace. Can I see it?"

She reached out to touch Kelcie's most prized possession. The necklace was the only thing of importance she had on her the night she was found. It was nothing special. A simple silver charm, a branch from a tree, but it was the only link to her past.

Kelcie recoiled.

Nobody was allowed to touch it.

Jenna took the hint. She lowered her offending hand, giving Kelcie an unwanted sympathetic smile. "Sorry. Um . . ." she hummed. "Want to be in our buddy group? We have room for one more. Has to be three."

"No, thanks."

"Why not?" Susan asked. "Someone already ask you?" Her expression was one of extreme disbelief.

"No." Kelcie looked out the window at the piles of dirty snow.

"Then why not?" Jenna sounded insulted.

Kelcie looked back at her. The truth was that for Kelcie,

friends never stuck. They found out she was in foster care and lived in a group home, or worse, their parents did, and then they blew her off. Said crappy things behind her back. That hurt way worse than not having friends.

So she lied. "I like being alone."

KELCIE WAS THE last off the bus, the frigid air seeping through her jean jacket and hoodie. As she slung her backpack higher on her shoulder, a woman fell in step behind her.

Kelcie glanced over her shoulder, seeing a silver BOSTON's FINEST patrolman's badge on the woman's lapel. Snow-white hair in a bun, a baseball cap, her hand gripping the top of a baton, the cop tossed Kelcie a lopsided sardonic grin that raised the hairs on the back of her neck. Police gave her the heebie-jeebies. Grilled for hours more than once for things she didn't do, and a few things she did, Kelcie never took it as a good sign when they came too close. She picked up the pace, scooting around bodies until classmates surrounded her.

The museum was busy and loud, with loads of parents with strollers and other classes roaming around. Kelcie slowed her pace, walking several steps behind the rest of her classmates, hoping they'd forget she was here.

"Stay with the group," someone called from up ahead.

She hung her thumbs on her backpack strap and stared at the blue veins running through the polished white marble floors as they jolted up a few flights of stairs, through an echoey muraled rotunda, and into a room that transported them into ancient times.

There were Egyptian pharaoh statues, chiseled stone tables with hieroglyphics, cabinets of jewelry from ancient Greece and Rome. It was all nice enough, but what Kelcie found in the next room was way more interesting.

Shields, swords, spears, knives, and staffs hung on the wall, all at eye level, all begging to be touched. Kelcie checked to make sure the room was empty, then ran her finger over the grooves on the pommel of a long sword. The placard said it was Viking.

Another glance over her shoulder told her she was still alone, her classmates' conversations and laughter wafting from the other room. The coast was clear. Kelcie set her backpack down. A thrill ran through her, shifting her pulse into overdrive as her fingers hovered over the grip. She knew she shouldn't touch it. Knew she would probably get caught, but that never stopped her before. Her lips curled into a mischievous grin as her fingers wrapped around the cold metal grip. The steel blade was so heavy it took two hands to lift the sword off the rack.

She lunged, thrusting the tip at a round wooden shield, careful to stop before it struck, then pivoted, taking a wild swing, almost cutting Elliott Blizzard's head off.

Kelcie dropped the tip of the sword, stabbing the marble. "What are you doing here?"

Elliott was Kelcie's assigned social services caseworker. She only heard from him for two reasons: she was moving again, or she did something wrong. It had only been a week ago that he brought her to Boston. She had a bad feeling this wasn't another one of those visits.

He wasn't in his usual navy-blue suit. He was dressed entirely in black, black turtleneck, black pants, as if he were going to rob a bank. All he needed was a black ski mask.

He frowned, taking the sword and returning it to the rack. "We have a serious problem and by we, I mean you."

His spiked dark hair and thin brows lifted on the word *you*.

Dread weakened Kelcie's knees. She was in trouble, but why? How? It had only been a week! "What problem?"

The temperature felt like it dropped ten degrees as the police officer from earlier stepped into the room.

"You're going to need to come with us," she said.

"Why?" Kelcie backed up, bumping into the shield.

The cop used two bony fingers to pull off Kelcie's sunglasses. The fluorescents hit her like a bolt of lightning. Kelcie blinked, wincing, waiting for the explosive pain behind her eyeballs to settle down, but her nerves only made it worse. She looked up through hooded lids at the officer, finding intense black eyes glaring down at her, so dark in fact Kelcie couldn't see pupils.

"Can I have those back, please?" Kelcie reached for them.

The cop shook her head, putting them in her pocket. "The woman who runs your new group home, a Mrs. Belts, reported her wallet and several pieces of her jewelry missing this morning."

"Mrs. Belts?" The heavy-set woman hadn't said two words to Kelcie since she moved in. This made no sense. Kelcie shoved her hands in her sweatshirt pocket. "She's wrong."

The officer picked up Kelcie's backpack, sliding the strap over her shoulder, like she was going to keep it. "You need to come with us."

"Why? I didn't take anything!" The last time something like this happened, Kelcie went willingly, was acquitted, but still ended up in juvenile hall until Blizzard could find another place for her to live. She could run. In the crowded museum, she could easily lose the cop and probably Blizzard, but if she did, Elliott would never bail her out again. He would abandon her, like her parents did. She couldn't afford to lose him too.

Jenna and Susan bopped into the room, giggling. They sobered when they saw Kelcie cornered.

"What do we have here?" Susan goaded.

"Should I get Mr. Katz?" Jenna asked.

The cop pulled a pair of handcuffs out from her belt, sending Jenna and Susan bolting out of the room. Kelcie crossed her arms, hugging herself, shaking her head.

"Those won't be necessary, Officer Grimes, will they, Kelcie?" Blizzard asked, setting a firm hand on her shoulder. "Come. Now."

Kelcie nodded. "Okay."

With Kelcie sandwiched between Blizzard and Officer Grimes, they went down the stairs, but turned right, heading farther into the museum.

"The exit is that way," Kelcie said, shooting her thumb over her shoulder.

"The car is parked in the back. We're going out by way of the basement," Grimes explained.

That sounded ominous. Was Mrs. Belts waiting for her with some made-up evidence? Kelcie ground her fingernails into the back of her clasped hands in her pocket. She was going to end up at the station, or worse, juvenile hall again.

Every school group they passed gawked. Fingers pointed. Teachers shifted their students, pressing them against the walls, moving out of the way.

Humiliated, her head aching beyond belief, Kelcie raised the hood on her sweatshirt and lowered her eyes to the floor, hoping that, at the very least, she would be able to leave Boston. Having been abandoned here, Kelcie should've known bad luck would follow her the minute she returned.

It wasn't until Officer Grimes shouldered an exit door with a sign on it that said *Employees Only* that Kelcie's internal alarm bells first pinged.

"We're not supposed to be back here. Why can't we go out the front and walk around the building?"

"It's fine, Kelcie." Blizzard tossed her a placating smile. "Just do as you're told."

Kelcie had no reason *not* to trust Elliott Blizzard. He had never lied to her before. In fact, he was the most frustratingly honest person in her life. *So, you were abandoned,* he said the day they met. *You will not only survive this, but be stronger for it.* Some of that was true. Kelcie learned to take care of herself, never to depend on anyone for anything, but that didn't mean she liked it that way.

Grimes padded along with authoritative, determined steps, as if she knew this museum inside and out. She led them through a maze of short corridors, passing several small offices, garnering confused stares from museum staff.

"Excuse me!" a man called as they rushed by. "Are you lost?"

he hollered. His chair squeaked, swiveling, and his footsteps plodded after them, but not before Blizzard forced Kelcie to take a sharp left, and then another into a supply closet.

"We're going the wrong way," Kelcie exclaimed, stopping. "Wha—"

Grimes slapped a hard, frigid hand over Kelcie's mouth as Elliott hoisted her off the floor. Stunned and panicked, Kelcie thrashed, yelling muffled cries for help, but the man's steps passed right by.

"We're not going to hurt you," Elliott whispered into her ear.

Officer Grimes' frosty breath tickled her other ear. "Unless you don't cooperate."

Was she being kidnapped? Who would pay ransom for *her*? The only person who cared if she lived or died for the past eight years was the one holding her hostage! Maybe this was a nightmare. She would wake up on the bus, covered in spitballs, with the word *loser* scribbled in permanent marker on her forehead. That had to be it . . . but still.

Kelcie struggled against Blizzard's impossible hold when Grimes poked her head out the door. They swapped hands over Kelcie's mouth as Grimes gave the signal that the coast was clear, and then they were on the move.

Across the hall from the closet was another door. Heavier. Thicker metal with a plate beneath a tinted window that said *KEEP OUT.* Grimes plowed through it with gusto. As soon as Blizzard was on the other side of the door, he kicked it shut, and hoisted Kelcie over his shoulder, pinning her legs.

Beyond the door was a steep stairwell. The only light came from fluorescents in the hallway seeping through the door's tinted window, leaving the landing and a few of the descending steps visible in haunting, muted shadows. Beneath that, nothing, only pitch black. Nightmare or not, Kelcie wasn't going down there!

She screamed. The high-pitched sound bounced off the walls, echoing in the cavernous stairwell. Twisting, flipping, bending, beating his back, Kelcie tried every imaginable way to break free, but failed miserably. Blizzard was too strong and refused to put her down. She was trapped.

"Scream all you want. No one can hear you now . . ." Grimes laughed, pulling out a flashlight as they started down into the bowels of the museum. With every stifled scream from Kelcie, Elliott only jogged faster until the stairs ended.

A tubular light turned on. Motion detected, Kelcie assumed. They were in a windowless tomb enclosed by concrete walls that looked built to stand up to a nuclear attack. It was dead quiet except for faint squeaks and scratching Kelcie suspected were rats running along the pipes spanning the low ceiling.

They stopped outside a huge round door made of reinforced steel at least two feet thick with a combination lock and large wheel. A vault, and the door was ajar.

Kelcie wrestled so much, Blizzard finally set her on her feet, but didn't let go. "Kelcie! Calm down!"

"Get control of her," Grimes snarled.

Kelcie swore she saw fangs! *This isn't real! It's impossible!* She stomped on Elliott's shiny black leather shoes, grinding her heel into his toes. His grip loosened enough for her to rip free. She took off running, but only made it to the bottom of the stairwell before Elliott somehow raced around her, blocking her path.

Kelcie held her hands up, backing down the stairs. "How did you do—?"

Blizzard cut her off, spinning her around, grabbing hold of her upper arms. "Listen to me. We can do this the easy way or the hard way. But I promise that if you do what you're told, you will have the answers you've been looking for since the day I met you. You *will* find out who your parents are."

Kelcie stretched, trying to get him off of her. "You're lying. If you knew who my parents were, you would've told me a long time ago. You know how important that is to me!"

"Maybe I would or maybe I wouldn't . . ." Blizzard let that sink in. "Maybe you've been kept clueless for a reason."

Kelcie's heart sank into her shoes. This was a nightmare . . . but what if it wasn't? What if . . . ? It didn't matter. There was no way she was going into that vault, not without a fight.

Blizzard must've seen the mutiny in her eyes, because the next thing she knew he was hefting her off the ground again. He suffered scratches, brute force pummeling, anything Kelcie could inflict on him, but it wasn't near enough to stop him from carrying her back down the damp tunnel, over the threshold, and inside the vault. Then, Grimes slammed the door shut behind them, plunging them into total darkness.

2

THE SCENE OF THE CRIME . . .

OOSE BUMPS SPREAD up Kelcie's arms as Blizzard set her on
her feet, keeping a firm grasp on her shoulders. She couldn't
see her hand in front of her face. Grimes dropped something
that sounded like Kelcie's backpack. She heard it shush across
the hard floor. At the same time, Kelcie heard clicking, like the
sound a card strapped to the spokes of a moving bike tire makes.
Bolts slid, then clanked.

Kelcie's breath caught. Grimes was locking the vault's door.

She started shaking all over, and not just because she was
terrified, which she was, but also because the temperature had
dropped. It felt like she was standing in a freezer.

"You sure this will hold up, Achila?" Blizzard asked. "What
if the place caves in?"

"It's a vault within a bomb shelter. Yes, it will hold up. You've
done your part. Now shut up, and let me do mine," Grimes
snapped.

"What part? What do you want from me?" Kelcie yelled.

A chain yanked. An overhead light flicked on. The small,
dank space was empty except for a medium-sized crate and a
crowbar that Grimes picked up and leveled at Kelcie. "What
I want is for you to be quiet!" She inched toward Kelcie, who
backed up until she bumped into Blizzard. "You're positive she's
the one?" Grimes asked, looking over Kelcie's head to Elliott.

"You better not have screwed this up, Blizzard, or I'll leave your body next to hers."

"I'm not the one! I'm nobody. I don't even have a real last name! Elliott gave me mine, made it up, didn't you, Elliott?" Kelcie glanced over her shoulder to see his furious you're-not-helping frown.

"Ignore her. She's the one!" Elliott growled.

Clueless, that was the word Blizzard used in the stairwell, and for a reason. What if this all had to do with her parents? All these years she told anyone who asked that her mother and father were spies, that they abandoned her in Boston to keep her safe. What if it was all true?

"Open the crate! Hurry up before we have company!" Blizzard snapped.

Company? The guy that followed them was probably still searching or maybe, with any luck, he sent security. Kelcie was about to yell for help, when she remembered what Elliott said— about knowing who her parents were, something she would know too if she did as they asked. A cold calm came over her. She could do this, whatever this was, if it meant answers.

Grimes went to work trying to open the crate. She wedged the crowbar into the seam, leaning all her weight on the bar.

The top jerked.

The lid hit the floor with a loud thud.

"Here we go . . ." Grimes said.

She hooked the crowbar on the edge of the front panel and gave it a hard tug. It crashed down, sending stale air and dust flying in Kelcie's face.

Before Kelcie knew what was happening, Blizzard clasped her wrists in one of his huge hands, holding them out in front of her, keeping a firm grasp on her shoulder with his other hand.

"Happy birthday!" he sang.

"That's not funny," Kelcie said, but then realization dawned. Fear nose-dived into shocked anger. If he knew all this time who her parents were, then he probably knew a whole lot more about her. "It's my birthday?" Kelcie gaped up at him. "You've known all this time that October first is my birthday?"

"Yes. You are twelve today."

"And you never told me?"

She never once heard the words *happy birthday*. Never had a teacher let her choose a special prize from the box because it was her special day. Never had she blown out candles on a cake.

"Stop looking at me like I killed your dog. I didn't know, not at first, anyway!"

"Excuse me, but we have more important things to be doing." Grimes reached in the crate and lifted a large block of what looked like smoking dry ice, only instead of white, it was black as ash.

Kelcie's head spun from the fumes. She struggled against Elliott's hold on her wrists, trying to get away from it, but he wouldn't let go! "W-what . . ." *cough-cough* ". . . is that?"

"Something as old as time, and equally unforgiving." Grimes carried an object about the size and shape of a basketball toward Kelcie. It was swaddled in folded layers of frayed black fabric that glistened in the light's dim glow.

Then the weirdest thing of all happened. Icy oversized butterfly wings grew out of Ms. Grimes' back. Her black eyes shrank to tiny dots, the rest solidly white. Her canines stretched until she had fangs longer than Count Dracula's. Water rippled from her feet over her body, freezing as it climbed to her neck, armoring her in ice that moved with her like a second skin.

Kelcie shook her head so hard her neck cracked. No way did Grimes just turn into Tinkerbell on ice. That was a giant leap too far. Reality-check time! This was just a stupid nightmare! "This isn't real! You're not real!"

"Oh, but I am . . ." Grimes leaned forward until their noses were almost touching. "I'm an ice fairy. As much as Disney would like you to believe otherwise, we're not always nice . . ."

Grimes jammed the ancient object into Kelcie's outstretched

hands. Ice spread from Grimes to Kelcie, locking them together and Kelcie's hands to the stiffening fabric.

"Get it off!" Kelcie tried to wiggle her fingers, but they were frozen to the object.

Then Grimes blasted Kelcie's feet with her free hand, freezing Kelcie's feet not only together, but also to the floor.

"Not going anywhere now. Let's begin," Grimes said.

The ice melted from Grimes' hand, freeing her from Kelcie. She took a few steps back. Blizzard moved beside Grimes, staring at Kelcie like an anxious dad on the side of a soccer field.

"You can do this, Kelcie," he said, his own pair of wings sprouting out of his back.

Kelcie eyes bulged. "You have wings too?"

He winked, his gloating expression filling Kelcie with rage. How could Elliott Blizzard have been a fairy all this time and Kelcie never known?

Her feet prickled, needles stabbing her ankles, losing feeling. Pretty soon, if she didn't break out of this ice, they would turn blue and fall off. Terrified and freezing, Kelcie gave in. It was only a nightmare. None of this could be real . . . *fairies aren't real*!

Her jaw chattering from cold or fear or both, she glared at Grimes. "Tell me what you want me to do."

"Simple, invoke *Ta Erfin*. Invoke your right to challenge!"

Ta Erfin. I am the heir.

"I-I am-m t-the heir?" Kelcie bit her lip, stunned. "W-wait? H-how d-d-did I know what th-that m-m-means?"

Elliott laughed. "Because you are the heir. Only the heir would know the ancient tongue. Even we didn't know what it means, until now." He smirked at Grimes. "And you doubted my word."

"Looks like you're going to live, Kelcie Murphy." Grimes beamed at her. "But in order for this to work you must repeat it exactly as I said it. *Ta Erfin!*"

"T-ta Er-feen," Kelcie repeated. "Heir of what?"

"Shush! Not now!" Blizzard shouted.

"Next phrase. *Vlast mian!*" Grimes bellowed at her.

The power is mine. Kelcie's brain was still stuck on the word *heir,* because if she was an heir, that meant she had a family. Or did. An heir could imply she was the next in line. Or the last. They could all be dead. *Blizzard said he has answers. If this is real . . .* but how could it be? *There is no such thing as magic.*

"Say it . . ." Grimes added another layer of ice. It crept up her arms and over her shoulders.

Kelcie gasped. "Vlast mee-an!"

Hot spikes stabbed the center of Kelcie's palms. For as long as it took to blink, it hurt, then the pain gave way to a rush of unbridled exhilaration. She took a deep breath, drinking it in. "What is that?" Then her eyes slammed shut.

A deep disembodied voice, so faint it sounded far away, rattled through her head, speaking in the same language. The only language Kelcie spoke was English, yet somehow her brain translated.

Another heir. He, whoever he was, sucked in a sharp breath. *Such potential! But, completely untapped. Interesting. Yes. I am willing to accept the challenge, but there is a price to pay. Are you willing to pay it?*

Kelcie laughed, her mind reaching the point of no return. There was absolutely no way any of this was real. Fairies. Magical objects. Ha! A talking ball of fabric asking her to pay for something she didn't even want. "Sure. Yes. Why not? How much?"

Agree and then ask the price? His chiding cackle was so loud it hurt her ears. *There can only ever be one. You succeed, and the other will perish.*

Her vision tunneled. Like a speeding train, she fell through nothing, empty space, hearing unexpected, terrifying sounds. Roars, growls, snarling, hisses, and zaps until a tiny light no bigger than a pin's head ignited. Like touching a plasma ball at the science museum, filaments stretched at lightning speeds in two directions. One, into the unknown emptiness before her. The other, straight for Kelcie.

The blast struck every part of her, chilling her blood until it stung, a cold, angry burning that culminated in an explosion that rocked the room, knocking Kelcie off her feet.

Alarm bells sounded.

"I'll carry it!" she heard Elliott say.

"No. I will!" Grimes growled. "Go! I'll handle things from here!"

"But Kelcie—"

"I'm in charge of this operation and I said go!"

The only thing she truly wanted were the answers Blizzard promised her, and Grimes just ordered him to leave!

Desperate to stop him, Kelcie found her voice. "Wait! Elliott! Don't leave!"

In the few seconds it took for Kelcie's vision to clear, Grimes melted the ice and ripped it, whatever it was, from her grasp. Kelcie had the sudden urge to cry. But why? It made no sense.

"Elliott? Elliott!" she yelled, but neither her caseworker nor the ice fairy were anywhere to be found.

Smoke billowed from charred spots on the ceiling. The door had been blown completely off its hinges. A smoldering bit of her destroyed backpack floated through a foot of churning water. Where did the water come from?

"What the . . ." She couldn't explain what happened, but her way out was clear.

Her clothes soaked, Kelcie pushed to all fours, hopping to her feet. She ran into the hallway, stopping dead in her tracks. Elliott was gone, but Achila Grimes flew above Kelcie's head, holding the ancient object. Kelcie knew she should go, Blizzard was getting away; if much more time passed, Kelcie would never find him, but for some inexplicable reason, she wanted that thing back!

Grimes accidentally bumped against the ceiling pipes, splitting the metal. Hot steam escaped, melting the ice on her shoulder, but she was otherwise occupied with the object. She rolled it down her back. Ice rippled, forming a cocoon, securing it in place.

"Hey!" Kelcie called. It was far out of her reach, but she couldn't stop staring at it.

Grimes looked down, her thin, frosty brow arching, a smirk

tugging at the corners of her mouth. "You really don't have a clue who you are or where you came from?"

Visions of the night she was abandoned rushed back to Kelcie, the same way it did in her nightmares.

Broken arrows. Black feathers. Blinding lightning followed by seismic thunder. Whipping wind. Her heartbeat so loud it was all she heard as she fell from an impossible height. Then she plunged. Water went up her nose. Filled her mouth. For the first time in her life, she couldn't breathe. All broken bits and pieces that made absolutely no sense.

Kelcie couldn't remember how she'd ended up in the water, or where she'd come from, or even her last name. She was immediately placed into foster care, and Elliott Blizzard dumped her off at a group home in upstate Massachusetts. Confused and afraid, she hardly spoke for months. Scrapes and bruises on her wrists took forever to heal. Alone in an unwelcoming world, she survived on the hope that one day her parents would come back for her, but they never did. This was her shot. Deep dream psychosis or not, Kelcie would play this nightmare out to the bitter end.

A guard ran into the room with his taser drawn.

"Hold it right there!"

He never got a shot off. Water cannoned from Grimes' hands, plastering him against the wall, freezing him completely from head to toe, face and all.

"He can't breathe!" Kelcie ran into the vault. She trudged through the water, shuffling her feet, soaking her sneakers, searching for the crowbar.

By the time she returned with it, Grimes was launching into the stairwell, her wings buzzing like an attacking wasp's hive. If Kelcie didn't go after her, she might never find out about her past, but she couldn't leave the guard.

Kelcie used the end of the crowbar to chip away the ice until he could breathe. She freed his arm next. As soon as his fingers wiggled, she stuffed the crowbar into his hand, and sprinted after Achila Grimes.

3

THE BREATHING TREE

KELCIE NEVER BELIEVED in magic. No superhero had ever showed up to make the world a better place. Guys hustling three-card monte in the park near her school in Worcester never tricked her. She found the ace of spades every time. The cop at the police station even tried the coin-in-your-ear gag the night she was abandoned. She'd poked him in the nose so hard his eyes watered, then she pocketed the quarter. But as she raced after Achila Grimes, hearing her razor-sharp wings slice through metal, finding a trail of museum staff she'd laid out with hail chunks, Kelcie conceded. She was most definitely wrong.

It took Kelcie a lot longer to get up the stairs than for Grimes to fly, but she heard screaming in the cafe on the first floor. By the time Kelcie arrived, Grimes was dive-bombing museum patrons.

Adults ran screaming. Kids threw syrup-smothered fruit cups and bowls of chunky applesauce, which Grimes happily slurped midair and spit back at them in frozen bits.

"Tell me who I am!" Kelcie yelled at Grimes.

"There she is." Grimes reeled back. "What took you so long?"

An ice spear grazed Kelcie's ear. She dove under a table and pinched the cut that was bleeding all over her only jacket. Now she was going to have to do laundry! Did this ice fairy have any idea how hard it was to get a machine in a group home? The irrational diatribe racing through her mind stopped short of falling over a cliff.

Bleeding.

Kelcie was bleeding! And it hurt. Really friggin' bad! This was real. All of it. And that meant with Blizzard nowhere to be found, the ice fairy was the only key left to finding out about her past. She couldn't let her out of her sight.

Museum docents in their fancy green jackets sprinted through the entrance, yelling "Stop!" until they got a glimpse of the fanged fairy flying over their heads, flinging icicles. They dove under the tables with the patrons.

"How do people get out of this place?" Ms. Grimes bounced from wall to window like a trapped fly. "Let me out of here!"

Kelcie crawled out. "I'll help you, but first, tell me who my parents are! Where do I come from?"

Guards flooded the room firing tasers at Grimes, missing badly, zapping a poor cashier and a big guy in a hairnet. Custodial staff and city gardeners, the museum's last line of defense, heaved brooms, mop handles, and cutting shears.

Grimes caught a pair of shears, letting out a joyful squeal. She rolled through the self-serve aisle, spinning like a drill, then torpedoed the giant glass wall.

Shards rained down.

Kelcie didn't hesitate. She threw up her hood and ran after Ms. Grimes. The fairy was easy to spot, heading for tree cover in the park. Kelcie dashed across a busy road without looking, nearly getting run over by a bus. She followed the sound of Grimes' buzzing wings, dodging strollers, leaping squirrels, tripping twice on black ice, tearing holes in the knees of her leggings.

The fairy landed on the end of a cobblestone bridge. Kelcie saw her glance back, flashing a devious smile.

But in the few seconds it took Kelcie to get to the bridge, the fairy vanished.

"No! Where are you?" she yelled. "Grimes?" Kelcie craned

her neck, checking the skies. "Elliott. Elliott! This is so unfair . . ."

Her necklace's silver branch charm skidded across her chest, lifting toward the bridge like a magnet drawn to its opposite charge. The charm yanked, digging the chain into her neck. Kelcie grabbed it and pulled it down, only to have it happen again.

Kelcie gave in, stepping onto the bridge, passing through something that made her hair stand on end. Then she tripped, stumbling, her bloody knees landing on hard tree roots.

"Ow . . ."

Her necklace still stretched, she got up slowly, straddling two roots for balance, and took in her surroundings.

She was standing in a river of bulbous roots, stemming from an enormous oak tree. The cobblestone bridge was gone. The park was gone. The strollers too. Not a single bird chirped from the branches, or squirrel climbed the tree. It was eerily quiet.

"Hello?" Kelcie yelled. "Elliott? Grimes? Anybody?"

Kelcie grabbed the necklace charm, holding it down, and climbed over the roots, toward the base of the tree. The trunk inhaled, expanding, then fell, exhaling with a long hiss. Startled, Kelcie stepped back. Never in her life had she seen a tree breathing before.

An unseen force tore the charm from her fist, tugging it toward the tree, taking Kelcie with it. She fell on the trunk, the tiny silver branch landing on the bark. Then, the branch grew roots. Kelcie tried to stand up but her necklace refused to let go.

The bark split open. Soupy yellow sap flowed, a raging river of light, bathing her shaking hands still clinging to her chain in a warm glow. Beyond that, deep within the fibers of the trunk, Kelcie could make out two fairy-shaped blurs, wings and all!

"Occupied," a synthesized feminine voice announced. "Occupied. Wait your turn."

Grimes and Blizzard waved. Kelcie's charm fell off the trunk and the tree zipped closed, leaving a gaping hole in her chest.

"Hey!" Kelcie kicked the tree. "Open up!"

But it refused, repeating, "Occupied. Wait your turn. Occupied. Wait your turn," until Kelcie wanted to blow her head off.

She glared at the tree, so angry tears welled up in her eyes, and then examined her necklace's charm. The roots were gone. It was nothing but a tiny branch again.

"The necklace . . ." A quick bark of laughter escaped. This necklace was the only thing she had from before. A link to her past.

She pressed her hand on the bark. Was this tree some kind of a portal to where she came from? Crazy, yes, but it suddenly made sense. Or did it? Was it possible that her life before Boston included mythical magical creatures, like Grimes and Blizzard, and that ancient object that blew the vault door completely off its hinges? What was that thing? It was powerful and dangerous, and Grimes took it.

"At least it's gone . . ." Kelcie could walk away like none of this ever happened, but then she would never find her parents or that object. "I am the heir . . ."

She stared at the tree, craning to see the top, but it was hiding in a sea of rolling dense white clouds. Clouds that in the park had been a blanket of gray. Kelcie heard squeaky wheels rolling on wooden planks and a mother cajoling a crying baby, but she couldn't see them.

The only explanation that popped into her head was impossible to believe. She was in some kind of a vortex, invisible to the people in the park, making her invisible to them. She could step off the bridge, test to see if she would be back in the park, but would she be able to come back? What if the tree disappeared altogether? She wasn't about to take that chance.

She gave the tree another pat, waiting for her necklace to lift, but it didn't even bobble. "Hello?" She rubbed the bark, feeling the breathing trunk rise and fall evenly, like it was asleep.

"Hello! Wake up!" she cried, knocking as hard and loud as she could. "Please?"

The tree let out an irritated exhale. Her charm lifted on its own.

"Yes!" This time, Kelcie knew what to do. She set it against the bark, holding it there until she felt the roots growing beneath her palm.

The trunk split open, and the sap parted, clearing the way to the hollow middle of the trunk. Kelcie tucked the charm beneath her sweatshirt, took a deep breath for courage, and climbed inside. Then the tree zipped closed.

4

THE ACADEMY FOR
THE UNBREAKABLE ARTS

A TINY LIGHT BLINKED above her head for twenty . . . long . . . painstaking . . . beats before a bell *rang*.

Palms sweating, heart racing, Kelcie pressed her hands against her sides, anxiously waiting for something to happen. Orange tree veins sparked on, lighting up like tracks on a roller coaster at night. The longer she waited, the more nervous Kelcie became. What if she ended up in a room full of ice fairies?

Kelcie forgot all about Grimes, Blizzard, or that object as sap poured in, swallowing her legs and arms until she couldn't move. All she could do was blink, which she did furiously, and scream, which she did as loud as possible when she shot straight up like a rocket heading for outer space.

After what felt like forever, she leveled off, moving slowly, flat on her back. Long shoot, sticky sap, Kelcie had only a split second to reach the conclusion that she was traveling through veins of the world's biggest tree. Unseen forces spun her one hundred and eighty degrees. A slot opened, and she was propelled through the hole, into another shoot, where she rode a steep incline, chugging inch by inch until she crested the top, and fell.

For several long, overwhelming minutes, she was dragged up and down, twisting and turning, bumping and banging, shuttled from chute to chute. Terrified and screaming at first, after her third downward spiral, she felt like she was flying. She hooted and hollered at glimpses of others riding in separate shoots running parallel or horizontal to the way she was traveling. This was way better than taking a train or a bus.

Kelcie slowed mid-descent. The sap drained off. The side split, then she was pivoted sideways and unceremoniously ejected out of the tree. She landed on her stomach, getting the wind knocked out of her, eating dirt. Gasping for breath, she rolled over. Before her were the bluest skies she had ever seen, and a merciless sun shining directly into her eyes. Wincing, she looked away, patting her pockets for her sunglasses only to remember Grimes stole them.

One bright spot was that her clothes were void of any residual sap-stickiness, but her head . . . Jackhammers pounded against her skull.

"Would you move?" A guy stepped over.

Kelcie tried but suddenly kids popped out of the tree from all sides. There were so many of them, she couldn't get out of their way fast enough. Every time she went to stand up, she would only get bonked down. A mortifying barrage of *excuse me*'s, *pardon me*'s, and *last straw, MOVE!*'s rang out.

Kelcie gave up, resorting to crawling, until she found an empty spot in the sea of legs a few feet from the tree. As she stood up, she glanced over her shoulder at the excited mayhem. Kids of all colors and ages dressed in a sea of fancy uniforms— white pants, black knee-high boots, and different colored fancy cloaks with the initials *AUA* stitched into the lapel—fist bumped, high-fived, and bonked shoulders happy to see each other.

"I can't believe school is starting up already. Feel like we just left for break," an older boy said as he walked by.

A school? This was the last place she expected to end up.

Kelcie panned every direction, up and down, right and left, searching for Blizzard and Grimes, but there was no trace of either one. Could she have been ejected from the tree too soon? She hiccupped a laugh. *Did I really just think that?*

They probably got here before Kelcie did. Maybe this was some kind of test? Like Blizzard was only going to bother to tell her anything if she found him? Definitely something he would do. The first time she asked him where the bathroom was at the police station he picked her up from, he said, "Life is hard. Figure it out on your own. Then you won't owe anybody anything."

The registration office was always Kelcie's first stop at a new school. She figured it was a good place to start but all around her was nothing but sprawling green fields, and more sprawling green fields. This campus was enormous. She stood on her tiptoes. Not a building in sight and no signs either. Kelcie would need to ask someone for help.

Snooty prep school kids were not very welcoming in her past. From the stern glares directed at her by this lot, these kids weren't going to be much different.

She smoothed her hair, straightened her jean jacket, and padded over to a group of older kids, standing in a tight circle. They were in matching blue cloaks. From the back, they looked like average teenagers, some tall, some medium, others short, two legs, two arms, a head, but as Kelcie got closer, she noticed something very peculiar. All of them had inhuman eye colors. Red, magenta, cyan, and yellow. They were also the prettiest people Kelcie had ever seen.

Besides their killer eyes, they had the shiniest hair, like it was conditioned with stardust. Their ears were perfectly sized for their heads, their noses stick straight and neither too big nor too small for their faces. Speaking of faces, not a single pimple marred their perfect complexions. Kelcie's hand lifted to her chin, which was still fighting three stress bumps. Just looking at these kids made Kelcie feel like she needed a total genetic makeover.

"What happened to you last week, Connor? I waited for two hours at the Sidral for you," an auburn-haired girl with shiny thick braids asked. She narrowed her cherry-red orbs and punched Connor's arm so hard he winced.

He raised his hands, surrendering. "Sorry, okay? My dah caught me sneaking out. I sent word, but your mum said you'd already left, Deirdre. What was Chawell Woods like? I heard they've been taking down the trees to build their own palace. Perhaps they think they can declare their own regent next."

"I never saw a palace. Most of them lived in small huts or caves near the lake. But we don't venture too deep into the woods. No reason to. It's enchanted. They can't get out."

"Did they resist?" a porky guy across from Connor asked.

Deirdre scoffed. "No resistance at all. How could they? It's the law now." She snickered. "I personally registered Killian and Ollie Lynch, and let me tell you—"

"Deirdre, no one wants to hear it," said a girl with a luminescent blond ponytail and matching yellow eyes as she walked with confidence toward them. She too was in a blue cloak, but hers had gold suns stitched on each collar tab.

"My father and his *fianna* were under orders directly from the Queen, Regan," Deirdre explained.

Regan batted her sun-kissed eyelashes at her. "Of course, they were. But that doesn't mean she would want her soldiers taking pleasure in others' pain."

"Like you would know what the Queen wants," Deirdre challenged.

Deirdre sounded like your average bully. Asking her where the office was would be not only futile, but potentially detrimental to Kelcie's health. She turned, hoping to ask Regan, but she was already walking away from them.

"I'm heading for the stables. Who's with me?" asked Regan.

Everyone but Deirdre and Connor went.

"She thinks she's so great because she's Alpha this year. This is what I think of our new Alpha." Deirdre stomped on a rock the size of a soccer ball, smashing it to bits.

"Whoa." Kelcie gawped dumbstruck, scooting backward until she bumped into the tree. "That's impossible."

Connor nudged Deirdre. "Look at her. Tester is pissing herself."

The tree unzipped. Someone plowed into Kelcie so hard she fell on her stomach, eating grass all over again. Worse still, whoever it was landed on top of her.

"Sorry." He scrambled off.

Kelcie rolled over, wheezing, finding a boy about her same age growing redder by the second. He reached a hand out to her. "You shouldn't stand so close to the Sidral."

She let him pull her up.

"Sidral," Kelcie said testing the word. She glanced over her shoulder at the tree that was forever spitting students.

As she let go of the boy's hand, Kelcie realized it was his only one. She tried not to stare, but all she was doing was staring. He either didn't notice or was too polite to say anything.

"I'm Niall. Niall O'Shea." Hidden behind his lopsided, black-rimmed glasses and shaggy brown hair was a mesmerizing pair of lavender eyes. He was dressed in all black, right down to his shoes.

Niall seemed helpful enough, so she introduced herself.

"Kelcie Murphy," she said.

"Are you lost?" Niall asked. "It's this way. We need to hurry though. It's starting soon." He took off quickly.

"Wait!" Kelcie called, running after him.

He led her down the hill, to a well-trodden path. The school's campus was the most beautiful Kelcie had ever seen. Green fields, dense woods, and if her aching eyes weren't playing tricks on her, medieval-looking towers.

Forced to sprint, she finally caught up to him at the bottom of a hill. "Niall, can I ask you a question?"

"No. I didn't lose my hand in a tragic accident. I was born this way. I'm used to it. Can't miss what you never had. And I can get through this test just as well as you can, okay?" he growled.

"Sure. But that wasn't my question."

"Oh." Niall slowed, turning red again. It was kind of cute the way he kept doing that. "Sorry."

"Um . . ." Easing into this, she decided to start with the basics. Kelcie cleared her throat. "Where exactly am I? I mean what is this place?"

Niall stopped walking altogether and straightened his glasses. "What do you mean? You don't know where you are?"

"A school, right? This brought me here." Kelcie held up her necklace. "Do you know what it is?"

"You're not funny." Niall stomped away, but Kelcie ran after him, pulling him to a stop.

"I'm serious. Just look at it."

"I've seen it."

He lifted a necklace out from underneath his T-shirt. Unlike Kelcie's, Niall's had a leather strap, and the charm had so many branches it looked more like a whole tree.

"But . . ." Niall lifted his glasses and scrutinized hers more closely. He picked it up, turning it over in his palm. "That's strange."

"What's strange?"

"Your bough only has one branch."

"Bough?"

"It's called a silver bough. You really don't know?" When he saw Kelcie's confused expression, he added, "They open the Sidrals." He let go of Kelcie's charm.

She stared down at it. "And Sidrals are how you travel from place to place?"

"Exactly."

He tucked his silver bough back beneath his shirt, not as if he wanted to hide it, but because it seemed the natural thing to do. Like putting away a monthly BART pass when you were done with it so it wouldn't get lost.

"Why does yours have so many branches?"

"Access to different places."

They started walking again, at a slower pace this time.

"Like keys to different doors?"

"Yes, but yours only has one branch, which is weird. It only goes there and back again. A single path."

"You mean with this I could only come here?" Kelcie glanced down at the charm bouncing on her sweatshirt. No. Not a charm. A silver bough.

"Yes. Or return where you came from. What part of the Kingdom are you from?"

Kelcie nearly tripped at the word *Kingdom*. It conjured medieval images of King Arthur and Camelot. "I'm from Boston, Massachusetts, in the US."

"Never heard of it. Where in the Otherworld is that?"

"Otherworld?" Kelcie frowned. "I don't know what other world you mean, but it's definitely in the *human* world." She laughed, but Niall didn't, which made her very nervous. He was serious.

"The human world?" Niall halted yet again. His lavender eyes grew impossibly wide. "The human world!" He smacked his forehead. "No wonder your branch has no knobs. In the name of the gods . . . I've heard stories of this happening before. Where did you get the bough? Which one gave it to you?"

"I've always had it. I assumed my parents gave it to me, but the truth is, I have no idea where it came from."

"Why not? Can't you ask them?"

"No." She didn't know Niall and wasn't sure how much she wanted to divulge to him, but she had to give him enough information to keep him answering her questions. "I've never met them before. Or maybe I just can't remember them. I don't know. It's a long story."

Kelcie shoved her hands in her sweatshirt pocket.

They continued on for a full minute before Niall spoke. "So, you're saying you found a Sidral in the human world that your bough opened, then just got in it? With no idea where it was taking you?"

"I was chasing . . ." Kelcie stopped herself from saying *an ice fairy* because it sounded too ridiculous, outlandish, just plain nuts.

"Chasing who?"

"Well . . . okay. I'm going to tell you. But don't laugh at me! Fairies. I was chasing a couple of fairies."

He gaped. "What kind of fairies?"

Odd question, but pertinent, Kelcie supposed, especially if Niall had encountered fairies before, so she went on. "One called herself an ice fairy. Nicked my ear with a frozen spear." She pulled her lobe down, showing him. "The other, I don't know what kind of fairy he was, but he had wings too."

"Fairies in the human world?" Niall spat. "Are they everywhere? Is the place completely infested?"

"No. I don't think so. It is absolutely not normal," Kelcie said. "I followed them into a park and saw them inside the Sidral, so I waited for it to open again and went after them."

"You purposely went after an ice fairy?" He said that like she was either incredibly stupid or incredibly brave.

"I need to find them, Niall. They know who I am."

Niall looked as confused as Kelcie felt. "You don't know who you are?"

Kelcie shook her head and repeated, "I need to find them."

"Oh. Well." His pursed lips cratered. "There might be a problem with that plan."

"What problem?"

"They would never, could never come here. They're from a very different part of the Otherworld. From the Lands of Winter. Their boughs wouldn't bring them here. They can't. It's physically impossible."

Kelcie was trying to understand this. "So, you're saying neither of them could possibly be here, at this school?"

Niall nodded. "That's exactly what I'm saying."

"And I can't go to the Lands of Winter because my silver bough will only take me back to Boston?" Kelcie's chest heaved with frustration. Blizzard said all that stuff just to trick her? If Kelcie ever found him, he would be one sorry fairy!

"Not even my bough will go to the Lands of Winter," Niall added.

"Of course not. Why should anything good ever happen to me?" Kelcie kicked a rock as hard as she could, sending it careening into a tree. It ricocheted off, hitting her in the shin. "Ow! You see!"

"But maybe it did." Niall gently picked up her charm again. "This bough could only bring you here, so whoever gave it to you meant for you to come here."

Kelcie gaped at him. Why didn't she think of that before?

A whistle blew.

"That's for us! We need to hurry." Niall took off running so fast Kelcie was forced to sprint after him to keep up. "There's a test to get in and we can't be late for it!"

A test? She didn't like the sound of that. Her headache worsened with each passing second without her sunglasses. "What kind of school is this anyway? What's it called?"

"The Academy for the Unbreakable Arts."

"Unbreakable Arts?" Those two words paired together made no sense to her. "What does that mean?"

"This school turns out the most magically powerful soldiers ever to protect the Lands of Summer."

"Magically powerful? They teach magic at this school?"

Niall flashed her an award-winning grin.

Kelcie took that as a *yes*. She smiled too. "Protect the Lands of Summer from what?"

"The Lands of Winter, where those fairies are from."

A panther leaped out of a tree above them as they exited the woods. Before Kelcie could scream, it reared and transformed into a guy. Maybe fifteen. Black, with dayglow green eyes and curls standing straight up. His uniform was the same as the others, only his cloak was red.

"Good morning, testers!" he sang. "Diccon Wilks, come to make your life miserable . . ."

Jogging backward, he waggled his eyebrows, then spun, sprinting down the hill, into a field packed with students sorted into lines by cloak color. Diccon stepped in front of the others in red. There were five lines in all. In addition to the many in red, there were loads in blue, black, green, but only two in yellow.

Kelcie gestured wildly. "Niall! That guy just shape-shifted!"

But Niall wasn't listening to Kelcie anymore. He was pushing his way through a group of kids their age, getting a good position close to a raised wooden platform. He grinned, peeping back to make sure she was following. As Kelcie shouldered through the throngs, a flock of enormous ravens whizzed overhead in a perfect V formation, nearly giving Kelcie a heart attack, settling in nearby trees.

A harsh whisper fell from the branches. "Uh oh. Roswen is already here!"

"Yes. She is! And you Ravens are LATE! Move it!"

A woman in a sleek white bodysuit hopped up on the platform. What she lacked in height she more than made up for in buff biceps. She had light brown skin and a full head of pink hair that was sectioned off and bound in knots. Her eyes were different than the students Kelcie had seen so far. They were a more normal shade of blue.

The birds chanted her name, "Roswen-Roswen-Roswen," as they came in for a perfect landing on the field where they transformed like the panther had into boys and girls, taking their places in line with others in black cloaks.

Kelcie shook her head, unable to believe what she was seeing. Could everyone here shape-shift? Was it a prerequisite to get in? Kelcie had never been anything but a short, skinny, over-freckled, painfully pale-skinned redhead her whole life. That Deirdre girl pounded a rock to dust with her foot. Kelcie couldn't do that either. She couldn't do anything extraordinary. She barely passed math last year.

Her headache worsened by the second. Her brain felt like a pincushion for nano-sized, needle-wielding elves. What was she doing here? Niall was wrong. This was a mistake. They put this necklace on the wrong person. It was the only explanation that made sense. Kelcie stepped out of line, but Niall caught her hand.

"Where are you going?"

Kelcie shook her head. "I shouldn't be here."

Niall looked perplexed. "Why not?"

"I can't do that." She gestured to the line of black-cloaked Ravenettes. "I can't do anything like that at all."

Roswen bonked her on the head with a clipboard. "Of course not. You haven't been taught to do those things yet." She pursed her lips at Niall. "Niall O'Shea. Regan's little brother, right?"

Niall stiffened. "Yes, ma'am."

She wrote his name down with an axe-shaped pen on her clipboard, then noticed a set of identical twin boys pointing at Niall's arm, swapping whispers. She cleared her throat, catching their attention, and shut them up with a single glare. "Got a rather disconcerting letter from your father this morning, O'Shea. Man named Thorn."

"Stepfather," Niall corrected, glancing at Kelcie with an uncomfortable hooded gaze.

"Said I wasn't to let you test. Thinks that arm of yours, the one missing a hand, should disqualify you from being a student here. Said it would be humiliating for your family, particularly your sister, when you fail the test."

Niall ground his teeth, trying to hold back yelling at Roswen about the obvious indignation, thereby making things worse for himself. Kelcie had no such worries.

"Why would he say that? What does it matter if Niall's missing a hand?" Kelcie blurted.

Roswen poked Kelcie's forehead with the butt of her axe-pen. "Not talking to you yet." She sighed at Niall. "He finished off saying it would be my head if you were to get hurt, or worse." Roswen leaned over him. "Are you going to get hurt? Will I be sending you home in pieces, Mr. O'Shea? I am rather attached to my head, you see."

"No, ma'am."

"What was that?" Roswen tapped his head with her pen.

"He said no," Kelcie shouted, loud enough that half the testers looked to see what was going on.

Roswen aimed the tiny yet razor-sharp axe blade at Kelcie's nose. "Did I ask you?"

Niall stared at his shoes, mortified, clamming up. Even after Roswen's humiliating tirade, he really wanted to test for this school, and truth was, so did Kelcie. "No, ma'am."

"Who are you?" Her stern frown shifted to Kelcie.

"Kelcie Murphy."

Roswen looked down her nose at Kelcie's clothes. "Testers are supposed to wear all black."

Kelcie removed her jean jacket and hoodie. Beneath was a blue and pink tie-dye T-shirt. "Ah, I could've sworn I put a black shirt on this morning." She shrugged. "I don't have anything but this." She didn't even have the money that was in her backpack to buy a new T-shirt. Come to think of it, she didn't have any money at all. Look at this fancy place. How would she pay for the tuition? Kelcie's mouth went dry. Her heart sank along with her spirits. This was hopeless. "Oh, um, actually, I should go."

She picked up her clothes.

"No, you shouldn't," Niall insisted, stepping in front of her.

She started around him but Roswen blocked her path. "What's the problem?"

Kelcie sighed. "I don't have any money. I can't afford to go here."

"There is no cost to go to this school," Roswen explained. "If you get in, and make it all the way through, you owe only your service, Kelcie Murphy. Are you willing to give that?"

Service sounded pretty reasonable to Kelcie, especially if this place led to finding her parents. "Yes, ma'am." Kelcie smiled, relieved. That was one less thing to worry about.

She wrote Kelcie's name on the clipboard beneath Niall's.

"Good. Time to get stabbed."

5

DEN ALERT!

S TABBED?" It was only after Kelcie agreed to test that she remembered Roswen had said something to Niall about getting hurt, or worse. Ending up in pieces. "She's kidding, right?" Niall shushed Kelcie without looking at her.

"Quiet down!" Roswen paced the platform until the chatter ceased. "Now that we're all here, Alphas, as usual you will remain with the testers. Students, lunch in Befelts Garden, after which return to your Dens and get settled. Dismissed!"

Roswen waited until they had all left the field except five who joined her on the platform. Among them were Regan, the blond girl from the Sidral, and Diccon, the guy who shape-shifted into a panther. All five wore gold suns on the collars of their cloaks. The Alphas, Kelcie assumed.

"Testers, welcome to the Academy for the Unbreakable Arts. As you likely know by now, my name is Roswen. I am in charge of everything you see on campus. Buildings, lakes, creeks, woods, trails, animals, minerals, herbs, and many, many vegetables. Everything you see here belongs to me. Pick a flower without permission, you will feel the sting of my pen."

Roswen hacked the tiny axe against the back of the clipboard, chipping shavings all over the testers' heads.

"You are GUESTS here for the afternoon. Most of you will NOT get in to AUA."

Kelcie could feel the tension in the air quadruple. She wasn't immune either. Butterflies beat the sides of her stomach. The jackhammer behind her eyes switched on again.

Roswen continued, "Most of you simply won't have any powers, and those who do, may not have the ones we're looking for. Here at AUA, we are training elite warriors."

Kelcie liked the sound of that more than she wanted to let on.

"Now then, step one is to bring any powers, if they exist, to the forefront."

"I heard about this part from my sister," Niall whispered. "Spriggans. That's what Roswen meant."

"Meant? Are you saying spriggans are going to stab us?"

A scowling girl leaned between them, her narrowed silver eyes darting from Kelcie to Niall. She looked like a warrior ready to take the battlefield in her black leather capris, black tank with three thin silver armbands on her upper left arm, and sword hanging off her hip. Her shiny black hair was pulled off her face in a perfect fishtail braid. Kelcie could never figure out how to do that with her own hair. "Shut it! I'm trying to hear," she whispered harshly.

Niall ignored her. "That's my sister, in the blue cloak." He nodded to Regan.

"No one cares," Fishtail hissed.

"Is there an issue, Brona Lee?" Roswen asked loud enough for all to hear.

"Yes, ma'am. I couldn't hear you because these two won't stop talking."

"No talking, Murphy. O'Shea, you should know better. Where was I?" Roswen glanced at her clipboard. "Right. Now, there are five Dens at the school, each associated with the powers we're looking for. Chargers, Adders, Cats, Ravens, and Saiga. Chargers are gifted with leadership and great strength."

To everyone's delight, Regan lifted a griping Diccon over her head using only one hand. Her eyes found Niall, and she promptly dropped Diccon, rousing laughter.

Niall shrunk behind Kelcie. His sister didn't know he was testing.

Roswen continued, "Ravens possess the ability of shifting to raven familiars."

A tall, gangly pale guy with a six-inch jet-black mohawk and beady aqua eyes rimmed in black eyeliner stepped forward. He ceremoniously clapped his hands above his head. Feathers sprouted from his forehead and spread over his entire body until an abnormally large raven stood before them.

"If that spriggan thing stabs me, will I be able to do that?" Kelcie asked Niall.

Niall elbowed her with a shush.

The Raven took off, circling the testers, his talons whacking the ones with slow reflexes before coming in for a perfect landing.

"Cats possess the gift of shifting too but can morph to any kind of feline."

Diccon Wilks shrank to a calico cat, rubbing against Roswen's leg, giving the sniggering audience a few meows for an encore after she kicked him.

"The Adder Den is for those who tap into the powers of the mind. Emphatic, telekinetic, telepathic. They vary the most."

Roswen's clipboard flew out of her hand and into the hands of a petite girl with shock-white hair at the end of the row of Alphas.

In her wildest imagination, Kelcie never thought she would find a school like the Academy for the Unbreakable Arts. She wanted more than anything to be like them. Anyone of them. She choked on a squeal. And there was still one more Alpha to go.

Roswen held her hand out, not bothering to look. The Adder Alpha smiled wickedly, winding her arm like a pitcher about to deliver a singing strike. The clipboard smacked Roswen's palm. She checked it once more before continuing. "And finally, the Saiga Den. The rarest of all, the elementals. Fire, air, water, earth."

Roswen stepped back, making room for the yellow-cloaked Alpha. "Killian . . ."

Killian was at least fifteen. His long black hair hung loose past his shoulders. Standing right above Kelcie, when he looked down at them, she saw that his eyes were two different colors. One blue. One brown. And unlike all the others Kelcie had seen so far, he had thimble-sized nubs an inch above his hairline. The beginnings of some kind of horns. Combine that with his angular jaw and crooked nose, he was the most imperfect person Kelcie had seen at AUA, and by far the coolest.

Testers backed away from the platform.

"I thought they were banished to Chawell Woods."

"How can they even get to the school? Their boughs were confiscated, weren't they?"

"Why would they be allowed to test at all? Why would the Queen ever trust one of them again?" The girl who said that scanned the testers, searching people's faces, but for what?

Kelcie nudged Niall. "What are they talking about?"

His eyes fixed on Killian, Niall scooted away from the others, taking Kelcie with him. "He's a Fomorian. Not long ago, one of them who was in our armies turned traitor. His name was Draummorc."

Niall lips pressed together into a tight thin line.

"Drom-morc . . ." Kelcie repeated. A sudden, unexpected shiver ran up her spine. "Scary name."

"Scary Saiga. He nearly burned Summer City to the ground. My father died getting my family out." Niall's cheek ticked, like he was struggling to hold back the memory of what happened.

"I'm sorry," Kelcie said.

Killian turned his clenched fist over. He unraveled his fingers, revealing a small handful of dirt. With his other hand, he twirled his index finger above his open palm, uttering a word so softly Kelcie couldn't hear.

A tiny playful tornado swirled, the dirt making it visible.

Kelcie was awed. "No one wants them here then?"

"This school trains fiannas who *defend* and *protect* our lands. Not destroy it," he said bitterly.

Kelcie felt bad for Niall. She completely understood his anger, but she was also confused. "If they don't want to fight for the Lands of Summer, then why would they be here? Maybe they want to prove they're not all bad."

"That's what my sister says. That one bad Fomorian's actions shouldn't condemn them all. She claims they're misunderstood because they're very . . ." Niall chose his next word carefully, ". . . secretive."

"What if I ended up one of them? Would you hate me?" Not that Kelcie would care if he did, did she? Most kids at school hated her. But she did care. She didn't want Niall to hate her.

Niall dismissed her question with a head shake. "You're not an elemental. It's a gift exclusive to Fomorians and they always have two different colored eyes."

Kelcie was relieved to hear that. For the first time, she loved her mud-brown eyes. Then again, who was she kidding? She probably didn't have any powers. She would end up being sent packing, all the way back to Boston without so much as an obligatory AUA T-shirt as a parting gift.

Killian jerked his hand, raising his arm. The twister spun off, growing until it was taller than Kelcie as it touched down in the middle of outraged, screeching testers. Gale force winds pushed outward. Kids toppled, Kelcie careening into Niall.

"That's enough, Killian," Roswen said in a stern tone.

A mission-accomplished smirk tugging on the corner of his mouth, Killian lowered his arm. The tornado dispersed with a whiny, disappointed hiss.

Whispers spread like a bad rash, repeating the same questions as before Killian did his little demonstration. She even heard the word *demon* from more than one person. Kelcie didn't realize she was holding on to Niall's arm until he cleared his throat.

"Oh. Sorry." What was wrong with her?

Roswen marched to the edge of the platform. "For those of

you who prove to have the necessary powers, you will then face the dreaded Bridge of Leaping."

Everyone groaned except Kelcie. She didn't see the big deal. Crossing a bridge? That didn't sound so hard. But this magic thing had her seriously worried. She rubbed her temples trying to alleviate some of the pressure pushing on her brain. It was getting worse by the second.

Roswen chuckled, amused. "And there you have it. Get over the bridge, and you're in."

"Hey." A stocky boy nudged Niall so hard he bonked into Kelcie. Black, with buzzed brown hair, the boy smiled nervously and a single dimple in his left cheek cratered. "You scared? I am. Sick about it." He hugged his stomach. "Can't believe I even made it in time. My father was hellbent on me finishing harvest with my brothers, and they were taking their own sweet time on purpose, just to needle me. I'm Zephyr Chike, from the Bountiful Plains. What about you?"

Niall opened his mouth to respond, but Zephyr kept talking. "I bet I'm an Adder. You know why?"

Niall didn't bother to try and answer.

"'Cause my mother knows everything I'm going to do wrong *before* I do it. Says she can read my mind. And my father says I'm just like her. So . . ." he shrugged, ". . . there you go."

Kelcie had fosters like that herself, but she wrote it off to their substantial experience with kids, general parental intuition, and Kelcie's miserable luck.

"Sounds like your mother just knows you too well," Fishtail braid interjected.

Kelcie rolled her eyes at her and couldn't resist saying, "Quiet, Brona. I'm trying to hear."

She scowled and gave Kelcie her back.

"It's nice to meet you." The boy held a strong hand out to Niall.

Niall shook it and introduced himself, then took Kelcie by surprise introducing her to Zephyr too, like they were old friends.

"Settle down," Roswen called. "Beyond the platform, you can see Ferdaid's Stone Circle."

Kelcie rose to her tiptoes to get a better look. The huge stones sat like a crown on top of the hill.

"One at a time, you'll proceed inside." Roswen hopped off the platform. "Shall we begin? Brona Lee, let's have you go first. I have a good feeling about you. But leave the weapon here."

Brona dropped her sword belt beside Roswen and sprinted up the hill, beaming with pride at going first.

"She has a good feeling about her because her mother is a goddess, someone called Macha. She told me like fifty times," a girl next to Kelcie said, her shoulder-length chestnut curls bouncing with her shaking head.

"Her mother is a goddess?" Kelcie said in disbelief as Brona disappeared into the stone circle.

Niall adjusted his glasses yet again. "Macha is one of the three Morrígna, sister war goddesses. Macha, strategy; Badb, vengeance; and Nemain, fury." He spoke with a different accent, pronouncing their names like MAKH-uh, BEV, and NEY-van.

Kelcie scrutinized the crowd. "Are there a lot of demigods here?"

Niall shook his head. "No. They're extremely rare. Kind of like humans entering the Otherworld." He arched a brow at Kelcie, smirking. "The birth of one is almost always foretelling, and with anyone related to those three, a bad omen."

"How do you know all that?" Zephyr asked.

"I read a lot."

"I bet you do," Chestnut Curls said, her condescending stare darting to his arm without a hand.

Niall brushed the snub aside, adjusting his glasses. Kelcie wasn't sure who she was more upset with, Curlicue for insulting him, or Niall for taking it.

A few seconds later, a spooky Raven arched up and over the circle, blaring a definitive *caw* before fading against the backdrop of the pristine blue skies.

"And that, testers, is what will happen if you have a shot at AUA. Lee, stand behind Gavin Puce."

Mohawk winked at Brona as she jogged to him with a stuck-up swagger.

"I'm Willow Hawkins, by the way, from the Lakelands," Curlicue said to Kelcie, as if that was someplace special. "Where are you from?"

"Boston."

A crease formed between her brows. "That's near Wild Rose Meadows?"

Out of habit, Kelcie was so used to avoiding questions, she nodded. *"Mmmhmmm."*

"I've been there. I love that place!" Willow looped her arm through Kelcie's, pulling her away from Niall. She leaned over, whispering in Kelcie's ear. "You really shouldn't be standing next to him."

She mouthed, *Missing hand.* "You probably didn't notice."

"Oh, I noticed," Kelcie fumed. She couldn't understand what the big deal was that Niall was born without a hand. Was it because everyone else in this place was so perfectly perfect?

"Your name's Kelcie, right? I heard you talking to Zeph. We're forming a fianna for the Bridge of Leaping. We have room for one more. Want to join? Zephyr's in. And Marta Louisa Lopez too."

Willow elbowed the back of another girl. When she turned around, Kelcie had to back up to talk to her. A foot taller than everyone else, she was a girl worthy of three names. Her brown hair was cut super short. She stared down at Kelcie with intense rust-colored eyes and a seriously intimidating frown.

"Well?" Willow asked. "You in?"

"No, thanks." Kelcie slid her arm out and walked back to Niall.

Willow scoffed at Kelcie, glowering. "You'll be sorry. You'll never get across with him as a partner."

"Willow, you're next," Roswen called. "The rest of you, line up! I want a straight line. I don't care if it stretches all the way back to the Sidral!"

Willow jogged the hill while testers jockeyed for position. Kelcie padded to the end, more than happy to let everyone else go first. Niall went with her, his gaze falling on everything but Kelcie.

When they settled into their spot, Kelcie nudged him.

"What?"

"If we get to the bridge, will you go with me?"

He shrugged, still refusing to look at her. "Willow's right." He lifted his arm. "You should go with them."

Kelcie snorted. "Not happening. Probably won't get that far, but seriously. You with me, or not?"

Niall cracked a smile. "Yeah. Okay."

Another Raven rose out of the stone circle.

"Lucky." Kelcie would give anything to be able to fly.

Willow took a victory lap too, and then joined Brona behind Gavin Puce. The two were instant best friends. Arms over shoulders, giggling like they'd known each other their whole lives.

After that, a steady stream of disappointed testers emerged unclaimed. The Alphas took turns escorting them out, except for Diccon Wilks, the Cat Alpha who scared the life out of Kelcie earlier. He seemed to have left altogether.

Marta Louisa earned a shimmering black cat who ran out of the circle, jumped in Roswen's arms, and burst into dust. Zephyr was wrong about being an Adder. A majestic black horse jumped the stones, galloping down the hill.

"What's he?" Kelcie asked Niall.

"Charger, like my sister." His voice tight, he was feeling the pressure.

Kelcie was too. She closed her eyes against the pain behind them. All she could think was what would happen if she failed? The silver bough would take her right back to Boston. Back to a group home and a boring school where students didn't shape-shift and there were no telepaths. Less than an hour at the school, and Kelcie knew she didn't want that life anymore. She wanted this life. Her head screamed, *Don't get your hopes up.* But her heart fought back with, *Your silver bough brought you for a reason. You belong here.*

"I'm not sure those little trees got it right," Kelcie overheard Zephyr say to Regan. "Shouldn't a Charger prospect be good with horses? I live on a farm with lots of them. Trust me when I tell you that they don't like me. At all."

She sniffed Zephyr. "Horses can smell fear and you reek of it. Don't worry." She gave him a pat on the back that nearly bowled him over. "We'll ride it out of you—if you get in, Chike."

It took well over an hour to get through most everyone. All the Alphas had testers standing behind them, except for Saiga. It didn't seem to bother Killian. He spent the hour throwing a rock into the air and using wind to catch it, never even looking to see what animals burst from the stone circle. With only Kelcie and Niall left, neither of whom had two different colored eyes, it didn't look like there would be any elementals at all.

Roswen shifted her axe-pen from Niall to Kelcie. "Your choice. Who's first?"

Of the one hundred and fifty plus who tested, only forty claimed powers. The odds were not in Kelcie's favor. She patted Niall on the shoulder. "You go first."

Niall took off his glasses and handed them to her. "Yeah. Okay."

With a fleeting glance at his sister, Niall slowly padded up the hill.

Inside Ferdaid's Stone Circle, Kelcie could swear she heard Niall having a one-sided conversation. Five long, painstaking minutes later, a large green snake slithered out, sidewinding down the hill until it smacked into the platform's post headfirst, exploding into glistening green dust.

"An Adder?" Regan's brow creased with surprise. She clapped along with the others, giving him a formal respectful nod.

Zephyr whistled through his teeth, cheering Niall on. Kelcie was happy for Niall too but nerves choked her. She didn't want to be left behind.

Niall joined the others standing behind the tiny Adder Alpha, holding his head high, tossing a confident smirk at the others still whispering and gawking at his arm. He was halfway to getting into the Academy for the Unbreakable Arts, to proving to all the naysayers they were wrong. Kelcie was really happy for him.

Her heart nearly jumped out of her chest as Roswen slapped her clipboard, shouting, "And lastly, Kelcie Murphy."

6

NO WAY OUT

KELCIE HANDED NIALL'S glasses to Roswen. "Will you please give those back to Niall?"

"Will do." Roswen tilted her head at the stone circle. "Get a move on."

A long time ago, Kelcie made wishes all the time. At first, for her parents to come back for her. When that didn't come true, she worried it was too big an ask, so she wished for easier things like more food, a better place to sleep, to be left alone. Those never came true either, so she stopped. Wishes were for fools. But as she climbed the hill, she couldn't help herself. That was how badly she wanted to go to the Academy for the Unbreakable Arts. *Please make me a Raven. If not, a Cat would be cool too. Or an Adder. Then I'd be with Niall. Really anything would be totally cool. I just want to stay.*

A sudden, chilling breeze raised the hair on the back of her neck a few feet from the edge, giving Kelcie pause. She set her shaking hand on one of the tall cold stones, debating the last step that would bring her inside. No one came out of Ferdaid's Stone Circle physically injured, but that didn't keep her stomach from twisting into an impossible knot, making her feel sick.

From the outside, it looked like your basic stone circle, not that Kelcie had ever been in one before. But she had seen pictures in books. Evenly spaced stones a few feet taller than Kelcie enclosed a soft bed of ankle-high grass. It was quiet. Too quiet. The only sound came from Kelcie's racing pulse crashing into her eardrums. *Just do it.*

A deep breath for courage and a few steps later, the standing stones creaked, widening, closing the gaps between them, trapping Kelcie inside. Her feet sank into the itchy grass. Exulted blue skies darkened to a gloomy, stormy gray. Lightning cracked. Thunder rumbled a foreboding warning. Sweat prickled, dripping down her sides.

Angry miniature trees, not much bigger than the average action figure, catapulted off the tops of the stones.

"Spriggans . . ." Kelcie mused, relieved. She let out the breath she was holding. They hardly seemed dangerous. "Aren't you cute . . ."

They ran at her from all sides, poking their sharp, toothpick-sized fingers at her feet and ankles, turning her into a human pincushion.

"Not so cute!" She kicked. "Quit it!"

Sap stuck them to her leggings. She tried pulling them off, ripping an even larger hole in the knee, giving them a new target.

"Ow!"

She spun, stamping, bonking into the stones, trying anything to get them off. Nothing worked. They wouldn't stop poking her!

Her blood *chilled*—like at the museum.

Her blue veins glowed, and *freezer* burned.

Kelcie hissed at the searing pain.

Then her ears *popped*. Green mist surrounded her head. She felt strange inside, like a valve she didn't know was there suddenly burst wide open. It was exhilarating.

"What's happening to me?"

Kelcie rode the wave, breathing through the surging energy. It waned, then vanished altogether, along with the green mist. Was that it? The spriggans' venom wearing off, proving Kelcie had no powers? Her shoulders drooped with extreme disappointment. For the first time in forever, she choked, holding back tears.

The stones creaked. Two parted enough for a black panther to enter, then closed again.

"Diccon Wilks?"

Kelcie's heart leaped at what this could mean. Was she a Cat too?

His fangs dripping, he growled, stalking Kelcie. If it was Wilks, he gave no signs of recognizing her.

The baby trees retreated to the edges of the circle to watch like spectators in the Colosseum in ancient Rome, come to see the gladiator eaten for lunch. Its head lowering, and freakish green eyes narrowing, the huge cat skulked toward her, chirping noises that Kelcie interpreted as *Dinner time.*

"Nice kitty . . ." Kelcie said. She didn't know what to do. She held her hands up, hoping something would happen, that her powers would suddenly manifest, the way they did in all the superhero movies, but nothing happened. She was about to end up Cat Chow!

The panther leaped.

Kelcie ducked, running across the circle, screaming, "Help!" Her shoe got stuck in the tall grasses, and she tripped. She threw her hands out on her way to crashing into one of the stones, but never made contact. Air pulsed between her hands and the stone. Startled, Kelcie gasped. Was she making this happen? Then she laughed! "Are you seeing this?"

The panther ignored her. Bulging neck muscles tensing, it crouched, ready to pounce. Kelcie scooped the air, feeling its tangible weight and sensing a strangely familiar connection.

Please work . . .

As soon as the panther charged, she pitched the wind. The cat dodged easily, but the spriggans weren't so lucky. Stick limbs cracked, smashing into the stones. Those left uninjured ditched their wounded and scaled the rocks, frantic to get out of the line of fire.

Meanwhile, the panther kept coming.

There was nowhere to run. Nowhere to hide. Adrenaline surged. Kelcie planted her feet, thrusting her hands, growling through her fear. "Stay back!"

WINDBALLS shot from her hands.

The first missed the panther by a mile, but the second hit with so much force that the panther flew headfirst into a stone. The animal morphed to a staggering, whimpering Wilks.

"Yo, boy . . ." He leaned on the stone to stay erect. A lump was already raising on his forehead.

"How . . . What. . . ." Kelcie jumped up and down, hooting and hollering, "I did that! Me!" She held her hands up, staring at them in disbelief. "They look normal, though, right? How crazy is this?"

Wilks flung a hand in her direction. "All done. You're good. Just stay back. Don't come any closer, Saiga."

"Saiga?" Her chest filled with cold dread. "But my eyes . . . I thought that was impossible?" What would Niall say? Would he speak to her anymore?

Gray skies pixelated to blue. The high noon sun broke over the circle, and the stones parted.

A shimmering white antelope with ringed horns dusted in pink and jade sprang from the earth, bleating in Kelcie's direction, then trotted right through the stones, declaring her potential Den to the rest of the testers, Alphas, and Roswen.

Kelcie couldn't move. She couldn't breathe. She *wasn't* human. At least part of her wasn't.

Niall's words flooded her mind. *Two different colored eyes. Elementals. Fomorian descendants.* At least part of her was Fomorian. They would all look at her differently, as if she was the enemy, but let them. Kelcie found her first clue about her parents, and to her, that was all that mattered.

Reactions were swift. Gasps and gossipy whispers greeted Kelcie as soon as she stepped outside the stone circle. The other testers gave her a wide berth, backing away from her as she padded toward Niall. She thought he would too, but he didn't. Niall stood there, staring down at her. She worried, chewing her lip, looking everywhere but at him, too afraid of what he was going to say. Maybe she did care more than she wanted to.

"Kelcie . . . look at me," he said with guarded trepidation.

She slid her eyes to meet his stare, wishing she hadn't. His jaw dropped. His brows shot straight up. "Your eyes . . ."

"What's wrong with them?"

He took off his glasses and looked closer. "They were brown."

She stepped back. "What do you mean, were? What color are they now?"

Brona's head jerked in a very bird-like fashion. "They're like his."

"I'm Killian Lynch."

Kelcie turned around and found the moody Saiga Alpha with one brown eye and one blue standing over her.

"Kelcie Murphy." He crossed his arms. "This is a surprise."

"For me too," Kelcie chirped.

"Stay focused on the next challenge. Block out anyone who gives you a hard time. They don't matter. Only getting over that bridge does."

"I will. Thank you."

As Killian started to walk away, realization dawned. Her eyes were like his. But how could they just change color? And for the first time in forever, they didn't hurt either. Neither did her head.

Testers and other Alphas cast glares in her direction. *So what?* It was the same way they always treated her when they found out she was a foster kid. Killian was right. *They don't matter.* Only getting over the bridge did.

7

DON'T. LOOK. DOWN . . .

ROSWEN LED THE testers through several practice fields and down a winding path around a dense grove that ended in a flower-filled meadow, on the edge of which was both a steep cliff and the infamous Bridge of Leaping. The whole way Kelcie brought up the rear, pretending not to notice the rest of the testers, Niall included, glowering over their shoulders at her and making snide comments. Kelcie was no stranger to feeling alone in a crowd of kids. *Ostracized* could've been her middle name, but Niall's snub hurt. She refused to care. If he didn't want to be her friend, so be it. She would get through this alone, like always.

"Where are the Alphas?" Kelcie asked Roswen when she caught up with the rest of the group.

"In boats under the bridge, waiting to rescue the sizable lot of you that will end up in the drink. Can't have you all swept out to sea. Talk about a mountain of paperwork."

"Drink?" Kelcie gulped.

She never swam. She never took baths. Only showers. She avoided standing bodies of water at all costs. The reason was obvious. She nearly drowned and had no interest in ever going through that again.

She stood back from the cliff's edge, her nostrils filling with salty sea air, refusing to look over. Niall was braver. He knelt at the very edge, staring down, perhaps contemplating his mortality. Kelcie would be. After a few minutes, he walked over to her, shoving his hand in his pocket. He spent a full minute blinking and staring at her before he finally deigned to speak to her.

"It's a thirty-foot drop. Churning currents. My sister's down there, in a rowboat with a super-long fishhook though."

"Oh, good to know." Was that supposed to make Kelcie feel better? "You can stop talking now."

He continued anyway. "And that bridge looks more like a plank. No handrails. Nothing but a thin board."

"Lovely. What's on the other side?"

"The preceptor's office. It's called the Shadow," Brona explained, unexpectedly joining them. "I met with Scáthach in her office when I visited over the summer."

Brona pronounced Scáthach's name Skah-hawk with enthusiastic awe, like she was a celebrity or something.

"Lucky!" Marta Louisa exclaimed, widening their circle. "Did you know her name means *the shadowy one?*"

Niall removed his glasses and started cleaning them with the bottom of his shirt. "Technically, yes, but in the old language her name could have also translated as *protector.* Then again, in the ancient texts in the library at the College of Mystical Beings in Summer City, they categorize her as a Goddess of Teaching."

"Whatever." Willow scoffed. "Here, she's preceptor."

"The principal of this school is a goddess?" Kelcie asked.

They all stared at her as if she'd grown three heads.

"What's a principal?" Marta Louisa asked.

"The same thing, I think," Kelcie answered, unsure.

"Gather round." Roswen waved everyone over. "As you probably figured out by now, that is the Bridge of Leaping." She nodded at the flimsy plank. "Get across, and you're in."

"That's it?" Brona asked skeptically. "What are the rules?"

"No rules, but a word of warning. I bet many of you are feeling suddenly very *powerful* after what you accomplished in the stone circle. The spriggan shock is potent, but it wears off quickly. To fully utilize your powers will take training. Years of training. Don't count on them to get you over that bridge." She looked down, catching the attention of as many of the testers as possible. "Count on each other."

With a wicked gleam in her eyes, Roswen stepped away from the group.

Testers latched on to each other like a barrel of monkeys. Kelcie had never been able to count on anyone before, and now, after finding out she was an elemental, she was one hundred percent positive that wasn't going to change. She hoped, though, that Niall would answer a few questions, since he seemed to be speaking to her.

"Niall, why do they call it the Bridge of Leaping?"

"It's modeled after the original enchanted bridge that had to be crossed for Scáthach to consider training you. Millennia ago, the school was on the Isle of Skye, which is now a part of a place called Scotland, from what I read. You've heard of that, right? It's in the human world."

Kelcie nodded. "Did you say millennia?" She sucked in a sharp breath. "That's one old goddess . . ."

Niall slapped his hand over her mouth. "She could be listening!"

"What's so special about the bridge?"

"It tosses you off when you step on it."

Kelcie examined her clenched fists. In the stone circle she managed to fire off a couple of windballs, but that would be useless. And what if Roswen was right anyway, that these new powers only worked because of what the spriggans did? Kelcie sighed, dropping her hands. She couldn't rely on them.

"Any thoughts on how we get across?" Niall asked.

"We?"

Zephyr's shadow fell over Kelcie. "Cú Chulainn jumped across in one leap, but he was a demigod and could do that."

That gave everyone the same idea, but Willow got to Brona first. "Do you want to be in our crossing fianna?"

"I would but I don't think I'd be much help." Brona walked to the edge of the bridge. "Thanks for asking though."

She clapped her hands over her head, and morphed into a raven. Jealous whines followed her as she soared over the Bridge of Leaping, skimming her claws on the plank for good measure. The irritated bridge bent, putting up a wall that she easily rolled around, landing safely on the other side.

"Wow." Kelcie was beyond impressed. "I really wish I could do that."

"Come on. Let's get this over with," Willow griped to Marta Louisa. She hooked Zephyr's arm, taking him with them.

Kelcie tucked her bough inside her shirt. She wanted to get this over with as fast as she could too. As she started toward the growing line, Niall stopped her.

"Let's let all of the others go first. We might learn something."

"We?" He said it again. Her heart backflipped. "You still want to go with me?"

"Yeah. I-I do." He half smiled. "Didn't I say as much?"

Kelcie wasn't satisfied. "You want me to get in to AUA? Even after . . . you know . . ." She sighed the word. "Saiga."

"You didn't know. It's not your fault."

That only made Kelcie feel worse. "It's not my *fault*?"

Niall raked frustrated fingers through his shaggy hair, making it stick straight up. "Look, I want us both to get in, okay?"

Kelcie's face grew hot from anger or something else, a tinge of happiness? She filed it under "too dangerous to dissect," and turned away from him, toward the others who were starting across. "Okay."

Watching turned out to be a good idea. They learned something all right. The bridge was temperamental and didn't want to be crossed. By the time it was Kelcie and Niall's turn, only half of the groups had made it. Speaking of groups, three was the magic number. With Willow's speed, Zephyr's strength, and Marta Louisa's height, they ran, shoved, and hurled their way across. It wasn't pretty, but it got the job done. Teams of four were too slow. Two didn't fare much better. Carrying too little weight, the bridge easily flicked them off.

As Niall and Kelcie prepared to go, those who made it regrouped into a row of skeptical spectators, making bets on how long they would last.

"I give them three seconds," Willow crowed.

"No way. He's only got one hand and she's a demon!" The boy behind her sniggered. "They won't last two seconds."

Wind whipped over the bridge. Nerves tightened Kelcie's chest, making it hard to breathe. Niall smartly removed his glasses, putting them in his pocket.

"Whatever you do, don't stop running, and DON'T look down," he instructed.

"You talking to me or yourself?"

He grimaced at the plank. "Good point."

Kelcie nudged him gently in the back. "Go."

"Okay! Don't push!" Niall shuffled on.

Arms out for balance, Kelcie followed, only making it a step before the windspeed grew tenfold, shifting direction too, hitting them head on, making it impossible to move forward at all.

"Stop!" Kelcie growled.

"What? Why?" Niall squeaked.

"Not you! I'm talking to the wind!" She yelled back, feeling like an idiot. She tried a silent plea. *Calm down, wind.*

Kelcie's foot slipped off the edge. She panicked, grabbing on to Niall's shirt. She leaned on him so hard Niall fell forward, gripping the sides of the bridge up to his elbows with incredible strength, keeping them both from going over.

"You need to get off me!"

Kelcie balanced enough to stand on her own. Niall hopped up, reaching back for her hand, but the plank shuddered. Kelcie crashed into him, knocking him flat. When the edge behind her lifted, she pushed him with all her might, driving him forward, off the other side of the bridge where he landed on solid ground.

She, on the other hand, was never going to make it. The bridge rose and fell, trying to flick her off. She lost her balance and was about to go over, her arms pinwheeling, when the wind *changed direction*. A sudden burst pushed Kelcie upright, keeping her from falling.

"Whoa!" someone cried.

"Did you see that?" another bellowed.

"Is she doing that?" gasped someone else.

Kelcie shifted her arms back to a T. The wind shifted again, hitting her from both sides. She was doing this. She was causing the wind to change direction, and it was awesome!

A rippling wave passed through the bridge. Kelcie hurdled three peaks on her way to diving headfirst off the end, belly flopping on unforgiving ground.

The sniggering boy from before hissed, "She doesn't belong here. None of them do."

Agreeing mumbles buzzed like bees over Kelcie's head.

But she was here, and according to Roswen, would have a spot at the Academy for the Unbreakable Arts. Kelcie lay completely still. She knew that when she got up from the cool grass the rest of her life would be a series of unending firsts. Like how for the first time, her head didn't ache. Her eyes no longer felt like over-inflated tires. They felt—right.

Balanced.

Normal.

An iron gate on the Shadow's wall creaked and a towering woman walked out with a foreboding stride. A long, glossy auburn braid draped over the shoulder of her black leather tunic. Swords anchored each hip, and Kelcie saw dagger grips sticking out of her boots.

Niall mouthed, *Scáthach.*

The preceptor lived up to her legend.

Kelcie hopped up quickly.

Tagging along beside Scáthach was what at first glance appeared to be a wolf, but it was unlike any wolf Kelcie had ever seen before. Lush green fur, except for its muzzle, which was white as fresh snow, and strapping feathers for a tail.

"The *cú sith* is not friendly, but he won't bother you so long as you don't bother him."

At first Kelcie thought his name was sue-sith because that was what Scáthach said, but then she added, "Striker, sit."

Striker obeyed, whining, unhappy about the order.

Everyone except Kelcie lowered their heads in a truncated bow. She was too busy smiling at Striker. She itched to pet him.

"No need for that. We don't bow, curtsy, or kneel at this school. I am Scáthach. And that is what I'm called. I only have one name, so use it." She paced, pausing before each of them. "The Academy for the Unbreakable Arts is my school, and it is only for the exceptional. Feel proud, for today all of you have earned a spot in our first-year class. A spot that will be tested each and every day."

After a disobedient glance at Scáthach, Striker trotted to Kelcie. He sniffed her fingers.

"Striker!" Scáthach snapped.

The next thing Kelcie knew, Striker's paws were on her chest, his tongue licking her cheek.

"Down!" Scáthach pushed him off. "Home!"

The cú sith trotted around Brona, startling her, then bumped Kelcie on the way through the gate. His head hung low, but by the way he panted, it looked like he was smiling.

"Did you rub roasted meat on your face, Kelcie Murphy?"

Everyone laughed.

Kelcie did too. "No, ma'am."

"Most unusual. Striker likes no one. Not even me sometimes."

"How do you know our names already?" Kelcie asked. In Kelcie's experience, it always took teachers weeks to learn new students' names, and her principals only knew the few who ended up in their office all the time.

Scáthach winked. "I'm gifted."

Brona stepped forward. "Thank you for this opportunity, ma'am. I won't let you down."

"I don't expect you will, Brona Lee." She pinned the whole group with a stern frown. "I don't expect any of you will. But year one will be the hardest year of your life. A few of you may quit. Others may not be asked back. Your path to success is simple. Work hard, study hard, follow orders. There are no second chances at AUA. Understood?"

"Yes, ma'am!" Brona answered.

Scáthach's gray eyes narrowed to slits. "Why is Lee the only one responding?"

"Yes, ma'am!" the entire class bellowed.

"Better. Roswen is waiting for you on the other side of the bridge. Dismissed."

Without looking back, Scáthach strode through the gate. A second later, it slammed shut of its own accord.

Kelcie breathed a relieved sigh as the plank transformed into a proper bridge with a cobblestone deck. There were even makeshift railings! Sturdy, thick ropes threaded through bird statues, resembling the brown eagles perched on the Shadow's gate.

As she padded across, she felt excited to have made it, but also scared and confused. Her day started with a field trip, her caseworker turning out to be a fairy, in cahoots with another fairy, who stole an ancient object that exploded an impenetrable vault door off its hinges when Kelcie touched it. None of that was a coincidence. They told her they had been planning that for a long time. But the fairies were gone. Niall said they couldn't come here. They had what they wanted anyway. The ancient object. If she was a part of their future plans, then they wouldn't have left her behind.

But one thing still bugged her. *Ta Erfin. I am the heir.* The heir of what?

8

A ROOM OF HER OWN

OVER THE NEXT hour, Roswen gave a tour of the sprawling campus. Kelcie saw two medieval towers with more broken windows than unbroken, and no door at all on the round one.

"The square tower is Direwood Keep, filled with classrooms that are rarely used. The round tower is called the Nether Tower, where Coach Blackwell will put you through your paces." Roswen paused, delivering a disgusted sigh. "Ignore the wear and tear if you can. I personally wouldn't want to step foot in those ancient structures. Any day now they may collapse on your heads, but Scáthach hates change, and hates parting with money even more, so here they sway, waiting for a strong wind to blow them down." She winked at Kelcie. "Moving on!"

Next up were lush green fields named for different kinds of trees, like Holly, Hawthorn, and Birch—and all busy. Students trained, sparring with swords and axes, throwing daggers, hurling spears, and shooting arrows at targets. It was the most beautiful thing Kelcie had ever seen. But all the while that little voice nagged, rationalizing—how could any of this be real? Always coming back to the same worry—what if this was only a dream?

Hours had passed. If she were in Boston, the field trip would long since be over. Would anyone notice she was gone? Or care? Mrs. Belts at the group home would report her as a runaway.

They always did, but if this was really happening, that didn't matter, not anymore. Kelcie had a place at the Academy for the Unbreakable Arts.

They returned to the woods Kelcie had been in before, when she arrived.

"I teach survival foraging in this part of the forest. Once a week, dinner will come from what we find together." Roswen sucked in a deep cleansing breath. "Do you smell that?"

Kelcie smelled the same thing she always smelled during summer in the woods. Sweet flowers and wet bark.

Niall sniffed. "Elderberries . . ."

Brona's head tilted. ". . . And knotweed?"

Roswen nodded. "Good. Looks like we found the smart ones in the first-year class."

Niall exchanged a competitive smile with Brona that didn't sit well with Kelcie.

As Roswen turned around, Kelcie glimpsed a black square in the middle of her back holstering a dagger. There were no straps like a normal scabbard would need to stay in place, and no matter which way she twisted or bent, the square never moved. It looked permanent.

After a swing past the stables, Roswen corralled the first years under a giant gazebo beside an elaborate garden called Befelts. "Other than one night a week foraging in the woods, this is where you will eat every meal. I cook them. Praise is highly recommended for your chef, even if you eat the same dish three times a week."

A chorus of *yes ma'am*'s followed.

Then Roswen passed out silver glass bottles of something called Zinger. "This will take the sting out of the cuts and bruises from the tests. We stock it in every Den. Drink enough of it and the healing apples will build your body's ability to rapidly heal on its own."

Kelcie gulped it down in three long sips. It tasted like the most delicious bubbly apple juice she had ever had. She felt an instant zing all the way down to her toes. The black-and-blue bruises on the back of her forearms, her scraped knees, the spriggan puncture marks, every scratch healed instantly.

When she was finished, Kelcie held it up like she was auditioning for a commercial. "Delicious and nutritious."

The bottle melted to sand, slipping through her fingers. "And environmentally friendly—instant recycling." She belched carbonation and gave a full-toothed grin to Marta Louisa and Willow, who wouldn't stop staring at her.

"You're really strange," Marta Louisa commented.

"And the mismatched eye thing makes you look possessed," Willow added.

"They're all possessed. Why do you think they call them demons?" a brown-haired boy exclaimed.

"Oh really, Tad? What about my dimple? That make me possessed?" Zephyr burped in Tad's ear. "Yup. There it is. I guess I'm possessed too!"

Niall surprised Kelcie, joining in, holding up his left arm with amused confidence. "Oh please. I win. And check this out." He sucked down a whole bottle, then belched the alphabet at Zephyr, singing the Z in Kelcie's ear.

She shoved him away, but was smiling when she did it.

Willow and Marta Louisa stared at all of them like they had grown three heads until Brona let one fly that was so loud the whole class whooped. Her hands launched above her head, declaring herself champion, earning the Raven yet another round of applause. Kelcie stared at her, envious. Was there anything she wasn't the best at?

Roswen slid the clipboard she was never without out from underneath her armpit and pulled the axe-pen from behind her ear. "A couple things. Your parents have been notified of your acceptance, except for yours, Murphy. Is there anyone we need to contact on your behalf?"

All eyes shifted to Kelcie. *Here we go.* "No, ma'am."

"No one at all?" Brona asked.

"Not an aunt or uncle?" Niall pressed.

"No one," Kelcie snapped, then felt bad for doing it.

"Great. Means my work here is done." Roswen stuffed her miniature weapon behind her ear, nearly taking off her lobe. "Check your silver boughs. Scáthach has officially accepted you into the school so you should see a new offshoot and leaf, the color of which matches your Den."

A yellow crystal leaf sprouted on Kelcie's silver bough.

"Schedules will be in your rooms shortly. Your fianna assignments will be listed on top. DO NOT come to me complaining that you don't like your fianna. It will not be changed. Ever. Got me, people?"

"Yes, ma'am!" the first years declared in unison, swapping nervous glances. The seed planted, dinner would be a mad dash to figure out who was in their fiannas. Kelcie included.

"Your Alphas will be here in a few minutes. They will get you settled in your Dens. I'll see you all at dinner."

HAVEN HALL LOOKED more like a mortuary than a dorm. Four stories of gothic delight with asymmetrical rooflines, rectangular windows with diamond-shaped panes, and no doors—no way in at all.

Killian and Kelcie stayed behind the other first years and Alphas as they crowded underneath the overhang of an archway. He had barely said two words to her on the walk over from the garden, but that wasn't surprising. Killian had all the makings of one of the moody older guys who existed in every group home she ever lived in. The artsy type, the one who figured out the matrix of life at birth and was either too shy to share it with anyone or didn't want to bother. A man of mystery. Cooler than cool. The kind who everyone developed a crush on, but Killian was at least fifteen, and Kelcie was twelve, and it was never going to happen.

"What was it you said when you made that twister?"

Kelcie asked him. She cupped her palms, scooping the air. Like in the stone circle, it weighed more than nothing. A lot more.

A deep crease cratered between his brows. "Mistral."

Her mind auto-translated. *Air*. "Mistral," she tested an underhanded wave. A gale hit Willow so hard in the back she barreled into Marta Louisa, laying them both out.

"Oops . . ." Kelcie cringed.

"What are you doing?" Marta Louisa snapped, hopping up.

"Nothing. I-me-no . . ." Willow stuttered, then aimed her finger at Kelcie. "It was her!"

"Don't be ridiculous," Gavin Puce warbled. His mohawk flattened against his cranium, smoothing to soft black feathers. "A first-year Saiga could never do that."

Killian jerked his head, indicating for Kelcie to follow.

Once they were out of earshot of the others, he whispered, "Did you do that?"

"I think, I mean, I, well . . . I didn't mean to," Kelcie admitted. "Am I in trouble?"

"No." Killian crossed his arms, sizing her up. "But Puce is right. You shouldn't be able to do that."

Footsteps came up behind them. It turned out to be Roswen. "Watch this . . ." she said in a very mischievous way.

"Chargers! All eyes on me!" Regan raised her silver bough, setting it against the wall. A tiny blue light flashed. A massive trapezoid-shaped wooden door materialized out of thin air. The horse chiseled into it neighed and bowed in greeting, then the door opened.

A first-year Adder tried to cross the threshold, but the horse reared, bucking her out. Roswen laughed so hard she nearly fell over.

"Good boy, Eremon." Regan patted the door, settling the horse down. She helped the Adder up. "Roswen told you to do that, didn't she?"

"Sorry, Campbell. Couldn't help myself," Roswen called, sobering. "Just proving a point. You're only allowed in your own Den. Your bough has no access to the others. If you want in, you have to be invited."

Beyond the door was an ornate spiral staircase with a smooth brass handrail that led sharply upward. "Let's go, Chargers. Bonus points for sliding up the banister."

Regan stepped over the threshold, straddled the railing, and was magically pulled upward.

Zephyr went last, hesitating so long the door started to close. "Uh oh!" He stepped inside, vanishing from view. As the door disappeared, Kelcie heard him howling with laughter.

Adders were next. In contemplative silence, the petite white-haired Alpha approached the wall. Her bough lifted off her chest of its own accord, leaving her hands free to meet the hissing cobra carved into the emerald glass door. A gentle scratch behind the hood and the snake coiled, the scales rasping as the door creaked open. Kelcie glimpsed an arched wooden bridge inside, the kind you'd see spanning a garden pond.

Niall waved to her as he cautiously crossed the threshold onto the bridge. For his sake, Kelcie hoped that this one was more stable than the Bridge of Leaping.

Real ravens soared out of the Ravens' iron door, greeting newcomers with harsh caws that sounded like curses. Brona showed off, transforming and flying through the door. The others ran after her, cheering her name, trumpeting how they couldn't wait to do that.

The Cat Den's door was guarded by a pacing black-spotted lynx. A tickle under the chin from Diccon, and triumphant roars welcomed the first years. Kelcie caught sight of them climbing a tree before the door slammed shut.

Finally, it was Killian and Kelcie's turn.

Facing the stone wall, Killian said, "Why don't you do the honors?"

Excited and nervous, Kelcie fumbled the charm a couple of times before it grew roots and the little yellow leaf lit up. A bronze door materialized with a beautiful white antelope pressed into the copper tones. It had thick horns with pronounced rings, a long droopy nose, and abnormally large eyes. The antelope stamped his hoof as if saying hello.

Killian flicked two fingers. The door glided to one side.

"Wow." Kelcie couldn't wait to do that.

Just inside was a spinning fireman's pole.

Killian half smiled. "You go first. Mind the bottom. Comes up fast."

Eager to try it out, Kelcie leaped on, sliding down into dense darkness. Unable to see past the end of her nose, she never saw the bottom coming. She hit so hard her feet came out from under her. Mortified, she hopped up as the lights flickered on, pretending that never happened.

Killian came up behind her. "Welcome home."

He padded down a short hallway that opened up to—an indoor pool.

"Ollie will tell you the pool is for him, but it isn't."

"It's okay. I don't like to swim."

A boy, younger than Killian but older than Kelcie, sauntered out of a room on the other side of the pool, drinking a bottle of Zinger, and rubbing his wet head with a towel. "Oh well, I guess I will have to make it my life's ambition to toss you in then."

He cackled diabolically.

Kelcie glared. "Don't even try it."

He made a face at Killian. "We got one?"

Killian shrugged. "Strange, right?"

"Strange," Kelcie agreed, leaving her the subject of curious stares. Questions stampeded through her mind. *Could we be related?* After all, they were Fomorian. She decided to wait on the interrogation for a few minutes. Ease into it.

"Um, who are you?" Kelcie asked the new boy.

"Sorry. Kelcie Murphy, meet my brother, Ollie."

Ollie gave a very dramatic bow. "Welcome to our humble abode."

Like Killian, Ollie had black hair and olive skin, but that's where the similarities ended. Ollie's hair was buzzed extremely short, showing off his oversized ears that wiggled with his smile. He didn't have tiny horn nubs the way Killian did either. Maybe it was an age thing. Kelcie rubbed her forehead, petrified at the idea of having a set of her own, but also intrigued.

A living room with comfy couches and plush chairs sat empty to the left. In fact, the whole place was very, very quiet. "Where's everyone else?"

"It's just us three," Ollie said.

"This place is all for us?"

Killian shoved his hands in his pockets, nodding.

"Where do we sleep?" Kelcie asked.

"Your room is this way."

Killian undid the buckle on his cloak, catching it over his forearm in a smooth move as he padded down a hallway. At the end, he pushed open the door to a huge room. The furniture was in multiples of four. Four beds, each big enough for three of her. Four oversized desks, the one at the end the only with a stack of books, and four wardrobes along the wall opposite the beds, the last full of bright yellow clothes.

Kelcie's eyes lit up. "All of this is for me? I don't have to share?"

"You're the only girl, and I'm pretty sure you don't want to bunk with us. Ollie snores." Killian smirked.

"I do not." Ollie flopped on her bed. "He snores."

Kelcie ran her finger down the books piled on the desk: *Magical Tools & Talismans, Moon Cycles to Live and Die By, Night Fundamentals: The Children of Winter, Don't Eat That! Foraging 101,* and *Beginning Crafting.*

"Those are *all* for Madame Le Deux's class except the foraging book," Ollie groaned. "She really piles it on. Get a head start on the moon cycles stuff or you'll be behind from the very first day."

"Thanks." The lights in the room dimmed. She glanced at the ceiling and was amazed to see what looked like the sky outside. "Are they screens? We're underground, aren't we?"

"Show her," Killian said to Ollie.

Without getting up from his bed, Ollie lifted his fist into the air and cried, "*Caenum.*" A black cloud raced in and a single raindrop pinged the ceiling.

It was made of glass. "You did that?" Kelcie asked.

"That's nothing." Ollie flipped his wrist, dangling his confident fingers, and the storm cloud let go. The rain plinking off the glass sounded like spoons tapping crystal, creating a playful symphony that filled the room.

Craning her neck, Kelcie beamed. "Wicked."

"The ceiling is made of sea glass from Lucent Bay. It mirrors the skies outside, directly above," Ollie explained.

"Beware. I accidently used my powers in a nightmare. Cracked a sheet in my sleep. Roswen made me clean out horse stalls for a month." Killian frowned, wrinkling his nose at the memory.

Kelcie made a mental note to sleep on her side.

"She won't need to worry about that for a long while," Ollie scoffed.

"Oh, she might. She just pegged a baby Raven from twenty feet, taking out a big kitty too."

"Really?" Ollie's jaw dropped.

"Really," Kelcie nodded. "You have water powers then?" she asked Ollie.

Ollie was about to answer but Killian cut him off. "Why don't you know that, Kelcie?" His sudden harsh tone startled her.

"How would I know that?" Kelcie retorted in an equally sharp tone.

"My big beautiful green eye." Ollie winked.

Kelcie took a closer look. His eyes were green and brown.

"Huh . . ." She walked into the bathroom, finding a small

mirror over the sink. She V'd her fingers, stretching her lids back, staring at her much richer brown and pale blue eyes.

"This is so freaky."

"Kelcie, you all right in there?" Ollie called.

She padded back into the room. "So my eye turned blue because I have wind powers?"

"Mistral. Air powers, not wind," Killian corrected.

Kelcie knew that. It was so strange to feel a part of something that she knew nothing about.

"Where do you come from, Kelcie Murphy?" he asked.

"Not Chawell," Ollie interjected. "We know all the Fomorian families, and none with anyone of age asked to come with us to test this year."

Kelcie grabbed the bedpost for support. *We know all the Fomorian families.* More than anything, she hoped that was true. "I'm from Boston, Massachusetts. It's a city in the human world. I don't know who my family is. I was hoping that you might be able to help me find them."

"The human world?" Ollie shook his head. "You're full of surprises."

"Is it possible they live in the woods?" Kelcie asked.

"Possible," Killian replied. "We were all banished there."

"After the attack on the capital, Summer City—" Ollie stopped himself. "Do you know about that?"

Kelcie nodded. "Niall told me. Someone named Draummorc."

"He was the most powerful Fomorian in Summer's armies," Ollie boasted.

"Who screwed us all," Killian grumbled. "After they locked him up, Queen Eislyn declared all our lands forfeit. Anyone with two-colored eyes was rounded up, herded like animals from all over the kingdom into Chawell Woods, the most remote part of the Lands of Summer where we wouldn't be a threat to Summerfolk ever again."

"You can't just take people's homes," Kelcie blurted, righteous indignation filling her soul with anger at this ignorant queen.

"You can if you're queen." Ollie threw a pillow at her.

Kelcie hugged it. "Is it terrible there, in Chawell Woods, I mean?"

"Not as bad as it was when we first got there. I'm fourteen now . . ." Ollie considered the math. "I was six then. We built houses so we could move out of the caves around the lake. There's a market now too. It's sort of home, I guess."

"It will never be home," Killian grated. "And it's not getting better. This summer they came to Chawell, registered everyone, collected blood samples."

She remembered those Chargers talking about that. "Why?"

"Tracking spell is my guess. To keep tabs on us." Killian bristled.

Kelcie didn't like the sound of that at all. "Wait! You said you were six, Ollie. This happened eight years ago. That's how long ago I was abandoned! That can't be a coincidence." Kelcie paced between the bed and desk. "Maybe my parents and I somehow got separated when they were taken there." She rushed to Killian. "Could you ask someone, like your parents? They might know of a family who lost a redheaded kid. I was four then."

Killian's shoulders tensed. "Our tubes are monitored. It could be a risk."

Ollie sat up, crossing his legs. "A huge risk." He agreed, his head bobbing up and down, then paused, conflicted. "Wait, what's the risk?"

Killian sighed at Kelcie. "You're an unknown in the Lands of Summer. Soon as I send that letter, you won't be. Are you sure you want me to do that?"

"I *am* an unknown. Even I don't know who I am. Please! It's worth the risk."

Killian nodded. "Okay."

"Thank you!" Kelcie smiled, hope blooming. "But I don't understand. Why are you here if the Queen did such awful things to your people?"

"Our people." Ollie grinned.

"Our people," Kelcie happily agreed. She had a people!

Killian leaned his back against the wall beside her wardrobe, crossing his arms. "Our grandfather isn't happy about it, but our parents were supportive when I asked to test. I was the first since Draummorc. I want to prove to the Queen she is wrong about Fomorians. That we are committed to the Lands of Summer, but she doesn't make it easy. After the registration, not a single kid wanted to test."

A red light spun above the desk.

"Incoming." Killian swiveled the door. Mounted on the back was a piece of slate where the word *Congratulations* was being erased. It was replaced by *Lynch, stop making it rain.*

"Oops." Ollie hopped up, launching his fist toward the ceiling. "*Nil caenum.*"

End water.

The rain stopped.

"What are those words?" Kelcie asked.

"Words that *spark* our powers. *Caenum* is specifically for water. You're like me. An air elemental," Killian explained. "I'll be training you. Alphas train their Dens."

Kelcie perked up. "Can we start right now?"

Killian smirked at her, shaking his head. "Tomorrow. Today is almost over. What else do you need to know?" He tapped the slate. "Announcements will appear on this board."

"Check it every morning first thing," Ollie added. "Scáthach changes fields all the time at the last minute and assigns extra laps if you're late."

The words wiped off once more, and new text appeared. *Schedules have been sent to your desk.*

There was a cumbersome *kerplunk* followed by a hissing *pop* that led to an overzealous *ding.* Kelcie hurried to open the top drawer and found two pieces of yellow parchment that smelled like sunshine. A schedule and a map.

She shoved her hand to the back of the drawer, running into an impervious, solid back. "How did these get in here?"

"Magically charged pneumatic tubes run all over campus. Classrooms, Dens, even the practice fields. Anywhere really. You can write home too. All you have to do is put the recipient's name and location at the top of the paper using this." Killian picked up a knobby stick with an end carved to a point from her desk. "Put the addressed paper in the drawer, close it, and your note will be vacuum-sucked to whoever's name is on it." He nodded to her locker. "All the clothes you need should be there."

Kelcie set the papers on her desk and padded over to the wardrobe that looked more like a gym locker.

Killian scanned briefly to make sure it was all there. "Sweats are for everyday. Dress uniforms only when they tell us. Swimming, sleep, and underclothes are in the drawers. If you're missing anything, please don't tell me. Send a note to Roswen."

Ollie moved to the door. "Keep your wardrobes super neat. Checks happen without warning. Scáthach is completely mental about everything being in its proper place, or it will be confiscated, and you'll have to beg for it back in front of the entire student body."

The red light flashed again, and another new message appeared. *The banquet will begin in five minutes.*

"Food!" Ollie cheered.

Killian gestured to her wardrobe. "Cloaks tonight. Get changed. We'll wait for you by the pole."

The two hurried out of the room.

A thrill ran through Kelcie as she ran her hand over the Saiga insignia on her cloak. She glanced at the little yellow leaf on her bough—the key to her Den—and smiled, genuinely happy for the first time in a long time.

9

DEAR OLD DAD

THE YELLOW CLOAK was lighter than Kelcie expected. The sleek fabric felt like bendable Kevlar. She glanced at her schedule again, noting she was in fianna three, then took a quick look in the bathroom mirror. She barely recognized the person looking back at her. Different eyes. Different clothes. A room of her own. *Could this day get any better?*

"Kelcie, come on! I'm starving!" Ollie called.

Kelcie was starving too, and excited to find out who was in her fianna, but as she paced through scrutinizing glares from upperclassman toward the first-year table, happiness waned.

The first-year table was colorful. Out of the twenty who made it through the test, there were five Chargers in blue cloaks, five Adders in green, five Ravens in black, and four Cats in red. She was the only one wearing a yellow cloak.

Platters of sweet-smelling bread, meat that Kelcie thought might be chicken, and salad made from purple greens and multicolored vegetables were being passed around the table. Her classmates were deep in animated conversations. Marta Louisa leaped on her chair, reenacting how she beat the Bridge of Leaping. Her fledgling cat-like reflexes were on full display as she dove off the table into a somersault, rolling up on all fours with her fingers shredding grass, bringing her to a hard stop. She earned a round of applause. Kelcie headed straight for the only open seat, next to Niall.

"Is this saved?" she asked him.

He nodded. "For you."

Relieved, Kelcie sat down, hungrier than she had ever been in her entire life. She was even more relieved to find out Niall was in her fianna. As she stuffed her face with everything that breezed by, she couldn't help noticing how handsome he looked in his Adder-green cloak, not that she would ever tell him that.

According to Niall, Zephyr and Brona were also in their fianna. Kelcie feigned enthusiasm at the mention of the self-professed demigoddess and legend in her own mind's name.

"Brona. Wow. That's fantastic."

Sitting on the other side of Kelcie, Willow demanded Brona's full attention, rapid-firing questions.

"Want to go for a run after dinner? Or maybe you could give me some pointers on shifting? How did you get so good at it?" Willow gushed at her. They looked like twins in their sleek black Raven cloaks.

"Been training my whole life. All day. Every day."

"That doesn't sound like much fun," Kelcie interjected.

"We didn't invite you into this conversation, Saiga," Willow snipped.

Kelcie couldn't help herself. She reached around Brona and yanked one of Willow's springy curls.

"Ow! What is wrong with you?" Willow squawked, sliding her chair farther away.

Niall shook, silently laughing. Zephyr spit peas, nearly choking. Kelcie smiled. Yeah. It was juvenile, but it was worth it.

"It wasn't fun, so much as important," Brona said, answering Kelcie's earlier comment. "My mother is—"

"A goddess, we heard the last five times you said it," Zephyr groaned, hoarding the dessert plate. Kelcie grabbed it from him, taking the last piece. Kelcie didn't know what to call it, but it was flaky and nutty and smothered in honey like baklava, only the bottom was chocolate.

"Just ignore him," Marta Louisa said to Brona, hissing at Zephyr.

He sank lower in his chair, licking chocolate off his fingers.

Willow twirled a curl around her finger. "What's the Island of Eternal Youth like, Brona? Is it all golden castles and endless facials? And does it really float in the sky? Servants waiting on your every need?"

"Bringing you silky moon shakes with fluff?" Marta Louisa added dreamily.

Brona crunched on a purple vegetable. "Yes to all of the above. After grueling workouts with my mother of course."

"I knew it," Marta Louisa purred. "What a life."

"I'd love to see it someday," Willow said, coyly. "Can you invite people, maybe during the break? It's a long time away, but think you could ask? I know my parents would be fine with me going."

Brona pushed the vegetables around her plate. "Um, I guess so."

"Really? Thank you!" Willow threw her arms around Brona. "Can you use the tubes? Or do you have some godly way to deliver a note?"

"Tubes work." Brona bit into something orange.

Kelcie was so involved in Brona's conversation she didn't notice Zephyr pilfering her dessert until more than half of it was gone.

"Hey!" Kelcie threatened him with her fork.

"Oh, did you want that? I thought you were done." He blinked innocently, immediately changing the subject. "Did it hurt when they changed like that?" He gestured to his own eyes.

"No. The opposite actually." She took a huge bite of the cake. "Roswen is a really good cook."

Brona leaned back in her chair. "Sweets are bad for you. They'll slow you down. I personally never eat them."

"Oh." Willow pushed her plate away, staring at her piece of the flaky chocolate goodness like it was public enemy number one.

"You don't want that?" Zephyr asked.

But Kelcie beat Zephyr to it, snatching it off Willow's plate. She sank her teeth into it before he could ask for half. "So good . . ."

"Wow. Not even my brothers move that fast," Zephyr chuckled.

"I've never seen anyone eat so much. Where do you put it?" Niall wrapped a thumb and index finger around her wrist. "You're so tiny."

"And I'm still hungry."

Zephyr leaned back in his chair, patting his bulging stomach. "Get it while you can. Morning meal is called bits for a reason. They don't want us puking during training."

Niall cautiously peeked over his shoulder. Then he did it again.

The third time, Kelcie asked, "What are you looking at?"

"Dierdre Crane and Connor Bones," Niall groaned their names.

Kelcie turned around, finding the two she saw when she arrived at the school glaring at her.

Crane said something to Bones that made him laugh.

"Don't look at them."

"Why not? They're looking at me." Kelcie made a face at Deirdre.

"Kelcie! Don't do that! Regan said Crane and Bones pick a first year to torture every year. It gets so bad that the person usually ends up quitting. I don't want it to be me and you don't want it to be you."

"Don't worry. If they try anything . . ." She balled her fist.

"You'll tell Scáthach." Niall pushed Kelcie's fist down. His hand lingered until he realized what he was doing, and he pulled it away.

Kelcie's cheeks warmed. Butterflies fluttered, getting stuck in digesting honey.

"You've obviously never dealt with a bully. Telling on them does nothing but make them torture you more."

Niall glanced over Kelcie's shoulder at Crane. "In dealing with malcontents, I prefer a diplomatic approach where no one gets hurt."

"Strange thing to say since we're at the Academy for the *Unbreakable* Arts," Brona said, deigning to speak to them.

"Maybe you're at the wrong school, O'Shea," Marta Louisa added.

"No maybe about that. Like her." Willow's lip curled as she stared Kelcie down. "Face it. Neither of you belong here."

Afraid it was gone, Kelcie raked her fingers through the air, feeling the mind-blowing connection. *Oh yeah . . .* It was still there.

"Niall," Kelcie shifted for better aim, "this is how I deal with a bully. Mistral."

She flicked her fingers, intending to knock Willow's plate on her lap. Wind whipped across the table, toppling food platters along with Willow, Brona, and Marta Louisa's chairs.

The first-year table erupted with laughter.

Honey streaked down Marta Louisa's scowling face. "There will be payback."

Half-eaten bones stuck to Willow's black cloak as she slammed her chair against the table. She peeled a white vegetable off her forehead. "You—demon!" She lofted a hand out to Brona, who was still on the ground.

But Brona didn't take it. She shook, silently laughing, holding on to her sides.

"Oh, it hurts." She heaved a breath.

Kelcie's lips quirked into a smile. Suddenly she was laughing too.

"Are you coming or not?" Willow snapped at her.

"Yes." Brona got up slowly, tossing a small smile at Kelcie.

Willow looped her arm in Brona's and whispered something in her ear. Brona's smile at Kelcie cratered into a deep frown. Whatever she said made the demigoddess angry.

"What?" Kelcie called.

But the two stormed off with Marta Louisa trailing after them.

"Murphy!" Roswen rushed up.

Kelcie stood at attention, knees wobbling with worry that she was about to be kicked out. "I'm so sorry! Please. It will never happen again. I promise!"

"Relax. We don't kick students out for beating on each other. That's what we teach here. But you're cleaning up the mess. Now." She folded her arms over her chest, tapping her foot, counting off the seconds it took for Kelcie to hop to it.

"Yes, ma'am." Kelcie started picking up the chairs.

Niall and Zephyr surprised her. They both got up and started on the platters.

THE LIGHTS SHUT off at ten. Kelcie was so exhausted her body felt like it was floating. She lay back and watched the night sky put on a magical show of its own. Everything was bigger in this Otherworld. Shooting stars arched through the uprights of a giant thumbnail moon. Mars drove by like a red balloon losing helium, while Venus floated past, a foggy white crystal ball. The sea-glass ceiling was definitely her favorite part of her new room.

As she saw the colorful gossamer rings of Jupiter entering the picture, Kelcie's eyelids grew impossibly heavy. She was drifting off into a deep, blissful sleep when her drawer went *ding*!

She slumped in the desk chair and opened the drawer. Inside was a folded-over piece of paper with her name on it in very scary print. KELCIE. The paper was so thick it felt more like fabric. The edges frayed, a tiny red drop was in the corner where a stamp would normally be. It looked like blood.

All the note said was Go to the stone circle. Immediately!

Kelcie sat back in her chair, stretching the parchment, mulling over whether she should go or not. She had a bad feeling this was about what happened at dinner. Willow, Brona, and

Marta Louisa would probably be waiting, ready to make her pay. Or maybe it was the preceptor, Scáthach. But Roswen said she wasn't in trouble, and the spooky stone circle at night didn't sound like anything a teacher would tell her to do.

Kelcie was headed back to bed, planning to ignore it when there was another *ding!*

Hurry! It's important! was all it said.

Important? Kelcie gulped. *What if it's from the fairies?* Curiosity always her downfall, Kelcie set the parchment down on her way to her wardrobe.

The campus was quiet, except for a few hooting owls and an occasional rustling from somewhere deep in the woods. Kelcie stuck to the familiar path, formulating a plan. She would peek into the circle, and if she saw Willow or Marta Louisa or Brona, she'd run. Simple. The only part she hadn't figured out was what to do if it was the fairies. If she called for help, she risked being caught out of bed after lights out, and losing her place at AUA.

She cautiously climbed the hill, circling the stones before wading through the tall grass inside. No one was there. It was empty. Willow probably chickened out. Relieved, Kelcie was turning to leave when the ground quaked.

She pressed her back against a stone to keep from falling over and watched with frightened awe as a face rose in the grass. A lopsided frown, a crooked nose, two narrow eyes, a thin scar beneath the left, and above the forehead, ringed horns.

A Fomorian.

The shaking stopped, but Kelcie was too afraid to move.

"Kelcie . . ." The man's voice was warm, like a soft, soothing blanket. "Is that really you?"

Her heart pounded so hard Kelcie worried it might leap out of her chest. "Who are you? What are you? And how do you know my name?"

"Please come closer. I need—see you." Lightning streaked through the sky at the exact moment a word dropped, like a cell phone intermittently losing its signal.

"Tell me who you are first."

Brown eagles swooped over the circle, peeling off high-pitched cries, then vanished into the dark skies as quickly as they came.

"You don't recognize my voice? You don't remember me at all?" Grass eyes shut. When they opened, the corners of his mouth turned down. He looked upset, like he might cry or something. "I'm . . . I'm your father, Kelcie."

"What?" She inched closer until he said, "Stop. Right there. I can see you now. I can't believe it. All these years! No one could tell me where you were or what happened to you. It was like you never existed. I started to believe . . ." He choked up. Ground water bubbled in his grass eyes. He was crying. He cleared his throat. "Are—all right? I saw you—a nightmare. Then—felt your presence—"

Lightning cracked, more intense than the last time. She checked the skies to see how much had blackened, to determine how long she might have before getting drenched and possibly electrocuted, but nothing had changed. Stars twinkled. The moon was still visible.

It was *unnatural*.

"Kelcie, please talk to me."

"I . . ." Kelcie desperately wanted to believe he was her father, but somewhere deep down she didn't trust this magical world, not after what happened with Blizzard and Grimes. "How do I know you're really my father?"

His lips pressed together. "You have a birthmark shaped like a crow in flight on your belly."

Kelcie rubbed her side where she did in fact have such a birthmark.

"And a pinky-leng—car on your right thi—" Lightning bolts threaded the stars, stealing his words. "From play—sword."

Kelcie fell to her knees. She did have a scar on her thigh. From playing with a sword? "I always wondered how I got that. It's really you?" She was talking to her father. Somehow. Surprising, but then again, after a day like she had, maybe it wasn't.

An emotional dam broke. Tears flowed freely down Kelcie's face. She didn't bother trying to stop them. "I-I was in the human world."

"The human world? How is that possible?"

"I thought, I thought you and my mother left me there. I thought that, that maybe you were dead." She sniffed, wiping her nose on her new Saiga sweatshirt. "I can't remember anything. Are you here? In this . . . Otherworld?"

"Yes. Of course. I'm—"

Lightning exploded across the heavens.

Kelcie ducked, throwing her arms over her head.

Her father gagged a scream like he was in horrible pain. "No! This connection isn't go—to last. I saw you through— You have to tell me what happened?"

She was trying to understand but with so many words dropping out . . . Kelcie shuffled closer until her leg touched the tip of his grassy nose, rattling off details as fast as she could. "These fairies showed up on my field trip! One was my caseworker, Elliott Blizzard. I never knew he was a fairy. The other was an ice fairy named Achila Grimes. They dragged me to this ancient artifact. I don't know what it was, but it was wrapped in shredded black fabr—"

"What?!" he yelled. "Ice—High Guard for Win— In the human world had—?"

Now, he sounded mad. Really mad. Stomach-curdling mad.

Kelcie shrank. "Not had. She has it." She started to cry again, but she wasn't entirely sure why. Maybe it was because he was so angry. "What does it mean? Where are you? I'll come find you. I can do it! I only need your name."

"You can't remember my name? You don't know me at all?" He sounded so upset.

Kelcie shook her head.

"Maybe that's for the best."

"What? No! Why would you say that?" Kelcie pleaded.

His mouth and eyes shut. It took several long distressing

seconds for them to open again. "You cannot come here. It's not safe. You have to go! You have to get out of the Otherworld! You have to run! And when you get to the human world, you have to keep running. Do not let them find you! Never let them find you! Never touch that—"

The sky exploded like the Fourth of July.

His order felt like a knife in her heart. After all this time, he was sending her away? He didn't want to see her? "Who are you? Who is my mother? Why won't you tell me?"

"It's too dangerous. You have to go."

Heartache twisted into bitter anger. Niall said fairies couldn't come to the Lands of Summer. Their silver boughs couldn't bring them. They wouldn't be able to find her even if they wanted to. Besides, at this school, she would learn to use her power. She would learn to fight. The next time she saw Achila Grimes and Elliott Blizzard, if there was a next time, she would be able to defend herself. She would be ready for them.

Kelcie stood up. "I'm at the Academy for the Unbreakable Arts. I tested today and I got in. And I'm staying. If you want to come and find me, this is where I'll be."

"Listen to me!" her father growled. The trembling earth crumpled into his cratered mouth. Fine lines cracked, shooting up the sides of his face. "—don't know what—done!" He spit gravel. "Kel—can't see—I love y—"

His face melted into the dirt.

The connection was gone.

Kelcie fell to her knees and beat the ground with her fists. "Come back! Please! Who are you?"

All at once the eagles returned, a convocation landing three to a stone, piping and squealing. Kelcie ran out of the circle. Before she made it to the bottom of the hill, a green streak cut her off.

Striker yipped, sprinting circles around her, keeping her from running. Scáthach wasn't far behind. Her loose hair was tucked into the back of her red robe, the tie crookedly cinched. The tattling eagles got her out of bed.

"Murphy, what are you doing out here in the middle of the night?"

Kelcie tried to fight back tears, but there were too many of them. Within seconds, she was a sniveling mess in front of the preceptor. If word got out, she would never live this down.

What was she going to say? How much could she tell Scáthach without losing her spot at the school? *Stick to the bare minimum.* "My father called."

Scáthach pulled a hanky out of her sleeve and passed it to Kelcie. "Through the stone circle? That's rather dramatic. Why not just send a note through the tubes?"

"He did, ordering me to come here so he could yell at me grass-to-face."

"What did he say that upset you so much?"

Kelcie sucked in a mountain of air, wiping her eyes with the silky fabric. "He was mad. Told me I had to go home."

Scáthach sighed. "It's not easy for Fomorians. I understand their reluctance in having their children serve."

It's not easy for Fomorians. Kelcie's father was a Fomorian. She was a Fomorian. As miserable as she felt with her father's refusal to tell her his name, or her mother's, she was elated just knowing that much about him.

Scáthach continued. "But I have a good feeling about you, Kelcie."

Striker wagged his tail feathers. He nudged Kelcie's hand with the top of his head, forcing her to pet him.

"This is your decision. You don't need his permission to be here. What do you want to do?"

Kelcie stroked Striker's soft fur, knowing exactly what she wanted. "I want to stay. More than anything."

"Good. Then I'll let this curfew break slide. Don't let it happen again."

"No, ma'am. I'm sorry. It was pretty scary too, with all that lightning."

"What lightning?" Scáthach looked up. "You saw lightning?"

Scáthach didn't see it? It lit up the whole sky.

Kelcie didn't want to sound nuts, especially after busting into tears. She laughed it off. "Oh, did I say lightning? I meant with all the eagles. They were really loud."

"Sounding the alarm, Murphy."

"Yes, ma'am."

After a few minutes of walking in silence back toward the dorm, Scáthach set a comforting hand on Kelcie's shoulder. "The hardest things to overcome in life are those things we cannot control."

Kelcie's whole life had been out of her control. That was a lot of things to overcome. "Yes, ma'am. Thank you for giving me this chance."

"You earned it. Never forget that."

Kelcie tried to hand Scáthach the soggy handkerchief.

"Keep it. By morning it will be nothing but a memory, like tonight."

On her way down the pole, Kelcie worried that she should have told Scáthach about the fairies. But if she did, would Scáthach order her to leave? Kelcie couldn't take that chance. The answers to who she was, who her parents were, were so close. She was going to find them, whether her father wanted her to or not.

As Kelcie took off her shoes, she was still furious at her father, but knowing he didn't abandon her, knowing he was trying to find her all this time, and hearing his last words to her, that he loved her, before the connection died, she knew she wasn't going to stay mad.

She climbed into bed, put her hands behind her head, and watched the night's sky through the ceiling. After all that happened, she was never going to be able to fall asleep. And it was quiet in her room.

Too quiet.

"I need some noise." Sleeping alone was a novelty. She wasn't sure she liked it. "And now I'm talking to myself. This is ridiculous."

Her drawer dinged.

Kelcie's heart nearly burst with excitement as she threw the covers off, jumping out of bed. Her father was having second thoughts. He wanted to see her too.

Before her feet landed on the floor, she heard a second *ding*.

"I'm coming!" she sang.

She yanked the handle and reached in, finding not one but two notes. Both on small white cards with a slithering snake sketch on the top.

The first said: *I CAN'T SLEEP.*

The second said: *ALL FIVE OF MY ROOMMATES SNORE.*

Kelcie slinked into the chair. They weren't from her father. They were from Niall. Disappointment faded into something else. Niall wrote her a note, and he forgot to sign his name. He wrote in all caps, not like he was yelling, like capital letters were the norm for him. She beamed at the cards, running her fingers over the print. It was pretty handwriting.

She quickly grabbed the pen but slowed as she reached for a piece of yellow paper. She didn't want to look anxious, not that anyone was looking at her.

The point of the pen hovered. Sticky sap dripped from the tip, ticking off the long seconds it was taking for her to compose a reply. Kelcie didn't know what to say. She had never written a note to a friend before, let alone a boy. What if she said the wrong thing?

She set the pen down.

But Niall was waiting for a response, wasn't he? He said he couldn't sleep. It would be rude not to write back. She gripped the pen, wanting to tell him what had happened tonight, that she had a father, that he was alive somewhere in the Otherworld, but it was late and way too much to say in a note, so she settled for something simple.

I can't sleep either. I've never had a room to myself before.
I can see the moon. Can you?

She closed the drawer. Then peeked to make sure it was gone. A second later she heard another ping.

I CAN SEE THE MOON TOO.

10

FIRST DAY BLUES

A siren whooped at dawn. Kelcie had been dressed for an hour in her yellow Saiga T-shirt and sweatpants. She didn't want to be late for her first day of classes, especially after being caught out after curfew by Scáthach.

During the last hour, she spot-checked the room, aligning her clean clothes and her dirty ones too, to be positive it would pass an inspection, then she made the mistake of perusing her *Night Fundamentals* book, hoping to find out something about the ice fairies. She found a whole hair-raising chapter dedicated to them. Nimble fairies. Ice fairies. Deceptor fairies, Shadow-melders, and on and on.

Kelcie only had time to scan the ice fairy pages. Chills alternated running up and down her spine at the end of every paragraph.

Scary item number one: Ice fairies could fly to heights that way exceeded Summer's Ravens' maximum altitude. In a battle fought before something called the Great Split, five ice fairies engaged an entire squadron of thirty Raven archers in some place called Loch Bas. Realizing they were losing, the five spirited to at least fifty thousand feet, into frigid temperatures, where they manifested a giant ice net within seconds. The Ravens never knew what hit them. Once the Ravens were dragged underwater, the fairies froze the surface. The whole squadron was lost.

Scary item numbers two, three, and four: They could manipulate ice into any shape, including weapons, which Kelcie had seen with her own eyes in the museum cafeteria. They had heightened senses making them evasive flyers, and honed eyesight making them deadly accurate sharpshooters.

Her fingers touched the healed cut on her ear. If ice fairies were supposed to be such a great shot, why did Grimes miss hitting Kelcie in the museum's cafeteria? There was only one logical answer. Because she never wanted Kelcie hurt so badly she couldn't follow her. She wanted Kelcie to enter the Sidral, but why? Did she think Kelcie would end up in the Lands of Winter? Or did she know Kelcie's silver bough would take her to AUA?

"Kelcie, we're heading for bits!" Killian called.

"Go ahead. I'll be there in a sec." Kelcie slammed the book shut.

She checked the message board on her door. Hawthorn Field this morning. After a quick glance at the campus map, she jogged to the fireman's pole, nervous and excited for her first day of classes. She was still getting the hang of riding it up. Last night she spun off into a huge puddle of mud from Ollie's rain shower, getting her dress uniform all dirty. This morning she tripped over an outstretched shoe.

Connor Bones seized Kelcie's elbows. "Look what we got here, Crane? A stumbling, bumbling baby Saiga." He wrenched her arms together, nearly ripping them from the sockets.

It hurt. Badly. "Let go!" Kelcie slammed her heel into his kneecaps, but he only laughed. "I'm warning you! I took down Diccon Wilks." She fisted her hands.

Deirdre laughed in her face. "Do it then, Saiga. Come on. I dare you."

Do it, wind! Get her! Kelcie concentrated.

The air stilled.

"That's what I thought. You've got nothing." Deirdre charged, taking several hard kicks to the stomach from Kelcie without even flinching. She grabbed Kelcie's bough, stretching the chain as far as it would go, and more, digging it into the back of Kelcie's neck. "And here it is. Our key to the Saiga Den." A simple tug was all it took for the Charger to snap the chain.

"Give it back!"

Deirdre dangled the charm in Kelcie's face. She popped her lip out in a fake pout. "Oh no. Are you going to cry?"

The sparking word! Kelcie forgot to say the word! "Not today. Mistral!"

The surge took control. Airballs fired from both fists, heading in opposite directions. Why? Kelcie had no idea. She was aiming only at Deirdre, who launched twenty feet, barreling into Regan.

Connor wasn't so lucky. He smacked into Haven Hall's doorway at the same time the Cat Den opened, landing legs spread on a tree branch in such a way that left him gasping and whimpering, "Mummy . . ."

A panther and a gray smoosh-faced cat jumped out the open door, their bodies shaking with laughter.

Kelcie ran to Deirdre, struggling to pry open the Charger's clenched fist crushing her bough, but it was like trying to bend a crowbar.

Regan didn't let go of Deirdre. She put her in a chokehold. "And here I was worried when you two didn't show up for bits. Give it back, Crane."

Regan tightened her hold. Deirdre's eyes bulged. She gagged, and finally released the necklace. Regan dropped her like a hot potato.

Coughing, Deirdre crawled to standing, glaring at Kelcie as she stumbled away.

"Thank you," Kelcie said to Regan. "I'm—"

"Kelcie Murphy. I know."

"Niall told—"

"No. I asked around last night after dinner, after I saw you use your powers." Regan bit her bottom lip. "But now that you mentioned Niall, he isn't speaking with me at the moment. See, I asked him to leave."

Regan's golden stare narrowed over Kelcie's shoulder. Kelcie looked back and saw the Cat Den's tree slingshot Connor Bones out the door. He tripped over his own two feet, unable to run away fast enough.

"Why did you ask him to leave?"

"Because he's going to get badly hurt. Because getting into AUA is hard, but staying in is much harder, especially for someone like him. He doesn't stand a chance. Trust me. I know what Niall can do, and this is beyond him. He won't make it through the rope climb in the first obstacle course. You and the rest of your fianna will start hating him by midterm when you're preparing for the melee."

"I could never hate Niall."

"You say that now." She sounded so cold, so matter of fact, as if the future was written in stone.

"Why are you telling me this?" Kelcie asked.

"I was hoping you and the others in his fianna would help me convince him to leave before this goes any further."

Kelcie shook her head. "You're underestimating him. He can do this. He's smart."

Regan crossed her arms. "You just met him yesterday. I've known him his whole life. And yes, he may be smart, smarter than I am, but in case you didn't notice, he's missing a hand. It's not right. He shouldn't be here."

"You're embarrassed?"

Regan looked away and Kelcie had her answer.

"Is that why you helped me? Just so I'd talk to him? Because I was doing fine on my own, and so will Niall."

"No. I helped you because those boneheads need to learn that we're all on the same side. But Niall's not going to be fine. I guess he'll have to learn that the hard way too." Regan hissed a laugh and let out a disappointed sigh. "Breakfast is over. Class is starting. You might want to run."

Regan left in a hurry. Kelcie shoved her necklace in her pocket, then sprinted down what she hoped was the correct path.

Blue skies, the air not too hot or too cold—Killian explained that the weather was usually perfect, with rain only at night and only when needed, unless Ollie wanted to show off. By the time Kelcie got to Hawthorn Field, the five fiannas were lined up and Scáthach was speaking from the platform.

"In my class, you will work tirelessly, without stopping, moving from one activity to another, building stamina. Obstacle courses, long runs, extreme exercise, whatever it takes to turn you into soldiers. All will be done together with your fianna mates," she bellowed.

Kelcie tiptoed behind Niall.

You're late.

"I know," Kelcie whispered.

"And at the end of this term you will be sent on an overnight to put what you've learned this year to use," Scáthach declared.

Joyous anticipation swept the lines until no one could stand still.

Regan said she almost died on the overnight.

"She's just trying to scare you off . . . Wait. You're talking to me in my head!" Kelcie wrinkled her nose. It was a little jarring hearing Niall's voice rattling her brain, like he was speaking to her through earphones.

Niall waggled his eyebrows. *Started last night.*

"Will you two ever be quiet?" Brona asked, loud enough for all to hear.

"I didn't say anything," Niall protested. *Not out loud.*

Kelcie stifled a laugh.

Zephyr cleared his throat. "Ahem. I'm supposed to say that, Brona. I'm the Charger. I'm the leader of this fianna."

"Then start acting like one," Brona clapped back. "Order them to shut up."

"Your performance on the overnight will be a big part of what

I use to assess whether or not you will be asked back for a second year."

Scáthach's voice grew louder with each word.

Kelcie glanced at the platform and cringed. Their preceptor stood directly above them. Scáthach looked ready for battle in a black unitard, swords crossed in a harness on her back. Her silver bough charm hung on a necklace of seven separate pieces of leather. It had so many branches and colorful leaves it looked like a blooming tree.

Her hands on her hips, her stern gaze shifted between them. "Let me be very clear. This class is about building trust. You must work as a team. That is what you will learn on this field, each and every morning. If you lack discipline, it isn't a singular problem. Your fianna will suffer the consequences alongside you. If you don't get asked back, it's highly likely that the rest of your fianna won't either. Understood?"

A chorus of *yes, ma'am*'s rang out.

Scáthach zeroed in on Kelcie. "Everything you do counts for the entire fianna."

"Me?" Kelcie panicked.

"Yes, you. You were late." Scáthach raised a disapproving brow.

"Because Deirdre—"

Scáthach held up a hand cutting her off. "No excuses. Find a solution, Murphy. Fianna three, ten laps around the field while the others stretch. Go. Now." She looked at the rest of the class. "Chargers, lunges. Alternating legs for a full minute each."

Scáthach didn't even give her a chance to explain. "So unfair . . ." Kelcie mumbled.

"It's completely fair. You were late," Willow said from the next row, sounding exactly like Little Miss Demigod. The two looked like twins in their black sweats and matching fishtail braids.

Kelcie's hands tingled. Frustration mixed with resentment in the pit of her stomach, churning until she felt like she was going to explode. The word *Mistral* shot through her mind, a hairpin trigger. Kelcie knew better than to let it come out of her mouth, but sadly, this time, it didn't matter.

A sudden burst pegged Scáthach squarely in the back, throwing her forward. She used the momentum to carry her into a perfect flip. Gasps transformed to applause when she stuck the landing.

"I'm so sorry!" Kelcie blurted.

"Seriously? You're apologizing?" Brona gawked at Kelcie. "You're pathetic, you know that?"

"You're mad at me for apologizing?" Kelcie threw her hands in the air, surrendering.

Scáthach jumped off the platform, right between Kelcie and Brona. Her glower flipped between them. "Fianna three, let's make that twenty laps!"

"Kelcie!" Niall griped out loud, embarrassing Kelcie even more.

Brona smirked. "Fine with me. It'll be a good warmup."

"Chike, get your fianna moving or you'll be running until the sun goes down," Scáthach ordered.

"Okay, fianna three! You heard Scáthach! Get a move on!" Zephyr bullhorned in Kelcie's ear. "Let's go, let's go, let's go!"

For the next thirty minutes, Zephyr made Kelcie stay out in front of him, threatening bodily harm every time she slowed down.

After that, Scáthach put them through a grueling workout, running all over campus, stopping at any possible flat surface to torture them with calisthenics until they were all bent over. For the first time, Kelcie was glad she missed breakfast, although by the time she got to Combat Training, she was positively hangry.

The first hour was hand-to-hand combat basics. Kicks, sweeps, punches, most of which Kelcie had a fair bit of experience at using, only she never knew they had such fancy names—like axe, butterfly, crescent, hook—or "proper" ways to throw them.

Their teacher, Coach Blackwell, had a wicked scar running from his forehead, up and over his bald head, and down the back of his massive neck. The only hair he had was on his face, a thick dark beard twisted at the chin. He grunted at the start of every sentence, making him sound perpetually irritated, and was extremely physical. He twisted Kelcie's arms and legs into what he called the correct position no matter how much Kelcie's joints protested.

During their first assessment spar, Brona landed so many punches and kicks all Kelcie could think to do was tackle her. But Brona morphed, slipping through Kelcie's mad grab. Her raven form circled, dive-bombing, her talons angled for Kelcie's hair.

Coach Blackwell blew a wooden whistle, but Kelcie wasn't ready for the match to be over. What was supposed to be an airball nailing Bird-Brona in the beak, came out a sweeping gale that turned the arena into a giant dust bowl.

When the air finally cleared, Brona transformed back to her human self, and dropped on Kelcie like a sack of potatoes.

"You lose . . ." Brona crowed.

"Murphy! Lee! There are no powers allowed in this class," Coach Blackwell yelled, rubbing his eyes. He crossed his arms, puffing his chest. "Three laps for fianna three around the outside the tower, then Lee, you pair with Murphy for grappling. Work out some of that anger in a more useful manner."

"I'm not angry," Kelcie spat.

"I am," Brona grumbled.

"Between these two girls, I'm gonna drop dead of a heart attack before the day is over!" Zephyr clutched his chest, staggering into Niall for dramatic effect.

"I can't feel my legs anymore." Niall cringed, limping after them.

Three miserable long laps around the Nether Tower, and they headed back inside for grappling. After an hour wrestling with Brona, and losing every round, the packed dirt on the floor turned Kelcie's red hair mud brown.

After that, they were finally ready to move on to sword skills. Kelcie's heart leaped as Blackwell pulled out his long sword and demonstrated the basics—lunges, parries, thrusts, advances, retreats, and so on until Kelcie was oozing excitement to get her hands on her own.

"Fagan, you're with me." Blackwell swatted Tad Fagan, the Charger in Willow and Marta Louisa's fianna on the back.

They disappeared into the storage room and returned with bins of short staffs.

"Staff up! Hustle!" Blackwell ordered.

Kelcie hurried to Tad's bin, which was closest. Fagan darted around the front of the bin, blocking her from taking one.

He flashed a fake ten-thousand-megawatt smile. "Sorry, Saiga. I'm all out. You'll have to get one from Coach Blackwell."

Zephyr snuck up on Fagan, shouldering him out of the way. "Like tipping grumpy steer back home."

He hooked his fingers over the lip of the bin, yanking it toward Kelcie.

"Thanks, Zephyr." Kelcie took a staff.

"Pick a partner. Let me see what you can do," Blackwell called.

After ten minutes of whacking at Niall and him whacking back, Kelcie couldn't take it anymore. This was so boring.

"When do we get real weapons?"

Coach Blackwell snatched a staff from the bin and attacked her. A well-placed cut coupled with a solid fake led to a simultaneous disarming and sound *thwack* on the back.

Kelcie ate dirt and was too humiliated to get up.

Coach Blackwell poked her with his staff. "You alive?"

Everyone laughed.

She nodded, moving slowly, the pain in her back still lingering.

"If that were a real sword, it would've hurt."

"It did, sir."

Everyone laughed again.

"You learn from taking hits with a staff, Murphy. You'll be bruised, but never cut. When you disarm me with one of these," he picked up her staff and handed it back to her, "I'll give you a sword and a shield to go with it. It won't be today, but if you're game for a little more punishment, I'll give you another try."

What do you have to lose?

It was strange to hear Niall's talking in her head, but truth was, she kind of liked it. She exchanged a quick glance with him for courage, gripped her staff like it had a proper pommel, and thrust at Coach Blackwell. He parried. A flick of his wrist and Kelcie's staff fell on the ground, rolling away in bitter disgrace.

"Who's next?" he challenged.

Brona waited until Tad Fagan and Marta Louisa walked away with their heads hanging in defeat to raise her hand. They sparred for three long minutes, covering the whole arena, until Brona ducked Coach Blackwell's jab, dropped to her knees, and somehow twisted his staff out of his hands. It was a genius move, like all of Brona's. Kelcie's chest burned with jealousy as Brona dropped her stick and held her grubby hand out.

"You were saying, Coach Blackwell?"

Blackwell rubbed his beard, contemplating her with an amused gleam in his eye. In the end, Brona got her sword, a shield, and an edict to spar with Coach Blackwell for the rest of the term.

"Sometimes I really hate her," Kelcie whined, realizing too late Brona was standing right behind her.

"So I've heard." Brona glowered.

"What's that supposed to mean?" Kelcie asked, but the Raven stormed off to join Willow and Marta Louisa, the heads of her fan club, to show off her shiny new sword.

11

DOWN THE DRAIN

EVERYONE ELSE WENT to lunch, except fianna three. Coach Blackwell volunteered them for clean-up, moving the staff bins into the storage room so they were out of the way for his afternoon classes. By the time they finished, Kelcie was so hungry the dirt floor looked appetizing.

As she and Brona shut the storage doors together, Kelcie tried an apology to end the weirdness between them.

"I didn't mean that I really hate you. I'm sorry about that. You're just really good, at everything."

Brona didn't answer. Her glare remained fixed on the exit. Once out the tower door, the Raven blew past her, acting as if Kelcie never said anything at all.

"Rude . . ."

Maybe she didn't hear you, Niall said coming beside her.

"She heard me all right."

Zephyr led the way down a different path, but then again, they all looked the same. After two forks, and fifteen minutes, they were no closer to Befelts Garden and lunch.

"I think we're lost," said Niall, wiping his sweaty brow.

"Zephyr went the wrong way. We need to backtrack. It was a left at that last fork. Not a right," Brona said. "The sun was positioned over my right shoulder on the way down to the Nether Tower." She lifted a tired finger. "Befelts is that way."

"Why didn't you speak up then?" Zephyr asked.

Kelcie saw a bent tree beside a large rock on the other side of a small glen that looked vaguely familiar. "Brona's wrong. It's this way." Kelcie walked around them, taking the lead. She left the path, cutting through the woods.

"My father is the best navigator in the armada. He taught me everything he knows," Brona griped.

"Of course, he is. Aren't your minions waiting?" Kelcie hollered. "Why don't you fly? They may be sacrificing a worm in your honor. You wouldn't want to miss it!"

"No! We are not separating. Rule number one from Regan last night. Fiannas arrive and eat together. And that's what we're going to do no matter how much it's going to kill me!" Zephyr cried.

Kelcie glanced over her shoulder, catching Brona drape an arm around Niall's shoulders. "I don't know, Chike. I think the two lovebirds would rather eat by themselves. You and Murphy want a table for two?"

"Hey! We're not lovebirds. We just met yesterday!" Niall protested, shaking Birdbrain off. If that wasn't bad enough, he drove the humiliating stake all the way into Kelcie's heart, finishing off his adamant rebuttal with, "We hardly know each other."

Kelcie turned back around and walked faster. Was Niall pretending to be her friend? It wasn't the first time it happened, or the twentieth. Why did she think a school in the Otherworld would be any different? But this hurt a whole lot more than those other times. *That's it.* Having friends was overrated. She was here to find her parents, and she didn't need any of them to do that.

And yet, they kept following her.

. . . and following her.

Past the angular tree, through another field where Kelcie glimpsed the stone circle on top of the hill. A left turn, and she would end up at Befelts Garden and lunch, but she could also cut through the stone circle, giving Kelcie a chance to look inside. She started up the hill.

"Where's she going?" she heard Zephyr ask.

"We can go left," Brona called to her.

"Brona's right, Kelcie!" Niall bellowed. "We don't have to go up the hill. Just as easy to go around! Save my legs more pain!"

But Kelcie kept going. Their footsteps steadfast behind her, and their conversations.

"It was impressive the way you disarmed Blackwell," Niall said to Brona. "Have you trained with other weapons?"

"Thanks. Yes. I started with a sword, then a bow once I started shifting. Spears recently."

Of course Brona wasn't nervous around him in the slightest. She wasn't nervous around anyone. Even Scáthach. She was tough and confident. Not the least bit insecure. The complete opposite of Kelcie. She really wished she had her old sweatshirt so she could pull up the hood.

A bed of grass moved as they neared the top. Spriggans shrieked at the sight of them, scaling the trees, taking cover.

"Skittish little things," said Zephyr.

"But extremely useful. The sap from a single shoot has strong healing properties. I've seen it seal up a deep stab wound in minutes. Can't break one off though. If you do, it's poisonous. They have to offer it to you," Brona explained.

"Offer to give you their arm or leg?" Zephyr frowned. "Why would they do that?"

"Their limbs grow back," Niall answered.

Kelcie caught Niall smiling at Brona in a way that made her feel ill. He was changing sides. He liked Brona more.

Midway up the hill, Brona said, "We should jog, or we'll miss lunch."

"You three should. Go ahead." Kelcie couldn't take it anymore.

"Figures you'd say that," Brona mumbled.

"What is your problem?" Kelcie spun around, fuming.

"My problem? What's your problem?" Brona took three long steps, invading Kelcie's personal space.

"I don't have one!"

"You hate me. I heard you earlier. And I know all about what you said to Niall last night. Don't pretend you don't know what I'm talking about either!"

"I *don't* know what you're talking about."

"Stop lying. At the test yesterday, when I went into the stone circle, you told Willow and Marta Louisa that I smelled like I just stepped off a year on a flaccobug skimmer." She took a menacing step forward. Their noses were practically touching. "And at dinner last night, you told Niall I was a know-it-all, and that I was lying about who my mother is!"

"First of all, you are a know-it-all! Second of all, I don't know what a flaccobug skimmer is, so why would I say that, and third, why would I care about your mother when I don't even know who my own mother is!" Kelcie couldn't believe she let that slip. It was Brona's fault. She made her so angry!

Brona looked surprised by the revelation, but from her smug expression, she wasn't backing down. "Willow heard you."

"Ahem," Niall said, raising a tentative hand. "Brona, Kelcie never said anything about you last night. And I was with her the whole time during the test. She never said anything to Willow or Marta Louisa about you either."

"I can vouch for that too, navigator girl," Zephyr chimed in. "With her the whole time."

"Oh," Brona said, sounding baffled, but didn't apologize.

Kelcie climbed the last bit of the hill and paused between two of the standing stones. Anger slipped away as nerves chilled her empty belly. Kelcie couldn't help herself. She needed to see if her father would feel her presence and appear again. Not that she expected he would, but knowing he was alive, and found a way to talk to her last night, she couldn't just walk by without taking the chance.

She peered in. Near the center, she saw a dark spot.

"Hello?"

"Who are you talking to?" Niall asked, leaning on the stone.

Kelcie ignored him, padding into the circle. Black muck bubbled like tar on a hot summer day in the center, burping odorless gas. Kelcie didn't remember that happening when her father's face popped up last night, but it was dark. She might not have seen it.

"Hello?" Kelcie called.

"Kelcie . . ."

She froze. Her heart stopped beating. She knew that voice. Deep. Gravelly. Much softer than in the museum, but still . . . it was the same voice she heard coming from that ancient object Achila Grimes took with her. If Grimes couldn't get here, then how did it get to the school?

"Kelcie . . ."

Barely audible, Kelcie got a fix on where it was coming from— the bubbling black spot.

Her fianna mates surrounded her.

"Who is that?" Niall asked.

"I told you to go ahead," Kelcie snapped.

"We don't take orders from you." Brona walked through the grass, staying close to the standing stones, inspecting the ground.

"Kelcie . . ." the disembodied voice whispered.

The tar slurped.

"Anyone else see that?" Brona frowned at the black spot.

Niall joined her. "Looks like a potion of some kind."

"Probably Bones or Fagan," Zephyr huffed. He made a cone around his mouth with his hands. "We're not falling for this, Crane!"

"Crane?" Niall worried.

"I bet she and those other two tosspots are watching from the woods. She and Bones cornered Fagan after they tried and failed to recruit me."

"For what?" Brona asked.

"To help them get Kelcie to quit." Zephyr shrugged. "They tried to tell me all this stuff about how Fomorians don't deserve to be trained at AUA. I told them that none of that mattered to me. In my family, we protect our own. Applies to my fianna too. Besides, I think it's cool we got the only Saiga."

Kelcie tossed Zephyr a shy, awkward smile, mainly because she didn't know how else to respond. It was the nicest thing anyone at this school had said to her.

"In class, Fagan was acting like a jerk to her too, evidence their recruiting tactics worked," Zephyr added.

Niall paced around the black spot. "And Fagan knew we stayed after Blackwell's class. They could've easily set this up in the time it took for us to finish putting the equipment away."

"I'm right here if you want to come and get me!" Kelcie yelled at the treetops.

Three seconds passed in silence. The muck blew a huge bubble that popped, sending goo in all directions.

Niall scooted away from it. "What do you think it is?"

"Kelcie . . ." The voice chirped from the tall grasses near Niall.

The gloomy muck whipped tentacles, lassoing Zephyr's ankle, yanking him into the sludge. His shoes vanished beneath the surface.

"Uh oh." He started dancing, swiveling his hips, flailing his arms. "I'm stuck! It won't let go!"

Kelcie put her back to Zephyr, hooking her arms through his, and heaved as hard as she could.

His leg sunk to his knee. "I can't feel my leg. I CAN'T FEEL MY LEG!"

Niall and Brona scrambled to help. Niall manned a shoulder. Kelcie stayed on the other one. Brona grabbed Zephyr's middle, anchoring him.

"Pull!" Brona growled.

The three heaved.

The sludge slurped. Zephyr's leg sank to his hip. He dug his free heel into the grass, using every last ounce of strength, but he was still slipping. "Don't let it eat me!"

"Kelcie . . . Kelcie . . . Kelcie . . ." Whatever was calling Kelcie's name was on the move, going away from them at a slow, steady pace.

Three spriggans raced into the stone circle, stabbing the muck like they had Kelcie during testing, zapping it. Yellow magic sparkled only to be swallowed in darkness, along with their twiggy limbs. Twisting and turning, snapping and cracking, the spriggans' frantic squeals reached code red.

"Murphy, take over!" Brona said.

Kelcie latched onto Zephyr's middle at the same time Brona let go, and morphed. She swept over the spriggans, catching their trapped twigs in her beak. Two broke free and ran screeching into the woods. But the last wasn't so lucky. A couple of glug-glugs, a toilet-bowl slurp, and the gelatinous gunk ate the poor little guy whole.

The sludge spit Zephyr out.

Kelcie and Niall fell backward with him onto the grass. The three immediately speed crawled, getting a safe distance away before looking back. Brona landed beside them as the muck gassed, then sank into the ground, disappearing from sight.

Suddenly, Striker was there, darting inside, finding the exact spot where the sludge had been. His front paws started digging like a cú sith on a mission to find a long-lost bone.

"Striker!" Brona cried.

"Striker! No! Come here!" Kelcie shouted, worried it, whatever it was, would reappear and take him like the spriggan.

Striker looked up. His head cocked at Kelcie. Panting, he trotted toward her until his back was beneath her fingers.

"You stay here," Brona said, grabbing him by the scruff of the neck.

Scáthach and Roswen weren't far behind.

"What's going on in here?" Scáthach asked.

"It tried to eat me!" Zephyr squalled. "I-I-no feeling . . ." He slapped his leg, babbling unintelligibly.

Roswen examined him. "What tried to eat you, Chike? There are no bite marks."

"Black! Sappy! And sticky, and . . . my leg . . ." Zephyr popped his knee.

Roswen whacked him on the back. "Spit it out, Charger."

"It ate a spriggan!" Zephyr finally blurted coherently.

"What ate a spriggan?" Scáthach asked.

"We heard someone calling Kelcie's name and came into the circle to investigate," Niall explained, pushing his falling glasses up his nose. They really were way too big for his face.

"There was a strange black liquid, over there," Brona added, pointing to where it had been rather than showing them, "but it disappeared, melted into the ground."

"A *shade mantle*, I suspect." Scáthach padded around the stone circle, gingerly tapping the ground.

"What's that?" Kelcie asked.

"Shadowed space. Anything that falls into it looks as if it has vanished for good. Doesn't last long though," Scáthach explained.

Zephyr nodded. "Yup. It was Deirdre Crane. She has it out for Kelcie."

Scáthach sighed. "This has her hoof prints all over it. Certainly getting more inventive this year. I better have Madame Le Deux lock up her stores."

"Kelcie . . ." the gravelly voice called from the edge of the stone circle.

"What keeps calling her name?" asked Niall.

They trailed after Roswen who went to investigate. She scoured the overgrown grass, capturing something in her cupped palms. "This is what you heard."

She shifted her top hand so they could see inside. A small bug cowered. No bigger than a thumbnail, it looked like a cross between a spider and a cricket. Eight legs, two long jumpers, a round head with antennae. Three beady red eyes.

It croaked Kelcie's name again.

"A memory beetle." Niall sounded disappointed he hadn't figured it out before.

"Very good," Scáthach said. "From the sound of the voice, Connor Bones is helping her."

The beetle hopped off Roswen's hand. Striker snatched it midair, and promptly ate it.

"Good boy," Kelcie said, giving him a thankful pat.

She wanted to believe it was nothing but a stupid prank, but the voice sounded so much like the one in the ancient object. Maybe she was just being paranoid. With good reason. Deirdre Crane came at her twice on her first day, which wasn't even over yet. It didn't bode well for the rest of the year.

"If only you would eat Deirdre Crane," Kelcie said to Striker. He licked her hand.

Scáthach grimaced. "Where is your bough, Murphy?"

Kelcie pulled the broken chain out of her pocket. "That's why I was late this morning."

"What? Crane tried to take your bough?" Niall fumed. "Scáthach, isn't there something you can do?"

"We all have our battles to fight, O'Shea. I can't fight them for Murphy, or I wouldn't be doing my job." She took off her own necklace, pulled one of the seven leather straps out and handed it to Kelcie. "String your bough on that and tie it around your neck. No one will ever be able to take it off unless you allow it."

Kelcie took it. "Thank you. But ma'am, what about the spriggan that disappeared?"

Roswen gave her a stiff swat on the shoulder that hurt. "Not to worry. Shade mantles don't last long. Be back in no time."

Scáthach scrutinized Striker, who was now rubbing against Kelcie's leg. "Very curious how much Striker likes you, Murphy. Lee too. Cú sith are extremely rare and they have very, very long lives. This one is not young. He had several before coming here to stay with me, of that I am sure. Have you three possibly met before?"

Kelcie rubbed his ears. "I've never seen anything like Striker."

"Me neither." Brona knelt beside him. He lowered his head and whimpered, invitingly. She stroked his ears too.

Scáthach's curious stare drifted from Kelcie to Brona as she spoke to Roswen. "Roswen, ask Madame Le Deux to dust the stone circle. Dry up any leftover shade mantle before other spriggans or students go missing."

"Will do," Roswen chimed.

"Murphy, Lee, visit Striker if you like. He tends to spend most of his time pacing the Shadow's cliffs. I have found him to be a very good listener." Scáthach left, whistling for Striker to follow. He whimpered, then reluctantly trotted to their preceptor's side.

Roswen clapped her hands. "Hurry along for lunch or you'll miss it. I have a schedule to keep. Students fed, then the horses. If I'm late, they get nasty. The horses I mean. And if they get nasty, you'll be scraping conk livers off the cliffs in foraging class tomorrow night and eating them raw for dinner."

12

MISTRAL IS AS MISTRAL DOES

L ET'S MOVE. I'M famished," Zephyr called over his shoulder, running ahead.

"Me too!" Brona jogged after him, leaving Kelcie in uncomfortable silence with Niall.

She walked slowly, carefully looping the charm on the leather strap. She clutched the broken chain she'd worn as long as she could remember in one hand and held up the new one in the other, letting the charm swing from side to side.

Niall took it before Kelcie could protest. He tied it off, then placed it over her head. "It's like mine now."

Kelcie started walking, refusing to acknowledge his presence. She looked up at the sea eagles swooping overhead instead.

"They're always watching. They're manifestations of Scáthach, connected to her," he said, cracking his knuckles against his thigh. "We did a good job back there. All of us. As a fianna. Working together. Don't you think?"

Kelcie sneered at him, then picked up a long stick, dragging it behind her.

"What are you thinking about?"

She was thinking about wanting to hit him with the stick but refrained. "Niall, you don't have to walk with me."

"I know that."

"Then why are you? You said it yourself. We're not friends. You hardly know me."

She whacked a leaf on a low hanging branch.

When she went to do it again, Niall caught her elbow, pulling her to a stop. "I shouldn't have said that. I really am sorry. I didn't mean it. I panicked when Brona called us lovebirds."

His glasses fell down his nose. He left them there, afraid to let go of her arm to fix them.

"I didn't like it either, Niall."

Although maybe a very small part of her did. Like her appendix. Something that could be removed, because Niall didn't like her, not like that.

"Okay then."

"Okay, what?"

"Okay, we both didn't like it. And now you're graciously accepting my apology for saying things I didn't mean. Because we are friends. Aren't we?"

His sad lavender puppy-dog eyes pleading with her made it impossible for her to stay mad.

"Fine," she groaned, trying to get moving again, but Niall blocked her path.

"Fine?" Niall scratched the back of his neck. "You're accepting my apology? We're friends?"

"Okay."

Niall shook his head, nearly losing his glasses. "Say it."

"Say what?"

"That we're friends. Say it like you mean it."

"Why? Why do I have to say it like I mean it?"

Because I don't like it when you're mad at me.

Kelcie's breath caught. Niall had a way with words, a good way. But Kelcie had less of a way, especially around Niall. Why was talking to him so hard?

"We're friends. Okay? Can we go eat now? I'm starving."

———

KELCIE WAS JUST finishing her lunch when she saw Deirdre and Connor leaving. This was her shot to give them a piece of her mind, and she wasn't missing it. She got up quickly.

"Where are you going?" asked Brona.

"Kelcie, this isn't a good idea," called Zephyr.

Niall groaned. "She's doing it anyway," she heard him say. She looked back and was surprised to see all three trailing after her.

"I won't lose my cool," Kelcie promised.

"Sure, you won't," Zephyr said with a heavy dose of sarcasm.

"I might," Brona countered. "These two messed with the wrong fianna."

Kelcie caught them outside Haven Hall.

"Oh, I, uh, forgot something in my room," Connor said, tripping over his feet, unable to get away fast enough. He vanished through the Charger door.

"Bones, seriously?" Dierdre scoffed. She narrowed her beady red eyes on Kelcie. "What do you want?"

"To tell you that if you try that again, I'm going to blow a windball up your nose so hard your brains will squirt out your ears."

Deirdre glimpsed the leather band on Kelcie's necklace. She crossed her arms, clasping her bulging biceps. "I don't know what you're talking about."

Zephyr made a noise of utter disgust. "That shade mantle trap you set in the stone circle? I stepped right in it, fellow Charger."

"Scáthach knows it was you," Brona added.

Deirdre heaved a laugh. "Oh please. If I set a trap for Murphy, she wouldn't be standing here." She leaned over Kelcie. "By the way, Fomorian, I asked my father about you. Seems you didn't get registered this summer. I took the liberty of filling him in on your name, classification as an air demon—"

"Don't call her that," Niall snapped.

"Why not? That's what she is, Adder." Deirdre looked down her perfect nose at Kelcie. "Someone from High Command will be here at the end of the year to finish the job, if you make it that long . . ."

Deirdre pushed Kelcie out of her way, storming off, her long auburn ponytail swishing like an angry windshield wiper.

"It was definitely her," Brona said.

"Definitely," Zephyr agreed.

But as they started walking back, Kelcie wasn't so sure. Deirdre had no reason not to cop to it. Scáthach already thought she did it, and she wasn't going to get into trouble anyway. Scáthach wanted Kelcie to fight her own battles. But if it wasn't Crane, then who?

She fingered her necklace, twisting the leather strap until it hugged her neck, still haunted by the sound of her name coming from that memory beetle. *Fairies can't get to the school. The object, whatever it was, isn't here. It's with them.* But she couldn't shake the feeling that this was all connected.

After lunch, the first years buzzed with excitement as Alphas brought them into the training facility to practice using their unlocked gifts. Bigger than a Costco warehouse, the massive structure was partitioned into five separate areas, one for each Den. Killian, who was carrying a heavy leather-bound book under his arm, motioned for Kelcie to wait behind, letting the others go first again.

"Welcome to the pride," Diccon Wilks roared. The Cat Den's space was filled with moving wooden planks and logs hanging from the ceiling at impossible to reach heights. "Assignment number one. An impossible leap. Assignment number two. Breaks those claws free! You're done for the day when you can do both at once. I want to see you kitties swinging from the scratching posts!" Wilks jumped ten feet from standing, latching onto a passing log with morphed claws.

The Raven Den's Alpha, Gavin Puce, had trimmed his mohawk so that it was more of a stripe down the middle of his shaved skull and his black eyeliner had been traded for shimmering gold.

"This is the nest for grounded little chicks," Puce said through clenched teeth biting down on a stick. The Raven space was filled with mounds of hay. He clapped his hands together, rubbing his palms. The look in his aqua eyes was pure evil. "Today we're popping tail feathers."

Brona raised her hand. "Is this class required?"

"Only one way out of it." Puce plucked the stick he was chewing on and aimed it at a hole in the ceiling above the Ravens' nest.

Brona pried her arm free from Willow. "I'll see you later."

She morphed and flew out without looking back.

"Where are you going?" Willow called in her wake. She exchanged an annoyed glance with another Raven girl behind her.

The Chargers were next.

"One hour here in the troop, then we move to the stables," Regan bellowed.

"Stables . . ." Zephyr looked like he wanted to cry as he followed Regan and the other first-year Chargers into the Charger Den's space.

As training began, noise exploded from all sides, bouncing off the ceiling, merging into deafening chaos. Ravens groaning. Cats screeching. Chargers were the loudest, chanting like football players readying to take the field, followed by loud grunting and earth-shaking crashes, and the afternoon had only started.

"That's it," the Adder Alpha, Arabel Wasp, moaned. "We can't work in here today. First years . . ."

The rest of her orders to them were delivered silently. They nodded, already starting to leave.

We're going to the Lazy Creek for meditation. Niall mouthed the word *boring*. He tossed her a shy smile as he passed by that made her feel like he really was sorry for what he said earlier.

The Saiga space was in the far back corner and wasn't much to speak of. Light hardwood floors, cobblestone walls. The only light came from small holes below the tall ceiling. It was empty except for a pile of cobwebbed-covered metal blocks in one corner and dusty buckets in another.

Killian closed the door and locked it. He padded to the middle of the floor and sat down cross-legged, setting the book he had been carrying with him in his lap.

Kelcie sat across from him. She had been waiting to deliver the bad news. "Deirdre Crane reported me to her father."

A crease formed between his thick brows. "What exactly did she say?"

Kelcie recounted the entire miserable conversation, including the part where it happened in front of her fianna.

"Not to pile on that with more bad news, but I heard back from my family. They didn't have any useful information on your parents. There aren't many of us left. If someone lost a child, they would know. None of them knew of any who left for the human world either. My grandfather doesn't even know how that would be possible. He said it would take divine intervention."

"Divine intervention? Like a god or something?" Niall had said something similar when she arrived at the school.

Killian nodded. "Maybe your mother or father is human? There are stories of humans being given silver boughs by deities. Invitations into the Otherworld. Maybe one of them was invited. When things went bad for us, he or she returned with you to the human world."

That had possibilities. Her father was Fomorian. He had horns. She saw them last night. If her mother was human . . . "That could all make sense. They put the bough on me because only one of us could get out."

"No. Others can ride with you in the Sidrals. You just need the right bough to open it."

"You mean when I left, they could have gone with me?" How fitting. Her father didn't want to be found, and her mother must've elected to stay in the Otherworld. It felt like being abandoned all over again.

Kelcie had been here only two days and already the pieces of her life were coming together, only the outcome was the same. They didn't want her.

"My grandfather said he would ask around a bit. See if anyone else might know something."

Kelcie thought about telling Killian about talking to her father last night, but if she divulged that he didn't want to be found, Killian might tell his grandfather, and he might stop looking. Killian was so worried about everything all the time. Kelcie couldn't risk that. She wanted to know who they were, no matter the consequences.

"Let's get to work." He placed his hand over the letter *M* chiseled into the cover of the book. "*Mistral.*"

A tiny gust of wind passed between him and the book. The *M* lit up.

Kelcie smiled. "Can I open it like that too?"

"Any Mistral can." Turning to the first page, he shifted the book so Kelcie could see it too. "Look here."

On the page was a series of drawings of a man wearing black. His dark hair was bound at the base of his neck, his long beard tied in the middle. His thin, ringed horns made him resemble a Saiga antelope, only instead of growing straight up, they arced over his head. Kelcie wondered if her father's did that too.

In the pictures, his hands moved in a synchronized, sculpting fashion, his feet shifting forward and back, creating an increasing number of tiny swirls which Kelcie took to represent wind.

"There are four elements. Besides *Mistral*, *Caenums* are water elementals. *Therans* manipulate earth. And *Ignis* wield fire. The connection each of us has to our element is fundamental but also unique. The words we use to call our powers spark invocation, but they do not control them. That's on you."

"Like light switches?"

"If that means turning on the flow of light, then yes. These images illustrate carving techniques specific to Mistrals." Killian stood, backing up a little to give them room. "Follow my lead. Use your hands to feel the connection to the air." Killian demonstrated, holding his cupped hands out, palms facing each other. His fingers pressed tightly together and tensed. "*Mistral* . . ."

Tiny blue glints mixed with the air bouncing between his hands like fireflies caught in the wind. "The blue you see is my connection to the air. I can slow it down." His brows lowered, the lights slowed, the air thinned. "Or speed it up." He concentrated again, and the wind pushed against his hands so hard he could barely contain it. "Now you try."

Kelcie mimicked the stance. "Mistral."

She felt the surge, and then the connection tingling through the center of her palms. The air bounced from side to side, building speed and strength. She wasn't sure how long she could keep her hands together. "Killian . . ."

"Good. You catch on quick. Now for the release."

He pressed forward slowly, opening his hands, blowing Kelcie's hair out of her face, tickling her neck.

She winced at her trembling palms. "My turn."

Killian was blasted off his feet. Flat on his back, he groaned.

"You are unexpectedly strong."

He sat up, rubbing the back of his head.

"At your age, I could barely manifest enough wind to blow out a candle. And Ollie . . . it took more than a month for him to draw a pin-sized drop of water from a bucket to his finger. You're an anomaly."

Kelcie interpreted that as abnormal, and not a good thing. "I can't seem to say or even think, you know, that word, without bowling someone over. This morning it was Scáthach."

"Really?" Killian laughed.

"It's not funny. If this were the human world, they would name a hurricane after me. Don't get me wrong. I mean, yay me for being good at something for a change. But too good and out of control is getting me in trouble. What do I do?"

He thought for a long minute, glancing a few times at different pages in the book. "Try slowing your movements down."

"I was hardly moving before." Any slower and she would look like the old folks doing tai chi in the park. "Are you sure you know what you're doing?"

He gave her a look of supreme annoyance. "Right now, you're letting it control you instead of the other way around. Ignite the power within and hold tight to it."

He clinched his fist. "Mistral."

The air flowed around his hand in a glistening, swirling display of power. "Then let it go . . . gently."

He flicked his fingers at the open book. A gentle breeze turned the page.

Killian took a step back. "Center yourself. Stay calm, and most importantly, concentrate."

"Got it." Kelcie fisted her hands, drawing them toward herself in a slow, methodical, contemplative, benign way. Her mind emptied. "Mistral."

Deep down, she felt her powers spark to life. Wind swirled around her clenched fists even faster than it did Killian's. She tightened her grip, digging her nails into her palms, trying to hold back the tide rolling inside of her. Then she stretched her arms forward, opening her hands, releasing.

Airballs hit the wall like bazooka rockets, blasting two enormous holes in the side of the building. Killian jumped in front of Kelcie, shielding her from falling rock.

When the dust settled, Killian stared, dumbfounded. "Wow . . . that was . . ." He never found the right word.

"Hey!" Arabel Wasp's soaking wet head poked through the left hole. "Seriously, Lynch?"

"It was me, actually . . ." Kelcie admitted.

Wasp thrust her hand out. Suddenly, Kelcie was flying across the room. She crashed into the door and sank to the floor, where she curled into a ball, worried a broken rib punctured a lung. "Ow..."

"Keep her under control, Lynch, or I'll speak to Scáthach," Wasp threatened before storming off.

Killian helped Kelcie up. "Wasp's a telekinetic."

"You don't say..."

After twenty more minutes, the holes in the wall were so big they merged into one. Roswen's pink head slid into view. "Murphy! What have you done?"

Killian leaned on Kelcie's shoulder, chuckling. "Lesson one when you're cleaning horse stalls: watch where you step."

Kelcie knocked his arm off. "Not funny."

"How...? This...?" Roswen wrestled, finally throwing her hands in the air. "Unbelievable!" She shook her head at the pile of rubble, but then stopped. Her head tilting, a slow deceitful smile tugging at the corners of her mouth. "But maybe, just maybe... I'll have to speak to Scáthach immediately. She will not be happy with you, Murphy, not at all, but... Picture it. Open concept. Decorative gargoyles on the rafters. Something to really liven the place up! It's time to bring in the trolls. Not the tree trolls. They haven't a creative mind among them."

"Is she still talking to me?" Kelcie asked Killian.

Killian shrugged in disbelief. "She looks happy about this."

Roswen kept going. "We need a real architect with vision. Rapshider! He designed Summer City's catacombs. He is a genius. Ancient though. I heard he doesn't travel from the Boline Islands much anymore. I bet I could lure him. Trolls will do anything for silver or gold. Have to raid the safe..." She twisted her pink ponytail, then paused, looking over at Kelcie and Killian with a startled expression. "Did I say all that out loud?"

"Yes, ma'am," Kelcie replied.

Roswen aimed her axe-pen. "You elementals are officially banned from here. Another hit to these old walls, and the lot of you will be squished like morning cakes. As it is, I'll be here all afternoon adding support beams. Go. Now. Move it outside!"

WHEN THE MISERABLE day finally ended, Kelcie propped her pillows so she could watch her desk, hopeful that her father would send her another note through the magical tubes. A note that said, *I'm sorry. You have every right to know who I am. My name is so-and-so. I live in this incredibly beautiful place, and I expect to see you very soon. Oh, and yes, you have every right to know who your mother is too. Her name is Mrs. so-and-so. She loves you very much and is here with me, excited to see you too. Much love, Dad.*

But the drawer never dinged.

Night dragged.

By the time the moon dipped from view, Kelcie couldn't keep her eyes open any longer. She sank into blind darkness, that place between sleep and awake where the path diverges, one leading to dreams, the other to nightmares. Weightless, but unable to move, her hands prickled as she stood on the precipice.

Willow, Marta Louisa, Tad, and several others from her class whose names she couldn't remember pointed at her sniggering, whispering, staring like she was standing there naked. Her throat closed with panic. She looked down and was relieved to find that she wasn't actually naked. She was in the clothes she had on yesterday, her jean jacket, hoodie, and leggings, only the knees weren't torn.

Kelcie wanted to turn her back on them and walk away, but she couldn't feel her legs. Or arms. Or any part of her body. Deirdre Crane strutted out from the behind the pack, wading toward her. Following were Niall, Zephyr, and Brona. All were in their dress uniforms, and all were chanting *Fomorian. Demon. You don't belong here.* Their voices void of any emotion whatsoever, but relentless and unyielding.

She told herself, *This isn't real. It's only a nightmare.* But their words broke through, leaving her bereft and angry.

Niall stepped forward. He wasn't wearing his glasses. His lavender eyes darkening, his expression hardened. *No one wants you here. Your parents don't even want you. Go back to the human world.* His voice was no longer monotone, but filled with vehemence, a rage matching her own.

Fury choked her. Kelcie tried to raise her fists, but they swarmed. Arms snaking until she was trapped. Her limbs frozen in place, all she could do was yell, "No!"

They lifted her off the ground, onto their shoulders, carrying her toward . . .

The Sidral materialized right in front of them. Branches waving, its trunk splitting open.

Goodbye, Saiga! Deirdre growled in her ear. They tried to shove her into the open Sidral.

"No!" Kelcie willed power into her legs. She braced them against the sides of the hole. Surging energy rivered. Her veins glowed blue, striping the backs of her hands, which she could suddenly feel. Kelcie crossed her arms over her chest. Filled with an unbridled hate, she was ready.

Deirdre slapped a hand over her mouth, cutting off Kelcie's ability to say the word to blow them off her. But Kelcie refused to let that stop her. She drew every bit of anger she could muster, letting it consume her soul.

The air sparked. Gusts blasted from all sides of her, warping through everyone including her fianna mates. One by one, they screamed in writhing pain as they dematerialized.

But her powers weren't done yet. Her fists raised on their own. Howling wind shot straight up like water from a firehose.

That's right. When the lids open, they will all die by your hand.

Light flooded. A shriek rang out. A rancid smell like rotten eggs permeated her nostrils. In her last sleeping heartbeat, she heard a deep, gravelly voice whisper,

Vas.

Prepare yourself.

The trial begins.

13

AN UNINVITED GUEST

THE NEXT MORNING Kelcie woke up to a disaster. Her room looked ransacked. Empty beds toppled. Books and papers scattered all over. Worst of all, her shoes somehow ended up on the bottom of the pool. Kelcie had to beg Ollie to get them for her. He did, but only after she promised to let him teach her how to swim. It was a promise she would never keep.

Killian helped fix the beds. Sliding the last against the wall, he offered another piece of advice. "Maybe you should try sleeping on your side so you're facing the bathroom."

"With my luck, my toothbrush would end up in the toilet."

Kelcie needed to get dressed or she would be late to Scáthach's class, but she kept flashing on the nightmare. After dealing with Deirdre and her antics yesterday, Kelcie wasn't surprised the Charger staged an insurrection into her dreams, rallying Kelcie's own fianna against her, all hellbent on tossing her out of school. But she didn't count on the lingering effects souring her mood.

In her first class, Kelcie didn't feel much like talking to anyone. She snapped at Niall when he repeatedly asked her what was wrong. He was only being nice. It wasn't his fault her subconscious decided to cast him in the role of the ultimate backstabber. After all, he was the one who convinced her to test in the first place. He had a good reason to hate Fomorians since his father was killed by one, but he didn't hate her, as far as she could tell.

More than that, all through her first class, she couldn't shake off the chill of hearing that gravelly voice again. It said, *That's right. When the lids open, they will all die by your hand.* A lid, like the top of something? *It isn't real. It was only a nightmare.* But it felt so real. *Die?* Kelcie didn't want her friends to die. She didn't even want that awful Deirdre Crane to die. Why would her subconscious say that? And in that weird voice she heard in the object at the museum?

Vas. Prepare yourself. The trial begins. What did it mean? What was that thing Achila Grimes and Elliott Blizzard stole from the museum? She felt so stupid. Why didn't she ask Blizzard what it was when she had the chance? Kelcie took several deep breaths, telling herself she was overreacting. It was just a nightmare. But what if it wasn't?

She thought about asking Niall, but she had so little to go on. There was only one person who could give her any information. Her father. She had to find a way to talk to him.

Throughout the day, Kelcie tried to sneak off to the stone circle, but it wasn't easy. After fianna training, she told Niall, Zephyr, and Brona to go ahead to Combat.

"I'm going to do a few more laps," she said.

"You're not going anywhere alone, Saiga. Go with her, Raven," Zephyr ordered.

Brona's face broke into a huge smile. "With pleasure."

Kelcie groaned the whole way.

Later on, she told them she had to go to the bathroom. No one wanted to go with her. She was forced to sprint the long way around campus, past Haven Hall, to get to the stone circle, only to rush back for afternoon classes at Direwood Keep. After all that work, her father never showed.

She considered talking to Killian about it during Mistral training, but there wasn't time. Her session ended abruptly when she knocked down two of the campus' oldest trees and a horde of furious spriggans chased them out of the woods.

That evening, during foraging class, Roswen headed for the same spot she and Killian had been earlier. Kelcie cringed, waiting for a spriggan onslaught, but they were nowhere to be found. Nor were the toppled trees. All that was left of the old oaks were two chip piles sprinkled with sawdust, like they had been attacked by starving supercharged termites.

"Whoa. What stinks?" Zephyr cast an accusing glare at Gareth McKnight on his left, the redheaded Charger from fianna two.

"It wasn't me!" McKnight protested.

His twin sister, Ginger, rolled her eyes. "It's always you."

"I hate you," Gareth neighed.

"I hate you more!" Ginger snapped.

"Be quiet. All of you." Roswen knelt. The class collectively gagged as she ran her hand through the chip piles. "Strange." She sniffed her fingers. "It's impossible. Smells like . . ."

Yuri Petrov, the bowlegged Raven from fianna four, pinched his nose. "'ike wha'?"

"Nothing. Leave it. Come on. This way." She led the class farther into the woods, away from the overpowering smell, then stopped, asking them to gather around. "Let's get cooking. Hopefully, you saw the board in your rooms and memorized what the five plants we're going to be having for dinner tonight look like, or we'll all be going hungry."

Kelcie frowned, having forgotten to check the board. Niall would have though. Brona too. They probably checked it ten times a day at least.

Roswen brought a dagger out of her back holster, tapping off assignments on her clipboard. "One, elderberries. Two, you're on oyster mushrooms."

Their graceful Cat, Delilah Quick, hummed. "Excuse me, can you give mushrooms to another fianna? I'm afraid I'm allergic to anything that grows from mold on the sides of trees. Or the ground. I break out in a rash."

Roswen's pink brow arched at her. "I can live with that."

"Three, sweet potatoes. Four, crabapples, and five, chickweed."

"No meat?" Zephyr whined, crestfallen. "This man can't live on produce alone."

She levied the dagger at him. "You will be tonight. Now . . . where was I . . ." She glanced down at the clipboard again, running the blade along her scribbles. "Right. Make sure you bring enough back for the entire class." Roswen produced an hourglass from inside her sleeve, set it on the ground, and turned it over. Sand poured through the hole way too fast. "You've got twenty minutes. Find it, you pass. If you don't, you fail. That simple. What are you waiting for? Go!"

Fiannas scattered.

Kelcie scratched her head, trailing after Brona. "Sweet potatoes grow underground, right? So, what are we looking for?"

"Leafy green plants with white flowers. I see them!" Brona jogged to a patch of green stems with delicate white flowers.

"That was easy," Kelcie clapped.

"Stop!" Niall yelled, rushing after them.

Brona hesitated but didn't look happy about it. "What? This is it."

"No, it's not. That's mephitis. It's called stink weed."

Before Niall could stop him, Zephyr sniffed the flower. He swayed, grabbing on to a nearby tree trunk to keep from falling over. "I-I can'th feel my th-ongue."

"You're lucky you're not convulsing. It's toxic," Niall explained.

"Am I going thue die?" Zephyr put his back against the tree, closing his eyes.

"No. But I doubt you'll taste dinner." Niall trudged along the path, searching. "The flowers are white but have pink centers."

The others followed him.

"Feel-th tho th-range." Zephyr stuck his tongue out and bit down. "It thothally numb."

As Niall kneeled in a patch of pink flowers, the tree next to him quivered. Kelcie met Brona's confused glance with her own.

"Niall, did you see that?" Kelcie called.

"See, what?" Niall answered, but didn't turn around. He was laser focused on the task at hand.

The trunk sank a foot.

Then another.

And another . . .

"O'Shea, behind you!" Zephyr shrieked.

Niall looked back, then down. He dove out of the way just in time. The entire tree was pulled into an underground wood-chipper. Shavings overflowed the hole, carrying the same nasty stench as the other piles.

Dirt cratered.

Hairy green hands with trowel-shaped claws surfaced in the muck. A few more scrapes and they were joined by their even hairier green head, with squared-off ears and an oversized mouth filled with jagged-sharp teeth, spitting bark slivers.

It crawled out, sniffing. Waist-high, with four bulbous limbs and warts all over its elongated snout, the creature was so ugly it was almost cute. It took one look at Kelcie and howled a delighted squeal as if saying, "Dessert!"

"Run!" Niall cried.

Kelcie did, but too late. Green arms stretched like they were made of rubber, hog-tying her legs. It hoisted her off the ground, then leaped into the hole.

It all happened so fast that if it weren't for Zephyr's quick reflexes, Kelcie would've been toast. He caught her armpits, keeping the burrowing monster from getting away with her.

Niall latched on to Kelcie's wrist.

At the same time Zephyr yelled "Pull!" to Niall, Brona morphed her hands, extending her talons, and scraped the only visible part of the creature left, the top of its head. A loud screech shook the earth. Its arms around Kelcie unraveled, snapping into the ground like stretched bungee cords being released.

Zephyr only had time to set Kelcie on her feet when the ground quaked. Greeny surfaced so fast that before Kelcie could turn around, grimy nails dug into her shoulders.

"Ow!"

Kelcie swung wildly. The others hurled rocks, sticks, leaves, but nothing worked.

"Hey! Wood goblin! Over here!" Roswen yelled, rushing toward them. She waved a leafy branch, scattering berries.

The goblin's black eyes bulged. A big sniff in Roswen's direction, and its head spun completely around, torn. The goblin's hold loosened, and Kelcie ran.

Niall caught up quickly. Zephyr took the lead while Brona flew behind them, marking the wood goblin's trail—it was almost on top of them.

"What do we do?" Kelcie gasped.

"The Bridge of Leaping!" Zephyr yelled.

Zephyr's plan made sense. It wouldn't be able to get onto the bridge without surfacing.

The ground crumpled around their heels. At the rate they were going, they were never going to make it. Kelcie looked back, and stumbled over a large rock, falling flat on her stomach. The goblin surfaced to its waist, grabbing her foot.

"Help!"

Niall stomped on the goblin's back. Its chin came down hard on the rock.

The wood goblin reeled. Blood soaked the stone and Kelcie broke free. She lunged out of the way before the goblin vomited black bile all over the rock. Or at least Kelcie thought it was bile. With a *slurp* and *pop* the rock sank, disappearing, like the spriggan in the stone circle. The wood goblin screeched at the sight of it, back crawling and digging, submerging beneath the earth.

"That thing puked up a shade mantle," Kelcie said confused.

"Where?" Niall asked.

But it was gone.

Unfortunately, the wood goblin wasn't. Brona swooped over a spot only a few feet away from them, rasping the alarm.

"The bridge! Now!" Zephyr ordered, already on his way.

Niall snatched Kelcie's hand and didn't let go until they stood on the cobblestone deck.

Striker whizzed past them, heading straight for the green goblin, who had emerged on the cliff's edge, close to the bridge.

"Striker! Get back here!" Kelcie yelled.

But Striker didn't listen. Yipping and growling, the cú sith circled too close. The goblin nabbed him by the tail feathers.

"Striker!" Kelcie sprinted back across the bridge at the same time Roswen rushed out of the woods, carrying a long spear. She threw so hard and with such precision, Kelcie winced anticipating the bull's-eye, but the goblin caught it in its jagged teeth. It spit it out, wheezing a laugh, then dug its claws deep into Striker's hindquarters.

Striker yelped.

"Let him go!" Kelcie demanded.

The wood goblin hissed, jerking its muddy chin at Kelcie.

"Is it proposing a trade?" Niall asked.

Kelcie had to do something, but what? With her lack of control, if she used her powers, the goblin and Striker would both go over the cliff.

The spear!

Zephyr grabbed it, hurling it to Brona. She caught it with her talons midair, flipped it tip down, aiming straight for the goblin's head, and let go.

The goblin dove one way and Striker went the other. As soon as Striker's green streak was clear, Kelcie roared, "Mistral!"

A hurricane force wind whipped the wood goblin across the strait. It smashed into the Shadow's cliff, and plunged into the churning water below. It would've been a triumphant win for fianna three, but the gust didn't stop there. The wind slammed into the Shadow's wall. A large section crashed to rubble.

Zephyr flinched as the dust settled. "That's not good."

First years ran out of the woods. Scáthach and Regan, along with other Chargers on horseback, rode into the field, heading straight for them.

Striker made a beeline for Kelcie. Relieved, she hugged him and checked him over. Other than revolting residual goblin stench, and a few scratches from its nails, he seemed fine.

"We need support in the channel," Roswen said to Scáthach as their preceptor dismounted beside her.

"Already there. Was that an actual wood goblin?"

"Yes."

Kelcie heard extreme splashing, followed by a hard *thud*, then a familiar "Stop or I'll make this hurt!" from over the cliff's edge.

She walked over and saw Coach Blackwell had hauled the goblin out of the water, into a small wooden rowboat. Blackwell was strapping on leg irons, its hands already bound behind its back.

Their coach gave a thumbs-up. "I've got the stinking vermin."

The goblin bit the bow, eating a huge chunk of wood, and lurched, trying to escape. The boat rocked. Blackwell leaped on top of it, holding it down.

"A little help!" Coach Blackwell yelled.

"Regan, lead the senior Chargers to assist him," Scáthach ordered.

Regan hesitated when she saw Niall. She jerked her head at Deirdre, letting her take the lead.

Deirdre smirked, more than happy to take command. "On me, Chargers!"

As her Den mates rode away, Regan jumped off her horse, and hurried to her brother, fussing over him. "Did it hurt you?"

"I'm fine, Regan." Niall's faced flushed with anger.

She didn't take his word for it. She checked him over. "Are you sure? Your glasses are broken!"

"So? They're just glasses. My fianna and I fought off a wood goblin! And won if you didn't notice!" he snapped, storming away from her.

"O'Shea! Your brother doesn't need you. He's perfectly capable of taking care of himself," Scáthach scolded. "Go! Now!"

"Yes, ma'am." Regan glowered at Niall's back as she mounted her horse. She kicked into a startling gallop, chasing the dust wake the others left behind.

Brona landed next to Kelcie. She morphed and stroked Striker's back. "We wouldn't let it eat you, boy." The Raven glanced at Kelcie, and said in all seriousness, "That was fun."

"Fun isn't the word I would use . . ." Kelcie said, laughing, then stopped.

There was something in Brona's mischievous expression that raised goose bumps on Kelcie's arm. She felt like she was having déjà vu, like she and Brona had a similar conversation before. But that was impossible, wasn't it?

"How did it get here? I haven't seen a goblin in these lands since before the split," Scáthach said to Roswen in a haunting tone that shook Kelcie to her core.

"I don't know. I've never seen one outside the Lands of Winter, and never wanted to again. Disgusting creatures." Roswen held lavender stems to her wrinkled nose.

Kelcie frowned at Niall, who looked concerned too. He said nothing could get into the Lands of Summer from Winter. But there it was, a Winter wood goblin ramming its bald head into Connor Bones, sending him crashing into the choppy waters. If a wood goblin could get to AUA, why not Grimes and Blizzard? What if they were here, but no one could see them? Could they be hiding on campus somewhere?

And then another much more terrifying thought occurred to Kelcie. What if this all had to do with her nightmare last night? *The trial begins.* Could this be the trial the voice talked about? Kelcie's stomach lurched into her throat.

She had more questions than answers, all of which she kept to herself. She couldn't even tell Niall. If Scáthach thought the wood goblin being at the school was her fault, she would kick her out, and Kelcie couldn't let that happen. Maybe it was a selfish decision, but there was too much at stake. She wanted to find her parents.

"Bones doesn't look like he can swim any better than the goblin," Zephyr laughed.

A sea eagle landed on Scáthach's shoulder. It whistled next to her ear.

"At least it didn't eat any of the students," Scáthach said, relieved.

"Only the two *trees* Murphy knocked down this afternoon," Roswen said, rubbing her pink brows like she had a headache.

Kelcie grimaced. "Sorry about that . . ."

"Yes, well, perhaps overzealous powers were as helpful as hurtful today," Scáthach said, frowning at the broken section of the Shadow's wall. "Once the goblin is chained, I'll take it to Summer City and turn it over to High Command. They can properly interrogate it and find out how it got here."

"First years, back to class!" Roswen ordered.

A FTER A TENSE meal of mushrooms and sweet potato stew roasted over a warm campfire, Kelcie slid into bed still hungry, and still reeking of wood goblin. The moon hung above her head, bathing the room in glistening white that reminded Kelcie of the ice fairy's hair color.

Her mind spiraled down a dark wood goblin hole. "What if Grimes and Blizzard wanted me at this school? And why was it my father could contact me once, but not again today?" She sat up, talking to the moon since there was no one else around to listen. "He said it shouldn't have been possible for him to talk to me, and then he freaked, asking about the object, and then freaked some more telling me to leave! What if Grimes and

Blizzard, or whoever they worked for, orchestrated that call? *Let my father speak, a tiny clue but more than enough to keep me here, for sure!*" Kelcie rolled on her side. "*But why?*"

One thing she was growing rapidly aware of was that she wasn't going to be able to figure this out on her own. It took her fianna working together as a team to stop the wood goblin. She needed their help. But could she trust them?

Kelcie got out of bed, determined to write Niall first, but as her pen hovered over the parchment, she saw his face in her nightmare. She heard him and Brona and Zephyr tell her to go home, that she didn't belong here. The seeds of doubt planted, she set the pen down.

Even if she asked him not to, Niall would tell Scáthach.

She looked up at the moon once more, this time making a silent wish to speak to her father again. She would return to the stone circle tomorrow, and the day after, and the day after that. Kelcie would keep this secret until she found out who he was and how to find him.

14

SWORD & SORCERY

SCÁTHACH DELIVERED THE wood goblin to High Command in Summer City. Since then, there had been no signs of other infiltrators at the school, and no more nightmares. But disappointing weeks passed without contact from Kelcie's father. She had come to terms with the fact that she was on her own, per usual. And per usual, she was failing most of her classes.

At every turn, she couldn't get control of her powers. More trees lost their lives. She buckled the Shadow's main gate, and worst of all, knocked over two sacred stones in Ferdaid's circle. Of all the Chargers, Roswen sent Deirdre Crane and Connor Bones to right them. They told everyone that would listen that the newest addition to the Saiga Den was a walking elemental disaster.

After desecrating the stone circle, Kelcie's Mistral lessons were officially suspended, and she was asked to not use her powers until Scáthach could come up with a solution.

Kelcie wasn't the only one in her fianna struggling either.

Zephyr was on edge all the time. The horse he had been assigned to, a mare with an attitude named Dimitri, bucked him off every time he tried to mount. That led to him taking his frustrations out on Kelcie, Brona, and Niall during Scáthach's class. He yelled so much on the obstacle course that Brona morphed and tried to harpoon him with her beak at least once a day. All of which led to more punishment laps from Scáthach.

Rope climbs were added to the obstacle course. Regan wasn't wrong about Niall having trouble with them. He had yet to make it halfway up without quitting. Kelcie hardly saw him outside of class because he spent all his free time on the practice field struggling to get up them.

Brona was the only member of their fianna who excelled at everything. She was Little Miss Popular too. Everyone wanted her to hang out with them, both in class and out. They jockeyed for position to walk beside her to classes. Even though Brona didn't say she wanted to leave their fianna to Kelcie or Niall or Zephyr, she did to others. Kelcie heard her on the way to the Nether Tower for Blackwell's class.

The other first-year Ravens flocked around her, forming a tight conspiring circle.

"All three of those scabrats are making you look bad, Brona," Willow challenged.

"Can't hurt to ask?" Igor Lopchick from fianna two offered.

"Do it, Lee," Yuri Petrov goaded, swinging a wing over her shoulders.

Brona shook her head. "Roswen made it clear day one. Fiannas wouldn't be changed."

"Scáthach would let you. You're a demigod." Sanura Shaker cooed.

Brona frowned. "I'll think about it."

It wasn't a *no*. And if Brona was allowed to leave their fianna, it would be a sure sign the rest wouldn't get asked back for year two. Kelcie never belonged here to begin with, did she? She wasn't like the others. She didn't even know these kinds of powers existed before a few months ago. She had stayed to find her parents and was at a complete loss at how to do that. She was a failure at everything she tried. Maybe, like Willow liked to remind her, she didn't belong in their perfect school, filled with so many perfect kids. Brona being the most perfect of all.

Kelcie crossed her arms, barreling into Brona's shoulder, eliciting an enraged "Hey!" from her, but didn't look back. By the time she got to the Nether Tower for combat training, she was angry and ready to hit something.

Coach Blackwell had dispensed swords and shields to more than three-quarters of the class. Niall and Zephyr had joined Brona, trading in their wooden ones for the real deal. Kelcie was forced to work with Gabby Arnold most days, a Cat shifter and the most uncoordinated person in their class. It was common knowledge that she had yet to morph a single nail to a claw. Her combat skills were no better. She swung wildly, whiffing most times, stopping to apologize so much that Kelcie never got any worthwhile practice in. Kelcie didn't want to hurt Gabby's feelings, but when Coach Blackwell switched to grappling, she asked for a different partner.

Sadly, Coach Blackwell paired Kelcie with Tad Fagan, making her immediately regret the decision. All one hundred and fifty pounds of him ended up squatting on Kelcie's stomach. He beat his chest like a primate in a frenzy.

"This was over before it started." Fagan laughed.

Her inner voice went to work propping her up, snarling things like, *Don't let him get the better of you. He's the one who doesn't belong. Not you,* and finally, *What are you waiting for?*

What was she waiting for?

Kelcie bucked, launching Tad up and over her shoulders. His dark hair fell like a curtain over his eyes and his hands planted beside her head, giving her the perfect escape. Before Tad knew what hit him, Kelcie whipped her arms around his left wrist, pinned his right foot between her legs, then executed a swift roll, breaking free.

Kelcie launched her hands in the air, dancing in circles. "Oh yeah! Saiga! Saiga! Saiga!"

Tad slammed his fist into the dirt. "No!" He yelled so loud everyone stopped their matches to watch.

"Murphy, good move," Coach Blackwell grunted. "Nice to see my time hasn't been wasted." Kelcie smiled. It was the first time

Coach Blackwell had ever complimented her. "The rest of you, back to work!"

Kelcie should've known Tad wouldn't take being beaten lightly.

Coach Blackwell moved on watching the others as they went back to their matches.

"Round two," Fagan declared. He grabbed Kelcie in a bear hug from behind, lifting her off her feet. "Take your wins while you can, Saiga. I heard Scáthach is kicking you out of school if there's one more incident."

Kelcie kicked his knees with her heels. Tad laughed in her ear.

"Parchment is going out to High Command right now. Your days are numbered. But you already know that, don't you? That's why you keep going to the stone circle, calling for your father. *Da, are you there?* Or no, wait. That's not the way you say it. *Daddy.* That's a new one. Daddy."

Adrenaline heaved her chest. *Show him who you are,* her brain snarled. But Kelcie refused to give in. Powers weren't allowed in combat class. *Who cares?* it challenged. Her inner voice took a noticeably deeper and darker tone, chipping away at her resolve.

"Do the tubes not work in Chawell Woods? Don't worry. Scáthach will find a way to tell him you're done here." Tad squeezed so hard her elbows dug painfully into her ribs.

"Shut up!" She threw her head back, striking his nose, hearing a satisfying *crack.*

"Gah!" His grip loosened, but not enough for her to break free.

Kelcie slipped her hands beneath his arm, trying to push him off. He tightened his grip, laughing in her ear. "Go back to Chawell Woods where you belong, demon."

Rage coursed through her, mixing with the adrenaline, driving her to a whole new level of angry, and it scared her. She was out of control. Boiling fury spilled down her arms. The veins on the back of her hands glowed red.

Kelcie gasped.

Fagan yelped, "Ow!" He threw Kelcie on the ground like a rag doll. "What the . . . ? Ah, jeez . . ." He shook his arm out. Kelcie's handprints were there in bright red, but already fading. "What did you do?"

"Nothing!" Kelcie insisted. She stared at her hands, unable to fathom how she burned him. "You win. I give." She held her hands up.

But Fagan didn't accept her surrender. He side-kicked her in the chest, sending her crashing to the floor with the wind knocked out of her.

"Fagan, that's enough," Coach Blackwell snapped.

"Yes, Fagan, that is enough," Kelcie groaned. In one move, she jumped to standing. Niall's *don't do it* and Zephyr's orders to *wind down!* fell on deaf Saiga ears.

Kelcie fixed on Fagan's smug smirk. "What? Are you going to c-c-cry? Sniff. Sniff."

She scooped air. "Not today. Mistral!"

An airball slammed into Fagan. He flew across the tower and into the storage room. Pegging the wall, the airball bounced, heading straight at Kelcie.

"*Nil mistral!*" Kelcie called, trying to stop it—too late. It belted her with so much force, Kelcie crashed into poor pathetic Gabby Arnold.

Mortified, she rolled off Gabby, whose nose was bleeding, and quickly helped her up. "Sorry."

Coach Blackwell stormed over. "Murphy! You know full well that powers are not permitted in this class."

"Yes, sir."

Fagan climbed out of the storage room, holding his gut. "She's not supposed to be using hers at all, Scáthach said."

Blackwell's jaw tensed as he turned to the rest of the class. "Dismissed. Get to lunch. All of you!"

Kelcie started to leave with the others when she felt the coach's firm hand on her shoulder. "Not you. You've got so much energy, you skip lunch. Run. Around and around. I'll tell you when you can stop."

KELCIE RAN FOR most of lunch, but it gave her time to think about what happened with Tad. She burned him. She stared at her hands, willing them to get hot a few times, but nothing happened. By the time Coach Blackwell told her she could stop, she knew it wasn't her. Fagan was probably trying to burn her with another potion she never heard of, like shade mantle, and it backfired.

Niall snuck a bowl of stew and bread out of lunch for her, which she gratefully ate on the way to Madame Styora Le Deux's Sword & Sorcery. Her legs felt like jello. Thankfully, sitting was mandatory in this class. The first month of classes had been held at night, outside, to talk about the various moon cycles, the positions of stars and planets, and how cutting hair when Mars was in retrograde could lead to permanent hair loss. Sounded a little out there, but then again, so was Madame Le Deux.

She spent an entire class on the transport trees, where Kelcie learned that Sidrals were all birthed from the seeds of the Tree of Life that grows on the Island of Eternal Youth. When the Otherworld was first inhabited, the various gods and goddesses handed out seeds to whomever held up their grubby hands. Seeds were planted without any consideration to proper urban planning. Kelcie remembered the others she saw traveling on her way to AUA. It hardly seemed like heavy traffic to her, but apparently, Sidral travel during rush hour in the larger cities became so congested they were forced to add additional slower, alternative means of transportation—like trains.

Another thing Kelcie found interesting was that the lands in this world were once a single giant continent like the human world. Kelcie learned all about Pangaea in Mr. Allen's fourth grade class. He was a good teacher, except when he pulled out his guitar. His off-key original titled "We All Live in a Place Called

Pangaea" still popped into her brain unbidden when Kelcie was least expecting it. In the human world, tectonic plates shifted, causing the single land mass to split apart into seven continents. In the Otherworld, the giant continent was called Alltar. And it was broken apart by war.

Madame Le Deux's cluttered classroom was at the very top of Direwood Keep. Herbs hung upside down, drying behind her desk. There were jars filled with strange labels, like leprechaun baby teeth, water horse droppings, and kelpie hair. Empty cauldrons hung on cranes inside unlit fireplaces in preparation for the class to brew their first potion, which was coming up.

Kelcie couldn't wait.

Down the center of the room were six tables, one for each fianna. Fianna three's was in the back, but that didn't keep Madame Le Deux from constantly peppering them with questions, many of which were impossible to understand because of her accent. Kelcie thought it was French, but after a while, it sounded a little Russian. It was confusing to say the least.

"Today, we dive deeper, deenkas." Her constant referral to her students as *deenkas* was always met with bemused frowns. No one knew what it meant or had the courage to ask.

Her long black cloak swallowed her wiry six-foot frame and swept the floor when she paced up and down the aisles. Her blond hair was always worn in a painfully tight bun, and she had piercing azure eyes that when narrowed had even Brona squirming in her seat.

She aimed a bony finger at Niall. "You, the name of the war being fought when the continent split was . . . ?"

"The Never-Ending War."

"Very good, boy weeth brokeen glassees. Who fought een thees war?"

"The Land of Summer and the Land of Winter, obviously," blurted David Dunn, a skinny, golden-haired boy in the Adder Den.

Madame Le Deux popped him on the back of the head. "Deed I call on you, snakey-poo?"

The class laughed.

He shrank in the seat. "No, ma'am."

"Snakey-poo ees right. Let's move on. 'orse-boy with cute dimple, deed eet end, the Never-Ending War?"

Zephyr scoffed. "Yeah, it did. Or the Abyss ended it for them."

Kelcie raised her hand. "What's the Abyss?"

"You don't know what the Abyss is?" asked Brona.

"Even farm boy knows what the Abyss is," Fagan said, flashing his perfect teeth at Zephyr.

Laughter rang out.

"I really hate that guy," Zephyr said under his breath.

"Of course, I've heard of it, obviously." Kelcie laughed it off. "I meant to say I've never seen it."

Niall smirked her. *Good cover.*

"I bet few in your class 'ave, Kelcie." Madame Le Deux frowned at Tad. "Let's start at thee beegeenneeng. Eet weell be on thee next test."

The class responded as one with a loud "Yes, ma'am."

"Why don't you tell us, Raven girl, seence you know so much?" Madame Le Deux instructed.

Why does she only remember your name? Niall asked Kelcie in her head.

Kelcie shrugged, smiling. It was nice being the teacher's pet for once.

Brona stood up to answer. "Alltar split in two in the middle of the largest river in the Otherworld. When it did, it created an unending waterfall between the Land of Summer and the Land of Winter called the Abyss. Nothing can cross, not even by air. Toxic gas rises higher than fairies can fly."

"Yes, Raven girl, deenka-doo. A golden sun on your forehead. Now, seet down."

"But there's more." Brona's eyes glossed over. "The river in the

Lands of Summer was renamed the Vanishing River. It's fed by three smaller rivers. At the confluence, where they merge, there's a reservoir filled with the softest, bluest water in all of the kingdom. If you follow it to the edge, where it crests into the Abyss, it turns syrupy, and pitch black like tar. One tragic slip of a foot off the bank, and the tar won't let go. You'll be sucked over, and then you're falling forever."

"Unexpectedly veeveed. You sound as eef you've seen eet," Madame Le Deux said quizzically.

Brona shook her head. "I've just heard stories about it."

Their teacher padded slowly back to the front of the class. "Let's see . . . a never-endeeng fall deevided thee lands so the fighting could stop. And yet, eet ees called thee Never-Ending War for a reason. The armies of Weenter still find ways to eenfeeltrate thee Lands of Summer. It ees why all of you are 'ere—to fight for Summer, ees eet not? Thees school ees the only one that churns out soldiers capable of standing up to thee armies of Weenter. Eet weell be your job to keep thee Summerfolk safe." She reached her desk and turned to face the class. "Who can tell me who leeves on thee cold side of the Otherworld? In Weenter?"

"Fairies, goblins, vampires, and banshees," Marta Louisa answered.

"Vampires?" Kelcie gawked.

Willow scoffed. "Didn't know what you were signing up for?"

Their teacher arched a thin, blond, unsatisfied brow at Marta Louisa. ". . . And many, many more. Next week we weell start weeth my personal favoreete, thee teeny Deepsa. Of all thee creatures een thee Lands of Weenter, they are thee most dangerous. Never see them unteel after you've been beetten. Then . . ." She wrapped her hands around her throat. "Too late." She smiled widely. "Be sure you've done your reading. There weell be a quiz."

After class was over, Kelcie left her textbook on the table on purpose, padding halfway down the spiral staircase before telling Niall she was going back for it. She wanted to ask Madame

Le Deux a few questions without anyone hearing. Her teacher was still at her desk.

"Kelcie, deed you need sometheeng?"

"I wanted to ask . . ." She wasn't sure where to start. "Have you ever heard of a round object about this big . . ." Kelcie used her hands to demonstrate the size of a basketball. "That could cause explosions and had something to do with lids?"

Madame Le Deux's brow knit. "Explosions? Leeds? Kelcie, you are Saiga. You should not be speaking of the eye!"

"Eye?" It never occurred to Kelcie that *lid* could be an eyelid.

Le Deux leaned over the desk, lowering her voice to barely above a whisper. "Come now. Weeth what happeened to your people after thee attack eight years ago . . ."

Eight years ago? Kelcie's heart raced. Everything kept coming back to the same time when Kelcie was abandoned. "When Draummorc betrayed the Queen?"

Madame Le Deux stared at her, the crease between her brow cratering deeper. The temperature in the room felt like it had dropped twenty degrees in a second. "The eye deestroyeed Summer Ceety."

Kelcie was even more confused. How could an eye destroy an entire city? It exploded the room on the museum, but a whole city? She knew it was powerful, but that . . . Her chest tightened.

"Could it be here? At the school?"

Madame Le Deux smiled dismissively. "No. Eets eempossible. But leesten to me. Eef you ask about the eye, eet weel be very bad for you 'ere. I would 'ave thought your pareents would 'ave told you that. Focus on your classees. Your powers. Get stronger. That ees what you need to be doing, deenka."

"Yes, ma'am." Kelcie picked up her book, still confused.

Niall was waiting for her at the bottom of the stairs. "Took you long enough."

Kelcie heeded Madame Le Deux's warning. "My book fell behind the desk."

15

POOL PARTY

KELCIE SPENT HER free hour combing her schoolbooks for information about eyes. Her *Beginning Crafting* described several potions and poultices that incorporated everything from dried dung beetle eyeballs to lullaby lashes plucked from a sleeping reindeer, but nothing that could burn down a city. When she exhausted her books, she snuck into Killian and Ollie's room. It looked a lot like Kelcie's, four beds, four desks, four lockers, but between Killian and Ollie's lockers was a shelf with a burgeoning library of textbooks.

She would have to hurry. They were still in combat class but would likely be back soon to clean up before dinner. After Le Deux's warning, Kelcie wasn't going to risk asking anyone about the eye, not even them. She ran her finger over the spines, stopping on an enormous book titled *Encyclopedia of Supernaturals*. She lugged it to one of the empty beds. A quick scan of the table of contents, and Kelcie found exactly what she was looking for, a chapter called "Evil Eyes."

"Score . . ."

But when she opened the chapter's first page, what she read made her rethink what her father had said about leaving. Evil eyes didn't come from curses or castings. They couldn't be manifested. They existed naturally in the universe in two forms.

Infectious, and thus could be avoided or removed, or *delivered,* usually by people—knowingly and unknowingly.

The latter, the delivered, were malevolent, destructive forces that emanated from the originator, and carried on after death, which Kelcie took to mean that an evil person's spirit could live on in their evil eye. What haunted her the most was what it said about the unknowing person. If the will of the spirit living on in the evil eye was stronger than the unknowing person bringing it forth, it could force the bearer to do its bidding. That meant an evil eye could force an unsuspecting person to do things they didn't want to do.

"Hey!" Ollie said, making her jump. "Trying to get ahead for next year?"

Kelcie slammed the book shut, faking a laugh. "Oh yeah. Just bored. Sorry. Probably should've asked first."

"Nah. But don't let Killian catch you in here without asking. He hates it when I touch his things."

Kelcie put the book back where she found it and left as fast as she could.

A FTER DINNER, NIALL and Zephyr invited themselves over to the Saiga Den to swim. Kelcie sat on the side of the pool, her feet in the water, rereading her Mistral book for the twentieth time, trying to find anything she might've missed to help her control her infuriating powers. She couldn't afford another incident like what happened with Tad Fagan in Coach Blackwell's class.

"I can't believe you're not in here every day," Zephyr said. He leaped off the side, belly flopping in the pool, splashing her.

Niall was a back floater. He snaked his arms, bumping his head into the sides, then moved in another direction.

Ollie sat cross-legged on the bottom of the pool with his eyes closed. He'd been down there for five minutes when Niall finally asked, "What's he doing?"

Zephyr shook his hair out. "Shouldn't he be dead by now?"

Ollie surfaced, spraying water all over Kelcie.

"Ollie! Your brother gave me this book!"

She held it up, letting what water the pages hadn't already soaked up drain back into the pool.

"Get in!" Ollie grabbed her ankle.

She slipped out of his grasp and scooted away from the edge. "No! I told you—"

"You don't like to swim," Ollie said in an annoying, high-pitched voice that was supposed to sound like Kelcie.

"Don't get her agitated, Ollie," Zephyr warned. "You'll end up blown into Scáthach's living room."

Ollie splashed him. "Who's up for a holding-your-breath contest?"

Niall swam to the side the pool. "You're a water elemental. You can breathe underwater."

"True." He whipped water in Niall's face.

Niall stared blankly at him, unsure how to handle Ollie at his obnoxious best. Kelcie would offer advice, but she hadn't figured it out yet herself.

"Why didn't you invite Brona Lee to swim? I saw her practicing with Blackwell. Brona with a sword . . ." He swam toward the side, drooling. "She's spectacular."

Kelcie dipped her feet back in the pool. "She's too busy with Willow and Marta, contemplating ways of changing fiannas."

Ollie hopped out, wrapped a towel around his neck, and strutted toward Kelcie, whistling a playful tune. "You're going in, Murphy. Right now!"

Before he could reach her, Niall zipped out of the pool with one hand, putting himself between them. "Back off, Saiga boy."

Ollie pursed his lips, making annoying kissing sounds, then danced all the way to his room, slamming the door shut.

"Killian must want to smother him in his sleep," Niall said, shaking his head.

Kelcie's heartbeat sped up. Niall was too close. She couldn't look at him—but all she wanted to do was look at him. Especially since he didn't have his glasses on. What was it about when he took them off that made her want to stare at him all the time? His eyes looked darker, a deep violet.

Kelcie set the book down. "This is depressing."

"Yeah. About that . . ." Zephyr swam over and set his chin on the edge. "We need to have a parley."

Niall's coordinated frown dropped Kelcie's stomach into her bare feet. "Okay."

"After the Fagan incident this morning in Blackwell's class, his entire fianna lodged a complaint with Scáthach." Zephyr's dimple dipped. "Normally, I'd be like, who cares, she never listens anyway, but it's the third complaint in the last three weeks about you using your powers in classes you're not supposed to. And Fagan told her you did it on purpose."

"Only after he kicked me when I was giving up! Did he mention that part?"

Zephyr shook his head. "Of course not. He's a lying sack of squid polish. But when she asked me what I saw, I had to tell her the truth."

"Which is?"

"I didn't see it."

"Neither did I," Niall added. "And Brona—"

"Hates me." Kelcie wrapped her arms around her knees.

"She doesn't hate you," Niall disagreed. "She hates us all."

Zephyr sighed. "She's worried about having a spot next year, and frankly so am I."

"Because of me." Kelcie turned away, unable to look him in the eye.

Zephyr hopped out of the pool and grabbed a towel. "Scáthach said it on day one. If one of us fails, we'll all fail. That's just the way it is. And that's the reason Ms. Demigoddess wants to change fiannas, not that they'll let her."

"You know I'm trying."

"Are you? You didn't have to use your powers in combat class," Zephyr argued. He scooped his blue T-shirt off the floor and slipped it over his head.

She was so mad at Tad for kicking her, but maybe she should've been more like Niall, and let it go. She broke the rule. Powers weren't allowed in combat class, and her fianna would pay the price.

"You've made your point, Charger," Niall hissed.

"He's right, Niall. I have to do better. I vow to never use my powers in that class again." Kelcie sat back down, dangling her feet in the pool.

Niall elbowed her. "You need to get them under control. A tiny airball up Fagan's nose would've been highly distracting and gone unnoticed by Blackwell or anyone."

Dismayed, Kelcie plunged her foot into the water, over and over, making teeny tiny whirlpools. "Killian has tried everything. Nothing is working."

"Is there anyone you can ask for help?" Zephyr asked. "Who in your family is a Mistral like you?"

Niall splashed him. "She doesn't know who her family is. She doesn't know who her parents are. She doesn't even know if they're dead or alive."

"Sorry. Forgot."

Kelcie looked from Niall to Zephyr, debating. Her father might be able to help. He was a Fomorian. These powers likely came from him. Could she risk telling them? Maybe she could. This eye-thingy, that was off limits, but Scáthach already knew she spoke with her father, so there was no danger there.

Kelcie stared at her elongated toes. "My father's not dead."

"What?" Niall accused.

"The first night I was here he sent me a note. Two actually."

Niall was so close she could feel his wounded stare. "You never said anything."

Kelcie sighed. "There was nothing to tell. He didn't want to see me, Niall. He wouldn't even tell me his name. Or my mother's. Or where he is. I've been back to the stone circle so many times, trying to find out more information. He never . . ." Tears threatened. Kelcie could barely speak past the lump in her throat. "It doesn't matter. He doesn't want me to find him."

"He has to be in Chawell Woods, right?" Zephyr asked.

"Not necessarily," Niall said, but didn't elaborate. "Do you have his letters?"

Kelcie nodded. "Be right back."

She retrieved them from the bottom of her wardrobe where she'd put them for safe keeping. Niall examined them closely, touching the red marks in the corner of each. "A drop of blood. Your father sent this looking for you. He didn't know where you were either."

Kelcie stared at him. "How do you know that?"

"This is from a locator spell. This is all you need. A locator spell is a direct line from sender to recipient."

"So she can send a note back to him if she uses the same parchment?" Zephyr asked.

He flipped it over. "Yep. Write on the back. Put it in the drawer. It should return to its sender."

Kelcie's jaw dropped. All this time, it was that easy? If it worked, then maybe she could ask him about the eye too. But then there was another problem. "What do I say?"

Niall's hand brushed hers on the edge of the pool. "Get your pen. We'll write it together."

THAT NIGHT SHE sent what she, Niall, and Zephyr thought was a well-crafted, respectful note to her father.

Dear Dad, don't worry. I know you don't want me to find you.

I'm writing because I need your help. I can't control my Mistral powers. I say the word, and then—splat. Trees. Walls. The gate on the Shadow. Nothing I try works. Killian (you don't know him, but he's our Alpha) is out of ideas.

Any advice would be greatly appreciated.
Your daughter, Kelcie

Kelcie pricked her thumb with Zephyr's knife, letting a drop fall on the corner of the parchment.

She was scared her father wouldn't answer, but more nervous that he would. What if he turned her down? What if he told her to leave again? Kelcie's hands trembled as she set it in the drawer. How could a person she never met have that kind of effect on her?

This was too important. Her fianna would fail if she didn't succeed. She took a deep breath for courage and pushed the drawer closed. When she opened it, the letter was gone.

16

SYLPH DANCING

A DAY LATER, KELCIE's drawer dinged, but what she found left her more confused than ever.

The handwriting was very different from her father's last note, with grand, swoopy letters, and rather than torn moldy parchment, the paper was opulent silver. This note wasn't from her father. And whoever it was from was messing with her.

You're not a Mistral.
Try again.

What's that supposed to mean? Niall asked while their fianna waited to take their turn on the dreaded rope wall.

"No clue, but I don't think my father wrote the note. The paper was different and so was the handwriting." Kelcie lunged, stretching.

"That means someone must have sent it for him the first time." Niall chewed his bottom lip, his stare shifting to Scáthach on the platform. She wasn't looking at their fianna, if that's what he was worried about.

"Who wrote it then?" Zephyr asked.

"No idea but when I asked Killian and Ollie if it was possible I was something other than Mistral, they laughed at me . . . a lot."

"O'Shea, excited to see you climb up that rope," Fagan shouted.

The rest of the class laughed. Kelcie glared at Fagan. His face fell and he turned away immediately, rubbing his forearms.

Kelcie stood from her lunge and stared at her hands, turning them over. Could Killian and Ollie be wrong? Did she really burn Tad Fagan in combat class? If she did, then what could that mean? If she wasn't a Mistral, like the note said, what was she?

Niall interrupted her elemental soul searching, asking, "Can I see the letter?"

"It disintegrated into dust after I read it."

Zephyr pulled his foot up behind his knee. "The other one didn't do that."

"Nope." Kelcie sighed.

"What are you all talking about?" Brona asked, returning from an extra warmup lap. The ten they were ordered to do weren't enough for the demigod.

"Um," Niall hummed.

"Nothing," Kelcie answered.

"Not important," Zephyr said, in an unnecessarily authoritative way.

Her silver stare filling with ire, Brona poked Zephyr in the chest. "I'm getting really tired of being treated like I'm not in this fianna too."

Kelcie couldn't believe her. It wasn't like she wanted to be in their fianna anyway. "Willow at it again? What do you think we did now that we didn't do?"

"Yesterday, you all went to the Saiga Den without me for a meeting, and now you're hiding something from me. Tell me what's going on!" Brona yelled so loud their whole class turned and stared at them.

A large shadow fell over Kelcie from behind.

Scáthach. Niall pointed up.

"Why is it that you four are always arguing?" Scáthach asked.

Zephyr opened his mouth to respond, but Scáthach shook her head.

"Here's what's going to happen for the rest of class. You're going to proceed in silence, except for your Charger. And then, after a perfect class, which I know you four will have today, you will run an extra ten laps so that this lesson sticks."

"Yes, ma'am!" Zephyr bellowed.

"Why is Chike the only one responding?" Scáthach asked, irritated.

Niall's eyes narrowed.

Zephyr smiled at him. "Right. Because you said I was the only one who should talk."

Scáthach pinched the bridge of her nose. "So I did." She shifted to speak to the rest of the class. "This course will be timed today. If it takes more than twenty minutes to complete, you'll do it until it doesn't."

Niall looked like he wanted to cry.

Their preceptor turned back to them with a stern stare. "The four of you are in a fianna for a reason. And I saw how well you could succeed if you worked together when Chike stepped in the shade mantle. And when the goblin was loose on campus. Teamwork. That's all it will take to get through this course in a timely manner. Figure it out, Chike. Get them working together."

"Yes, ma'am."

The course began with a steep, downward-moving ramp they had to run up. Ten feet before it leveled off, transitioning into two twenty-foot-long, two-inch-wide shaking balance beams. A pole ride down to the ground, then a game of hopscotch across sinking squares. A rope swing over a flaming mud pit led to hurdling beds of flowering snapdragons that in the Land of Summer both snapped and had razor-sharp teeth like dragons. They got through the rest of the course in record time when they hit the rope wall.

Niall backed away. *You all go first. Then you can pull me over the top.*

"Good call!" Zephyr went up the rope with all the ease of a guy with super strength. He straddled the top of the wall in seconds.

Brona flew up to join him.

Kelcie grabbed the rope, hoisted up, setting her feet flat against the wall, and climbed, making it to the top in a couple of minutes. Niall jumped up as high as he could, hugging the rope. He braced his feet on the wall.

Just as they started to pull him up, Scáthach bellowed, "Time! Fiannas three and five, go again!"

Regrouping at the bottom, Zephyr started toward the beginning of the course.

The four fiannas who finished the first time stood off to the side, smugly watching as they started again.

This time when they got to the rope wall, Niall grabbed Zephyr's shoulder. His brow creased, the way it did when he would talk to Kelcie in her head. He made a move to punch the wall but stopped short.

Zephyr popped him on the arm. "Smart, Adder. Let's do this!"

Zephyr grabbed the rope. He climbed, slower this time, punching holes in the wall. Niall used the cracks as footholds, making it to the top seconds after Zephyr.

Brona waited this time until Kelcie was halfway up to morph. She flew beside her, squawking like a drill sergeant. The four jumped off the top, landing on the other side of the wall together only seconds before Scáthach called time.

"Well done, fianna three. But why is it you're always breaking things? At least this time it wasn't Murphy."

Kelcie smirked a smile.

"Oh, and you may speak again," Scáthach said.

"We did it!" Kelcie exclaimed.

"Of course we did," Brona boasted, grinning widely.

Niall breathed a relieved sigh.

"I think we need a group hug!" Zephyr pulled them all in, whether they wanted to be hugged or not.

As Kelcie let go, she heard a shriek so harsh it drowned out everything else. It abruptly shut off at the same time her eyes slammed shut on their own accord.

Her heart raced. "What's happening?"

Dvan, she heard the disembodied, gravelly voice from the ancient object say. Kelcie's brain translated. *Two.*

"What do you mean, what's happening? Let's go," ordered Zephyr, chuckling somewhere nearby. "Niall, you count."

Zephyr sounded as if he was moving away from her. Kelcie's hands started to sweat, her breath panting from worry. She opened her eyes to find Scáthach jerking her head.

"Get a move on, Murphy."

"Get a move on . . ." Kelcie shook her head, trying to defog her brain. The laps. "Yes, ma'am."

As she started running, she looked up, finding blue skies. She pinched her arm. It was a dream. It wasn't real. But how could she have a dream while she was awake? And why did she keep hearing that voice? *The trial. There would be a cost.* Was it a warning that the second trial was about to happen? A gentle breeze lifted the hair on the back of her neck, sending chills down her spine.

Kelcie swept their surroundings, watching for signs of another wood goblin. As they rounded the Nether Tower on the first of ten laps, Kelcie yelled, "We should stick together."

"Good idea," Zephyr agreed. "Side by side in case Scáthach is watching!"

The sun was at the ten o'clock position in the sky, giving plenty of visibility in the woods. Eagles swooped above the treetops. Ravens screeched in the distance, probably practicing formations on the far fields by the Shadow. Spriggans scurried up trunks when passed by. Everything seemed blissfully normal.

When they made it to the last lap without incident, Kelcie picked up the pace, relieved. She was overreacting.

A massive *boom* halted them in their tracks.

"What was that?" Zephyr asked.

A whooping sound rose up and over the trees.

"Is that . . . ?" Niall asked, craning his neck. "The door to Direwood Keep?"

Black iron with seven silver knots, the keep's door was unmistakable as it ascended, spinning like a rock hurled from a trebuchet, arching above their heads, crashing down in the middle of the woods.

"Yup. Probably Le Deux's class," Brona suggested.

Kelcie had a very bad feeling.

Trees cracked, falling away from the path, only to be dragged forward, scooped up by an invisible force and crushed to bits. At first Kelcie thought, *gustnado?* A mini tornado, they come out of nowhere. One lambasted her fosters' side yard in Leominster after a freak storm. But it spiraled down the path with a face sculpted from mulch and a mane from shredded leaves, while spindly ballerina stick-arms played snatch and grab with everything in its the path.

"Oh, do forgive me you poor, unfortunate, yet incredibly delicious birch, oak, and elms, but I desperately need your assistance if I am going to kill *the heir* . . ." She crooned like a Disney princess, except for the part about killing Kelcie. She growled that bit.

"Is that a sylph?" Niall gasped.

Kelcie swallowed a scream. "What's a sylph?"

"You really need to start doing the reading for Le Deux's class!" Brona griped. "It's—"

"Doesn't matter right now!" Zephyr sucked in a sharp breath. "It's heading straight for us! RUN!"

They tripped over each other hoofing down the path, but crunching, grinding, whooping, and hysterical cackling was coming up fast.

"Oh, don't be that way. I have to do this. Why exhaust your bony legs! Stop and face me so you can just die already!"

Kelcie took a sharp turn, heading into the woods, trying to lead it away from the others.

Sea eagles took to the skies, screeching the alarm.

"Where are you going?" Brona shrieked, sprinting after her.

"It's chasing me!" Kelcie cried.

"Why? Why did it call you the heir, Kelcie?" Niall huffed coming beside her.

"I repeat. Doesn't matter. What chases one, chases us all! Follow me!" Zephyr overtook her, jumping over obstructions like an Olympic hurdler, moving so fast the others could barely keep up.

When they reached the empty practice field, Lady Windbag fired. Woodchips, rocks, stray spriggans unable to get out of her way in time. A shard cut Niall's arm, and another hit Kelcie's side.

"We need cover!" Brona yelled.

Zephyr raised a finger acknowledging a brilliant idea without losing step. He zigzagged, cutting through the field, spinning into another glen, and down a short path that forked. He led them left, stopping them just short of the paddock and stables, motioning for them to hide behind trees and stay quiet.

Kelcie tried holding her breath, but after running so fast it was nearly impossible.

"Get back here and face me!" the sylph roared like a freight train.

Zephyr hurled a rock, and she took the bait, spinning after it, and away from them.

Kelcie and Niall exchanged a relieved glance.

"Brona, get help," Zephyr ordered.

"I heard that . . ." Lady Windbag sang.

Brona shifted and took off, making it to the treetops before being swatted out of the skies. She crashed down in the middle of the paddock.

"Bad birdie . . . no help will come for the heir!"

"Brona!" Kelcie crawled through the paddock's fence, dodging frenzied horses, to get to Brona's side. She was conscious, but still on the ground, and holding her ankle. Icicles dangled from the bottom of her braid. Through chattering teeth, Brona warned, "She's one cold wind."

Kelcie helped her up.

Brona wasn't putting weight on her ankle. She wasn't going to be able to run or fight.

The sylph squealed way too close. "Oooh, I hear horsies. They taste so yummy!"

"No!" Zephyr tore a plank off the rail fence, clearing a way out for the horses to get out, but the stubborn beasts corralled in a corner, ears flickering, tails stiff, refusing to leave.

"Dimitri . . ." Zephyr waved at the beautiful brown mare. Dimitri neighed, jerking her head back and forth with a re-sounding *are-you-kidding-me?*

Zephyr stamped his foot, raising a fist in the air, clearly giving Dimitri an order.

Reluctantly, the mare dashed forward. Zephyr captured her mane at the same time he swung a triumphant leg over her back. Dimitri reared.

"Please. I'm trying to save your life!" Zephyr cried, falling forward and hugging her neck.

Niall slapped Dimitri on the butt. She took off at a full gal-lop, racing out of the paddock with Zephyr barely hanging on, but managing to whistle through his teeth, hailing the others to follow.

"Aha!" Lady Windbag blustered through another section of the fence. "Dumm de dum dum DUM! There you are . . ." She moved into the paddock, hovering twenty feet above the ground, turning in on herself, an amorphous mass of wreckage in limbo, deciding what shape to take next.

The temperature dropped. The water in the troughs froze over.

Niall prepared for battle, pocketing his glasses.

"What do we do?" Brona whispered.

"What are you doing here?" Niall called out.

Two snakes forming lips pressed together as she took in her

surroundings. "My, my. I'm not in Winter." She shimmied. "This is Summer!" She squealed with delight. "Oh, once the heir is dead, I'm going to tear down everything in sight. When I finally return to Winter it will be to a hero's welcome! Ice capades in my honor!"

"Heir?" Niall's grim expression flipped to Kelcie.

"Now might be a better time to talk to us in our heads!" Brona snapped at him.

Kelcie stepped away from them. "Let my friends leave. Please. Then you can do whatever you want to me."

"No." The sylph spun, raining down wood shavings all over them.

Niall and Brona dove for cover behind a barrel. Kelcie crouched, tucking her head under her arms.

"Look at you. Short. Puny," the sylph gurgled. *"Let my friends leave,"* she mimicked. "You sound like a shrieking harpy."

"Well, you sound like garbage disposal trying to choke down a fork!" Kelcie countered.

"Garbage disposal! How dare you! I have a beautiful voice! Oh, I'm going to take my time killing you . . ." Lady Windbag flattened, flipping on her axis, spinning like a giant circular saw preparing to carve Kelcie into thinly sliced steaks.

Kelcie, Brona, and Niall threw anything they could find at her—rakes, buckets, manure, all of which ran through a spin cycle, ricocheting right back at them.

"Piece by piece . . ." the sylph hummed, gliding back and forth, digging fine lines through the paddock, backing Kelcie, Niall, and Brona up to the barn, leaving them nowhere to go without risking the horses still inside.

Fight air with air, Kelcie!

"But I can't control it!"

"Don't. Let it FLY!" Brona yelled, as if she heard Niall too.

Kelcie ran away from them, forcing Lady Windbag to change course. With a hellish "Wheee!" she drove forward for the win, weed-whacking the back of Kelcie's hair before Kelcie could dive out of the way.

Kelcie stumbled to standing, fists raised. She felt the surge racing through her veins, and for once, let it fly. "MISTRAL!"

A huge gale plowed into the sylph, pushing her back before happily joining her ranks. "That tickles . . . My turn!" Lady Windbag touched down.

Dust whipped. Kelcie couldn't see.

"Your fault, heir. I'm afraid the two friends will die first . . ."

"No!" Kelcie ran blind at the sylph only to be blown into the side of the barn.

There was so much dust it was impossible to see, but from the sounds of their screams, Niall and Brona were no longer on the ground.

"NOOOOOOOO . . . put them down!" Kelcie yelled.

She squinted, blinking furiously and watching in horror as the sylph spun them higher into the air.

"Morph, Brona!" Kelcie called.

"I-I c-can't s-see!" Brona cried, her teeth chattering so hard she could barely speak.

N-neither c-can I! It's s-s-so c-cold . . .

Zephyr rode Dimitri into the paddock. "Put them down!"

Dimitri reared.

Zephyr fell off, only to be caught by the frigid gasbag.

"Kelcie!"

Then Lady Windbag took Dimitri.

"Enough!" Kelcie raised her hands, hoping to use the wind to knock at least one of them out of the sylph's grasp. But then she had a second unbelievable, impossible, ridiculous thought.

Niall must've been thinking the same thing because she heard him say, *Y-you're n-n-not a M-Mistral. Trrrry again. You're n-n-not a M-Mistral.* He repeated. *You're not a Mistral!*

"I'm not a Mistral." Instead of the cold surge in her gut, Kelcie's blood boiled. She threw her arms up, calling, *"IGNIS!"*

Her hands ignited.

"Holy!" Kelcie flinched, waiting for it to hurt. But the feeling was the exact opposite. She felt awakened.

Alive.

And strong.

"I don't like fire! I DON'T LIKE FIRE!" Lady Windbag shrieked. She dropped Zephyr, Niall, and Brona, but not poor Dimitri.

"The horse!" Kelcie demanded, holding out her blazing hands.

"Turn the fire off!" she countered, wisping frost.

Kelcie savored the fear she heard in the sylph's warbling voice. She tasted bittersweet revenge at her fingertips. Revenge? She shook her head, trying to make the feeling stop. It wasn't her. She didn't want that. She only wanted the horse to be okay.

"Drop my horse!" Zephyr demanded. "Do it, or the Saiga fires!"

Kelcie hesitated too long. The sylph whipped a wind tentacle at Niall, lassoing his ankles, dragging him toward her.

"No!" Kelcie roared. Her arms exploded like flamethrowers, igniting woodchips, consuming Lady Windbag's oxygen until Lady Windbag was nothing more than the distinct smell of a chlorine pool and a small puddle of black tar.

"Nil ignis!" Kelcie's breath caught as the fire reluctantly died. Her fingers tingled warmly. She stared at her hands unable to wrap her mind around what happened. Exhilarating wasn't strong enough to describe how good that felt. But it wasn't supposed to feel good, was it?

Sea eagles dropped from the trees around the paddock on what was left of the fence railing, a sign their preceptor was on the way.

"Are you okay?" Kelcie said, helping Niall up.

"I'm fine," he said angrily, stepping away from her.

"Dimitri?" Zephyr called. "Dimitri?" He jogged around the paddock. "Where did she go?"

Neigh . . . The horse's cry softened until it silenced.

"It's coming from there." Brona pointed to the tar.

Kelcie inched closer. "Like the spriggan in the stone circle."

"You stupid shade mantle!" Zephyr yelled at it. "Give me back my horse!"

Brona caught him before he went after her. "I don't think that's shade mantle, Zephyr."

He fell on his knees. "She's my horse. My responsibility. Dimiiiiitriiii . . ." he wailed, clutching his chest.

Niall pulled his glasses out of his pocket, slipping them on, still glowering at Kelcie. He opened his mouth like he was about to let her have it when Scáthach ran into the paddock with two long flaming spears. Coach Blackwell was right behind her, carrying a bow, an arrow pinned and burning at the tip.

"The sylph, where did it go?" Scáthach demanded, her gaze shifting to every compass point on the ground and in the sky.

"What is a sylph exactly?" Kelcie asked.

Coach Blackwell kept the bow taught. "Nasty air spirit."

"Nasty is right," Brona said, setting her foot down, testing her ankle.

A sea eagle piped, telling Scáthach what she needed to know.

"It's gone." Scáthach planted her spears, putting the fire out. "But how?"

"Kelcie roasted it," Zephyr explained, wiping his nose on the bottom of his sweaty blue T-shirt.

"Roasted it?" Coach Blackwell asked.

"More like torched," Niall corrected, putting his glasses on. "Tiny flame. Big burst of fire. It was . . ."

"Brilliant," Brona finished, beaming at Kelcie.

"Fire?" Coach Blackwell scratched the top of his bald head, leaving long red marks. "I don't understand. I thought you wielded air, Kelcie."

Kelcie stared at her shoes. White at the start of school, they were now a putrid shade of manure brown. She threaded her fingers together behind her back before looking up. "I thought so too."

"More than one element?" Blackwell rolled the flaming arrow tip on the ground, snuffing it out. "I've not heard of another since Draummorc."

Scáthach passed him the spears, her concerned gaze locked

on Kelcie, which was understandable, considering Kelcie could not only blow the school over, but burn it down.

Kelcie tucked a piece of hair that had fallen out of her ponytail, only to feel that her hair was no longer in a ponytail. The sylph had chopped at least six inches off.

"Dimitri, speak to me." The black goo sloshed, inching closer to Zephyr.

"I thought Zephyr hated horses," Kelcie whispered to Niall.

Chargers bond with their horses. They're like siblings. One day you hate them, the next day they're your best friend.

Kelcie wouldn't know. She never had a sibling, not that she could remember.

Scáthach's face turned paler than normal. "Is that—?"

Coach Blackwell poked the goo with the bottom of a spear. He tried to pull it out, but it was stuck. "Never in all my years . . ." He stumbled as the spear was torn from his grasp, sinking into the bubbling tar, disappearing with a final subtle *plurp*. "Did you see that?"

"I think it's water from the Abyss," Brona explained.

"How did it get here?" Blackwell hissed, pulling Zephyr back several paces.

"Excellent question." Scáthach's stern gaze lingered on Kelcie so long she started feeling sick. This was bad. The preceptor had the same look every principal had right before they called Elliott Blizzard and unceremoniously kicked her out of school. Only there was no one to call, not anymore. If she was sent back to Boston, what would she do? With her new powers, Kelcie might be able to eke out a living in the park juggling windballs or igniting her hands. Tourists might cough up some serious cash if she could keep from blowing them to Timbuktu or barbecuing them.

"It's disappearing," Niall exclaimed.

The Abyss water receded, pulled by an invisible force, until it was gone.

"No!" Zephyr cried. "Dimitri . . ." He stamped the ground where the waters were seconds before.

"Dimitri?" Scáthach gasped, surveying the paddock. "Where are the horses?"

Niall answered for them, "Zephyr got the rest of them out."

"Except for Dimitri. She disappeared in the Abyss water." Zephyr scraped the dirt with his shoe, sniffling, trying to pull himself together.

"Brona's hurt," Kelcie said. "Her ankle . . . she was flying to get help when—"

Brona stomped. "I'm fine. I heal really fast."

"Good. Chike, find Regan O'Shea. Have her rally the rest of the Chargers to gather the horses. Put them in the barn until the fence can be repaired," Scáthach instructed.

Zephyr nodded and hurried off.

Scáthach knelt down, taking a closer look at the dirt patch where the Abyss water had been. "Where is it coming from? Where are these Winter creatures coming from?"

Brona *hmm*ed. "The Sidral?"

"No. It hasn't been used since the start of school. They are sneaking on to this campus and we need to figure out how."

"Kelcie," Niall said, out loud. He stared at her. *Heir? You need to tell Scáthach and the rest of us what's really going on here. Now!*

Although she didn't appreciate his imperious tone, Kelcie knew he was right. She knew she was going to have to come clean— about everything. Maybe Scáthach could help stop whatever started with Grimes and Blizzard at the museum. If anyone would know what to do, it was Scáthach, wasn't it? Ancient herself, she might even know what that artifact was.

"Scáthach, I'm not sure . . . well, I asked Madame Le Deux . . . she said something about lids . . ." Kelcie cleared her throat. She was parched. If she had a glass of water—

Coach Blackwell tapped her on the arm with an arrow. "Murphy, just spit it out."

"Do you know anything about—an eye?"

Blackwell dropped the arrow, and left it there. "Balor's eye?

Why would you bring that up? What is going on here, Murphy? Wielding fire and air. Who are you, Kelcie Murphy?"

"I don't know." Kelcie scuffed her heel in the dirt. "That's why I asked."

Niall's eyes narrowed to slits. His lips pressed so tightly together they turned white. He was mad, really, really mad. Seeing him like that, Kelcie's heart cracked in half. Why was he so angry with her? Not that it mattered. From the look on Scáthach's face, Kelcie wasn't going to be at the Academy for the Unbreakable Arts much longer.

Scáthach gestured to the opening in the paddock's fence. "Murphy, O'Shea, Lee, follow me to the Shadow. Coach Blackwell, send Chike when he returns. I think it's time we all had a little chat."

17

KING BALOR'S EVIL EYE

THE WALK TO the Shadow was the longest of Kelcie's life. It wasn't yet lunchtime, so campus was busy. The rest of the first years were inside the Nether Tower in combat class, but the upperclassmen were on the practice fields. They stopped sparring to stare at Kelcie, Brona, and Niall padding after Scáthach, heads down, in silence—an obvious walk of shame.

Killian sheathed his sword and started toward them, but Scáthach sent him back to class with a head shake.

There was one friendly face. Striker greeted Kelcie with a howling smile at the cliff's edge. He was a welcome sight. She stroked his back, trying to keep her nerves at bay as he walked between her and Brona, through the gate. They followed a cobblestone path that wove around trees as if the trees were there first. All the while, sea eagles piped in greeting from their perches on the wall's ramparts where they kept watch, except for on the part Kelcie had blown down. Roswen hadn't gotten to that yet.

In the middle of the grounds was a simple castle with four round towers marking the corners. With a wave of Scáthach's hand, a drawbridge lowered over the moat.

"This way." She crossed it in two long strides.

As Kelcie entered the castle, she glanced over at Niall, but he kept his eyes fixed on Scáthach. Oddly enough, it was Brona who was looking at her, giving her a small reassuring smile.

Bronze heads with gaping mouths carved into vaulted arched ceilings frowned down on them.

"She's the one who blew down our wall!" a head with an abnormally long handlebar mustache griped.

"Why is Scáthach bringing her insi—?"

Scáthach stabbed the spear into its mouth. "Why I brought you four with me when I left the Isle of Skye is a mystery to me, and always will be."

"We watch your hallways!" Handlebar Mustache called. "And your back!"

Cubbies lining the walls were filled with axes, spears, swords, bows, full quivers, and shields. All shiny and stacked neatly from shortest to tallest. It looked more like an armory than a principal's office.

"Are those fairy nets?" Niall asked, pointing to metal mesh blankets hanging from pegs.

"Yes. Good eye, O'Shea."

"I knew that," Brona uttered.

Kelcie tried to lighten the mood. "Quite the arsenal. Never took up knitting?"

"Once. About ten thousand years ago. Skye was frigid. I needed a scarf. Made for a very long, very miserable day." Scáthach paused beside the last door at the very end of the hallway. She glanced at Striker faithfully glued to Kelcie's side. "Patrol," she ordered.

Striker gave Kelcie a last nuzzle then trotted back the way they came.

"Come in. Take a seat. Don't touch anything."

"Yes, ma'am," Kelcie said at the same time as Niall and Brona.

Scáthach's office was as heavily fortified as the hallway. Shields were mounted above the door, a bow and quiver sat beside an old rust-colored leather sofa, but it was the sword hanging on the wall above Scáthach's desk that caught Kelcie's attention.

With a ruby-red grip, the sharp obsidian blade was serrated

and double-edged. Kelcie had never seen anything like it before. It was the very definition of Otherworldly.

Brona sat on the sofa. Kelcie took one of the two seats facing Scáthach's desk. Niall slid into the other, still staring at Scáthach grimly. Beside the desk was a cupboard with many shelves, all brimming with wooden scrolls. A teapot hanging over a lit fire in the fireplace boiled. Scáthach brought over a tray from the table beyond the sofa, poured five steaming cups, and offered them around.

Kelcie and Brona each took one, and exchanged curious glances, sniffing.

"Nothing poisonous." Scáthach smiled. "Chamomile. Calms the nerves."

Scáthach watched as Kelcie took a sip, making her wonder if this wasn't some kind of a trust-test, or if there was something besides chamomile in it, like a truth potion.

Coach Blackwell escorted Zephyr into the room. Blackwell was about to sit down when Scáthach stopped him with an arched brow.

"Can you please return to the paddock and be sure Roswen doesn't require assistance?"

Coach Blackwell chuckled a grunt. "You could just tell me to leave, Scáthach."

"And here I was trying to be polite."

After he was gone, Zephyr snagged a cup of tea and sat down beside Brona. Scáthach picked up a scroll from the cabinet behind her and set it down on her desk. She took a long sip of tea, then unraveled the scroll, scanning it from top to bottom, ending with a dissatisfied hum.

"Murphy, your file reads like a blank page. No emergency contact information. An orphan, according to Roswen. She also wrote down that you likely, although she could not be sure, came from Chawell Woods."

"Kelcie is from Chawell, isn't she?" Brona asked.

"I'm not actually." Kelcie glanced at Niall, waiting for him to tell them the truth.

He crossed his arms, refusing to look at her.

"I'm from the human world."

Zephyr fumbled his teacup, spilling it in his lap. He hopped up. "Oooh, that's hot!"

"You lied?" Brona said.

"You never asked," Kelcie answered, because it was the truth.

Brona sank into the sofa, conceding the point.

"I knew," Niall offered.

"And my Den mates too," Kelcie added.

"My mind is blown. I didn't even think that place was real," said Zephyr, sitting down slowly with a new cup of tea. "No one is from the human world!"

"Humans are, Chike." Scáthach leaned forward in her chair, picking up a spear-pen from the top of her desk. "And it isn't entirely human. Humans only pay attention to what is important to them. Anyone from Winter or Summer could walk among them and they'd never know it."

That was very interesting information and explained a lot about several of Kelcie's more bizarre foster parents. She wondered if they too had been part of Grimes and Blizzard's scheme.

Scáthach threw the scroll into the fire, wooden rods and all. "It's apparent I need to speak with Roswen about her record keeping. Let's start over, shall we?"

"What does it matter where Kelcie is from?" Niall asked.

"Because when Winter attacks, they must use the human world as a stopgap to transport here. In defending our borders, it is our biggest vulnerability. It is the only place with Sidrals that can transport to both Lands. A stolen bough, and they're in. Only they don't usually get far. Our Sidrals are, as you know well, Mr. O'Shea, heavily monitored."

"You told Coach Blackwell the Sidral wasn't used since the start of school," Kelcie said. "So, I don't understand. How are they getting here?"

Scáthach pulled a piece of paper out of her desk. "That's what we are going to try and figure out. Let's start over, Murphy. You're not an orphan because you told me your father was communicating with you your first night here. And now you're asking about King Balor's eye."

Niall shifted uncomfortably in his seat.

"Yes, ma'am," Kelcie answered.

"Fomorians do not toss that word around lightly." Scáthach whipped the pen around her fingers. "What is it you were afraid to tell me? Afraid to tell your own fianna, since they look as surprised as me by all of this?"

Kelcie's knee refused to stop bouncing. She nearly spilled her tea setting it down on Scáthach's desk. "I don't know what King Balor's eye is, but I suspect it might be causing all this trouble. It's a long story."

"And no one is leaving this room until we've all heard it." Scáthach aimed the pen at the paper. "Now, start from the beginning. The very beginning. *Your* beginning."

"My beginning? That's the problem. I don't know my beginning." Kelcie took a small sip of tea, trying to settle her nerves, but it didn't work. She leaned over the desk to whisper to Scáthach. "Do they need to be here?"

Scáthach's brows reached for the skies. "You fought a wood goblin and a sylph together. I do believe they have your back, Murphy. But I'll leave that up to you."

Niall and Zephyr glowered in her direction.

"Spill it, Murphy," Brona blurted.

"Okay." Kelcie took a deep breath for courage, then launched into everything she knew about herself—leaving nothing out. Not the frigid, terrifying fall the night she was abandoned, when she nearly drowned in Boston Harbor. Or how at her first home in Burlington she slept on the porch every night for two months to avoid the goons threatening to shave her devil-red head if she came inside. After that came Leominster, which was decent but only lasted a few months. Then was Rockport, when she had had enough and ran away. She lived with a bunch of other kids in an abandoned house. She spent the summer picking tourists' pockets on Main Street until she got caught and spent her first night in jail. Then it was a winter in Worcester, when she spent every night in an old car because things were too scary in the group home she was placed in. The "too scary" part was where she drew the line. Kelcie never wanted to talk about that house again.

Throughout, she heard Niall's feet shuffling, Zephyr's breath seizing, and Brona moving forward to sit on the edge of her seat. Kelcie couldn't look at them, or Scáthach. She stared at the stone floor, tracing a scratch shaped like a lightning bolt with her shoe, knowing her fianna mates would never look at her the same way again. Kelcie continued, unloading her entire life story, spending as much time as possible on her last day in Boston, about how her caseworker tricked her, about the ice fairy and holding the artifact she now guessed was actually King Balor's eye, and about how it was now in the hands of Winter.

She told them that her father wanted her to leave the school, return to the human world, and never stop running.

"He never got to tell me it was an evil eye or what it could do because the connection went dead. I thought it was some kind of cursed box or something. I heard this voice talk about lids. I tried to ask Madame Le Deux about it. She told me it was bad for Fomorians to ask about *the eye*. That's when I realized it wasn't a box. That eyes have lids too."

Scáthach listened, taking copious notes the whole time, then set her pen down. She stared at Kelcie, then at the sword above her desk. When she turned back around, she balled up the paper and threw it into the fire.

"That bad, huh?" Kelcie asked.

"No. The contrary actually." She didn't elaborate beyond that. "My turn to talk now. What do any of you know about King Balor's eye?"

"It burned down Summer City," Niall started.

"And how did it do that?" Scáthach asked, tapping her spear-pen on the desk. "Who was King Balor?"

"A Fomorian king, right?" Zephyr offered.

Niall tried to answer but Brona beat him to it. "Thousands of years ago. He waged war on our people, who were called the children of Danu at the time. He—"

"He was killed by his own grandson," Niall interjected, because Brona was stealing his limelight.

"I was going to say he was a cyclops!" Brona growled. "And that his eye was a weapon!"

"Yes," Scáthach said. "When it was fully open, it blasted civilizations from existence. That is how Summer City burned, Mr. O'Shea."

"When fully open?" Kelcie asked.

Scáthach set her pen down, then stood up and walked to the far end of the office, way in the back, under a circular staircase. She returned with another scroll, this one much larger than Kelcie's school file. The rods were ruby red, like the sword's grip, the ends engraved with a symbol. A spiral with an arrow through it, only the arrow had no feathers, rather pointed tips at both ends.

Scáthach unraveled it, turning it horizontally, then placed it on her desk. "This scroll was delivered to me at the same time as that weapon." She glanced over her shoulder at the sword. "Never knew why, but it seems that destinies are colliding. All of you may look."

Kelcie got up first. The others followed her lead, crowding the desk.

The scroll was about King Balor's eye! Divided into six separate panels of art. In the first, the closed eye was still in the giant cyclops head, but his head was no longer attached to his body. His broken body lay slumped on the ground on the other end of the panel. Between head and body was a decimated Fomorian army.

The next four panels depicted various stages of King Balor's eyelid opening, and the destruction caused on the right.

Scáthach pointed to the first panel. "After Balor died, his eye was carved from his severed head and used as a weapon. That much I knew, but the intricacies documented here of how the eye works are very enlightening. As you can see, there are four lids that cover it. With the raising of each comes different kinds of mayhem and destruction."

"It looks like a game show from hell," Kelcie said, earning blank stares all around. She could just hear the cheesy announcer in her head declaring the not-so-lovely prizes.

Behind lid number one, you win a small brush fire.

"Like a warning shot over the bow of a ship," Brona commented.

Number two, a violent tempest.

Unlucky lid number three, and you get to freeze your enemies into solid stone.

And finally, should you make it all the way through the game show from hell, you raise eyelid number four. TOTAL ANNIHILATION!

Niall put his finger on the last image. "This was how the city burned."

Scáthach nodded. "For millennia the eye had vanished. Some thought it was in the Lands of Winter after the Abyss split All-tar in two. A balance of power, so neither side could use it. See, Balor's eye is intensely loyal, making it useless to any who are not the Fomorian king's heir." She tapped on writing at the very bottom of the page. "The heir holds that power until he or she is either dead or challenged by another heir. That challenge begins with an invocation. The heir holding the eye, repeating the phrases—"

"*Ta Erfin.* I am the heir." Kelcie swallowed hard. "*Vlast mian.* The power is mine."

"You didn't?" Niall asked.

"I did," Kelcie confessed. "That ice fairy made me! She froze my hands to it! I couldn't stop her. I couldn't . . ." But that wasn't entirely true. Kelcie could have refused, although she would probably be dead if she had. A gruesome death too. Frozen in a block of ice. Suffocating in that vault. Stabbed with an ice spear . . . or worse . . . no. Kelcie shook her head, refusing to let her brain spiral.

Brona stared at Kelcie's face as if seeing her for the first time. "Then Kelcie's father is—"

"Draummorc," Niall blurted, less surprised than Kelcie would've expected.

Scáthach pulled a book out from behind her desk. She flipped through until she found the page she was looking for and turned it around for Kelcie to see.

"This is Draummorc at the time of his graduation. Is that who you spoke to in the stone circle?" Scáthach's question dangled like a guillotine before beheading.

Kelcie took a closer look. Crooked nose, a lopsided smile rather than frown, ringed horns, but no scar on his face. It definitely looked like him. "I think so."

"You're the daughter he claimed was missing when he was captured. No one knew he had a daughter," Scáthach explained.

Emotions choked her. Kelcie sat down in her chair, whispering his name.

"I'm sorry, but you win the award for the worst life so far, Kelcie." Zephyr shook his head. "I just want to hug you. Can I?"

"Stay put, Chike," Scáthach ordered.

"Is it strange that I'm kinda jealous?" Brona asked no one in particular.

"Very," Zephyr smirked, cratering his dimple.

Niall finally looked at Kelcie, to better interrogate her. "Is there anything else you haven't told us, Kelcie? Something else that the fairies said that might be important?"

Kelcie didn't like his accusatory tone. "Elliott said it was my birthday and that they had gone to a lot of trouble putting this together. Years in the making. Maybe they're responsible for abandoning me in the human world. Whoever *they* are."

Kelcie was so confused. Her father was public enemy number one, the traitor responsible for Niall's father's death. She couldn't fathom why anyone would do something so horrible as burning down a city full of innocent people, yet he told her he loved her.

"*They* are most definitely Winter," Niall growled. "But why wait for a certain age?"

"You have to be at least twelve to test for the Academy," answered Brona.

Kelcie's mouth fell open. She'd guessed right. "They wanted me here. Maybe they gave me my bough the night I was abandoned. Elliott was there to pick up the pieces."

"That makes sense," Zephyr agreed, his expression hinting a sympathetic smile.

"Except, I haven't seen the fairies or the eye since I left Boston. Achila Grimes had it with her, iced to her back, when she went into the Sidral with Elliott."

Scáthach leaned back in her chair, chewing on the tip of her spear-pen. "None of this explains how a sylph or wood goblin got on to our campus without me knowing. A fairy of any kind would most definitely have been seen traveling in the Sidral, and by my eagles as soon as they exited."

She dropped her pen on the desk, dismayed.

Brona leaned over the old scroll. "Maybe the Winter incursions have nothing to do with the eye. I mean, look." She ran a finger down the scroll. "None of these things have happened. If the lids were opening, there would be smoldering fields, people turned to stone, catastrophic oblivion."

"Excellent point," Scáthach agreed.

Brona beamed.

"What did the eye look like?" Zephyr asked.

"Round, about this big." Kelcie demonstrated with her hands. "I never actually saw it. It was wrapped up. But—" She hesitated, biting down on her lip. If she revealed the rest, there was no way Scáthach would let her stay at the Academy.

"But what?" Scáthach asked, sounding as dismal as Kelcie felt.

When Kelcie remained mute, Niall pulled out the guilt-guns. "This is life or death, Kelcie. No matter the consequences, you have to tell us everything."

"How much worse can it get?" Zephyr smiled.

"When I touched the ancient object, a voice spoke to me. I heard the same voice before the wood goblin. And then right before we ran laps after class, before the sylph."

"King Balor's voice?" Niall croaked.

"His spirit lives on in the eye," Scáthach explained, leaning forward. "What did he say?"

"He was counting. One, before the wood goblin. Two, before the sylph."

"What's he counting?" Brona asked, intrigued.

"I don't know." Kelcie shrugged. "But we all heard that sylph say she had to kill *me*." Kelcie wanted to crawl under a rock and not come out until break.

"And the wood goblin went straight for Kelcie too," Zephyr added.

"So, they were tests. To see if you're worthy of wielding the king's power instead of your father." Brona shook her head. "You really have all the luck, Saiga."

"You're seriously two eggs shy of a full dozen, you know that?" Zephyr said. "Maybe three."

Brona seemed oddly pleased, like it was a compliment, and what scared Kelcie the most was that Zephyr looked like he meant it as one. *Academy for the Unbreakable Arts, only those who relish danger and despair for the rest of their lives may apply.*

"Ahem." Zephyr cleared his throat. "To recap, if we're correct, Kelcie is in a battle with her father for control of the deadliest weapon ever used in the Otherworld. Fairies may or may not have smuggled said object into the Academy. AND King Balor, with nothing left of him but a giant eyeball, is transporting our Winter enemies into school to see if Kelcie's worthy of said power. Now for the big question. If said transfer of power happens, what does that mean?"

"That Kelcie could open the lids, and destroy the school," Niall answered.

Kelcie glared at him. Was he trying to get her kicked out of school?

"True. But the eye is a weapon. It shouldn't be able to transport Winter creatures into the school without me knowing. And where is the Abyss water coming from?" Scáthach snapped her spear-pen in half. She stood up and threw it into the fire, then paced, staring into the flames.

"What if the eye fell into the Abyss? Could that have something to do with it?" Brona asked.

"Then it would never have been seen again," Scáthach explained, tapping her long index finger to her lips. "Or so we all believe. Ponderings for a later time because we're talking when we should be taking actions." She shifted to look at Kelcie. "Murphy, what did you want when you came here?"

Kelcie suddenly felt like she was back in that doctor's office who wanted to know about her feelings when she got headaches. Probing questions were the worst. "Um, I-I wanted to find out who my parents were."

"And so, a piece of that puzzle is solved. Your father's name is Draummorc. He is in Summer City in the most secure prison in the Lands of Summer. The fact that he was able to speak to you at all is very disconcerting. I will have to let High Command know they may have a breach." Scáthach sat on the corner of the desk with a dismal look on her face. "He told you to leave, and now you know why."

"I get it." Kelcie should've seen this coming. She rose out of her seat, using the chair's arms for balance. "Would it be okay if I took some of the clothes? It's really cold in Boston right now and the cloak would come in handy."

"She doesn't have to leave, does she?" Brona panicked. "I can take an ice fairy if I could borrow a few more quivers. Coach Blackwell is stingy with ammunition."

"You can't send her back!" Zephyr crossed his resolute arms. "That place, the human world, it isn't safe! Did you hear what happened to her there? I'm in charge of our fianna, right? I say she stays. We're in this together. That's what you said, right, Scáthach?"

"O'Shea, what say you?" Scáthach asked.

"She should stay," Niall said, startling Kelcie.

"Good. Then Murphy, I put it to you once more, the same question I asked the night you spoke to your father. This time, your answer should be with an understanding of what is at stake." The preceptor's gaze shifted to her fianna mates. "What do you want to do?"

Kelcie understood. It wasn't just her own life at risk, it was theirs too. Brona mouthed, *Stay*.

She half smiled. "I want to stay."

"That's settled then." Scáthach hopped up. "Now, what I want is fourfold. One, to search the school from top to bottom to make sure that eye is *not* here. I'll do a surprise inspection as soon as we're done. Two, the second you hear that voice in your head, Murphy, you or someone in your fianna finds me. My guess is that whatever trial the eye is putting you through, it isn't over."

"Yes, ma'am."

"Three, this conversation shall stay between us. I don't want anything said to anyone—no siblings, no Den mates, no one. All of it. Nothing about the eye, nothing about Draummorc." She glanced at Niall, Zephyr, Brona, and then Kelcie, who all nodded. "The last thing I need is Deirdre Crane's father showing up with High Command. It is the last thing you need as well, Murphy."

"But shouldn't they send a battalion or something?" Zephyr asked.

"Battalions of soldiers can't stop the eye," Scáthach explained. "Otherwise, it wouldn't still be a threat thousands of years after it was cut out of Balor's head. Trust me when I say we've all had a hand in trying to destroy it, yet here we are again."

Scáthach walked to the board on the back of her door and wrote something on it, but at the angle Kelcie was sitting, she couldn't see what it said.

Zephyr raised his hand. "Can I get back to my room before inspection? I might've left my dirty clothes on the bathroom floor."

"No, you may not." Scáthach sat back down on the corner of her desk next to Kelcie again. "The fourth thing."

"Yes, ma'am," Kelcie said.

"You must get a handle on your explosive powers. You're not alone in this. I am your teacher after all. It's my job to give you the tools you need to succeed. Madame Le Deux has been con-cocting something that may help diffuse things, but it isn't ready yet. In the meantime, the impulsive reactions and rule breaking when you're confronted with situations like the one with Fagan recently are not acceptable."

"Yes, ma'am," Kelcie repeated with conviction she hoped would stick.

A knock at the door made them all jump, except Scáthach.

Killian entered, his brow sweating, a sword resting on his shoulder. He grimaced at Kelcie as he came to stand at attention before Scáthach. "You asked to see me?"

"Yes." Scáthach stood up. "Lynch, this afternoon Murphy wielded fire."

He fumbled his sword.

"My sentiments exactly. I suspect she is a pulse elemental."

"What does that mean?" Kelcie asked.

He stared at her like she was a lit stick of dynamite. "That you can wield all four elements."

Kelcie barked a laugh. "No way." She stared at her hands.

"I . . . you mean to say . . . are you sure? There hasn't been . . ." Killian said, tripping over his own tongue. "I mean, Kelcie?"

"Yep! Epically did away with a sylph. It was special." Brona winked at her.

Kelcie felt like she had leveled up. Maybe she had. She had spilled every humiliating bean in her past to Scáthach, and her fianna, and still they all wanted her to stay. Now, Scáthach was telling her that she was going to be able to spark all four elements! The worst day of her life had morphed into the best day of her life. The Academy for the Unbreakable Arts really was a magical place.

Scáthach padded toward Killian, picking up his sword along the way. "Tomorrow, you will test her on the last two elements and report back to me. Two simple tests only. Melt a rock. Dump water from a bucket to cool it. That's it."

"Yes, ma'am," Killian said.

"Murphy, beyond that, you are to do no elemental magic—for now. Do NOT utter the words for wind or fire. Don't even think them."

"Yes, ma'am," Kelcie droned, frustrated. If the fairies returned, she would need to be able to defend herself.

Scáthach must've seen the mutiny in her eyes. "You will learn to use your powers, Kelcie, at a pace I'm comfortable with. Madame Le Deux's plan is going to work." She didn't elaborate on what that plan was, and by her exasperated expression, wasn't going to. "Not to put too fine a point on this, Murphy, but if a student were to get hurt or worse by your powers, it could end my ability to train Fomorians for the Queen's armies for good."

Kelcie saw Killian's concerned frown. She would never do anything to hurt her people. "That's a very fine point," she replied.

"Not to mention Roswen is already paying that Rapshider five times what he's worth to fix a bloody hole in the training den. And his bid for repairing a simple rock wall . . . !" She stabbed the cold stone floor with the sword, chipping off a piece of slate. "Murphy's mishaps have given the woman the excuse she needed to make repairs I've long been putting off. At this rate, the coffers will be empty come break."

"*Murphy's mishaps* has a nice ring to it," Zephyr said, laughing.

Kelcie glared at him.

"You may return to class, Killian," Scáthach ordered.

Kelcie could tell he wanted to stay, but he slid his sword into the scabbard on his belt, saluted with a nod, and left.

Scáthach padded behind her desk. "Fianna three, you must

start working together better. Much better. No more bickering. No more tardiness. I want to see absolute conviction and conformity."

"Yes, ma'am," Kelcie, Niall, Zephyr, and Brona said in unison.

Roswen stormed in the door, her axe-pen cocked at Zephyr. "You broke the paddock fence?"

"To save the horses!" Kelcie exclaimed.

"There really was no choice," Brona added.

"We all contributed to the damage," Niall admitted.

Roswen snorted and spun on her heel. "Well, then together, you four will help me fix it. Now!"

18

A PULSE ELEMENTAL

ON THE WAY to the paddock, Kelcie slowed to walk beside Niall, who still hadn't said a word to her. His brow furrowed, the muscle in his jaw ticked.

"I'm sorry," Kelcie said, testing the waters to see if he was speaking at all to her.

Niall took his glasses off and shoved them in his pocket. "For what?"

"For not telling you everything. I should've trusted you." They walked in silence a bit longer. "Did you know Draummorc was my father?"

Niall sighed. "I don't know. Maybe. I mean, why else wouldn't he tell you his name?"

"Why didn't you tell me?"

"Tell you that your father might be the man that killed mine? Because I didn't want it to be true. I still don't!"

Kelcie cringed at his sharp tone. "You hate me now, right?"

He stopped walking. "No. I'm just so angry, okay?"

"Angry at me?"

"No. I don't know," he murmured.

Kelcie took a step back, but he closed the distance between them, his grimace filled with regret. "I'm sorry. I don't want to care that your father is Draummorc. But I really wish he wasn't."

Kelcie wished he wasn't either. "I can't change that."

"I know." He started walking again. Kelcie kept pace, still unsure of where she stood with him. "Not being able to tell my sister feels like such a betrayal."

"Tell her. It's okay. Scáthach won't mind, I'm sure."

"We were given orders, Kelcie. Disobeying orders at AUA is no different than when we go on active duty. No, I can't do that." Kelcie nodded. "I'm sorry."

"I am too," he said, his expression resigned. "Let's hope Scáthach finds the eye during the inspection. If she does, it will all be over, and no one ever needs to know that your father is the traitor."

WITH INSPECTIONS GOING on, all students were orered to their Dens. Kelcie spent the afternoon sitting around the pool with Killian and Ollie interrogating her about fighting the sylph and sparking fire.

"We need to get word to Grandfather. A pulse elemental is at the Academy! He should be the one training her," Ollie insisted, his feet dangling in the pool. "He'll come back if he finds out."

"No, he won't, but he can help her during break. Kelcie, you should come to the Woods," Killian said. He leaned against the wall, biting into an orange fruit that crunched like an apple. "I'm hoping to be commissioned at the end of the year with the rest of my fianna. If the Queen doesn't get in the way. But Ollie can bring you with him."

"Yes! That would be so fun!" Ollie splashed her. "You can stay at our house and Grandfather can work with you."

It was the nicest invitation she'd ever gotten in her life. "But my bough—"

"Crane reported your existence. How could they keep you from going to the one place in the Lands of Summer you're supposed to be?" Killian said.

"I'd like that." Ollie and Killian were fast becoming more than Den mates. They were the older brothers she'd never had but always wanted.

"Awesome." Ollie hopped out of the pool. "You know, Kelcie, you should be able to breathe underwater." He waggled his caterpillar eyebrows at her. "Let's test it, shall we?" His green and brown eyes twinkling with mischief, he lunged.

"Not in this lifetime!"

Kelcie sprinted into her room, locking the door, refusing to open it for anyone until Scáthach showed up to inspect it.

She told Kelcie she'd checked the grounds herself, but there were no signs of illegal fairy infiltration, the missing horse, the missing spriggan, or Balor's evil eye.

"What does that mean?" Kelcie asked.

"It means we must stay on our toes. If you hear his voice again—"

"I'll report it right away. Yes, ma'am."

"Good." Scáthach tilted her head at Kelcie's desk.

It was littered with crumpled parchments. "An essay on nimble fairies for Madame Le Deux's class. They're very fast." Kelcie nodded, expecting leniency since it was a school assignment.

Scáthach nodded along. "Yes, I'm aware. Wind sprints seem fitting, then, for failing this part of inspection, don't you think? Twenty, I'd say." To Kelcie's dismay, Scáthach wrote it down on Roswen's clipboard.

Later, at dinner, Kelcie heard Scáthach did recover a couple of surprises on her inspection. Deirdre Crane's stash of mirror dust was confiscated, and she and her fianna were forced to clean the stalls in the stables for a month. Poor Marta Louisa got hit hard when Roswen ate every piece of her illegal box of candy, forcing her to watch.

Meanwhile, word of fianna three's battle with a sylph spread all over school. Tables were tense with speculation on how a Winter creature broke into the AUA campus again, but also surprised that a first-year fianna was able to stop it. All of the Alphas breezed by offering congratulations, including Regan, who made a point of pinching Niall's cheek to mortify him. Before heading to the Cat Den, Delilah Quick stopped by, whispering in Zephyr's ear, then sashayed off with her panther tail swishing see-you-later.

"Nice tail," Niall called.

Kelcie bopped him on the back of the head for that.

After the table emptied, her fianna peppered Kelcie with questions about King Balor's voice. What did it sound like? Were there warnings it was coming? Did it hurt when the eye contacted her? That last one left her speechless, not because she didn't have an answer, but because the truth was it was the most powerful she ever felt. What if the strength in her powers came from touching the eye? From the very first time in the museum, she felt the unbridled exhilaration of what it was capable of, and wanted it for her own.

Kelcie simply said, "It doesn't hurt."

"Tell us about the human world. Was it really that miserable?" Zephyr asked.

"It wasn't all bad." She told them about how she could load up on candy for a year trick-or-treating on Halloween, and about snowball fights during winters in Massachusetts. "I miss snow. I miss the smell outside right before it snows the most. The air is so heavy too, and cold."

"You like winter?" Zephyr accused.

"Winter isn't a place or a people. It's a time of year. There are four seasons in Mass. Fall is such a magical time. Between summer and winter, the leaves change color and fall off the trees like they're bowing to winter."

"I don't think I'd like that," Niall grumbled.

"It's fine because winter thaws to spring. Leaves grow back. Baby animals are born. Flowers bloom."

"Sounds magical," Brona said dreamily.

"Yeah. And then comes summer. Everyone wants to be outside, soaking up the sun. Except me, of course. Hopping in pools to keep cool. And popsicles from the ice cream truck are the best, if you have some money."

"Sounds like summer reigns supreme," Zephyr chuckled.

"As it should," Niall agreed, smirking.

They clinked Zinger bottles.

Kelcie sopped up the last bit of rosemary chicken delight with baked womperill bread. She was about to pop it into her mouth when she mistakenly asked, "What's a womperill?"

"Rolled apoi droppings," Zephyr said.

"Droppings? As in excrement? As in poo?" Kelcie set it down.

Niall laughed at her. "It's a plant."

Zephyr banged his spoon on the glass bottle, grabbing everyone's attention. "I have something important to say. We need to be on alert and at our best," his voice dropping three octaves on the word *best*. "Every morning from now until the end of the year we get up an hour early and train."

"Good." Brona brandished a rainbow carrot. "We need this. Maybe we should get up two hours early."

Kelcie wanted to cry. "I need sleep more."

Niall nodded in agreement. "Mentally fit is as important as physically fit. I vote for more sleep."

"I'm not taking votes. This is an order. Butts on Hawthorn Field at six."

Brona's carrot threatened Kelcie. "Maybe you and me should meet at five thirty. I might be able to help you with your control prob—"

"You heard Scáthach. She can't," said Niall.

Brona flung the carrot at his busted lens. "I was asking Kelcie."

Zephyr picked it up and flung it back at her. "We're supposed to be getting along! Keep your carrots to yourself!"

"Niall's right, Brona. I can't risk it." Kelcie didn't want her fianna to get into more trouble because of her. "Scáthach is working on it with Madame Le Deux. They'll come up with something, I'm sure."

"Since when do you rely on adults for things?" Brona challenged.

Kelcie scowled at her. Brona had just dropped her own self-reliant life in her face like a gauntlet, daring her to pick it up. But if she did, her time at AUA would be over.

Thankfully, Zephyr stepped in. "No, Brona. That too is an order."

Willow, Marta, and Sanura Shaker, another Raven first year, swarmed Brona. Willow folded her arms around Brona's neck. "Your drawer pinged!" she shrilled. "I bet it's your mother!"

Brona's shoulders drooped. She sagged out of her hold. "Oh really?"

"I bet she said yes. Will you go check right now? Please? I can't wait to tell my sister that I'm going to the Island of Eternal Youth for break! So much cooler than her stupid trip last year to boring Great Falls . . . which she wouldn't let me go on, by the way."

Brona hesitated. She picked up another carrot. "We're in the middle of a fianna meeting. I can't leave yet."

The girls glared at Zephyr. "What? Something on my face?"

Brona kicked him under the table. Niall squinted at him.

"Oh yeah, no. We're not done yet," he said sternly.

"No problem." Marta Louisa wrapped an arm over Willow's shoulders. "Let's wait in your room for her."

As soon as they were gone, Brona's face fell like she remembered something horrible. "I'll see you guys in the morning." She sprinted toward Haven Hall.

"What was that about?" Zephyr asked.

"I think . . . she's anxious," Niall explained cryptically.

Kelcie fought hard against a sudden urge to go after her. "I think that Brona is worried about whatever could be in that letter, and that Willow and Marta Louisa went back to Brona and Willow's *shared* room to wait because they have plans to open it for her."

19

WHO SMELTED?

WITH NOTHING LEFT to hide from her fianna or Scáthach, and knowing King Balor's eye wasn't on campus, Kelcie slept well for the first time since she arrived at the Academy. She crawled out of bed an hour early and met her fianna for the extra workout, thankful for uniforms. She used to make fun of private school kids in their plaid skirts, white shirts, and fancy saddle shoes. How comfortable could they be? But after weeks of rolling out of bed into clean yellow sweats, Kelcie was a fan. She never had to worry about what she was going to wear. She looked freshly plucked from a lemon grove every single day.

Brona hardly spoke. Her hair was in a messy ponytail. Dark circles cratered beneath her silver orbs. Something was definitely off. After the workout, she skipped bits. Then, after Combat, Brona went back to Haven Hall, missing lunch, claiming she wasn't hungry.

"I bet it's because of what Crane said. She told everyone that the whole sylph adventure never happened, that we made it up to hide the fact Kelcie's crazy air powers caused all the damage," Zephyr explained.

"Nah. Brona only cares what Scáthach thinks. And she knows the truth."

"Kelcie's right. There's something else bothering her," Niall squinted.

"Like what?" asked Zephyr.

He squirmed in his seat. "Don't know. But I can just, um, *feel* it."

"Like *sense* it?" Zephyr frowned. "You better not start that touchy feely stuff on me, O'Shea."

"Never. Guys have no emotions, am I right?" Niall held his fist out.

Zephyr hesitated.

"Well, Neanderthals, this is where we say goodbye. Le Deux moved class until after dinner so Killian's testing me with those other two elements."

"Can I come?" Niall asked.

Kelcie didn't see why not. "Sure."

Zephyr raised a hand. "Count me in."

The three hurried to the training building. When they arrived, Ollie hopped up, smiling as always but Killian stood in such a way as to block them from entering the building.

"Why are they here?" His head jerked from Niall to Zephyr.

Kelcie shrugged. "To watch."

"We don't let anyone in the Saiga training space."

"By we, my brother means he," Ollie said. "Where's Brona by the way? Shouldn't the whole fianna be here?"

"She's not here. And they're coming." Kelcie ducked underneath Killian's outstretched arm.

"Excuse me," Zephyr said, taking her lead.

"Pardon me," Niall added, doing the same.

"Maybe we could make an exception this time," Ollie said, traipsing after them.

But Killian wasn't allowing it. He stopped Kelcie outside the Saiga's metal door. "It's bad enough you let them in the Den. I kept my mouth shut because Ollie said they were harmless. But this is different. I don't want them in here."

I told you day one. Secretive, Niall said in her head.

Kelcie crossed her arms. "I thought you said you came to the Academy to build trust between Summerfolk and Fomorians?"

"I did, but this is different. This is about our powers."

"I can test the other elements outside without you, if that's what you want. The sparking words are—"

"Don't repeat those out here." Killian raked his fingers through his hair, bumping his growing horns. Two inches long, the tips were needle sharp.

"Fine. But just this once," he relented, flicking his fingers, casting the wind hard enough to push open the door. They were greeted by the sound of metal scraping rock.

"Great. Just great," Killian groaned. "Roswen said the trolls would be done with the repairs by now."

Kelcie's mouth fell open at the sight of them.

From the smallest coming up to Kelcie's knees to the tallest at some seven feet, the trolls all wore matching blue overalls. Some fat, others thin, they were hairy all over, except on their faces.

The hole wasn't much smaller, and she could see why. The trolls stood in a brigade line, sweat pouring down their puffing cheeks as they cradled heavy rocks in their sagging arms, waiting while a particularly stout, gray-haired troll with tiny glasses on the end of his pointy nose dished teaspoons of cement out of a wheelbarrow.

Rapshider, Kelcie presumed.

The old troll smoothed the cement with a delicate touch like it was icing on a fancy wedding cake.

"Should we find somewhere else?" Kelcie asked.

"No. Scáthach wanted us to test here. But let's make it quick. Ollie, get water."

While Ollie used a pump in the corner of the room to fill a water bucket, Killian lifted a hunk of steel from the large dusty stack on the side of the room. He set it down in front of Kelcie. Ollie lugged the filled bucket over with one hand, using the other to wave the spilling droplets back into the bucket before they hit the floor.

Killian turned to Niall and Zephyr. "You two, over there." He pointed at the farthest corner.

Niall and Zephyr grumbled under their breath the whole way.

Killian's mouth moved, but he spoke so softly, Kelcie couldn't hear him either over Rapshider's high-pitched scraping.

"What?"

"He said Earth is a particularly finicky discipline," Ollie shouted. "But don't worry. Our mother is a Theran. We've seen how this works."

Rapshider finally set the stone and blew a whistle. The trolls dropped the rocks, padding off for what looked like a long over-due break. The room fell silent.

"Do all Fomorians have elemental powers?" Kelcie asked.

Ollie opened his mouth to answer but Niall beat him to it.

"Yes," Niall said with confidence.

"How would you know anything about our people?" Killian asked.

"Regan told me. She said you've taught her a lot of things. She likes you. Likes all Fomorians, I mean."

Killian chewed on that as he knelt down beside Kelcie. "Theran is a deeper connection to the earth and the elements it is made up of. Place your hands on the steel."

She did as Killian instructed.

"Picture it in another form. Melting is a common use. Therans typically work in crafting. Find the source of your power, that same pull in your gut. Then say the sparking word, *Theran*."

"Take your time," Ollie said. "Don't feel rushed. It can be hard—"

"*Theran . . .*"

The metal warmed. Molecules bounced around so fast they jolted Kelcie's hands. Solid melted to liquid almost instantly.

"Whoa!" Ollie cried. "That was fast!"

But it didn't stop there. The smelt gassed, filling the room with thick black smoke. Killian grabbed Kelcie's shoulders, pulling her hands off, breaking the connection.

"Ow! You're hot!" He dunked his hands in the water bucket.

But Zephyr yanked the bucket out from under Killian. He tossed the contents on the blistering hot smelt, sending nox-ious smoke billowing out the hole at the trolls, smothering their lunch in black dust. They dropped their sandwiches, yelling in a language Kelcie couldn't understand.

When the dust settled, the trolls made rude gestures at them, then grabbed their trowels, shovels, picks, and hammers, and trudged away.

"Did they just quit?" Kelcie worried.

Niall pushed his foggy glasses up his nose. "Yeah. I hope Roswen didn't pay them in advance."

Zephyr shook his head, sending soot flying. "Another item added to Roswen's long list of Murphy's mishaps."

Kelcie didn't need another ding in her scroll. "Maybe we should stop."

"Are you crazy? Who cares about the building? Kelcie, you're a pulse elemental!" Ollie gushed. "This is HUGE!"

"What use is it to have more powers when I can't control a single one?"

Killian face lit up. "Don't worry about that right now." He clapped his hands. "Ollie, get another water bucket."

Ollie did as Killian asked, setting another filled bucket in front of Kelcie. He held his open hand over the water. "Try this. Caenum." The water rose out of the bucket to kiss his palm, remaining there until he eased his hand down. "Water in this form is *calm*. You have to be too."

"Calm," Kelcie repeated, letting out an audible breath. She slid her palm over the bucket, and took another deep breath, exhaling slowly.

Zephyr scooted into the corner.

Niall smirked at him. "It's not a lot of water. What's the worst that can happen?"

"I'm not taking any chances."

Kelcie stayed focused on the bucket, and whispered, "Caenum."

Killian and Niall flinched expecting the worst, but the water didn't move.

"Try again," Killian said.

This time Kelcie closed her eyes, trying for true meditative Zen. "Caenum." She raised her hand and opened her eyes at the same time. The defiant water remained frustratingly flat.

"Yeah, well, I hate you too!" Kelcie stuck her tongue out, seeing her reflection giving it right back to her.

"Maybe a little less calm?" Niall suggested.

Kelcie would tell that bucket who's boss! She thrust her arm and stamped her foot, sending ripples through the water, then yelled, "CAENUM!" When nothing happened, she did it again. "CAENUM! CAENUM! CAENUM!"

Kelcie kicked it over. She glowered at Ollie—not that it was his fault, but she was irrationally angry and in need of blaming someone. "Why won't it work?"

"Well, if I had to guess . . ." Ollie stuck his fingers in the puddle, raising a trail of droplets beneath his hand, and flicked it at her. "You're afraid of water."

"I'm not afraid of a bucket of water!"

Ollie shrugged off her ire. "Whatever. Water is water."

"This is ridiculous!" Kelcie stomped in the puddle. "CAE-NUM!"

Ollie laughed. "It can smell fear."

"Water doesn't have feelings," Niall said.

Killian shook his head, laughing. "You don't understand."

"Enlighten us then," Kelcie snapped.

"Our powers come from a fundamental connection to the particular element. It isn't simply about casting a thought willy-nilly into another person's mind. It's much deeper than that."

Zephyr padded next to Niall. "Arrogant, much?"

"Then you obviously know nothing about where an Adder's power comes from," Niall exclaimed, insulted. "It's the same thing, it's just that our connection is to people, not things."

"Chargers too. We connect with horses and our muscles." Zephyr flexed.

Ollie, Kelcie, and Niall laughed. Killian started to leave.

"Where are you going?" Kelcie asked.

"The test is over. I'll report back to Scáthach."

Kelcie's chest tightened. "What will you tell her?"

"That you are a pulse elemental. But that you're going to need a real teacher. Until such time as there is one, she's right to keep you from using any of your powers. It's just too dangerous."

20

A GLOVE THAT FITS

A week later, Kelcie worried about Brona. The Raven was being way too nice to her. She waited for Kelcie before and after every class. During combat training, she asked Coach Blackwell if she could work with her. With the first sweep that landed her on her back, Kelcie figured that Brona was only looking for a new punching bag, but by the end of that practice, Brona taught Kelcie a combination foot-hook and jab that had Coach Blackwell both falling over and losing his staff at the same time, earning her a real sword and shield.

Kelcie loved the way the weighted steel grip felt in her hand and couldn't wait to show Ollie and Killian before lunch. On the way out of the Nether Tower, she made sure to thank Brona. "I owe you big time."

"So, you do." Brona hummed. "You can pay me back and get something for yourself at the same time. Let me help you with your powers."

"You're an amazing teacher, but . . ." Kelcie hesitated. It had been a full week of not using her powers at all. She could feel them, rolling around inside her, anxious for action. But she was afraid of what would happen when it all went wrong. "You know I can't."

"You're walking out of combat class with a sword and shield after practicing with me for *one* day. Don't you trust me?"

"Of course, I trust you. I don't trust me." Kelcie bit her lip. "And the truth is, if I get kicked out, I have nowhere else to go."

Brona seemed to accept that, and dropped the subject.

After lunch, on the way to Sword & Sorcery, Willow and Marta Louisa jogged by Kelcie and Brona on the trail. Willow looked over her shoulder at Brona. Marta Louisa cupped her mouth so they wouldn't hear what she was saying to Willow. They started giggling.

"You can go walk with them if you want," Kelcie said.

"I don't want." Brona slowed, not wanting to get near them.

"I thought you all were best buds? The she-women Saiga hating clu—"

Brona flinched. "You think I hate Saigas? Hate you?"

"No. Of course not. Sorry. But why are they acting like that?"

"I don't want to talk about it."

"Maybe I can help. I owe you, you know, for the sword."

"You can't help. No one can." Brona morphed and flew into the open window of Le Deux's classroom at the top of Direwood Keep, ending the conversation.

MADAME LE DEUX started class by dropping a heavy book on her desk.

"As promeesed, we wheel start our fhirst potion today." She flipped the book open without looking at the page she turned to. "Many of you probably theenk potions are mageec. Only weetches can eenfuse mageec eento potions. And we all know weetches exeest only in the Lands of Weenter." Her bony index finger lifted with caveat. "Or maybe you don't. You wheel learn about that next year."

She glided up the aisles, staring down her nose at each fianna's table. "Potions are not for the eempatient. They take time. Some, a day; others, a year. In thees class, potions are comprised of mysteecal eengreedients combined at the proper time een order to achieve a parteecular goal. There ees no hocus pocus een-volved. ONLY careful planneeng."

Madame Le Deux stopped beside Kelcie.

"The potion we wheel take on ees called a maskeeng. A type of *glamourie*. Can anyone tell me what a maskeeng potion does?"

Niall's hand shot up, as did David Dunn's, one of his Adder roommates. Stocky, and with his golden hair tied into a ponytail at the base of his neck, he looked like a prepubescent Viking.

"Yes, thee wheat-haired snake thees time."

"A single drop will hide the appearance of an object it's dripped on, blending it seamlessly into the immediate environment."

He tossed a cocky grin at Niall, his ruby stare filled with conceit.

"Like a chameleon?" Kelcie asked.

"Very good." Madame Le Deux patted her head, then paced between tables. "Open your books to page thirty."

Books plonked. Pages flipped.

Kelcie scrolled through the ingredients, her jaw dropping at how complicated this was going to be. The potion had to be started on the exact day the moon was full. Then, the ingredients added at different times over three months, with the final component, something called a hoffescus stone, to be dropped in on the night of a new moon, when the moon wasn't visible at all.

"It's going to take three whole months to make this," Brona exclaimed.

"On that page you wheel find thee leest of eengreedients. Burdock rhoot. Pookagrass. Mantle hyssop flowers. Snake oil. All but thee hoffescus stones and burdock rhoot can be found on thee shelves here or een Befelts Garden. Thee burdock rhoot grows near running water. Hoffescus stones are the rarest of rare. Found only at thee bottom of Morrow Lake on thees very campus. Glamourie eesn't possible without them. If you fail to get one, you fail thees assignment."

Niall raised his hand. "What part of the bottom exactly? That lake gets deep."

"Yes, eet ees. But alas, I can tell you no more. That would be wrong. On thees page you wheel see a descreeption of thee eengredients. Could I seemply geeve you these theengs? Yes. But you must learn to recognize them in thee Otherworld. The hoffescus stone ees small, and striped red and white."

Kelcie imagined it looking like a peppermint candy.

"Now then, weeth thee time we 've left, you may set up your cauldrons on your deseegnated fireplaces and search thee shelves for eengrediants. Eef you put zem on your table, then they belong to your fianna. No stealeeng from each other or shareeng!" She paced toward the door. "I wheel be back een a meenute."

Madame Le Deux left the classroom.

In the aftermath of the mad dash for the shelves, other fiannas snagged the pookagrass and mantle hyssop flowers first, leaving fianna three with only snake oil and a necessary trip to Befelt's Garden.

"We can put the cauldron up," Brona suggested.

"I've got it." Niall smirked, shooting his hand out at the shelf. The cauldron lifted, floating through the air, over the table, heading for their fireplace.

"Look!" Kelcie whacked Zephyr and Brona, who were too busy arguing over who was getting which ingredient in the garden to notice.

Kelcie clapped.

Brona too.

Zephyr launched his fists in the air. "Check it. Our Adder has telekinesis and is a telepath. What about yours, Fagan? Huh, Dunn? Give us a show!"

Fagan glowered at Dunn.

"Shut up, Chike," Willow snapped.

Marta Louisa meowed right next to Niall's ear. The cauldron missed the hook in the fireplace. It fell with a clank and rolled to fianna one's table, where Tad Fagan stomped it to pieces.

Fagan kicked it to Niall's feet. "At least you have one hand you can use to pick that up."

"What did you say?" Kelcie heated with anger. The air sparked around her.

"Oh, is the *demon* going to hit me with a little wind?"

"Don't call her that!" Niall growled.

Fagan stepped in front of her. "Do it. I dare you. Destroy Madame Le Deux's classroom. That'll be the end of your days at AUA."

"Blast him into tomorrow," Brona hissed, morphing her fingers to talons.

Kelcie's breathe heaved. In her mind's eye, she blasted him across the room. Saw him career into the shelves. Saw broken shards from busted vials stab him in the back. His blood dripping on the floor—and gasped.

She stepped away from him.

She had faced the same kind of bullies loads of times before in the human world, but never had she felt this angry. Her inner voice yelled, *End him.* But Kelcie would never want that to happen, would she? She would never want to hurt someone, not like that. Was this the effect of touching the eye? Was this King Balor's fury spiking hers, or was she changing?

Kelcie shook her head, refusing, and swallowed her rage, hating the way it tasted. "I can't." She opened her hand. "He's not worth getting in trouble."

"Time to go!" Madame Le Deux shouted from the doorway. "Class ees deesmeessed. Except Kelcie. I need to speak weeth you. Your fianna can stay too."

"Look at that. You didn't even have to do it to get in trouble. She wants you out of here too. Mission accomplished . . ." Fagan sang on his way out, waving goodbye.

"If you haven't noticed, Kelcie is Madame Le Deux's teacher's pet," Brona yelled after him.

"Thanks a lot," Kelcie said to her.

Brona rolled her eyes. "I mean, I don't think you're in trouble."

After the rest of the class left, Madame Le Deux picked up something off her desk and padded toward Kelcie.

Kelcie dove into a preemptive apology. "I'm sorry, ma'am."

"For what?" Madame Le Deux's smile was so bright, Kelcie had to blink. "I understand you're steel 'aving deefficulty adjusteeng to your new powers."

Kelcie slumped down in her chair.

"Deenka-doo, up. Up. Now."

Madame Le Deux pulled Kelcie's chair back with her in it, popping her on the back, forcing her up. She lifted her chin so Kelcie had no choice but to look at her. Le Deux stared into Kelcie's eyes, examining them one at a time, then stepped back. "Thee powers buried witheen you fight for control."

"That makes no sense," Brona said.

"It makes perfect sense," Niall countered. "If they're fighting to get out, pressure would build."

"And then boom," Zephyr added with exploding hand gestures.

"Eh-xactly. I 'ave sometheeng that wheel help. I made these for you." Madame Le Deux draped a pair of fingerless gloves made of a lightweight black mesh over Kelcie's arm. Copper threads crisscrossed the fabric, stitching cylindrical obsidian stones, sculpted to points on both ends, to the back of each. "Try them on."

Kelcie did as instructed. The mesh was light as a feather and the stone fit perfectly into the groove between her index and middle finger.

"Thee obseedeean wheel channel your powers and tame them."

"Are you Fomorian?" Brona asked Madame Le Deux.

"What does that matter?" Kelcie asked.

"Do I look Fomoreean?" Madame Le Deux leaned over Brona.

Niall and Zephyr cowered behind Kelcie, but Brona didn't back down.

"Then how do you know it will work?"

"Who ees the teacher here?" Madame Le Deux shouted. She softened, turning her attention back at Kelcie. "Geeve eet a try, Kelcie. A leettle weend at those dried flowers. Chop. Chop." She clapped her hands.

"Okay. Here goes . . ." Kelcie raised her fists, aiming the stones at the flowers.

"Hold up!" Zephyr dragged Brona and Niall to the far corner of the room, way out of the line of fire. "Okay." He clapped, cheering Kelcie on. "Go on. You can do this, Murphy."

"Please work," she wished, then whispered, "Mistral."

The surge raced down her arms. When the power hit her hands, the obsidian glowed midnight blue. Kelcie braced for the inevitable typhoon that would blow every bottle on the shelves behind her teacher's desk off, sending them crashing to the floor.

But it never happened.

Air puffed at the flowers. They swayed ever so poetically.

Kelcie stood still as a statue, waiting for a possible second wave—that never came. "It worked!" She turned to Madame Le Deux, happier than she had ever been in her life. "Thank you so much!"

Madame Le Deux gave a firm pat on the shoulder. "You see? Eet wheel keep them bridled."

"Brilliant!" Niall exclaimed.

"Never take them off," Zephyr ordered.

"I don't like it." Brona glowered at the gloves like they were public enemy number one.

"Why?"

"Because—" Brona started to answer Kelcie but Madame Le Deux pinched Brona's arm and didn't let go. "Ow!"

"Raven girl, you always 'ave to be thee very best at every-theeng."

"Let go of me," Brona hissed, wincing.

Madame Le Deux sniffed, releasing her. "Jealousy ees a beeeter peel to swallow. But choke eet down, or leave."

Brona dropped her book on the table. "Why would I ever be jealous of *her*?"

She stretched taller, spreading her arms, then morphed, and flew out the window.

"Way to rain on my parade!" Kelcie yelled after her.

Madame Le Deux took Kelcie's hand, patting the back of her new glove. "Those birds are so deesloyal."

O N THE WAY back to Haven Hall, Kelcie drove Niall nuts puffing air in his ear.

"What is eating Brona?" Zephyr asked.

"I don't know, and I don't care," Kelcie said, admiring her new gloves. She could use her powers now, except water. Caenum. She was going to pretend that one didn't exist.

A crowd blocked the entrance when they arrived at Haven Hall.

"Why is the whole school out here?" Kelcie asked.

Necks craned, everyone was pointing and laughing at Brona, who stood beneath several pieces of paper dangling from the arch above the doorway. With tears pouring down her face, she jumped, trying to pull them down, but an invisible force kept lifting them out of her reach.

"Uncatchable strings," Niall groaned.

Brona turned at the sound of Niall's voice. She took one look at the three of them heading for her and flew away.

"Did you read them? Her father's as tired of her as we are," Willow said, high-fiving Sanura.

"Move it!" Kelcie shoved Shaker out of her way, then bumped through the others until she was close enough to read the first one. *No, Brona. No word. I told you I will let you know. How is school?* Then another that said, *Stop asking. Go for a run. Hit something or someone. You'll feel better. You always do.*

"*Brona, no,*" Willow read aloud, her curls bouncing with every pause in her highly dramatic recitation. "*Your mother has not been in touch. Why would she? She's never been in your life and never will be. Please stop asking and focus on your studies and training. I've had all of this I can take.*"

"Big surprise. Brona Lee has been lying this whole time," Deirdre Crane guffawed.

Regan pushed past Crane to get to Willow. "Did you put those up there? Because I want them down now!"

"Where do you get off telling me what to do? You're not my Charger or my Alpha."

Regan cast a scrutinizing yellow glare at Gavin Puce. He answered by laughing and blowing her a kiss. He wasn't going to do anything about the situation.

"You're all just jealous of her!" Kelcie yelled.

"Jealous? Please! She never trained with Macha. The goddess probably isn't really her mother. She's just a liar, and as pathetic as the rest of you." Fagan sank his teeth into his bottom lip. "Looks like she was put in the right fianna after all."

Kelcie didn't care about getting in trouble. She didn't care about anything other than wiping that smug look off Fagan's face. Kelcie aimed a fist at him.

Don't do it, Kelcie! Niall moved to stop her, but Kelcie ducked under his outstretched arm.

"Mistral!"

"No!" Fagan cowered, slamming his eyes shut, bracing for a wild gust that never came. Air puffed a gentle cool breeze in his sniveling face.

Everyone laughed, this time at Fagan.

"Booya!" Zephyr chuckled.

Regan laughed. "Nice one, Murphy."

"I was hoping for something a bit more . . . more."

Of course you were, Niall's laughter filled her head.

"Move aside. Move!" Roswen shouldered through the students until she got to the front. Her pink hairline rose in appreciation as she spotted Kelcie's new gloves. "Well . . . Murphy. Haven Hall is intact. Glad to see those are working for you." When she saw the dancing letters, her lip curled. She took out her axe-pen and threw it, cutting the strings with a single pass. "We do not invade personal space or touch anyone else's things! EVER! Whoever is responsible for this, when I find out who you are, which I will, you'll be shoveling manure for a month. Let that be a warning to all of you! Got me?"

A chorus of *yes, ma'am*'s rang out.

Kelcie picked up Brona's letters, holding them above her index finger.

Niall leaned away from her. *Seriously? Do you have to try that one out?*

"Ignis."

A single tiny flame lit.

Inside, Kelcie was screaming, *I DID IT!* Outside, she did her best to play it cool, relishing her classmates' surprised expressions as she set the letters on fire. She dropped them on the ground, letting them burn, guarding them until they were ash.

"How did she do that?" Gareth McKnight asked his twin sister, Ginger.

"I thought she was a Mistral?" Ginger said.

Crane's beady red eyes narrowed. "What is she?"

Kelcie caught Killian smirking. He was enjoying their shock as much as she was. She wiggled her fingers at Crane. These gloves were going to change everything.

Killian's breeze scattered the ashes.

Niall sighed. *I think we figured out why Brona's been so irritable.*

"What do we do now?" Zephyr asked.

"Leave it to me." Kelcie started down the path. "I think I know where she might be."

21

SUNSET AND STRIKER

THE SUN WAS going down as Kelcie crossed the Bridge of Leaping. A delicious cool breeze greeted her on the small isle, whipping her hair off her face. She found Brona exactly where Kelcie would be under the same circumstances, on the cliff's edge, petting Striker. The cú sith whined a hello, wagging his feathery tail as Kelcie sat down beside her.

Brona picked up a rock and threw it in the water. "I don't want to talk."

Striker rolled over, stretching. Kelcie rubbed his belly, making him coo. "I just came to pet Striker."

Brona leaned back on her elbows. Her eyes were ringed red from crying.

Kelcie settled on her elbows too, stretching her legs. Sunlight glinted off the obsidian on her gloves as she held one up. "Why don't you like these?"

Brona flicked the obsidian. "Because they limit your powers."

"I don't care about that. I lit a tiny flame to set your father's letter on fire and didn't burn the school down. That's all that matters."

"You lit my father's letters on fire?" Brona frowned at her.

"Sorry."

"It's fine." She hurled another rock, waiting for the plunk

before talking again. "I don't know why I care," she sighed, sitting up, and nodded at the gloves. "You think a tiny flame would've stopped that sylph?"

Kelcie considered that. "No, but I don't want to lose my place here. Or for you and Zephyr and Niall not to get asked back because of me."

Brona wrapped her arms around her knees. "I don't know if I want to come back."

"You have to be kidding me. You're the best fighter I've ever seen. You can shift in a snap. That's, like, third-year stuff."

Striker curled his tail feathers through Kelcie's bent legs. A weird shiver ran up her spine, another déjà vu in the way he did that.

"After what happened . . ." Brona choked a sob. Her head dropped into her crossed arms, hiding her face.

Kelcie stretched an arm around her shoulders, hoping Brona didn't peck it off. Instead, Brona leaned into the hug, crying harder. Kelcie's heart broke for her. "Yeah. I could've told you Willow was two-faced from the minute I met her."

Striker poked Brona's leg with his snout. She laughed, sniffling. "His nose is cold." She raised her head, setting her chin on her bent wrists. "If Macha really was my mother I'd want to stay, fight it out, never give up, but all I want to do is go home. I miss it so much."

"*If* she was your mother?"

"I can't remember her. My father told me who she was when I started morphing."

"You never met her?"

"Nope. Not once."

"I can't remember mine either. At least you have a dad who cares about you. Did he teach you to fight?"

She nodded. "He's the best."

"You going to follow him into . . . what did you call it, the armada? Is that like the navy?"

She picked a long blade of grass. "He's, um, not in the armada exactly. I kinda lied about that too."

Kelcie shifted to face her. "Really?"

"You can't tell anyone this."

Kelcie held up her hand. "I swear!"

"He's the privateer Tao Lee."

She said his name as if Kelcie should know who he was.

"The Chameleon?"

Kelcie shrugged. "I'm not from here, remember?"

"Oh right. Well, they call him that because he can sail in and out of places completely unseen. He's brilliant."

"Your father's a pirate?"

"No. A privateer."

"What's the difference?"

"He sails with letters from the Queen. The armada can't arrest him."

"So he's a pirate with permission to plunder?" Kelcie was intrigued.

"Exactly." Brona laughed. "And he lets me help him."

"Um, hello! That is way cooler than a goddess for a mom. That is something to brag about. I would love to be a pirate, except the sailing part. All that water." Kelcie shivered.

"I live on the water." Brona flopped on her stomach to stare over the edge of the cliff at the churning sea below. Kelcie did too.

"I really miss it. It's hard to sleep here. I'm used to a bed that rocks all night. Ach! Gads." She sat up, huffing. "I don't think I can sleep in the Raven Den tonight. I can't face them. Especially Willow."

"Oh, I know that feeling."

Brona looked down at Kelcie. "If you let me, I really can help you with your powers."

"You're relentless." Kelcie rolled over. "If Killian couldn't help—"

"Killian couldn't teach you because he's not like you. I know what it's like to have your powers come on all at once. Mine did the same thing."

Kelcie propped up on her elbows. "I can't risk it."

"Risk, what? Greatness?"

Kelcie laughed at that. She sat up. "There's nothing great about being me."

"Scáthach could've kicked you out, but she didn't. Do you know why?"

"She felt sorry for me. Like you do."

"Ha! You have me confused with your boyfriend, Mr. Sensitive."

"He's not my boyfriend."

"He certainly acts like he is."

Kelcie's cheeks burned. "He does?"

"Oh yeah. He's got it bad." Brona laughed. "And I don't feel sorry for you. I don't feel sorry for anyone. Honestly, for the first time in my life, I'm scared. That sylph swatted me out of the skies like I was nothing more than an annoying jackal fly. Nothing has ever done that before. I felt so helpless. You saved us, Kelcie. Saved me." She picked another blade of grass, tearing it in half along the seam, handing one to Kelcie. "And this trial with the eye, these mysteriously appearing Winter creatures, it isn't over."

Kelcie tickled Striker's nose with the blade of grass. "I haven't heard King Balor in a long while. Maybe it is over. Maybe I failed. From what I've heard, my father has no trouble controlling his powers. Why would an ancient evil eye choose me over him?"

"It isn't over. You know it, and so do I. Niall, Zephyr, and I are counting on you. And you can't use your powers to their full potential with those ugly gloves on."

"They're not ugly."

"Hideous." Brona wrinkled her nose at them. "But, for a while, until you get a handle on things, you can wear them in class and only take them off when we train."

That had possibilities. "Where? If I break one more thing . . . if anyone finds out—"

"Leave that to me." Brona smiled.

Sea eagles posted on the Shadow's repaired wall took to the skies, shift changing with another convocation returning from main campus. The gate opened. Kelcie and Brona jumped to their feet, exchanging worried glances.

Kelcie almost didn't recognize Scáthach as she padded toward them. She was out of her usual unitard armor. She wore a casual blue linen dress with a soft pink wrap over her shoulders. Her wavy auburn hair hung freely down her back. It was strangely unsettling seeing their warrior teacher looking like she was about to go on a date.

Scáthach whistled. Striker hopped to attention and jogged through the gate.

"Hello, you two," she said. "An hour until curfew. You should be heading back."

"Yes, ma'am," Kelcie said.

"Just leaving," Brona added, sighing heavily at having to return to the Raven Den.

That gave Kelcie an idea. "Scáthach?"

Scáthach crossed her arms. "Yes, Kelcie. Brona can sleep in the Saiga Den tonight. But only tonight."

Kelcie's mouth fell open. "How did you know what I was going to ask?"

Scáthach smiled. "Teacher intuition."

22

BARBECUED GRINDYLOWS, IT'S WHAT'S FOR DINNER

A S KELCIE AND Brona skipped across the bridge, Niall and Zephyr stood up, dusting off as if they'd been there awhile. "What are you two doing here?" Kelcie asked.

"We followed you. To, you know, make sure there were no more run-ins with scary creatures from the Lands of Winter," Zephyr said.

Niall preemptively held his hands up in surrender. "Not that you two can't take care of yourselves."

Brona smiled a genuine smile at Zephyr. "Thanks."

As they started walking, Niall pulled out a piece of paper from his pocket. "I brought the ingredients we need from Befelts Garden for the potion. We should stop on the way to Haven Hall. Full moon's tomorrow. I want to start the masking potion so there is no question that it will be done on time."

"Overachiever." Kelcie elbowed him.

"Niall's right. It's worth a huge portion of our grade," Brona added, walking with a renewed spring in her step. She skipped ahead.

Zephyr walked backward, arms stretched. "Enlighten us, Adder. What do we need to add tomorrow?"

"The snake oil and mantle hyssop flowers. But we can pick the pookagrass too. It has to be dried before we add it in a couple weeks, when the moon is in waning, along with the burdock rhoot, which I know grows near the Lazy Creek. I've seen it there during meditation. Then the last thing is the hoffescus stone."

"All right then. It's getting dark out. We better hurry," Zephyr ordered, breaking into an unappreciated jog.

"He has to be kidding me . . ." Kelcie had nothing left.

Beyond the pergola where they ate all their meals was Befelts Garden. Kelcie had never been inside before. To the left, the words *Sow Pretty* were painted on a wooden arch. Beyond were fruits and vegetables planted in raised beds. To the right, an old sign that said *Herbaceous Horrors* dangled sideways on a leaning post.

"This way?" Kelcie pointed to the Sow Pretty veggie gardens, hopeful.

"This way," Niall said, padding into the Herbaceous Horrors.

Gravel crunched beneath their feet on a path that wound in a heavenly scented spiral through herb beds of sweet lavender, minty sage, and bitter rosemary. Lanes broke off. Arrows directed traffic three different ways: Cooking, Medicinal, and Deadly.

Something howled in Deadly. Then its pack joined in. Kelcie inched backward, bumping into Niall.

He laughed. "Wolfbane." He shook his head disapprovingly. "You really need to start doing the reading for Roswen's class."

"Why is it howling?"

"It's twilight," Brona answered, dancing into Medicinal.

Kelcie read off the placards identifying a few of the gazillion things that were growing. "Verbana, henbane, mugwart, belladonna, helleborus, yarrow comfrey. Where exactly is—"

"Mantle hyssop flowers!" Brona pointed to a section of ten-foot leafy green plants with drooping purple flowers tucked way in the back, beyond several other beds of flowering greens.

"Perfect timing. They're asleep," Niall whispered, pulling out a pair of scissors.

"The herbs howl and the flowers sleep?"

Brona shushed her. She leaned over and whispered in Kelcie's ear. "Lots of Summer flowers do. Takes a lot of energy to bloom every day."

"Okay, then how do we get to them without waking them up?" Kelcie whispered back.

Brona waved, indicating for them to follow her.

"Hold up," Zephyr said in hushed tones. "Do you see how dark it's getting? I can barely see in front of my face. Curfew, people. You and Niall go for the flowers. Saiga and I will get the pookagrass. I heard the pond in the center of the garden is for grindylows. That's what they eat. Has to be a patch near it."

"I hate those things," Niall hissed.

"Me too. But they love pookagrass. I know. We've got a pond filled with them at home."

As Kelcie and Zephyr rounded the first bend, he stopped. "Don't get too close to the water, no matter how many times they whistle at you. They might look cute, but their bite is worse than the spriggans' jab."

"Lovely."

A few minutes later they arrived at the small pond. Zephyr nodded to waist-high white stalks covered in prickers growing along the backside of it.

"That's pookagrass?" Kelcie stared at her new gloves, wishing she brought a pair of scissors.

"And those are the grindylows."

The pond brimmed with the ugliest slithering things Kelcie had ever seen. Grindylows were frog-like in size and shape below the neck. But above it, they resembled possessed chicken-cats with downturned yellow beaks, round yellow bug eyes, and wiry black whiskers.

One leaped from the water, whistling, "*Phhuuwwwweeeeet-Phheeew!*"

The others joined in, putting on quite a water show, trying to get Kelcie and Zephyr to pay attention to them. Floaters piped a lively tune, setting a beat for others that backflipped out of the water with perfectly pointed webbed feet.

Kelcie laughed.

"Careful," Zephyr warned.

"Yeah, yeah." They were hilarious.

Kelcie sidestepped around the edge, moving close enough to the pookagrass to pick some. She pulled off a glove and stuffed it in the top of her sweatpants for safekeeping.

"How much do we need?" she asked Zephyr.

The pookagrass rustled a few feet away. Dark sludge oozed between shafts into a dip in the mud beside Kelcie. It burped odorless gas. Kelcie's stomach seized.

"Zephyr! Is that what I think it is?"

"Is that what?" Zephyr called from the other side of the pond. She took a giant step away from it—into the water.

Sharp teeth sank into Kelcie's thighs. Beaks stabbed her ankles.

"Ow!"

She yanked one grindylow off by its springy legs only to get bitten or poked by another daredevil singing diva.

"What did I tell you?" Zephyr threw his hands in the air. "Have you lost your—"

After that Zephyr sounded like he was yelling at her with a mouth full of marbles, ". . . *uman-ma-buma-dah* . . ."

Kelcie's vision clouded. She submerged into an all-consuming darkness, a place she'd been before, in the basement of the museum, when she held King Balor's eye.

The light at the end of the long dark tunnel was bigger this time, hotter, and uncomfortably close. Like in the museum, energy shot from it in two directions. One tendril racing away from her, and another that nailed her dead center in her chest.

Her soul filled with unearned confidence, a feeling of unimaginable power. It was everything she ever wanted, and yet something to be more than feared. Kelcie didn't fight against it though. She let it in, her breath glinting like sparklers on the fourth of July, teetering on the brink, but on the brink of what?

A taste of what awaits you when you win. King Balor's gravelly voice was louder than before. *I can feel how much you like it.*

Kelcie did like it. Who wouldn't love feeling like they could drive the miserable universe to its knees with a simple glance? But the universe wasn't miserable right now. In fact, it was pretty fabulous. Kelcie was going to have a sleepover with Brona tonight. She had her new gloves. Her fianna was working together, and more than that, they were friends. Good friends.

I have another present for you, King Balor shouted, demanding her attention. *Can you hear him?*

"Kelcie . . ."

Her father. His whisper daggered her heart. It was so faint, so far away, and filled with so much warmth it made her angry. He hurt so many. Did he expect her to be happy to hear his voice again?

"How is this possible?" Kelcie asked.

Don't lose focus on the prize, Kelcie. You want to take it away from him.

"No. I don't. I don't want it!"

Her breath coalesced, the sparklers drawing a three-dimensional map of a vast, beautiful city. A flame lit at the lowest corner. A sea of fire rolled like a tidal wave through the districts, turning everything to ash. Kelcie heard the screaming. She felt the anguish—so many lost. Her father hurt Niall's father. He did horrible things to innocent people.

"Kelcie . . ." her father pleaded. He sounded so far away.

She spit the only name he deserved. "Draummorc."

He holds the power. He will use it again unless you take it from him.

"Don't listen to him, Kelcie," her father growled. "It was him! It was always him!"

The pipeline shooting in her father's direction exploded. He cried out in pain. King Balor was hurting him.

For what he did he deserves to rot in his prison cell. The evil spirit's sentiments were a haunting reflection of her own. *Prove your worth. Take it from him.*

All at once, feeling returned. There was so much pain. Her leg. Her hand. Her heart. *This isn't real,* she told herself. It was a dream, a nightmare, a lie.

Kelcie screamed.

Balor laughed. *"Trisan."* Three.

Somewhere off to her left, Zephyr shouted, "Kelcie! Snap out of it!"

Her eyes flew open. Her entire leg, grindylows and all, was encased in hard crystal rock. Their tiny limbs were frozen, eyes bulging, teeth and beaks stuck in Kelcie's skin.

"What did they do to me?" Kelcie cried.

"It wasn't the grindylows! It rolled out of there!" Zephyr pointed to where Kelcie had seen the Abyss water.

"It was the eye!" Kelcie panicked. "I heard King Balor. Trisan. This is the third trial! You have to get Scáthach!"

"We can handle this, Kelcie. It's just some kind of crystal." Zephyr took a step back. "I'm going to break it off. Hold on."

"Hold on to what?" Kelcie wasn't about to touch the thorny pookagrass. It was bad enough her leg was a grindylows pincushion.

Zephyr kicked Kelcie's leg so hard the ground quaked. The quartz dented, but instead of breaking off, it sprouted chutes, weaving around Kelcie's other leg, locking the pair together. "Zephyr! You're making it worse!"

Another chute drove up her abdomen, over her shoulder, and down her back.

Zephyr chopped off a section on her back, throwing it in the pond. The crystal floated to the top, chuting in all directions.

"Uh oh!" Zephyr scooped as many snapping grindylows as he could out of the pond before it was completely covered in crystal.

Those left behind were a horrifying picture beneath the quartz, beating the glass ceiling, trying to break free until they stopped, frozen in facets.

"Could you make any more noise?" Niall exclaimed. "You woke—" He took one look at Kelcie and stopped talking.

Brona was right behind him, carrying handfuls of screeching purple mantle hyssop flowers. "Is that gossamer quartz?"

"It's the third trial! I heard Balor. You have to get Scáthach!" Kelcie squirmed.

"This is not a trial. It's not even from Winter," Brona said. "Grows all over the caves beneath the Dandelion Cliffs."

"The grindylows aren't going to last long." Niall pulled a small knife from his shoe. He knelt down beside the pond, reached back to stab when Brona stopped him. "When you cut one facet, two more grow."

"How do we get it off?" Kelcie panicked.

"No idea," Brona said, shrugging.

"Melt it like you melted the steel in the training den," Niall said with confidence.

"Are you sure?" Zephyr asked. "She might melt her feet off, and what about the grindylows?"

Brona peered through the quartz. "They're already dying."

"What?" Their bug eyes started rolling up into the back of their chicken-cat heads. Suddenly Kelcie remembered what Balor said. *Prove your worth. Take it from him.* King Balor wanted her to use her Theran power. But if she didn't, the grindylows would all die!

Kelcie placed her ungloved hand on her quartz-encrusted leg. She took a deep breath, focusing on the bonds in the crystal, willing them to break. Then she whispered, "Theran."

Red ignited beneath her palm, shooting through the crystal formations, bouncing off the facets, leaving a sparkling trail. The crystal turned black and avalanched off in large chunks. The grindylows fell off her leg into a pile, their tiny corpses smelling alarmingly like grilled chicken. The pond melted, but Kelcie's overzealous powers didn't stop there. Before Kelcie could say,

"Nil Theran!" the entire pookagrass patch smoked, turning brown. It was all dead.

Surviving grindylows crawled out of the steaming waters onto the shores, their tiny flippers fanning their beaks, their hind legs kicking air.

Niall helped Kelcie out of the water. "You have bites all over you."

They itched already. "I heard Balor's voice! We have to get Scáthach!"

Roswen rounded the corner and gasped, "Gossamer quartz? Here! In my garden?" She levied her axe-pen. "Which of you did this? Who brought this to school? And who destroyed my beds? Murphy!" Her voice rose to a fevered pitch on Kelcie's name. "Where is your glove?

Kelcie patted her stomach, finding it right where she left it, curled over the top of her sweatpants. She put it on as fast as she could. "We need to speak to Scáthach."

"About why you were in my garden making a huge mess?" Roswen's nostrils flared. "I'll be speaking to her about that. You four, honestly, look at this!"

"It rolled out from the pookagrass," Zephyr said.

"From Abyss water!" Kelcie exclaimed.

"Hold on. I didn't see any Abyss water," Zephyr countered.

"But I did!" Kelcie waded through the dead pookagrass, but there were no signs of it. "It's gone."

Roswen shook her head. "Nice try, Murphy, but gossamer quartz is a Summer nuisance. You invasive weed!" she yelled at the dead pookagrass. "Someone brought this here. Look at the grindylows. Charbroiled. They were supposed to be for a special stew at the end-of-year feast."

"You were going to eat them?" Kelcie asked, disgusted.

"Why do you think we keep them on the farm?" Zephyr asked.

Roswen knelt down beside one of the lucky ones. She pulled out a dropper and bottle of Zinger from a pack on her belt. "This has Crane's hoofprints all over it," she said, dribbling a few drops in its mouth.

"Yes, ma'am," Zephyr agreed.

Brona and Niall exchanged shrugs.

Kelcie would love to let her take the blame, but it wasn't Deirdre. "Please. You have to listen to m—"

"Enough, Murphy." Roswen frowned. "What are you four doing in here anyway?" she asked, continuing to treat the surviving grindylows.

"We need pookagrass and mantle hyssop flowers for a potion assigned in Madame Le Deux's class," Niall explained.

"Madame Le Deux?" Roswen sounded surprised. "A masking potion? Can't remember the last time she had first years making that."

"Do you want us to help?" Kelcie offered, wrinkling her nose at the smoldering corpses and growing cluster of grindylows huddled together beside the pond.

"No. Can't keep you out after curfew. I'll get Coach Blackwell down here." Roswen handed the last bit of the pookagrass to Kelcie. "For your potion."

Kelcie hesitated. "Don't they need it?"

She shoved it into her hand. "Take it. I'll get more planted at midnight. It'll be ready for their breakfast tomorrow. Back to the Dens. Hurry up."

WHEN THEY REACHED Haven Hall, Kelcie said, "We need to talk. You have to believe me. It was the eye." She filled them in on everything, the part about hearing Draummorc, and most importantly, the part about taking the power from him. Kelcie leaned against the stone arch for support. "This was another one of his tests. Summer, Winter, whatever, I know it was."

"I'm sorry I didn't believe you." Zephyr sighed.

"None of us did," Brona said.

"What else was Kelcie supposed to do?" Niall countered.

"How many more are there? And then what happens when the trials are over?" Brona asked. "And where is this stupid eye?"

"There are four," Niall said as if he'd known this all along.

Kelcie stared at him, dumbfounded. "How do you know that?"

"Because there are four elements."

Kelcie's mouth fell open. "You're right. Balor is testing my elemental powers. First air with the wood goblin, then fire with the sylph—"

"And earth with the gossamer quartz," Brona finished.

"If that's true, then water's next, right?" Zephyr asked.

Kelcie laughed. "Good luck with that. I don't have any Caenum powers. According to Ollie, unless I get over my fear of water, I won't. So, I guess that's where this test is going to end anyway."

"Maybe it shouldn't," Niall said with determination.

Did Kelcie really need to point out the obvious? "Niall, this thing killed your father."

"I'm aware." He passed the potion ingredients to Zephyr and set his hand on Kelcie's shoulder. "We don't know where this eye is. Scáthach couldn't find it. But King Balor is still connecting with you. His spirit is still making things happen."

"And your point is?" Kelcie asked, growing impatient.

"The only way to get our hands on the actual eye is if you finish the trials. Then, the fairies will put Winter's plan in motion. And if you're controlling the eye—"

"You think I can destroy it."

Niall nodded as if this wasn't a new thought, as if he planned this all along. This was why Niall didn't want Kelcie kicked out of school. This was why he told her to use her Theran power in the garden. She was angry at him, more than angry, but also terrified.

"You want to let this all play out," Zephyr asked.

"Brilliant." Brona smirked triumphantly.

"No. Not brilliant." If Kelcie did, what would she be giving up? King Balor said it from the beginning, that there was a price to be paid. What if that price was too high? What if it meant the lids opening and people being hurt because of her? "If you haven't noticed, King Balor's evil spirit is in control here, not me. And even if I was, how would I destroy it? Scáthach said it's been around for thousands of years!"

"We'll find a way. We have to finish this!" Niall said emphatically.

"I get you want revenge, Niall, but . . ." Kelcie shook her head. "I don't want to finish this. I want the whole thing to stop. Come up with another plan!"

Brona raised a finger. "Do we tell Scáthach?"

"Tell her what? Roswen didn't believe a word of it," Niall answered.

"All we have are more questions than answers." Zephyr sighed loudly. "We keep this to our fianna, for now."

KELCIE WAITED FOR Brona to get her clothes for the sleepover, then brought her down the fireman's pole. Ollie was waiting. He had snuck some dessert back from dinner and shared it with Brona while Kelcie downed Zinger in a futile attempt to get the grindylow bites to stop itching. It was the first time Kelcie ever saw Brona take a bite of anything remotely unhealthy. Worse, she giggled at every dumb joke Ollie made so he never left them alone until it was lights out.

Brona hopped into the empty bed next to Kelcie's. Kelcie couldn't believe she was thinking this, but she kind of wished that they could be roommates for longer than a night. That would never happen though. Scáthach had been very blunt. They only got one night to hang out, and here they were wasting it, already in bed, too tired to stay up.

Within minutes Brona was grumbling in her sleep, snapping about a loose jig as Kelcie's own slumber-curtain fell. The nightmare began in a familiar place. Cocooned in a flurry of feathers, bathed in warmth, and riddled with pain. Sailing over Boston's wide bay, Kelcie cried, knowing what was coming.

Please, I can't swim! Kelcie pleaded.

Whoever carried Kelcie let go.

Eyes closed. Falling. Screaming. Bracing for the gut-wrenching impact she was never prepared for when it came. Air burst from her lungs. She submerged so deep her ears popped. Confused in the darkness, she didn't know which way was up. The water was so cold it burned.

"Kelcie!" Brona's voice sounded underwater. "KELCIE!"

Kelcie woke up with a start, her brow beaded with sweat.

"You were having a nightmare." Brona sat down on the edge of her bed. "What was it about?"

Kelcie's chest ached from fear. She panted, trying to catch her breath. "The night I was abandoned."

"When you fell in that bay you talked about in Scáthach's office? Niall's pushing you probably freaked out your psyche."

"No. It's always the same nightmare." Kelcie hated talking about it, only with Brona, it felt strangely okay, normal even. She sat up to shift her pillows. "I'm afraid to go back to sleep."

"I've got an idea." Brona ran to the far side of her bed and started pushing it toward Kelcie's.

Excited, Kelcie hopped out of bed and helped. The beds clanked together, side by side, making one big one. They both slid under the covers, inching close to the crack in the middle. On their backs they watched the stars twinkling. Brona called out constellations Kelcie had never heard of as they passed overhead, like Gwyn and Gwyrthur, brothers who fought over the love of a woman, and Corvus, the soul of a giant called Bran.

A strange familiarity, déjà-vu-ish, gave Kelcie goose bumps. She rolled on her side, facing Brona. "Brona, is it possible, like maybe when we were really little, that we knew each other or something?"

Brona's eyelids drooped, and she yawned. "I've had that same feeling since we met. It's been bugging me. I even asked my father last night. He said he didn't know any freckle-faced, red-headed little girls. And that Draummorc never had a daughter, not that he remembered. He said he knew him a long time ago. They both went here, you know."

"Really?" Kelcie glanced around the room as if seeing her den for the first time. "My father lived here in this Den then." Ollie or Killian could be sleeping in his old bed. Her lids grew heavy too, but she worried her subconscious would drag her back to that horrible night. She stiffened, stirring Brona.

"What's wrong?"

"I'm still scared."

Brona found Kelcie's hand. Looping her pinkie through Kelcie's, she held on, like it was the most normal thing to do. "Don't worry. I can fly. I won't let you fall."

23

SKEWERED

TIME MARCHED ON, and with it, Kelcie's luck took a turn for the better. Other than being called a demon now and then, the school bullies were too busy with their own work to bother her. There had been no other insurgents from Winter on campus. No declarations from the eye's voice for trial number four. Kelcie's fear of water might be the one thing that saved her after all.

Without changing seasons, Kelcie marked passing time two ways. First, Killian's nubs had grown five inches into real horns with ringed ridges and deadly sharp points. Ollie explained that by seventeen guys' horns were full grown.

"When do I get mine?" Kelcie had asked him.

He had scoffed at her. "You don't. Girls don't have horns."

Kelcie decided right then and there that if she ever met the person responsible for doling out Fomorian genetics, she would lodge a formal complaint, because that was just sexist.

Second way of marking time, the looming first-year overnight. Scáthach told them little about it, only that failure meant no chance of being asked back for year two. There would be a melee to decide which fianna got to go first, a melee that could happen at any time. Their preceptor was going to thrust it on them, like a pop quiz. That meant preparing every day like it could be the next, leaving the entire first-year class bickering from nervous anxiety and in continual states of exhaustion from over-training.

Powers were allowed in the melee. Chargers, Cats, and Ravens packed the training facility whenever they were out of class. Adders, Niall included, fled into the woods because of the noise. Roswen locked the Saiga space and boarded up the hole in the wall after Rapshider's workmen abandoned him. Not that it mattered. Kelcie was still barred from using her powers without her gloves on.

They did give her more freedom to say the inciting words. But how many times could she light the cauldron fire with her finger in Madame Le Deux's class, or flick a teeny tiny puff of wind in Niall's ear when they grappled in Coach Blackwell's class? Although the latter was amusing. It completely threw him off his game. Kelcie pinned him every time. What could he say? She was blowing in his ear?

But with Willow constantly transforming her arms to silky black wings, and Marta Louisa morphing her legs into panther hindquarters whenever they were ordered to race to Haven Hall after combat class, Kelcie was beginning to resent not being able to take the gloves off.

After Combat, Kelcie, Niall, and Zephyr exited the tower, excited for lunch.

"Anyone seen Brona?" Kelcie asked.

"Yo! Saiga!" the Raven cawed. Her back against a tree, a spear, sword, bow, and three quivers of arrows at her feet, she was battle ready.

"Planning an invasion?" Kelcie asked, jogging to her.

"A girl can only dream, but no. You and I have a date."

"A date for what?" Niall asked.

"Down, boy. Not that kind of date." Brona waved them closer so no one could hear their conversation. She lowered her voice to barely above a whisper. "We have the melee coming and Kelcie needs to be able to take off those gloves."

"Why?" Niall asked.

"No one will be suspecting it," Zephyr answered. "Like having our own secret weapon."

Niall frowned at him. "You know about this?"

Zephyr crossed his arms, a smug smile flirting across his lips. "Brona asked me permission."

Niall shook his head. "I don't like it. What if she damages more school property and gets kicked out? We should ask Scáthach first, and then you can work with her afterward."

Kelcie stomped on Niall's foot.

He hopped, wincing. "Ow! What was that for?"

"For talking about me as if I'm not here. Don't I have a say in this?"

"You want Brona to train you? Is it worth the risk?" Niall asked the same question she had been asking herself.

Kelcie glared at the gloves, nodding. "I'm tired of wearing these handcuffs."

"Air only," Zephyr added. "That's what we agreed."

"Yes, oh mighty Charger," Brona said bowing ridiculously.

"I'll come," Niall volunteered.

"Nope." Brona waved a dismissing finger at him. "We don't need distractions. We need alibis. Go to lunch. Anyone who asks, we went on an extra run or are in the Saiga Den not swimming. Whatever works."

"I got this," Zephyr said, shoving Niall. "Move it, Adder."

Kelcie picked up the sword to help Brona with her loot. "Save me something, Niall. Anything . . . a crumb. . . ."

No. You stamped on my foot. You get nothing. He stuck his tongue out at her.

Brona saddled her bow on her shoulder, slung the quivers' straps on the other arm, then picked up the spear. "This way."

"Where are we going? And what do you need your bow and arrows for?"

"Beyond the Lazy Creek, and to shoot at you."

"What?" Kelcie stumbled over a tree root, nearly stabbing herself with the sword.

Through dense woods with no path, Brona led Kelcie to a part of campus she had never been before. Tree branches grew together, forming makeshift canopies that blocked the sun most of the way. Sweat from combat class dried so quickly that for the first time since coming to AUA, Kelcie was actually cold. Sparrows, finches, and thrushes sang, trading branches. Squirrels the size of cats and chipmunks the size of squirrels sprinted here and there, without a care in the world. The occasional pair of love doves cooed at each other.

"Is this still campus grounds?" Kelcie asked.

"I don't know, actually. But the eagles aren't here, otherwise the smaller birds wouldn't be. Or the rodents. They would eat them. And the spriggans don't like sparrows because their limbs are the perfect size for nest building. I do believe I've found us a very private spot. You're going to love it!"

The spot was an old stone building, although calling it a building was being generous. There was no roof. With four leaning walls in various states of decay, a strong wind was going to bring it down on top of them. Kelcie let Brona go through the empty doorframe first.

"You want to work on air in here?"

Brona dropped her quivers in a corner. "I know. It's perfect."

"Perfect for a funeral."

Kelcie put the sword down near the quivers, leaning it against the wall. Brona slid the bow over her head and pulled an arrow from one of the quivers.

"Take the gloves off."

Kelcie hesitated.

Brona shot an arrow at her. Kelcie barely dove out of the way in time. "Hey! You could've hit me!"

Brona snatched another offending projectile. "I'm going to hit you if you don't take those gloves off!"

The arrow nicked Kelcie's earlobe. Hopping to her feet, Kelcie grabbed her ear, saw blood, and then saw red.

"Are you trying to make me mad?"

"Maybe I am. Not like you can do anything with those stupid gloves on." Brona's lip curled into a taunting sneer. "You're pathetic, and scared."

"I'm not scared," Kelcie said with less conviction than she'd hoped for.

"Wrong." Brona poked Kelcie's nose with her bow. "You're afraid of everything. Afraid of getting kicked out. Afraid of your own power. Afraid you might be Draummorc's daughter, and afraid you might not be because then you'd be back to square one. And more than anything, you're afraid of water. So afraid you have nightmares about falling into it almost every night."

Lesson one, no more sleepovers for Brona.

"You've been letting others tell you how to do things and how to feel each and every day."

"Like who?"

"Killian, for one."

"He's my Alpha. He's supposed to be teaching me. And he knows how to use his elemental powers."

"Which are different from yours. And now Madame Le Deux. She tells you to put on handcuffs, and you do it. No questions asked."

"I have to trust someone, Brona!" Kelcie yelled.

"I know!" she yelled back. "But the person you need to trust most is yourself!"

"What are you talking about? I do trust myself."

"No, you don't. You used to, when I first met you. But you've changed. I heard what you told Scáthach about your life in the human world. Alone. Moving from place to place. Afraid, but surviving. You are a survivor. You're strong. But also angry."

"I have a right to be angry."

"Yeah. You do. But you're not anymore. It has been replaced by fear. Happened the second you hit Scáthach with a wind gust. I mean, she's the best warrior of all time! It was a great move. But you freaked. *I'm so sorry*," she whined, doing an infuriating impersonation of Kelcie. "With every little thing that went wrong you shrank away from who you are. Went utterly soft. Why do you think that is?"

Kelcie tried to answer but Brona held up a hand in her face. "That was rhetorical. I'll tell you why. You're trying so hard to please everyone else that you've forgotten to be true to who you really are."

"You said it yourself. I don't know who I am!"

"I don't mean who your parents are. They don't define you, do they?"

"Are you talking about yourself or me? Because I remember you telling everyone that you trained with your goddess-mom on some hoity-toity island."

Brona let another arrow fly. Kelcie dove out of the way.

"Yes. And I was wrong! It was because of you that I figured out it didn't matter. None of it. Not who I was or who my parents were. You're a pulse elemental who fought off some seriously dangerous Winter creatures—with my help, true, and I guess Niall and Zephyr deserve a few accolades—but I digress. You fought and won. That's you. Who you are. No matter your parents. But it's like you've forgotten."

Kelcie stared at the obsidian rocks on the back of the gloves. "I didn't think about those things. I just did them."

Brona dropped her bow and arrow and threw a punch.

Kelcie blocked it, shoving her off. "Hey!"

Brona launched a side kick at Kelcie's stomach. Kelcie caught her by the calf, twisting, sending her into the overgrown wild-flowers. Worried what Brona was going to do next, Kelcie stayed in a ready stance.

"Exactly! Just like now." Brona hopped up, unfazed, with a blue buttercup in her hair. "Deep down, Murphy, you're a hero."

"Ha! Yeah right." Who was she kidding? "This is your inspiring speech that is going to tame my air powers?"

"It's true. Shocked me too. You're hardwired to act. As my father would say, it's part of your being. Your soul."

"He said that about you. Not me."

"Oh no." She crossed her arms. "I told him all about you. But then he said something useful for once. He said your powers reminded him of the first time I morphed, and *bang*! I knew exactly what to do." She picked up her bow, slid another arrow out of the quiver.

"We're seriously going to keep doing this?" Kelcie had a bad feeling about what came next.

"Remember when you were angry all the time? Filled with delicious rage that turned your Mistral powers up to maximum velocity? You shut down those feelings because that kind of power is scary. And destructive. And it all happened too fast."

Kelcie tested her weight in her stance, ready to dive out of the line of fire. "That's the first thing you've said that I agree with one hundred percent."

"I get it because it happened to me too. I involuntarily morphed on my seventh birthday. It was terrifying."

"You spontaneously crowed?"

"Ravened. Don't confuse us with crows. It's disrespectful." Brona pinned the arrow on the string. "Crows have a different beak. Ours are bigger, curvier, much more graceful. Crows stick to treetops and fly short distances, flapping furiously like idiots. We soar to great heights and with brilliant grace ride the thermals." At Kelcie's confused expression, she added, "The updrafts of warm air. We glide in wide circles without having to flap much at all. It's my favorite thing, riding the thermals."

"I wish I could do that."

Brona smiled a huge smile. "Good, because that's what I'm going to teach you."

"I can't morph."

"No, you can't. But you can fly. That soaring feeling is where I go for focus—for control. When I couldn't morph back to myself, my father explained that it was the universe telling me to fly. He said, *Find the place where you feel perfectly balanced. Ride the wind. And when you feel confident and free, land, holding on to that feeling as tightly as you can. Then, with no fear, only confidence, command your body to morph back.*"

"And it worked? Just like that?" Kelcie had a hard time believing it would be that easy for her.

"Not the first time or second. I partially morphed a few times. Slept with a set of talons and one foot one night, an arm and a wing on another night, but after a while, it became as simple as breathing." Brona looked sternly at Kelcie. "The first part of our challenge is to find your perfectly balanced place."

Kelcie was confused. "Are we going to get to an air lesson any time soon?"

"That's part two. I live on a boat. We talk a lot about wind. Wind is just moving air caused by differences in pressures. My guess, your Mistral power changes air pressure. Your movement I bet should be less thrusting fists out, and more . . ." She held her palms up, facing each other, pressing them together. "Like this, I think. Concentrate your power while pushing your hands together, increasing the pressure. Then decrease as you separate them." She pulled them apart. "Be the pressure. Choose a speed, then send it on its way." She pushed her hands forward.

"That wasn't the way Killian's book demonstrated it. It was all fists and—"

"And didn't work because his powers aren't as strong as yours. So, let's try it my way." Brona paced. "What gives you a serious adrenaline rush? The thing you do that gives you the kind of feeling you never want to end?"

Holding the evil eye. The power riding Kelcie's veins, burning, but in a good way. It was the most alive she'd ever felt. She couldn't tell Brona that, but maybe she could use it.

"I've got it."

"Got, what?"

"I don't want to say."

Brona smirked. "If this is about O'Shea, then by all means, keep it to yourself." She cringed. "Take off your gloves."

Kelcie set them against the wall behind her for safekeeping.

She flexed her fingers. She'd been wearing the gloves so much, her hands felt naked. She had ugly tan lines three-quarters of the way up her fingers.

"Good." Brona smiled wickedly. "Close your eyes."

Kelcie did.

"Take your mind back to that place and time. The very second. Can you see it? Feel it?"

Kelcie took a deep breath. She saw Achila Grimes iced in armor, slamming the eye into Kelcie's hands, freezing them together. In her mind's eye, a blue light flashed. A pinprick at first. Her breath quickened in panic, whistling through her teeth.

Kelcie's hands started shaking.

"Let go of the fear," Brona instructed. "Let the adrenaline crash through you. Relish the stomach tightening that comes with it. Don't let it faze you."

Scenes flashed through her mind. Elliott Blizzard revealing he'd been lying to Kelcie her whole life. Deirdre Crane yanking Kelcie's bough off her neck. Fagan calling her a demon a million times over. She felt it. Overwhelming power and unbridled confidence. "Okay."

"Say the word."

"Mistral." It was more of a whisper.

Brona squealed. "Open your eyes."

Kelcie gasped. "Bah . . . uh . . . holy . . . are you seeing this?" Crackling blue energy surrounded her entire being, like she was the nucleus in the center of an atom.

"Yes!" Brona beamed, as if this were all her doing. She blew on her nails and rubbed them against her heart. "I knew it."

Kelcie shifted her hands so her palms faced each other. The energy ponged back and forth. She pushed them together. Speed accelerated, pressure building on a cushion of air. It felt like squeezing a marshmallow. "Now what?"

"Blow the hair off my face."

Kelcie hesitated. "I don't want to hurt you."

Brona stepped closer. "You won't."

"Okay . . ." Kelcie parted her hands. Pressure decreased to a bending feather. Pivoting her stance, shifting her left hand to face Brona, Kelcie pushed, releasing. A gust shot off, whipping Brona's loose hair harder than Kelcie intended, but she was left standing.

"I did it!" Kelcie hugged Brona.

"You did it." Brona laughed, pushing her away to pick up her bow. "Now, we work. I shoot. You stop me with your powers."

"Say what?" Blood drained from Kelcie's face.

Leather scraped as Brona plucked an arrow from one of her three well-stocked quivers, sending chills up Kelcie's spine.

"Do we have any Zinger with us?" Kelcie backed up, bumping into what was left of the building's western wall. "It's a long way back to campus . . ."

"Zinger, really? Won't help. I hit you in the heart with one of these lovelies," she flicked the head, "you're dead. But it will never get that close. You can do this, Kelcie." Brona threaded the arrow. "Go back to your Niall happy place. I'll wait."

Kelcie closed her eyes. When she opened them, Brona didn't hesitate. She released.

"Mistral," Kelcie yelled. With a quick hand sweep, she sent the arrow off course.

It plinked off the wall.

"You could've killed me!"

"No, Saiga brain, I couldn't have. You didn't let me. And lookie lookie, the ruins are still standing." She cupped her ear. "I'm waiting for another thank you."

The walls were still standing and Kelcie was still alive. "I really did it." She stared at her hands.

"You have to learn to do it without closing your eyes. That's death in battle."

"How do I do that?"

"Sense memory. Memorize that feeling until it comes back to you instinctually." Brona picked up another arrow. "Ready?"

Kelcie shifted her feet, waved her hands, leaving a trail of blue sparks. She smiled at Brona. "Bring it on."

24

ICE CAPADES

AFTER TWO HOURS, Kelcie packed up Brona's weapons, flinching at the drying cuts on her shoulders and legs. She managed to bat away arrows straight at her, but needed way more practice if she was going to impress anyone at the melee. The last thing she did before she left was put on her gloves, hating the feeling of the obsidian draining her, but there was no getting around wearing them.

"I wish we could stay longer," Kelcie said.

Brona slung her bow over her shoulder. "We need to get back. I haven't read the chapter for Le Deux's class."

"What chapter?" Kelcie asked, horrified.

"I guess you have to read it too." She laughed.

As they started back, the golden sun dipped near five o'clock, that was if Kelcie was reading it correctly. There were no clocks at the Academy. No bells chiming to start or end class. No phones to check. Telling time was done by the sun and moon, day and night. Kelcie wasn't very good at it. They could be missing dinner. Her stomach growled in protest.

"Glad Le Deux moved class to after dinner tonight," Brona said, passing her the sword.

A subtle thumping tapped to the beat of Kelcie's pace. "Do you hear that?"

"Hear what?" Brona tilted her head, listening.

It was still there, a smothered, repeating thump.

"It's coming from over here." Kelcie turned back toward the direction they just came.

Brona's footsteps jogged after her. "I don't hear anything, and you're going the wrong way."

"I know . . ." After a minute, the banging was so loud, Kelcie swore she was standing on top of it. "You don't hear that?"

"No. Nothing. And I'm ravenous."

Brona spun around to leave only to have her feet slip out from under her. She landed hard on her back. "Ow!"

"Is that . . ." Kelcie knelt beside where Brona fell. She brushed off leaves, moss, and dirt, finding a cold slippery surface. "It's ice . . . only . . ." She stared at her own reflection framed in a smokey haze. "It's tinted. I can't see through it."

Brona's reflection appeared beside Kelcie's.

Thump.

Kelcie pressed her ear to it. "Something is beating down there."

Brona lay on her belly, putting her ear to it. Her mouth opened and shut several times before she got up, nonplussed. "I don't hear anything. Looks like an old piece of sea glass."

"Oh my gosh!" The beat grew louder and faster. Kelcie's heart raced, catching up to it. "It's not sea glass! This is the stuff that covered the eye in the museum when Grimes took it out of the crate! I'm positive!"

Kelcie heard a deep, gravelly growl that had the same chilling effect as a spider crawling up her back. Her neck stiffened. Her shoulders lifted around her ears.

"It's the eye!" Kelcie pounded the ice with her fists. "What if the ice fairy hid it here when Scáthach searched the school?" She stomped on it, but it wouldn't break. The ice was too thick.

"Only one way to find out . . ." Brona morphed her foot. She scraped her talons across the ice, carving long, snaking grooves.

The ice melted, but not to water. It skipped liquid, moving directly to gas, just like in the museum.

Swallowed by black smoke, Kelcie coughed so hard she couldn't speak. Her head fogged. Her limbs numbed.

Brona was coughing too. Then she slumped.

"Brona . . ." Kelcie's eyes watered. Trunks danced the cha-cha.

And then the lights went out.

KELCIE, WAKE UP," she heard Niall say. But she didn't want to wake up. Everything hurt. A tongue licked her. Her stomach . . . she swallowed hard, but there was no holding back the tidal wave of nausea. She turned over and puked.

"Ew," Zephyr crooned. "Brona, come on, Raven. Up. Up."

"Just leave me. I didn't read the chapter." Brona sounded like she swallowed a grindylow.

Striker rubbed his side against Kelcie, yipping.

"I be—" Kelcie vomited again.

Niall nicely held Kelcie's hair back until she stopped retching and opened her eyes. Things slowly came into focus. Trees. Darkness. Striker's white muzzle. Zephyr's torch. Niall's concerned magenta stare.

"It's night?" Kelcie tried to stand but her knees gave out.

Niall wove his arm around her, keeping her upright. "Almost curfew."

"How did you find us?" Brona asked.

"We were worried when neither of you showed up to Le Deux's class. She dismissed us to go find you. She didn't want you getting in trouble with Scáthach. We found Striker's trail at the edge of the woods you two walked into and figured he was looking for you too. What happened?"

"What happened?" Kelcie repeated. "The eye." Clarity returned. She stamped the ground, trying to find the spot where the black ice had been.

Brona crawled over. She sat cross-legged at Zephyr's feet, holding his legs to stay upright. "It was all good until Saiga lost her mind . . ."

Brona filled them in, beginning when they parted ways, taking them through the grueling yet highly successful workout she put Kelcie through.

All the while, Kelcie stomped and slid her feet, finding nothing but dirt. No black ice. No eye. It was gone.

"In the museum, the eye was encased in something like smokey dry ice." She looked back at her fianna who stood there watching. "Brona scraped it, and whoosh. Black smoke. Lights went out."

"You think whoever has the eye was hiding it here?" Niall asked.

"That's what Saiga said right before . . ." Brona groaned. "Man, I don't feel so good." It was her turn to throw up.

"So gross." Zephyr slammed a hand over his eyes. "We need to go back. It's really getting late. We can't be out after curfew."

Kelcie opened her mouth to argue, but Zephyr shut her down. "No. If it was here, it's gone by now. And I'm not so sure that whatever you scraped wasn't a fungus. Slick silver is cold and slippery."

"And uses a potent toxic gas as a defense mechanism," Niall added.

Brona wrinkled her nose. "Can we please stop saying fungus or fungi or anything beginning with *fung*?"

"It wasn't a fungus!" Kelcie exclaimed.

Zephyr's right. We can come back tomorrow. Together this time. Niall gave her a resigned stare.

Striker whined his agreement with Niall.

"Okay. Fine."

But Kelcie wasn't okay. She was right, and she would return tomorrow and the day after that, and the day after that. For the rest of the school year if that's what it took. And when she found the eye, she would destroy it. But even as she thought it, hesitation crept in.

25

TAKE THE PLUNGE

OVER THE NEXT two weeks, Kelcie returned to the woods many, many times, but never heard the sound again. Niall suspected the thumping was her own heart after the massive workout, first time controlling her air powers and all. But still, doubt lingered.

Her fianna had transformed the old building into a makeshift clubhouse to prep for the melee. Zephyr had a stack of boulders and anvils to lift. Niall brought down smaller equipment—a handful of knives, a basket of throwing stars, bowls of stink pellets he had made from leftover wood goblin dung—weapons light enough for him to lift with telekinesis.

Brona and Kelcie worked outside the building, so as not to accidentally kill Zephyr or Niall. Early on, Brona had shot arrows at Kelcie. But in recent days, Brona changed up the curriculum, pushing Kelcie headfirst into offense training with high-velocity air swipes and concentrated airballs, which, in their invisible air form, were impossible to see coming.

Kelcie and Brona returned to the clubhouse in time to see Niall stretch for a knife, snagging a stink pellet instead. He flicked it at the ground, groaning in frustration.

"The melee's tomorrow, and my telekinesis has a mind of its own!" He kicked the grip. "What time is it?"

Brona pinched her nose. "Dhat's what we were comin' to tell you. Time to go."

Zephyr set down a two-hundred-pound boulder, causing a small tremor and the building to creak. "Morrow Lake time."

The hoffescus stone needed to be added to their masking potion before midnight.

"Who wants to dive for the stone?" Zephyr asked as they started back.

"Not me," Kelcie said.

"I'm not the best swimmer," Niall added.

Not surprisingly, Brona volunteered. "I'll go."

MORROW LAKE WAS on the far side of campus, beyond the stables. By the time they got there, the other first years were leaving. Only a few stragglers remained.

"What's going on?" Zephyr asked Mellis Gear, fianna five's Charger.

In blue trunks with a towel around him, Gear shivered uncontrollably. His orange eyes were bloodshot, and goose bumps blanketed his beefy brown arms and chest. "Th-they're n-not d-d-down there."

"The w-water is f-f-freezing too," Gabby Arnold complained, tightening the straps on her red robe.

"This is some k-kind of joke Madame Le Deux is p-p-playing on us," Fagan griped, joining them.

"Did anyone get to the bottom?" Niall asked, staring at the dark lake.

David Dunn shook his head, squeezing out his blond ponytail. "Too deep."

"I was afraid of that." Niall raked his fingers through his hair.

The others all gave up and left, leaving fianna three with a quandary.

"Maybe if none of the fiannas have one, Madame Le Deux will just give them to us," Kelcie said.

"Oh please." Brona kicked off her shoes and morphed. She flew to the center of the lake, then straight up about twenty feet where she transformed mid-plummet, diving stick straight into the water.

Kelcie gripped her hands tightly, her fingers scraping the stone in her gloves as the splash smoothed over. The lake was so dark, she couldn't see Brona at all.

An explosion shook the ground. A giant cloud mushroomed over the Nether Tower. The eagles raced overhead, flocking to the scene, piping a siren's call.

"Should we . . ." Niall started, but Kelcie never heard him finish his sentence.

A curtain fell. In the familiar hollow darkness, King Balor's eye opened, his power splitting, feeding both Kelcie and her father yet again, only this time the tendrils to her thickened, and those to her father thinned. She was winning . . .

Cheturi. Balor rattled inside Kelcie's brain.

Four.

Get in the water, Kelcie.

"Stay away from her!" Kelcie's father growled, then suddenly screamed in pain so loud Kelcie felt it in her bones.

There is nothing to fear, Kelcie.

"I will never get in the water. Never!"

King Balor had the nerve to laugh. *You will do as I say, or your friends will suffer the consequences.*

Kelcie's vision returned. She stepped farther away from the water. "No-no-no! This can't be happening!" She grabbed Niall's arm. "I heard him."

"Who?"

"King Balor! This is the fourth trial! We have to get Brona out of there. He's going to hurt her!"

"Hurt her, how?" Zephyr panicked.

"I'll get her." Niall's brow creased. Precious seconds ticked by but Brona never surfaced.

The bushes on the far side of the lake shushed as three eels slithered out, doubling in size before entering the water.

Uh oh, Niall croaked.

"Brona! Get out!" Kelcie yelled.

Brona finally surfaced, raising her fist into the air. "I got it!" She dipped, submerging. Then popped up, flailing.

"Hel—!"

She went under again.

Zephyr ripped his shirt and shoes off as he sprinted into the water. He swam to where Brona went under and dived. Brona popped up twenty feet away, thrashing, gasping for air, an eel curled over her shoulder, dragging her back down. Then Zephyr surfaced, wrestling with an eel wrapped around his neck.

"I've got an idea!" Niall kicked his shoes off, diving in.

"This can't be happening . . ." Kelcie watched in horror. She had never felt so helpless in her life.

"What do I do?"

Trade places with them, Kelcie, King Balor instructed. *Fear nothing. Not water, not air, not fire, or earth. You are the heir. You will wield my power. You will do* my *bidding.*

Kelcie slapped her hands over her ears. "Get out of my head!"

Brona surfaced with the eel coiled around her body, rolling with it, stealing a breath before submerging again. The eel was tightening around Zephyr's throat; he was losing the battle, rasping breaths. Niall treaded water, hand raised, fist clenched. He jerked his arm, using his telekinesis. The eel choking the life out of Zephyr gave an inch. Another yank, and it unraveled from his neck, disappearing under the water.

"Brona!" Kelcie inched into the lake, her shoes submerging.

The boys spun, looking for the Raven, and were jarringly dragged under.

The water stilled.

None emerged.

"Niall! Zephyr! Brona! No! Please! Stop this!"

You can save them, King Balor hummed.

Kelcie ripped off her gloves and walked into the water.

That's it, he sniggered.

She sidestepped, arms out, moving deeper into the water until she slipped off a shelf. Her feet no longer touching the bottom, she panic-doggie-paddled, somehow making it into the middle of the lake. "I can't swim!"

You don't have to.

She choked on lake water, bobbing under, submerging once, twice. On the third time, she instinctively opened her eyes. The eels snaked circles around her. They doubled in size again, now twice as long as Kelcie was tall. One ensnared her body, trapping her arms. Another captured her legs, immobilizing her. The last whipped back and forth, growing larger by the second, keeping Niall, Zephyr, and Brona from getting to her.

Down-down-down, she descended to the murky depths. Mud stirred, making it difficult to see. Air escaped her lungs in tiny bubbles until it was gone. Kelcie shook her head, straining against the eels. None of her powers, controllable or not, were going to save her now.

Breathe, Kelcie.

Having expected to hear King Balor's nasty growl, she was surprised by Niall's voice.

You have to breathe! He yelled at her. He tried to swim toward her, making it close enough that she could see the anguish in his face. *Please . . .*

Kelcie wheezed her last, muttering, "*Caenum.*"

Green sparks lit her last exhale. Her lungs relaxed, vacating for a long overdue nap. The deep-seated desperation for air fled. She was breathing—no—she didn't need to breathe.

The eels released her. Niall pulled Kelcie out of the way as the largest unhinged its jaws, but it wasn't after her. One after another, from larger to smaller, the other two swam into the enormous gawped jaws, voluntarily being swallowed whole, like a Russian nesting doll. Then, the monster-sized eel went after Zephyr.

Brona's feet morphed. Her talons scraped slimy skin as it zoomed by, leaving a bloody spill. Zephyr landed a solid punch on the gaping wound. The serpent's body seized, recoiling, then surfaced long enough for Niall to pull a long dagger from a scabbard beneath his shirt.

When the eel submerged, the boys attacked. Zephyr punched its nose at the same time Niall sliced off its tail. It thrashed, its body twitching on the surface, slithering for shore.

Niall, Zephyr, and Brona were stellar swimmers, beating Kelcie to shore by minutes. When she crawled out, still shaking, the eel was gone.

"Where—where did it go?" Kelcie panted.

The silence was ominous. It was still out there, somewhere.

"I take it that was trial number four?" Brona asked.

"Yes." Kelcie spit lake water.

"How do you feel?" Niall pressed.

"The same. I don't feel any different."

Zephyr looked nervous. "What does that mean?"

Kelcie shrugged. "I don't know."

Zephyr glanced around. "Scout, Brona. See if the eye is around here."

Brona circled, returning quickly.

"It's not here. No one is. There's a massive fire at the Nether Tower."

"Let's go!" Zephyr cried.

Brona flew, while Kelcie and Niall sprinted, trying to keep up with Zephyr and failing miserably.

"Niall, do you think whoever has the eye can open the lids now?"

"No. Remember, Scáthach said it has to be the heir. But what that does mean is that we can expect a visit from whoever has it sometime soon." Niall smiled.

"How can you be happy about this? Did you not hear what those fairies did to me the last time I saw them?"

"It's going to be okay."

"No. No, it's not."

The fire was almost out when she and Niall arrived. The entire student body watched Ollie hover a rain cloud over the Nether Tower. The roof was gone, smoke billowing out the loops.

"I'm going to speak to Scáthach," Kelcie said.

Niall followed her.

They passed Roswen huddled with Rapshider, taking copious notes on her clipboard as the old troll grumbled with gusto.

"Yes! That's exactly what I'm thinking. Something modern. Raise the roof, put in soundproofing—"

Scáthach was speaking to Madame Le Deux and Coach Blackwell.

"Unbelievable." Their preceptor shook her head. "Seems I'm destined to have an entire new campus by the end of the year."

"Eet was a seemple acceedent. They deedn't mean to do eet," Madame Le Deux explained. "Haytreed een leequeed form ees potent. All the feeleengs, a leetle fire, and"—she shrugged nonchalantly—"kaboom."

"Your *acceedent* blew the roof off my training tower!" Blackwell snapped. He rubbed his hairy cheeks, leaving sooty streaks in his beard. "How about I use your classroom for grappling for the next two months?"

"Wouldn't eet be more practeecal to do that sort of theeng on a lawn?" Le Deux stepped toward him, wielding her bony finger. Coach Blackwell slid backward, bumping into Roswen. "There are fields all over thee place. We're standeeng on one right now!"

Ollie waved the cloud away and jogged over. "Fire's out."

"Well done, Lynch," Coach Blackwell grunted, locked in a staring competition with Madame Le Deux.

"Murphy, did you need something?" Scáthach asked.

"Why are you and the rest of your fianna all wet, and where are your gloves?" Roswen asked, padding over.

"Ah, zee hoffescus stones," Le Deux crooned, joining the conversation. "Deed you get one?"

"Yep." Brona shook her leg. The hoffescus stone dropped from the bottom of her sweatpants. She picked it up. "We were the only ones."

Le Deux tapped Brona on the head. "Good, deenka."

Kelcie cleared her throat. "Scáthach, we need to speak with you."

Scáthach frowned down at her, her tightly pressed lips quirking with anticipation. "Retrieve your gloves. I'll see you and your fianna at the Shadow directly."

THE SUN SET behind the Shadow, casting an inviting orange halo over the island that was beautiful but did nothing to settle Kelcie's nerves. Scáthach was on the Bridge of Leaping, waiting for them.

"Why such long faces?" Scáthach asked. "Tomorrow's the melee. I would think you'd be huddled, strategizing, or resting up."

"Ma'am, we have something to report." Zephyr stiffened to attention.

Her arms crossed, Scáthach remained unnervingly silent as he told her about the eels, Kelcie hearing King Balor's voice, and their theory that it wanted her to use all four of the elemental powers, which she had now done. As Charger, it was Zephyr's job to speak for the fianna, and he had gotten much better at it. All facts, no emotion. Kelcie probably would've cried reliving the brush with drowning. As it was, when he explained that he and the others would've died if Kelcie hadn't entered the water and sparked her water powers, she teared up.

Scáthach gripped the bridge's railing, staring at the churning waters below.

"Will you inform the Queen's High Command? Has Draummorc been interrogated?" Niall asked, his voice oddly authoritative.

Scáthach turned to face them, nodding. "He has. Nothing to report there. And yes. I will communicate with the High Guard directly. I suspect we'll be hosting visitors from Summer City in the next few days. They'll likely wish to speak to you, Murphy."

Kelcie felt sick. "Will they make me leave school?"

Scáthach clasped her hands behind her back. "Let's not dwell on that."

Easy for her to say.

"Whoever has the eye will be coming for you, Murphy. We must allow this to play out in order for them to show their hand. Then we capture them, and the eye."

"It's the only thing to do," Niall said, acting as if this wasn't his plan all along.

Kelcie felt like a worm on the end of a fishhook. "So, I'm bait."

"Murphy, the Alphas and teachers will be on watch. But this confrontation has been looming since you agreed to the challenge. A destiny of your own making. The fairies tricked you into this, and you have a right to feel trapped. It's Winter's way. They will stop at nothing, even using a child. But it changes nothing. Do you have the strength to stand up with your fianna and face your destiny?"

"I don't know," Kelcie answered because it was the truth.

"Yes, you do," Brona said, salivating for a fight.

"We got you," Zephyr added.

We won't let you fail, Niall said.

Kelcie wished she had their confidence.

"I will escort you back to Haven Hall, and then speak with the teachers and Alphas. You four should get some rest. The melee begins at dawn."

26

MELEE

KELCIE WOKE UP the next morning trying not to think about the eye. Or the fact that Winter would be coming for her any day now. But it was all she could think about. What scared her most of all was that her fianna was in the middle of this. Every trial put them in peril, and whatever came next would be no different. Her father had been right all along. She should've left when he told her to.

Her father.

Draummorc.

Did he say that because he didn't want her to take the power of the eye from him? Or did he really care about her? She tried to push that thought out of her mind, but her heart refused to let it go.

Kelcie met her fianna on Hawthorn Field with her sword and shield in hand. In only her sweats, she felt very underdressed. The others wore armor. Stunning bronze helmets with braided decorative designs. Matching forearm and calf guards. Leather chest plates over their T-shirts. Even Zephyr had a hand-me-down set from a great-grandfather.

Only one weapon was allowed, and everyone chose swords, except Brona. Her quiver full, she planned to show off today, and Kelcie couldn't wait to see her in action.

Of the four Cats in the first-year class, Zephyr heard from Regan who heard from Diccon Wilks (at the weekly Alpha reports to Scáthach) that only two could fully shift, Marta Louisa and, shockingly, Gabby Arnold. Which also explained why only those two wore special back scabbards to harness their swords so they could easily shift.

Kelcie helped Niall strap on his chestplate. The leather stiff and polished to a shine, it looked brand new. Stamped into the middle was a family crest with the O'Shea name inscribed in a ribbon. He had a special piece for his handless arm, a leather guard with a cup on the end, topped with a metal cap. He jabbed with it a few times, testing it.

"Feels good."

Coach Blackwell called Kelcie over. At his feet were several charred pieces of armor.

"These survived the fire. Smell of smoke, but still sturdy. Choose some. Return them after the melee clean."

"Thank you!" Kelcie strapped on a chest plate that was a little too big and smelled like barbecued ribs, but she was happy to have some protection.

Niall picked up a tarnished helmet and plopped it on her head. "Very nice."

"How can anyone see out of these?" Kelcie lifted it up.

The whistle blew.

Kelcie and Niall jogged over to Brona and Zephyr, who were already on the field, staring down their classmates. All eyes turned to Scáthach. She stood on top of a freshly built hill.

"This is a defining moment for all of you at the Academy for the Unbreakable Arts. It is time to test your training in an actual battle. Fianna will be pitted against fianna in a match of Queen of the Hill. One fianna defending." She nodded to Fagan, indicating they earned top spot. "The other four attacking, all vying for the throne. Once disarmed, you are OUT. I don't want any extra bloodshed." Scáthach rubbed her hand along her chin.

"As you are well aware, the winning fianna receives the honor of going on the first overnight, but what you don't know is that the first overnight begins tomorrow morning."

Excitement spread. Swords beat shields.

"Fianna one, take your position."

Scáthach stepped aside for Tad to stand on the X at the top of the hill. Kelcie could barely see his face beneath his massive helmet. He raised his fist. Willow, Marta Louisa, and David fanned out, each taking a ready stance on a different side of the hill.

"You make a lovely queen," Zephyr called to him.

Tad blew him a kiss.

As Zephyr turned, his face fell into a deep, deep scowl. "Her majesty is about to lose his head. Huddle up."

Fianna three formed a tight circle.

"We stick to the plan. All the other fiannas will be racing up the hill to challenge. We let them wear down the Queen and his ladies in waiting. Kelcie, don't take off your gloves until—"

"You give the signal. I know."

Brona smirked a smile. "This is going to be fun."

Nervous adrenaline pumping, Kelcie wholeheartedly disagreed.

"Prepare!" Scáthach called from the sidelines.

Shields and swords raised, legs bending, ready to run, fiannas chanted their numbers.

"Attack!"

Battle cries sounded. The field erupted in chaos as fiannas charged the hill. Some stopped to fight each other, leaving half the class embroiled midway up.

Scáthach wasted no time calling out the names of the disarmed. "Eryn Hansen, out. Ginger McKnight, out! Igor Lopchick, out. Gareth McKnight, join your sister! Move, people! Off the hill!"

Fianna five's Charger, Mellis Gear, broke through the lines with Gabby Arnold at his side. Marta Louisa transformed into a lion and pounced. Gear slid down the hill, losing his sword.

"Gear, you're out!" Scáthach called.

Before Gabby could get near David, he kicked her shield so hard she dropped it. Gabby's yellow eyes wild, she saddled her sword, shrank to a spotted lynx, and pounced. She leaped over his shield, onto his chest, knocking him down, then morphed back, pulling her dagger, ready to strike. His eyes narrowed. Gabby fell off him, losing her weapon, holding her head, tearing in pain.

"What's Dunn doing?" Kelcie asked Niall.

"The Scream," Niall explained. "Gabby got too close. Dunn can't talk to anyone unless they're within a foot of him."

"Arnold, out. Rose, out! Webb, out. Petrov, out!" Scáthach rattled off.

Kelcie saw David narrow his eyes at Sanura Shaker next. She grabbed her head, wincing long enough for David to side kick her sword out of her hand.

"You've got Dunn," Kelcie said to Niall.

"Works for me." Niall swung his sword in a circle, itching to go. "Chike . . ."

Zephyr nodded to Kelcie.

She slid her gloves off, tucking them in the back of her sweatpants, careful to keep her hands hidden behind her shield.

"You've got this," Brona said, swatting her on the shoulder with her bow.

"Let's go, fianna three! Take that hill!" Zephyr raised his sword and charged.

Kelcie jumped over Sanura, heading straight for Fagan, but Willow got in her way. Metal clanked. Their swords locked, Willow threw a vicious front kick, driving Kelcie down the hill, nearly ripping her sword from her hand. Kelcie went to drop her shield, ready to blow Willow out of the way, but her arm got caught in the strap.

Talons shredded the back of Kelcie's sword hand at the same time as Willow's blade slammed down on Kelcie's shield, jarring it loose.

"Thanks!" Kelcie let it fall.

"No, thank you!" Willow side kicked her middle, bending Kelcie over.

She barely ducked Willow's next thrust and was forced to stumble backward, retreating.

She glimpsed Brona and Marta Louisa facing off nearby. Her bow and quiver harnessed to her back, Brona morphed into her Raven form. At the same time Marta Louisa turned into a sleek jaguar. Brona swooped, scraping the jaguar's back, lifting off before Marta Louisa's swat could come anywhere close to her. Brona morphed a few feet from the ground, pinning two arrows, letting them fly. The jaguar dodged one, but not the other. Marta Louisa transformed with an arrow sticking out of her right shoulder. She ripped it out without flinching and pulled her sword.

But Brona was just too fast. She flipped over her, her pinned arrow grinding into Marta Louisa's back. The whole thing was over in seconds.

"Lopez, you're out!" Scáthach called.

Willow attacked in a chaotic blur of thrusts, jabs, swipes leading to a sweep that dropped Kelcie on her back.

"You're going back to Chawell Woods on a stretcher." Willow lifted her foot to stamp on Kelcie's sword hand, but Kelcie hopped up, thrusting, forcing Willow to block with her shield. Kelcie's other hand spun air.

"Mistral!"

Wind sliced across Willow's back. Springy brown ringlets fell to the ground.

Willow gasped, "My hair!" Screaming like a banshee, she raced at Kelcie. A well-timed sidestep and planted heel was all it took for Willow to trip, her momentum being her own worst enemy.

On her way down, Kelcie hurled a windball, hitting her midback. Willow slid down the rest of the hill on her stomach. Kelcie was there when the Raven rolled over, the tip of her sword hovering over Willow's chest.

"Hawkins, out," Scáthach bellowed.

Kelcie rushed back into battle, finding Niall and David in the middle of a heated fight.

Shields gone, sword against sword, they volleyed. Dunn swung a two-handed downward strike that Niall blocked with the metal plate on his arm guard, but Dunn continued to press, leaning into the downward slope of the hill, sending Niall to his knees. Kelcie panicked until she realized he did it on purpose. In a brilliant move, he pushed, sliding the metal cap along the blade, then used his sword like a staff, shoving Dunn off balance. Dunn tumbled down the hill.

Niall didn't let up. He chased after Dunn, stomping on his back before he could get up, pressing the tip of his sword between David's shoulder blades.

"Dunn. Out," Scáthach called.

Kelcie, Niall, and Brona hiked the hill, heading for Zephyr, who was going one on one with Fagan. Heavy clanks on shields sounded like giants swinging metal baseball bats at each other. But Fagan showed signs of tiring. Sweat beading down his face, shoulders drooping, Fagan plowed into Zephyr with his shield.

Zephyr swept, latching his foot around Fagan's ankle, taking his feet out from underneath him. Fagan went down hard, still holding on to his sword, but it was over. Zephyr stepped on his wrist, ripped the weapon out of his grip, and held it up in triumph!

"That's right, AUA first years! Zephyr Chike and fianna three are the Queen of the Hill!"

He stabbed Fagan's sword into the dirt.

Scáthach blew her whistle. "Well done, all of you. Fianna three will be the first to go on the overnight."

Some grumbled, but most everyone clapped, Gabby Arnold hardest of all. Except Tad Fagan, of course, who stayed down, pretending he was too injured to get up.

"The rest of you will go one a week, in numerical descent. All of you are dismissed, except fianna three."

The others left the field.

"Murphy, did I see you use your air powers on Hawkins?"

"Yes, ma'am," Brona answered for her. "I taught her. She was good, wasn't she?"

"Mistral only," Zephyr blurted.

"That is what you've been doing in Atrecus' old place in the Fringe." Scáthach hummed, her index finger falling on her pressed lips.

"Killian and Ollie's grandfather?" Kelcie asked.

"He used to be a teacher here." Her tone was laced with regret. "I was impressed, Murphy, and given time I have every confidence you'll conquer the others as well. You have your gloves?"

"Yes, ma'am," Kelcie said. She pulled them out and put them on, cringing at the tug she felt in her belly.

"Good. Take it slow. Fianna three, as I said, you'll be leaving tomorrow morning. You can bring nothing but the clothes on your backs. And trust me when I tell you there is nothing you can do to prepare. Get some rest. You're going to need it tomorrow."

27

A NOT—SO—DESERTED ISLAND

IT DIDN'T TAKE long to get ready to leave the next morning. Scáthach and Coach Blackwell were waiting for Kelcie and her fianna beside the Sidral. An armload of weapons lay at Blackwell's feet, a bow and arrow quiver, an axe, a spear, and a dagger.

Scáthach checked the morning sun. "It's getting late."

"It's barely dawn," Kelcie yawned.

"It's getting late where you're going." Scáthach held her hand out. "Pass me your silver boughs."

One by one, they turned them over, except Kelcie. She gripped the charm in her gloved hand. Her father was alive, and traitor to the Lands of Summer or not, the charm was her only key to the Otherworld, and him. Taking it off was a nonstarter.

"You can't take it with you on the overnight. Those are the rules. If you don't hand it over, fianna three fails," Scáthach explained.

It'll be okay, Niall promised.

Kelcie had a bad feeling he was wrong, but she untied the leather strap just the same, and reluctantly handed it over.

"This will be a test of your strength as a fianna," Scáthach explained. "I'm sending you to a small island called Tech Gaoth. Each of you will have a specific task to perform on this journey, something cooked up for you as individuals as you work together for the common goal: to get to the silver bough at the very top of the mountain, hanging from a branch of an ancient oak Sidral, one of the oldest in all of the Otherworld. That bough used on that Sidral will return you home. You simply have to get there."

"What happens if we can't?" Kelcie asked.

"We'll come and get you," said Coach Blackwell, handing Brona her bow and quiver. "But that would mean you failed."

He gave Kelcie a spear, Niall an axe, and Zephyr a sword.

"A spear?" Kelcie questioned.

"I'm giving you different weapons because on missions it is rare that one solely needs a sword," Blackwell explained. "And Scáthach allows only one each."

Scáthach continued, "Remember your training. Work together. Listen to your Charger."

Their preceptor gave Zephyr a final "you-got-this" swat on the back and set her blooming bough against the tree.

The trunk shrieked and unzipped.

One at a time, fianna three jumped into the bright yellow goo.

A LL FOUR FELL out of the Sidral at once, landing on top of each other in a giant whining pile.

"Stop moving!" Zephyr griped, his voice coming from under Niall's armpit.

"You people really need to watch your sugar intake! Get off me," Brona barked at all of them from the bottom.

With each attempt to get up, Kelcie got sucked back down. She finally backed out, crushing Niall's glasses, and promptly skidded across a patch of ice into a mound of snow.

"Is that frozen tundra?" Niall gasped, shivering.

"Snow!" Kelcie squeaked, ripping off her gloves. She packed a hunk of frozen white bliss into a snowball and launched it at Niall, pegging him in the face. His mouth fell open, laughing, and he started making his own.

"I want some of that." Zephyr ran over, scooped a huge heap, and dumped it on Brona's head.

Brona gasped. "It's so cold!"

"How is Scáthach doing this?" Zephyr asked.

"Illusionary magic. I've read about it. None of it is real," Niall explained.

"Who cares? It feels real!" Kelcie hit him in the side of the head with another snowball. "Who knew the overnight was going to be so much fun?"

The tree unzipped again. A golden-brown sea eagle escaped the Sidral before the trunk solidified. It soared overhead, circled, and landed in a nearby tree.

"She's watching," Brona warned.

"Where'd it go?" asked Zephyr, worried.

Kelcie pointed.

The large bird's golden eyes lit up like a camera flash as it locked on them. Kelcie put her gloves back on.

Zephyr padded a few feet beyond the Sidral. "Watch out over here. Massive drop."

Kelcie peeked over. It was at least a hundred feet down to the angry white-capping water below.

Gray clouds hung low overhead. Freezing wind blustered off the ocean, adding another layer to Kelcie's goose bumps. The forest before them was dense, the trees barren, their branches straight and stiff. They looked like corpses. No birds chirped. No rodents scurried. Other than the sea eagle, there was no life at all—at least, not that Kelcie could see. It felt more like a graveyard than a sleeping forest waiting for spring.

"Scout, Brona," Zephyr said in his Charger voice.

Glossy black feathers smoothed over Brona's crown. Her Raven form took off, flapping hard against the fierce wind, then soared out over the angry sea. She vanished in a swell of chilling fog.

Kelcie looked over her shoulder, clocking the sea eagle's gimlet stare.

The clouds let go, not just rain, but hard chunky sleet, pounding the ground. Niall looked up with a huge smile on his face as if it were raining marshmallows, until a hard ice drop smacked him in the forehead.

"Ow . . ."

The ground rocked and rose under their feet. Trees creaked and shifted, swapping places like castling pieces on a chess board. The wet ground opened up beneath them, taking Kelcie's footing with it.

She slipped into the deep crack, flailing for anything to stop her fall, finding nothing but air.

"I've got you!" Niall caught her wrist. "Hold on!" he cried over the loud, heavy rain. The earth shook even harder like it was trying to eat her, then suddenly stopped.

Zephyr reached down. "Give me your other hand!"

She tried but everything was slippery from the rain, and her hand kept skating off.

"Stop the rain!" Niall challenged.

The thought never occurred to her. "I can try." Kelcie used her teeth to pull off the glove on her free hand. She reached up the way Ollie did. Lightning spiderwebbed. Thunder cracked so hard Kelcie's heart skipped a beat.

With a mouthful of glove, she called, *"Nil caenum!"* It came out more like *eel came man.*

The rain came down harder, her supposed connection to water literally laughing in her face.

"Give me your other hand!" Zephyr yelled again, reaching down as far as he could, but it wasn't far enough. "Climb, Saiga!"

With Niall's grip cutting off her circulation, Kelcie did her best to brace her feet on the wall. She pushed off, taking a mad swing that Zephyr miraculously caught. He and Niall pulled her up and over the edge, finally releasing their death grips. Kelcie rubbed her wrists, trying to get feeling back into her arms.

The quaking started again, harder this time.

"Run," Zephyr bellowed. "This way!"

Chasing after Zephyr and Niall, who were heading for a

grassy clearing beyond the tree line, Kelcie removed her other glove and tucked them in her pocket. She needed to be ready for anything.

The moment they stepped on green, the earth stilled. The rain ceased. Kelcie bent over, catching her breath.

Zephyr leaned on Kelcie's back, doing the same. "Water powers, useless. Check."

Kelcie picked ice chunks out of her hair and flicked them at him.

Niall's gaze remained fixed on a black spot in the sky that was growing larger by the second.

"Brona?"

Brona came in for a shaky landing, skidding to a halt beside Zephyr. She morphed and fell over, clutching her right calf where both ends of a spike the size of a chopstick were visible.

"Frinxballs! It hurts!"

Before Kelcie could get to her, Brona ripped it out with a shriek. She shivered so much frozen flakes broke off her ponytail and long eyelashes. Niall pulled up her pant leg to reveal a dime-sized hole in her calf.

"Who did that to you?" Kelcie asked.

"Selkies."

"Selkies?" Zephyr withered at the reddening wound. "And I sent you to scout. I am so sorry, Brona." He tripped over a jagged rock, backing away. "Oh," he covered his mouth. "I, um . . . don't do well with blood."

"It wasn't your fault. Scáthach did this on purpose. I know she did. I can't fully morph injured. It's too dangerous." Brona winced. "This was my task. To teach me to function grounded, like you tosspots. Gah! I hate this!"

"Great! There will be something for each of us then," Kelcie groaned, kneeling beside her. She kept an eye on their surroundings, the ominous pit in her stomach growing larger by the second.

Niall gently examined the wound.

"It's not that bad," he assured her. "But we should find some water to wash it as soon as possible. I'll wrap it for now to keep dirt out. Zephyr, tear off a piece of your shirt."

Zephyr ripped a piece of Niall's shirt off and held it out to him. "Here you go."

Niall glowered, snatching it from him, then began patching up Brona's leg.

"Birdie, what did you see?" Zephyr asked.

Brona pushed up on her elbows, wincing in pain. "Selkies in seal and human form completely surround the island. The rain came down even harder over the water and froze on my wings. They got off a shot." She winced again. "But I saw the tree. Huge. Not going to be fun climbing it to find the silver bough. Not to mention the hike up the mountain. With a bum leg, I can't fly or walk easily. But at least I know where it is."

Kelcie helped Brona up, leaving a steadying hand on her shoulder.

"What else did you see?" Niall asked.

"The island is only about three square miles, and sits a hundred feet above sea level on all sides. The only way up the mountain is that way." She nodded away from the forest, beyond the edge of the grassy field where more trees clustered. "I saw a bridge that led to a path."

"A bridge?" Kelcie griped. "Scáthach has a thing for bridges, doesn't she?"

"Metaphors for connections to people, places, and things. In this case, how well connected are we that we can work together to get across it," Niall explained.

"You really have spent too much time in your own head," Zephyr chuckled.

Kelcie braced her feet. "Do you feel that?"

A slow and steady beat. Like hooves. Heading their direction. She held her breath, waiting, worrying they should already be running.

"Yeah. I think it's coming from over there." Brona shot her arm out.

Wild boars broke through the trees. But these weren't your run-of-the-mill angry piggies. Ghostly white, as large as rhinoceroses, they stampeded straight for them. Their yellow eyes glowed as they lowered their four tusks to perfect gut-wrenching positions.

28

ADDER SPEAK

ZEPHYR PULLED OUT his sword. "Run!"

But Brona couldn't run. She could barely walk.

Kelcie and Niall hefted her onto Zephyr's back and raced across the field, but they weren't moving anywhere near fast enough.

Wheezing grunts grew louder until the boars sounded right on top of them. Kelcie glanced over her shoulder, barreling into Niall, who wrapped her in a bear hug to keep her from falling off a cliff.

"The bridge is right there!" Brona exclaimed.

Twenty feet away, it boasted six giant selkies mid-leap, three on each side, carved from solid ice.

Carrying Brona's weight was no issue for Zephyr. He still beat Niall and Kelcie to the bridge, but when he stepped on, a barrage of arrows sailed across, driving him back.

The massive boars fanned out, corralling at the edge of the chasm. Still glowing, they exhaled yellow mist that made Kelcie's eyes water.

Zephyr set Brona down. "The only way out is to cross this bridge and the selkies don't want us crossing."

Seals circled large flat rocks in churning seas forty feet below. Three crawled out, barking. A wave crashed over, smothering them. When the water receded the seals were gone. In their place were beautiful women in clamshell bikinis, brandishing shiny bronze crossbows. Bins of darts like the one Brona pulled out of her leg were strapped to their thighs.

Zephyr grinned. "Is it crazy that I can't stop looking at them at a time like this?"

Kelcie kicked him in the shin. "What do we do now, Charger?"

"Not kick me!" He hopped.

The boars tucked their heads, scraping dirt.

Then they charged.

"Kelcie, light them up!" Brona exclaimed, hobbling to Niall.

"No, air!" Niall argued.

"No, fire!" Zephyr ordered.

"Fire . . . it is," Kelcie squeaked with excitement. She hadn't uttered the word for fire in so long. She thrust both hands out, bellowing as loud as she could, "IGNIS!"

"Whoa!" She recoiled as fire flooded the field, igniting grass, trees, and boars.

The boars screeched at the top of their lungs, running in all directions, including at them.

Kelcie cringed.

"I told you all, air!" Niall shouted.

"Mistral!" Sparks swept with Kelcie's arms as she made a giant circle, connecting with the frigid wind blowing off the ocean.

The boars hit a wind wall and were stopped in their tracks.

Again! Niall said. *Into the crack where you fell!*

Kelcie did it again. Then again and again until their frantically scrambling hind legs went over the edge. With a last push, their front hooves slid on the ice, and they vanished into the gap.

Kelcie fell to her knees, exhausted.

"Impressive, Saiga," said Zephyr.

"I taught her that." Brona cringed, reaching for her leg.

Blow darts shot from the rocks below, nearly taking out Niall. "I think they're trying to get our attention," he said from his tucked position.

Zephyr inched forward. "Hello. We see you. Can you please go away so we can cross the bridge?"

Malibu Barbie selkie threw her long bleached-blond hair over her shoulder, waving at Niall. She smiled sweetly at him and sang a melancholy tune in a language Kelcie couldn't understand. At the end, her voice rose in a lilting pitch.

"Is she asking a question?"

Zephyr crossed his arms. "Anyone understand selkie?"

"I, um . . ." Niall walked to the edge, his cheeks blooming red. "They'll let us cross, but they want something in return."

"What?" Brona asked. Then to the selkies. "What do you want?" Louder, as if hurting their ears would help them translate.

Malibu Barbie pointed at Niall, then Kelcie, then Brona, and Zephyr, finally placing her hand over her heart.

Niall looked down at her. "They want to know our story, why we're worthy of crossing."

"You got all that from . . ." Kelcie mimicked the selkie's graceful moves. ". . . that?"

Niall shook his head. "They aren't speaking selkie. It's more ancient. In the beginning, the Otherworld spoke a common tongue. There are volumes and volumes dedicated to it in the library at the College for Mystical Beings. The librarians taught it to me so I could read them."

"And look at that. All that seemingly useless work is now paying off." Zephyr's cheeks puffed. "Tell them about how we saved the school from the wood goblin, oh, and the sylph. That'll do it."

Niall swayed, chewing on his lip. "I don't think I can do this. You'll laugh at me."

"We would never laugh," Kelcie said.

"No promises." Brona sunk to the ground, turning paler by the second.

"Turn around. All of you." Niall tucked his arm beneath his armpit.

"Why would we do that?" Brona asked. "I can barely move."

"Turn around or the answer is NO!" Niall snapped.

Kelcie didn't like the idea of turning her back on heavily armed selkies, but she did as he asked. Zephyr blocked Brona's view.

"Okay. Do your stuff," Zephyr said.

The selkies whooped, smacking the water, beating their crossbows on the rocks. Kelcie heard Niall clear his throat and take a deep breath. Then he began to sing.

It was the most beautiful sound Kelcie had ever heard. She broke her word and turned around to watch him. They all did. It was impossible not to.

Niall didn't see them. He was facing the selkies, his arms raised waist high, his eyes closed, singing in a language Kelcie didn't understand in the slightest. But it came out of him as if he spoke it every day.

Based on the playful melody and his gestures toward each of them, she guessed he was explaining who they were. When Niall got to Zephyr, they *ooh*'d with glee.

"What's he saying about me?" Zephyr asked with a big grin.

With Brona, they bowed their heads, and when it came to Kelcie they grew quiet. He continued, singing evenly at first, then dropped an octave, hinting at danger. His tune changed, rising in key and volume. He belted the words, and moved to a frenetic rush, the melody growing higher and higher, until it came crashing down in a bold note that he held for what seemed like forever.

The selkies broke into a huge round of applause, clapping and whistling. Seals barked, slapping fins.

Kelcie touched his shoulder. "Niall, that was amazing."

"Beautiful, man." Zephyr sniffled, patting him on the back so hard he nearly knocked him off the cliff. "Sorry. Sometimes I don't know my own strength."

Brona paled. "Yeah. Yeah. Can we go now? I need water."

"You have ten seconds to get across," a selkie said in perfect English. "We offer only one chance."

"Let's go! Hurry!" Zephyr ordered, reaching for Brona. He grabbed her arms, lifting her off the ground and onto his back as if she weighed nothing. He hit the bridge at full speed and slipped, realizing too late the deck was made of ice.

"Whoa!"

Falling on his knees, Zephyr's yells turned to yelps as he speed slid across with Brona hanging on to him by morphed talons, digging into his shoulders. Niall skated across as fast as he could. Kelcie took a running start, falling on her knees, beating them all easily to the other side.

Once on solid ground, the bridge vanished, and they stopped to catch their breath and figure out what to do next.

"I need to make a poultice for Brona's leg," Niall said.

Zephyr checked the sun's position. "We need to find a water source, and shelter too. It's going to be dark in a couple hours."

"The cave is that way." Brona pointed to a trail leading straight up the mountain. "Same way we have to go to get to the Sidral."

Kelcie saw the eagle watching them from a tree growing sideways out of the mountain side. "You think Scáthach is sitting in her office, eating popcorn and laughing at us?"

"I would." Zephyr chuckled. "Except at Niall's performance." He wrapped an arm over Niall's shoulders. "You should do that at school. Girls would be all over you."

Niall turned bright red. His eyes slid to Kelcie's, which was a good thing because if he looked at anyone else, she would've popped him one.

"Let's get moving," Zephyr said, giving Brona his back. "You stick me with those claws again, you're walking, missy."

"I thought Chargers were made of tougher stuff than that," Brona teased, using Niall's bent knee as a stepstool to climb on Zephyr.

"I don't like the sight of blood, especially my own!"

After an hour trudging uphill, Kelcie was exhausted but had no right to complain. All she was lugging was Brona's bow.

Zephyr had it the toughest, carrying Brona the whole way. He spent the time taking his mind off the climb by telling stories about his family. His father's family had farmed the same spot for the past twenty generations. He had six siblings, including a twin, four aunts and uncles, and thirty cousins, all of whom lived and worked together. Only a few had ever left for school, and only one for AUA. His great-grandfather.

"They disowned him for it, like he betrayed the family for fighting for our kingdom rather than plowing the fields." He hefted Brona higher on his back. "They gave my youngest sister my bed. I've been relegated to the barn over break since I didn't earn my keep all year."

"That hardly seems fair," Niall offered. "You're training to defend the Lands of Summer. The Bountiful Plains is a kingdom in the Lands of Summer. So by that logic, you're training to defend and protect them."

Zephyr laughed. "Tell my father that."

The cave was around the next bend. Carved into a hill, it was cold and damp but big enough for all of them to fit inside for the night. Brona leaned against the cold stone wall and slid down until she could sit. Kelcie set her quiver next to her.

Zephyr vanished into the darkness in the back of the cave and returned quickly. "It's safe. Shallow with no other entrances or exits."

"There isn't much daylight left." Niall frowned at the dimming skies.

"Water," Brona mumbled. "And fire. It's freezing in here."

"I got the fire," Kelcie said, whipping her gloves out.

Zephyr clapped his hands. "Brona will stay here." He pointed to Kelcie. "Torch and I will get wood for the fire. Niall, you look for food and water."

Fifteen minutes later, Zephyr and Kelcie returned with armloads of wood and dried leaves. Kelcie built a pyramid with the larger logs and stuffed the leaves inside.

"You do this before?" Zephyr asked, impressed.

"I guess in a place that never gets cold, you only need fire to cook."

Zephyr smirked. "And my ma does most of that."

"Winter in Mass is so cold you can freeze to death outside, especially at night. There was this homeless guy in Rutland. An army vet. His name was Tidas. He showed me how to build a fire." Kelcie swallowed hard at the memories of her time in Rutland. "I would sometimes stay in the park until really late at night." She sat back on her heels and examined her work. "In that particular group home, it was safer to go back when everyone was asleep."

Kelcie held up her index finger. "Ignis." A tiny flame lit. She used it to light the fire, then blew it out. She wiggled her finger. "This would've come in handy."

A few seconds later, the fire popped and cracked, giving off much appreciated heat.

"That's rough." Zephyr sat down cross-legged.

"You get used to it," Kelcie said.

Zephyr warmed his hands over the growing fire. "We're like opposites. I mean, I have too much family always telling me what to do and when to do it, and you've had all this time to figure things out on your own. To be on your own. That's why I came to AUA. Figure out who I was away from them."

"Nice bonding moment, guys . . ." Brona inched closer, warming her hands over the fire. She licked her cracked, dry lips. "But where is Niall with the water? I'm dying here."

Niall shuffled into the cave with two bowls made from woven reeds. The one cradled in his hand was filled with water. The other held in his teeth contained a handful of white flowers. He passed the water off to Kelcie and removed the other bowl from his mouth. "I found a well, but it took a few minutes to make the bowls."

Kelcie helped Brona to drink first. Niall knelt beside her, crushing the flowers with a rock.

"You made those?" Kelcie could barely tie her shoelaces.

Brona let out a satisfied exhale. "I really don't need that, Niall. I should be better by morning."

Kelcie took a sip of the water and passed the bowl to Zephyr.

Niall used what was left to work the flowers into a paste. "This is yarrow. It will help stop the bleeding and stave off infection."

"Fine. But if it stings, I may bite." Brona winced as he carefully removed the bandage and spread the white muck over the wound. Kelcie was awed by the way Niall managed to do that with incredible dexterity, using his arm and fingers. Niall wasn't missing a hand. The rest of the planet had an extra.

"Please tell me you found something to eat too . . ." Zephyr whimpered.

Niall reached in his pocket and pulled out a handful of small green fruit. "Ripe mayapples. It's not much but we won't starve."

"What? No meat?" Zephyr frowned, eating his in three bites. "Not that I'm ungrateful, but that was completely unsatisfying."

Not long after that, exhaustion won out. Kelcie added logs to the fire and was just about to curl up beside it when Niall got up and hurried to the cave entrance. His back to Kelcie, she could tell he was rubbing his arm.

She walked over to him and saw an ominous look on his face. "What's wrong?"

"I don't know. I thought I heard something. Or felt something."

He rubbed his chest like it hurt.

Kelcie glanced outside the cave but didn't see anything. "Maybe it was the eagle."

"Yeah. I'm sure that's all it was. Come on, let's get some sleep."

He padded back toward the fire. Kelcie did too, but knew one thing for certain: morning couldn't come soon enough.

THE DREAM STARTED off in the strangest way. In sunless, starless darkness, Kelcie smelled the same noxious fumes from the museum and the Fringe, then the unmistakable sound of a vacuum cleaner. Kelcie tried to move, but she had no arms or legs. Only consciousness.

She jostled, moving blindly, like she was being carried. Footsteps crunched. She smelled piney, floral lavender. Heard grindylows catcalling. She was in Befelts Garden.

Kelcie's heart returned with a vengeance, beating against her chest, as realization dawned. She *was* the eye, and it was on the move.

"Killian!" It was Ollie. He sounded frightened. "Where is my brother? He was gone when I woke up this morning. All of his things are gone! What did you do to him? Tell me now!"

"Sounds like he went home. Crawled back to Chawell with his horns between his legs. I suggest you follow after him, like a good little demon."

It was Deirdre Crane.

"Stop lying." Kelcie heard a clank. "That's your sword. Your initials are on it. Now I'm going to ask you again, where is my brother?"

Water gurgled. Rain beat the ground. There was a massive struggle. Then Ollie made small, frustrated noises, like he was being held. A thud led to Ollie groaning like he had been kicked in the stomach.

"You cut me!"

Kelcie knew that voice too. Tad Fagan.

"How would you like to lose a finger? That would make it hard to control your water powers, wouldn't it? Or maybe a hand?" Crane hissed.

Noooo! Hate turned Kelcie's blood cold.

Open my eye, Kelcie. Let me see.

It was King Balor.

No, Kelcie. Don't, her father's voice said. *Don't listen to him.*

"Get away from me!" Ollie cried.

"Deirdre . . ." Fagan sounded unsure.

"What? You think this demon deserves your sympathy?" Crane screamed. "Hold him down."

"I . . ." Fagan was reluctant.

"No!" Ollie cried. "Help me!"

How could Fagan be so spineless? What was behind eyelid number one? Kelcie envisioned the scroll in her mind, her finger panning the page . . .

And behind lid number one . . . Fire. But the garden . . .

"No! Please! Don't!" Ollie screamed.

Kelcie had no choice. "*Ta Erfin*. I am the heir. *Vlast mian*. The power is mine!"

The lid raised. Through Abyss water and threadbare mesh she could make out Ollie on his knees. Fagan on his back, pressing Ollie's head to the ground. Crane with a dagger, reaching for Ollie's hand.

King Balor's sight, not Kelcie's, but she was controlling it. Power burst from all around her, dampened by passing through the Abyss water and the fabric. Still, it was more than Kelcie needed.

Fire ignited the path.

Deirdre looked over her shoulder. Her cherry-red eyes went wide. "Run!"

Deirdre and Tad ran one way. Ollie another. Kelcie's sight followed Deirdre and Tad, and so did the fire. Deirdre's pants caught. Tad's shoes.

Kelcie's vision slid left, trying to see if Ollie got away. Befelts Garden erupted in flames with Ollie in it.

"Stop! Stop! *Nil ignis!*" The lid slammed shut. Kelcie's breath was heaving, but she was relieved the eye listened. Ollie . . . he would be fine, she told herself. He was a Caenum. Water would put it out. He would be fine. The garden would be fine.

Her father screamed in pain, then silenced.

"Draummorc?" Her cry was met with silence. "Dad?"

Was he gone? Had he lost the power for good?

"Is this all a dream or is this real?" Kelcie asked King Balor.

What do you think?

He laughed like a madman.

Kelcie took that as a bad sign. "Wake up!" she yelled at herself. "You have to wake up!"

Balor cackled again.

"Draummorc! Help me!"

Oh no. Your father cannot hear you anymore. I will not let that happen.

Footsteps padded on soft ground. Whoever was carrying the eye was on the move. This seemed to go on for some time.

Then, Kelcie smelled musty, earthy, moldy decay, and heard lapping water. Morrow Lake? Striker yipped. She heard him race by, again and again.

"Find one?" It was Marta Louisa.

"No! How did they get a hoffescus stone and we can't even get to the bottom?" That was Willow. "What *are* those?"

"Ick! Eels!"

Hissing and slithering multiplied.

"Wait, wasn't there only two? What just happened?" Marta Louisa gasped. "Gross! They puked up another. And another!"

Striker yelped somewhere not far away.

"They're going after Striker!" Willow cried.

The grappler eels you failed to kill are hungry for cú sith, King Balor taunted. *Let's see what's going to happen, shall we? Follow them.*

"I have no legs . . ."

I wasn't speaking to you. He was speaking to whoever was in possession of the eye.

Kelcie would've vomited right then and there, if she had a stomach or a mouth. She wasn't in control. This had all been a game King Balor was playing, all this time, to use her. But she would never say those words again. She would never open the next lid!

Whoever held the eye started running. Kelcie bounced all over the place. Hissing grew so loud it sounded like a cicada invasion.

Striker howled over and over, back and forth, like he was pacing, like he was trapped.

"Stop them! Please! Don't let them do this!" Kelcie pleaded.

I can stop them. All you have to do is let me see.

"I can't. I can't. What if I hurt Striker?"

Pain exploded in Kelcie's chest.

You don't trust me? After all I have done for you? I have given my power over to you. You are my chosen heir. And this is what I get? Your father abandoned you. He never wanted you. No one has ever wanted you until me.

Before AUA, Kelcie might've believed him. But not now. Scáthach told her her first night at this school that she wanted Kelcie here. Zephyr said he thought they were lucky to have a Saiga. Brona was like a sister to Kelcie now. And Niall, he was somehow, even with Draummorc being her father, still her friend. Her best friend.

"You're wrong."

Am I? I can play that card too!

Kelcie exploded in pain. It hurt so much she couldn't tell him to stop. Striker's howl echoed in the emptiness.

The pup will die . . .

It was only eels. Why not give him what he wanted? More than that, there was no way she could let Striker die. "You better not hurt him! *Ta Erfin.* I am the heir. *Vlast mian.* The power is mine . . ."

The lid lifted.

Still veiled in murky water and thinned linen, Kelcie saw Striker surrounded by grappler eels. He had one latched on to his hindquarters in his jaws, and was struggling to rip it off with his teeth, but more were coming. Too many more.

The eye cast a blistering tempest. It whipped across the field, sweeping the eels over the cliff and into the waters between campus and the Shadow. Striker sprinted onto the Bridge of Leaping, drawing Kelcie's attention. The gale hit him, blasting him off the bridge and into the recently repaired wall. Another violent gust barreled into the gate. The hinges snapped. The gate sailed up and over the castle. The wall cracked and crumbled.

"Stop! *Nil mistral! Nil mistral!*" Kelcie screamed.

You may have the power to open my lids, but only I have the power to close them.

Trees ripped from their roots sailed into the Shadow's towers. Eagles were caught up in the tempest, and cast out over the sea.

You want me to stop? King Balor asked.

"Yes! Please . . ."

The drawbridge door went the way of the eagles.

Then the wind slowed and the lid slammed shut, plunging Kelcie into emptiness again.

"I don't want to do this anymore. Please, stop. Let me wake up." Balor didn't answer. Her carrier was moving again. Boots stomped on hard floors. From the short distance, Kelcie guessed they were inside the Shadow.

"Draummorc? Dad, please make him stop."

You want to talk to your father? After what he did?

"I don't want this. Give it back to him."

No. And if you don't do as I ask, I will kill him. And if you still deny me what I ask of you, my allies will kill them all, everyone you care about, one by one, until you give me what I want when I want it. You will hear them scream . . .

Kelcie heard Regan.

"What are you doing in here?"

Chaos erupted. Fighting broke out. Arrows swished. Metal clanked.

Let me see, Kelcie! Balor growled.

"No! I won't let you hurt them!"

Kelcie . . . her father sounded so weak.

Farewell, Draummorc. You daughter doesn't care enough about you to save your life.

This time, when the light exploded in the darkness, her father barely screamed, as if he had nothing left. But she heard him breathing, and knew he was still alive.

Your turn.

Kelcie choked. Pain exploded everywhere. She couldn't think straight.

I won't hurt them, Kelcie. Just let me see. One more time and I'll give you a rest. His tone softened, cajoling. *Come now. I promise you, I won't hurt them. I never lie. I never break a promise. And if you do as I ask, your father will live. If not . . . well . . .*

Draummorc cried out.

King Balor promised. She wanted to believe him. She had to believe him. She didn't want her father to die. "*Ta Erfin. Vlast mian.*" Another lid opened. Kelcie made out a blurry Regan tied up on the sofa. It looked like Scáthach was barreling through her office door.

Kelcie heard a hiss and a seismic *crackle*.

Then Kelcie screamed.

KELCIE WOKE UP with a start, toasty warm beneath the early morning sun. She clutched her terrified, jackhammering heart, unable to catch her breath.

"Where am I?" She sat up, confused.

Tall grasses. She was in the middle of a field, the sea eagle a few feet away. She swept the landscape. Blue and white wildflowers bloomed. She heard a stream not far off. Turning around, she saw the cave up the hill about a hundred yards away.

"How did I get here?" She must have sleepwalked. "Was it possible it was a bad dream?" she asked the eagle. It didn't move.

Kelcie stumbled to her feet, taking a closer look. The bird's head was lowered. Its wings spread. Its beak cocked as if it were about to squeak. Kelcie touched the wing. Cold. Hard. It had turned to stone.

"Oh no . . ." The eagle was a manifestation of Scáthach's power, and if the eagle was a statue, that meant . . .

Her fianna . . . what if the eye got them too?

Kelcie sprinted to the cave. Brona and Zephyr slept back to

back, leaning on the wall. Niall was curled up by smoldering coals, peacefully sleeping. She grabbed his arm. He was still warm. Still breathing.

"Niall! Wake up!" Kelcie shook him.

"What's wrong?" He fumbled for his glasses.

"I think I turned your sister to stone!"

29

BETRAYED

A FEW MINUTES LATER, all four stood around the sea eagle, staring like it was a statue in a museum.

Zephyr tapped the bird's head. "Why would it turn to stone?"

Kelcie's insides dropped into a bottomless pit. "The eye. Three of the lids opened. I think it was me."

Kelcie couldn't stand still as she told them about her nightmare. About what she saw at the school. About hearing Balor. And worst of all, about what she did. "This is all my fault! We have to get back to school. Now! We have to find a way to fix this!"

Kelcie was in full-on panic mode, but the others were taking way too long for her liking to comprehend the gravity of the situation.

"Are you saying the third lid opened? That my sister," Niall scrutinized the petrified sea eagle, "and Scáthach turned to stone?"

"But how? You're here?" Brona asked, like it was the most ridiculous thing she ever heard. She used the statue as a way station for her wounded leg. "Maybe it's just a statue of a sea eagle and you just had a bad nightmare."

"Featherhead is right," Zephyr agreed.

Brona punched his shoulder.

"Ow!"

She grimaced, seriously regretting the decision, shaking out her fingers.

"What? It was a term of endearment," Zephyr insisted.

"How can you all be so calm? I'm telling you our school is in trouble! I wasn't the only one King Balor was talking to," Kelcie shouted.

Niall fell to his knee, placing his hand on the eagle's chest. His expression went grim. "Kelcie's right. I feel a heartbeat."

Kelcie added her hand beside his. "That means it's still alive in there, so Scáthach and Regan must be too."

"Have you noticed it's hot all of a sudden? And balmy. And look at all the flowering plants," Zephyr said.

Niall stood up. "This was all freezing tundra yesterday when I was foraging."

"Okay. I believe her. Saiga did it. She opened the lids. It seems, Adder, your great plan of her winning the eye from her father has backfired in all our faces," Brona hissed.

Niall chewed on his lip, his sorrowful gaze falling on Kelcie.

"Time to go home," Zephyr said. "We have to get to the Sidral. And then we have to kick some Winter butt because I'm telling you right now, I'm getting my second year at AUA if it's the last thing I do."

The oak tree was two miles straight up. The landscape had changed. Unlike last night, the woods on the mountain brimmed with life. The trees were no longer barren. The branches hung low, weighed down by an overwhelming number of bright green leaves and heavy fruits. Sparrows chirped. Bugs buzzed. The sea air smelled salty and sweet at the same time. Summer had returned to Tech Gaoth.

Zephyr set his hand on the pommel of his sword as they trekked through dense woods. "Where are the boars?"

"It was all created by Scáthach. There's nothing dangerous here, I guess," Brona said.

Along the way, they volleyed plans back and forth. All went from bad to worse.

"Dropkicking the eye into the ocean isn't going to end it. It survived the Abyss," Kelcie explained. Then there was the absurd offer by Brona.

"Can you not cook it the way you did the grindylows? I bet Roswen would be happy to add an evil eye to her year-end stew."

"I have a feeling that's been tried at least once over the *thousands* of years this thing has been tormenting the worlds." Kelcie's chest tightened with worry she would never hear her father's voice again. If only she had listened to him. "We have to come up with something new."

In the end Zephyr and Niall decided on a measured infiltration. Gain reconnaissance information on Winter's position, find resources for battle with the other fiannas, and then, find the eye so that Kelcie could talk to her father. She was hoping he would be able to give her a hint at how to destroy the eye. She would have to bargain for that with King Balor. She had one lid left to do that with. The lid that would unleash total annihilation and destroy the school.

Not long after, the path, which had been winding upward, leveled off.

"We're almost there," Niall said, rubbing his elbow.

"You can sense it?" Kelcie asked.

Niall nodded.

"What does that feel like?"

"I'm not sure I can explain it. It's unlike anything I've ever felt. All Sidrals give off energy that Adders can pick up, at least that's what Wasp says. But this is stronger, older, feels unbreakable."

The trail ended at a ring of tall bushes. Single file, they passed through the only open sliver, finding a giant oak tree. Like the one in Boston, the tree was so tall Kelcie couldn't see the top. Leaves larger than her hands fell like rain as they approached. Massachusetts woods were filled with oak trees. A single large acorn bonked Kelcie on the head. She picked it up, like she always did, and put it in her pocket. *Just one for luck,* she thought; the rest were for the cat-sized squirrels running up the trunk to get away from them.

The ground around the tree vibrated, and there was an audible hum coming from it.

"How do we find the bough?" Niall asked.

"Brona, can you morph yet?" Zephyr asked.

"I can try." Brona set her bow and arrow down, testing her leg. She rolled her shoulders and sucked down a deep breath. For the first time, Kelcie saw a hesitant look float across her face. But it didn't last long. She slapped her hands over her head, and her Raven form took to the skies, circling the tree, going higher and higher until Kelcie couldn't see her anymore. A minute later, she returned with a silver bough in her beak. She passed it to Kelcie and morphed.

The bough resembled Kelcie's, one branch, only one place it would take them.

"This whole thing has been too easy," Brona hummed. "Scáthach is definitely asleep at the wheel."

Wind blew. The leaves shushed.

Brona scowled at Kelcie. "Take those stupid gloves off. We need to be ready."

But Kelcie wasn't ready. That was the problem. Nevertheless, she shoved them in her pocket, then set the silver bough against the bark.

Roots grew from the charm, digging into the trunk.

As soon as the tree split open, Zephyr shifted Kelcie aside and pulled his sword. "I'll go first."

A FEW SECONDS LATER they spilled out of the Sidral at the Academy for the Unbreakable Arts.

There wasn't a soul in sight. The school was quiet.

Eerily quiet.

Kelcie checked the sky. The sun was just coming up over Haven Hall. "It's dawn."

"Everybody must still be sleeping," Brona said.

"Haven Hall. Move, team," Zephyr commanded in hushed tones.

On the way they passed Befelts Garden. The fire was out, the garden's charred remains still smoldering, but there was no sign of Ollie.

"Roswen is going to kill me," Kelcie pointed out.

Sadly, no one argued.

At the archway, they realized they couldn't get into their Dens without their boughs. Niall closed his eyes. When they opened, he didn't look happy. "Wasp says they can't get out. Boughs aren't working. Every part of this school relies on Scáthach, like the sea eagles. The magic that runs the school comes from her. She made it all happen, so with her turned to stone, none of it is working."

"Then we're on our own," Brona commented.

Kelcie heard shuffling behind them. Collectively they turned, ready to pounce, but she saw Striker limping up toward them. His tail feathers dragged. He lowered his head, whimpering. He was bleeding from bite wounds on his hindquarters, his side, and shoulder.

"He's hurt." Kelcie rushed to him, checking the wounds. "The eels did this. I'm so sorry, Striker."

"Let's go to the Shadow," Zephyr said.

Because of his wounds, Striker jogged more slowly than normal along trails and through fields, pausing at the Bridge of Leaping. He glanced back, meeting Kelcie's gaze as they caught up to him. The gate had been blown off. A huge section of the wall was nothing but rubble.

"Oh yeah. If we get out of this alive, Roswen is going to kill you," Brona said.

On the outside, Kelcie put on a brave face, laughing it off. On the inside, her stomach knotted with every step they took bringing them closer to the castle. She could already smell that special magical scent the air had right before snow. The ice fairy was here, and probably Elliott Blizzard too. Kelcie wanted to strangle him.

Brona nocked an arrow. Zephyr hefted his sword higher. Striker darted around them, all taking the lead, while Niall and Kelcie brought up the rear. Niall wanted them to walk in and act like they were surprised at what was going on. Feel out the landscape. How many Winterfolk, what kind were they dealing with, and most important, where was the eye? It was the dumbest plan Kelcie had ever heard. They were walking into a trap, that much was obvious.

The drawbridge was gone, the fortress wide open. The eagles normally on the wall had fallen off. They were now petrified lawn statues.

The hallway was an icy mess. Icicles dripped from the rafters. The weapons were frozen in blocks of ice. Brona slipped. Zephyr caught her before she fell and hurt her leg even worse, but the damage was done. They were heard.

The door to Scáthach's office opened.

Madame Le Deux stepped out, wearing her signature knowing smirk. "Well, well, look who's back from a very successful overnight."

30

A WINTRY WELCOME

KELCIE DREW COLD air between her palms, rolling it into hard packed airballs.

Wait, Niall said.

She really hated this plan.

Fairies rushed into the hallway, joining Le Deux. Two appeared out of nowhere beside Brona and Zephyr. They were identical twins with matching Orange Crush–colored pixie cuts. Another ran at Niall so fast he left an ebony streak. Elliott had traded in his clothes for sleek black leather armor. Two long swords harnessed to his back crossed around his leather-capped fairy wings. Kelcie would've told him he looked almost cool, if she didn't hate him so much.

Achila Grimes in her glorious ice armor set her beady white eyes on Striker. She blasted the cú sith, catching him midstride, immobilizing his back legs.

"Get away from him!" Kelcie threw a curveball.

Grimes dodged right, into the curve. Her ice armor broke off in giant chunks, only to instantly be replenished.

"Why make this difficult?" Grimes asked.

Kelcie ran, hoping to draw her away from the others. Ice darts skimmed Kelcie's ears. Kelcie got off two shots, slamming Grimes into a painting of a half-dressed Celt. Cackling in a way that grated on every one of Kelcie's nerves, Grimes heaved an ice boomerang, nailing her legs, tripping her up. Kelcie crashed to the floor. The next thing she knew, her arms were frozen together behind her back in unbreakable, frigid ice cuffs.

Grimes' knee dug into Kelcie's shoulder blades. Her frosty breath froze Kelcie's nose, as she leaned down and said, "All of your friends will die if you don't do what we say when we say it, got me?"

She yanked Kelcie up by her elbows and marched her back the way they came.

In the seconds Kelcie was gone, the rest of her fianna had been taken down.

The Orange Crush twins wore camouflage unitards. Their roguish sparkling brown eyes danced with mischief as they gripped Zephyr and Brona's shoulders, shoving them forward, showing Kelcie the iron shackles binding their wrists and ankles. This was the dumbest plan Kelcie had ever heard, and if they lived through this, Kelcie would make sure Niall never lived it down.

"Kelcie!" Elliott sang, holding Niall's arm in a painful position behind his back. "I'm so proud of you. Your powers are blossoming. These two lovely creeper fairies are Latchkey and Nevver." He tilted his head at the Orange Crush twins. "Or Nevver and Latchkey. I can't ever tell them apart."

"Fianna, meet Elliott Blizzard, my pathetic caseworker from Boston." Kelcie struggled uselessly against the frozen cuffs.

"Ouch. That hurts." Blizzard faked a cry.

"Shut up, Blizzard!" Grimes snapped. "Get irons on that boy."

"But he's missing a hand." Blizzard groaned at the inconvenience. He pursed his lips, shrugging, shackling Niall's ankles instead. "That'll hold him."

The last in the room was Madame Le Deux herself. Kelcie stared at her teacher. "You're helping them?"

"Of course I am, only—"

"Hold up," Zephyr interrupted. "What happened to your accent?"

Le Deux's blond hair fell out of its tight bun, darkening to black as it stretched down her back. The tips of her ears elongated to points. Her face widened. Cheeks puffed. She shrank a foot, until she was barely taller than Kelcie. Much too big for her, her cloak fell off. Beneath, she twinned with Blizzard, in black leather armor.

She's a changeling.

Stunned, Kelcie looked at Niall. "A changeling? What's that?"

"You always have all the answers, Adder. A changeling can take the form of anyone they come into contact with. I left that part out of the reading assignments this year, but this one was always reading ahead." She ruffled his hair.

"And you've been manipulating the eye all year, hiding it in the Fringe!" Brona snapped.

"Never to be outdone by O'Shea. Yet another bright one." She twisted the silver bough around her neck. "I'm afraid Madame Le Deux never left Paris this year. My name is Pethia."

Kelcie saw her own bough around Elliott Blizzard's neck. In fact, all of the fairies had her fianna's boughs. "You used our boughs to break into the school?"

"Guilty." Blizzard winked.

Niall ticked off Winter's starting lineup, which Kelcie assumed Brona and Zephyr heard too: *The nimble fairy, the weakest in the bunch on me. A strategically placed foot, and he'll go down. On Brona and Zephyr, mirror creeper fairies, which means their powers are linked. One turns visible, they both do. And finally, the dreaded ice fairy on Kelcie.*

Grimes reached into Kelcie's pocket, pulling out her gloves. "Put these on."

Kelcie shook her head no, fisting her hands, making it impossible for Grimes to force her.

Grimes shot ice at Zephyr's face, covering his mouth and nose. He couldn't breathe.

Striker's hind legs vibrated against the sides of the block of ice. Water pooled. Any second, he would be free, but Kelcie couldn't wait. Zephyr's cheeks sucked in. His eyes bulged impossibly wide.

"Fine!" Kelcie let Grimes wrestle them on, feeling the obsidian settle between the bones in the back of her hands, and drain her. "Get the ice off of him! He can't breathe!"

"I say let him suffocate," the Orange Crush twin holding him said.

"Latchkey . . ." Blizzard sighed a sound of supreme stupidity.

"I'm Nevver, idiot!"

Blizzard rolled his eyes, and held a vibrating hand over the ice, warming it until it melted off.

Zephyr gasped. "I'm okay . . ." He breathed heavily.

"Party pooper." The real Latchkey pouted.

"Latchkey, get the Raven inside," Grimes growled, flashing her elongated incisors.

She lifted Brona up, carrying her into the office. Nevver went next, shoving Zephyr. Blizzard lifted Niall by his armpits, carrying him as finally Kelcie was allowed to enter. The first thing she saw in Scáthach's office was Roswen kneeling on the floor, her hands bound behind her back. Her pink hair fell in large chunks out of a ponytail; her left eye was swollen shut. The black plate she always wore on her back had been removed. Beneath where it had been, four small nubs shifted in synchronicity.

"Yes, Frost was a fairy. And that is what happens to fairy traitors in Winter. They have their wings clipped," Grimes explained. "Once they're gone, so are their powers. But I hear she's turned into quite the chef."

The fairies had the nerve to laugh. Roswen looked over her shoulder at Kelcie. She tried to speak, but ice-webbing bound her lips together.

Scáthach stood as still as a statue, sword in hand, midstride beside the door. Regan's statue form was in the chair Kelcie sat in the last time she was in this office. Her pallid expression left Kelcie filled with guilt and bursting with rage.

Blizzard coopted the edge of Scáthach's desk. He picked up

her spear-pen to use as a pointer. "Nice work, Kelcie." He waved it at Scáthach.

You have to save her, Niall said in her head, staring at Regan. Kelcie looked at him.

You have to destroy the eye. His gaze lifted to the sword above Scáthach's desk. *It's obsidian.*

"What?" Kelcie blurted. The obsidian was on her gloves, but . . . and then she got it. The small obsidian stones in her gloves shut off her powers. If these small stones could do that to her, the amount in that sword's blade might be enough to drain King Balor's powers, and maybe, with some long overdue luck, end the eye.

"Hey!" Blizzard poked Niall. "Stop talking to her!"

Grimes pressed her long fingernail in Kelcie's cheek. "What did he say to you?"

"Nothing. He's scared, that's all."

Pethia disappeared behind a suit of armor and returned with a metal box. "He should be." She opened the top and pulled out the eye. It was still wrapped in glistening, frayed black fabric. Abyss water leaked all over the floor. Several of Scáthach's shields vanished into the empty darkness. The changeling saw it in time, hopping away before she fell in too.

When Kelcie saw through the eye, she was beneath that fabric, but also a layer of Abyss water. All this time, the water was trapped in the folds of the fabric. But more than that, Balor's actual eye was hiding in the nothingness. She tried to keep from looking directly at the sword, but it was there, the edges of its serrated blade darkening her peripheral vision. If Kelcie was going to end this, she would have to drive that blade into the heart of the eye. Only thing was, she had no idea how she was going to do that.

Striker broke free and charged into the office.

"No, boy. Go outside!" Kelcie demanded.

But Striker wanted "the ball." He lunged at Pethia, falling headfirst into the inescapable waters.

"No!" Kelcie cried. "Get him back! Get him back right now or I swear—"

Pethia set the fabric down, soaking the waters up. "Nothing that falls in ever comes back out."

"Can we get on with this?" Latchkey griped. She used Brona's stomach as a footrest, fanning her sweaty neck with her enormous hands. "It's hot in here."

Don't think about Striker right now. Ask them what they want. I need time to tell Brona and Zephyr the new plan.

Kelcie swallowed the lump in her throat, choking out, "What do you want?"

Grimes answered. "Simple. For you to open the last lid and end the school forever."

"What?" Kelcie gasped.

Lid number four: total annihilation. The school would go up like Summer City.

"Really? Winter is going to burn down a school. That's how you want to use something as powerful as King Balor's evil eye?" Brona scoffed.

"Weren't you listening in class, Little Miss Know-it-all?" Pethia *tsk*ed. "This school turns out the only soldiers capable of standing up to ours. With Scáthach dead and the special breed of spriggans torched, the Lands of Summer will lose the ability to unlock powers. The Never-Ending War will finally be over. And we will win."

Grimes pulled Kelcie to her by the shoulders. "Here's the way this is going to work. You will open the fourth lid. End Scáthach, and then I will fly you over the campus, and you will burn it down." Frigid nails bit into Kelcie's arms in warning. "Once I'm satisfied, we'll let your friends live. Now I'm going to release your hands. If you try and take those gloves off, I will kill your Charger first. Then the Raven, then—"

"Stop with the theatrics. I get it," Kelcie growled. "You're worse than Blizzard."

Blizzard tapped his knife on Niall's chest, mouthing, *Enough.*

As Grimes thawed her ice cuffs, Kelcie met Niall's narrowed, determined stare and nodded. It was go time.

Niall looked up Blizzard's nose. Elliott's face grew redder with each passing second until he screamed, his hands flying to his head.

"What's wrong with you?" Nevver looked at him like he was possessed.

Zephyr broke the chains between his hands, then ripped the leg irons off and leaped on Nevver at the same time Brona morphed, slipping right through Latchkey's hands. She dive-bombed Grimes, giving Kelcie the time she needed.

Kelcie jumped on the desk. On a wild pass, Brona swept the sword, her talons making a mad grab for the blade, scraping it enough that it slid off, falling, right into Kelcie's outstretched hands.

The ruby grip lit on contact. Kelcie felt a strange pull as she leaped off the desk, ready to end the eye, but her feet never made it to the floor. The room spun and when it stopped, everything faded . . .

31

REMEMBER WHEN . . .

KELCIE STOOD OUTSIDE a simple cottage. It was dark but the moon was full and bright.

Three black birds swooped down, two flapping, one riding the thermals, like Brona. They perched side by side on a high branch in a tree, silently staring in the second floor window.

Lightning rocketed, startling her. The birds barely noticed. They were entranced by the scene in the window.

"Kelcie, Brona, if I have to come up there one more time!" a woman with a thick lilting accent yelled from inside the house.

A shiver ran down her spine at the mention of hers and Brona's names together. Kelcie padded up the porch stairs to the wooden front door. She tentatively touched the knob, but her hand passed right through, like a ghost.

Kelcie gasped. Maybe she was dead. That was fast. She never saw it coming. Or maybe this was all Balor's doing again. It wouldn't be the first time he hijacked her consciousness.

She heard giggling from inside. The crow cawed.

Kelcie walked through the door, finding a modest home. A staircase before her. Men's voices lofted from behind a door to the right, girls' soft laughter from a room at the top of the stairs.

An old woman burst out of the kitchen at the end of the hall, wrestling with the strings on her apron. Stout, with a bob of gray hair, she muttered to herself, "In all my years . . ."

What startled Kelcie the most wasn't the two ivory horns molded into a torc and hanging around the old woman's neck, but that Kelcie somehow knew without a doubt that the horns belonged to her *doyan,* her grandfather who died in the war, and that the left horn's tip was broken because *she* accidentally broke it when she was two. A story her doyen repeated to her whenever she got mad at her, like now.

Doyen . . .

She was Kelcie's grandmother.

"Oh . . . I remember." Kelcie choked. She tried to touch her grandmother, but her hand passed right through.

Kelcie followed her up the stairs and into her bedroom. Moonlight streamed through the window, giving the bedroom a warm glow. Doyen ripped the covers off a giggling mass in the middle of the bed.

There they were, Brona and Kelcie.

Warmth flooded. Kelcie couldn't wait to tell Brona she was right. They did know each other. But who were they to each other?

Little Brona's silky black hair was so long it was hanging off the bed. Kelcie's thick red mane was braided down her back. They were on their bellies in matching blue nightshirts. A tiny flame flickered on Kelcie's little finger. A book lay open between the two of them.

"Are you trying to send me to an early grave?" Doyen blew out Kelcie's finger. "What have I said about fire in bed?"

"Don't," Kelcie answered.

"So why do you keep doing it?"

Brona closed the book. "Because she can."

"You've got too much of your mother in you, Brona," Doyen said. Her furious glower shifted to the black birds watching outside the window.

"I wouldn't know." Brona gave her a cheeky grin.

"Oh, Miss Sass. Do you want me to send your father up?"

Brona pulled the covers over her head.

"Didn't think so." She turned, her face a picture of disappointment. "Bug, do you not love your old doyen?"

Kelcie hopped up and hugged her. "I'm sorry. No more fire. I promise. I love you, Doyen."

She patted Kelcie on the back. "That's better. Now go to bed. Your fathers are leaving in the early morning, and you'll want to be up to wish them goodbye."

Draummorc must have been one of the voices Kelcie heard downstairs. She wanted to go but didn't want to leave her old room yet. White shelves overflowed with books. Pictures of her and Draummorc littered the nightstand beside her bed, him holding her, hugging her, her sitting on his lap, and her as a baby, touching his horns while he kissed her belly. Maybe Balor was wrong. Maybe he did want her.

"I want to go with them." Brona threw off the covers and jumped on the bed. "Where are they going?"

"No place you can go, I'm afraid. To the very ends of the Lands of Summer, in search of something I'm very hopeful they do not find," Doyen sighed. She caught Brona mid-jump and tossed her down on the bed. Doyen tucked her in before she could get away.

"Then why are they going?" Kelcie asked as she sank under the covers.

"You'll have to ask them in the morning. Sleep."

Doyen left, shutting the door. The room dimmed into total darkness. Kelcie's smaller self and Brona rolled over to go to sleep. Brona reached for Kelcie's hand. When she found it, she locked her pinkie with Kelcie, as if this was the way they slept together every night.

Kelcie's breath caught.

She hated to leave but was desperate to see her father. Kelcie floated out of the bedroom, down the stairs, through the door at the bottom. She found herself in an office with two men. One dark haired and very tanned from years at sea. Brona's father, Tao, Kelcie remembered. The other had a thick red beard, shaggy red hair like Kelcie's, two long, ringed horns, and eyes like Kelcie's, one blue and one brown.

"Da." Kelcie's heart ached.

Her memories flooded back. Her father was indeed Draummorc. He and Tao Lee stared at a map spread over her father's cluttered desk.

"It's buried in the bottom of a well in this cave." Kelcie's father touched the map. "Can you get your ship in this cove?"

Striker poked his head out from beneath the desk.

Kelcie smiled as more memories returned. She sniffed, holding back tears, not wanting to miss a thing. Striker belonged to her father. Scáthach said Striker came to her around the same time as the sword. But how did he know Kelcie would end up at the school?

Kelcie wanted to crawl under the desk with him, but she wasn't really here, was she?

"Won't be easy, Draum. The rocks in that cove are impossible to see. They'll gut the hull. But if you can raise the sea level . . ."

Draummorc nodded. "That's what I was thinking."

"Do you know what we'll face in that cave?" Tao asked, sounding bleak.

"No. But the eye is there. I know it. I can *feel* it."

Doyen entered the room carrying two steaming cups. "Tea, for the idiots."

"Maya," Draummorc chastised. *Mother.* "Queen Eislyn believes Balor's eye is our only chance at ending this war, once and for all. We're so close."

"The Queen has no idea what she's talking about. And don't lie to me. You want it, Draum, as much as the Queen. Admit it. Your blood as heir is drawn to it. You know this. You have to be stronger. King Balor's spirit lives on in his eye. And it has only ever brought death and destruction and misery to our people. You should leave it alone. Tell her it wasn't there."

Kelcie's grandmother set the tea down.

"Maya . . . I can't."

"Fine. Why listen to an old lady? I'm only your mother." She left, leaving the door ajar.

Kelcie stared at where her grandmother had been. She was right. He should've listened to her. Yet something else needled at Kelcie. All this time they called Kelcie's father a traitor, but did no one know the Queen made him go after it? The attack on Summer City was as much her fault as his, wasn't it?

Tao sat down in the chair across from the desk. "Maybe she's right, Draummorc. Legends tell of harrowing devastation every time. Didn't those other heirs believe they could control it too? What makes you believe you can?"

"I can. Trust me." Draummorc sat down in the chair beside him. "I need the best navigator and that's you. But I will understand if you say no."

Tao got up and looked over the map. "You know I would never let you do this alone."

Relief washed over Kelcie's father's face. "Good."

Little Kelcie and little Brona peeked in the door. Striker rushed to greet them.

"Shouldn't you two be in bed?" Draummorc scolded, smirking.

Little Kelcie ran to her father. "Yes. But we want to come with you tomorrow."

He picked her up. "No, Bug."

"Not tomorrow. Another trip," Tao said to Brona. He pushed a whining Brona out the door, following her to the bottom of the stairs. "Up to bed. Get some sleep."

He squeezed her shoulders. Brona started up the stairs, but stopped, sticking her tongue out at him. "I have to wait for Kelcie."

Little Kelcie's fingers grazed a gash on his cheek, just below his eye. "I'm sorry I scratched you. I promise to let Doyen cut my nails when she tells me they're too long from now on."

"You have a good heart, Kelcie. It was an accident. Already forgiven." He hugged her and kissed her forehead before setting her down. "Sweet dreams. I love you."

"Love you too."

Tears came to Kelcie's eyes. She couldn't stop them from pouring down her face. She wanted to hug her father, to scream at him not to go, to leave the eye where it was. To tell him that it would take him away from her and Niall's father away from him. But her hands passed right through him.

As the girls went up the stairs holding hands, Kelcie heard her father say, "For two guys who made the mistake of falling in love with women we could never have, we ended up with something pretty special."

"Yeah, stubborn attitudes and sleepless nights." Tao laughed.

TIME ELAPSED. THE days and nights passed in blinks. Doyen chasing after Brona and Kelcie, who spent most days playing with wooden swords and climbing trees. Still, why were these memories coming back to Kelcie now? What did that sword do to her?

The fast-forwarding stopped when her father entered the house with a grisly look on his face, a round object draped in tattered black fabric beneath his arm. Kelcie blanched. He had found the eye. Doyen came out of the kitchen and dropped a bowl. The ceramic broke into a million pieces, sticky rice spilling all over the floor.

"You did find it. I've been hearing of fires burning the plains, tempests at the docks. These are the plagues when the lids open, Draum. Was that you?" Doyen's voice rose to a fevered pitch.

Draummorc stared at his mother, melancholy-eyed, opening and closing his mouth like he was trying to speak, but nothing came out. Seemingly frustrated, he stormed into his office.

Doyen hurried after him, shutting the door. "Well?"

Kelcie walked through it, finding her grandmother flailing her arms, desperately trying to get his attention.

"What's the matter with you, Draum? Speak to me!"

Her father completely ignored her. He pulled a book on the back shelf. The wall jerked, revealing a hidden room. Kelcie glimpsed an arsenal inside. Draummorc returned with two long swords and a metal box, large enough for the eye. He saddled the swords in crossed scabbards on his back, then placed the eye in the metal box, securing the top.

Doyen gasped. "You brought it here?"

He started to leave.

His mother caught his arm. "Do you not want to see Kelcie? She's been waiting all day. And where is Tao? Where is Striker?"

"I have to go. The king demands it," her father answered stiffly.

Kelcie shuddered. The ancient king's grip on her father was shocking. *Is that what he would do to me?*

"We have no king, Draummorc! We have a queen! What are you saying? What are you planning to do? Look at me!"

He looked at her. His eyes glowed with power. Wind whipped, scattering the papers on his desk. A pitcher toppled, crashing to the floor, the water rushing to her father like an elemental magnet.

"You're not in your right mind!"

His expression unyielding, he said, "Your son is mine now."

Kelcie started at the sound of Balor's scratchy voice.

"Give me that!" Her grandmother tried to take the box from Draummorc.

"Mistral." With a wave of his hand, he threw his mother against the bookshelf. She fell to the floor, struggling to get up.

No! Kelcie tried to help her but she was still nothing but a ghost.

Little Brona and little Kelcie ran into the room.

"Doyen!" Kelcie said to her grandmother, then saw her father. "Da, you're home!"

She tried to hug him, but he pushed her away.

"Da?" Kelcie asked. Her surprised frown shifted to her grandmother limping toward her. Tears threatened. She called, "Da?" again, louder this time.

"Where's my father?" Brona asked.

Draummorc looked down at Brona with an expression that terrified Kelcie. Her younger self recognized something wasn't right and pulled Brona away from him.

He left without looking back.

The room emptied, but Kelcie stayed. Her stomach aching, she glanced around her father's office, filled with his special things. She sniffed her father's pipe on the desk, trying to remember her life with him, the way he was before this. Maybe she was too young when she was separated from him, or maybe it would take time.

She needed to get back. She had to destroy the eye.

But how? She decided to try leaving. She passed through the wall into the night.

A blink later, Kelcie smelled smoke, but there was no fire in sight. A raven and a crow landed on the grass beside her. Kelcie tripped getting out of the way as they morphed into two cloaked women, both dark haired and silver eyed, like Brona. Kelcie held her breath, trying to keep her pounding heart from leaping out of her chest as pieces of her memory came rushing back to her.

Mother?

Her mother was Nemain, one of the three Morrígna sisters Niall told her about her first day at AUA. Brona's mother, Macha, and Kelcie's mother were sisters.

If that wasn't mind-blowing enough, Kelcie remembered her doyen telling her the reason Kelcie never saw her mother was because she was a war goddess, an omen on the battlefield, and for war goddesses to have children meant only bad things for their children. They never returned out of fear. "What kind of mothers curse their children?" Doyen had said. Yet they had come back. Just moments ago Kelcie saw them through the window in her old room.

Brona and Kelcie should never have been born.

"This is madness, Nemain. If we're seen—"

"Then leave, Macha. I won't leave my daughter to be a pawn in this war. Draummorc has been captured. She will not stay here! And your daughter is here too. She's in danger."

"But the eye has been thrown into the Abyss," Macha exclaimed. "Tao is on his way back from there now."

"It will return. I have *seen* it. So has the Queen's seer. She's on her way now. Kelcie is the only heir left. They plan to lock her up, like Draum. I won't let them do that. One day she will be the one to destroy Balor's eye, but that won't be for a long while. Until then, she needs to be kept safe."

"What do you plan to do?" Macha asked.

"I will take her to the human world."

"You will leave your daughter to humans?" Macha made a disgusted face. "What would they make of her powers there?"

Yeah! Kelcie tried to yell. *Listen to your sister!*

"I will handle that."

What did that mean? Kelcie had a bad feeling she was about to find out.

"Brona should be with her father. I will take her to Tao. But they don't know us. How will we get them to come with us?"

Nemain removed her cloak. "We're their mothers. We'll find a way."

Black feathery wings sprang from Nemain's shoulder blades, the tips of which extended a foot above her head, the bottoms so long they dragged on the ground. She pushed the door open and in one leap, she flew up the stairs.

Shocked, afraid, and awestruck, all Kelcie could think to say was, "Whoa! I want wings!" She raced after her.

Instead of turning left to enter Kelcie's room, Nemain swept right. Macha followed, her wings making an appearance as she turned. Between their scowls and spooky outfits, Kelcie wouldn't be surprised if her younger self ran from the room screaming.

"What? Your plan is to scare little me to death?" Kelcie asked, knowing they couldn't hear her.

She passed through the door ahead of the gruesome twosome. Doyen was in bed asleep, her head bandaged, a half-drunk cup of tea on her night table. The girls were in sleep clothes, looking out the window where miles away a fire raged.

"I have a very bad feeling," Kelcie said, leaning her head on Brona's shoulder.

"Me too." She hugged Kelcie.

The door burst open. Nemain and Macha entered.

Doyen sat up in bed. "Back again, are you? My son isn't here."

"He's not coming back. He's been captured," Nemain said. "We're here for the girls."

"What?" Doyen gasped.

Kelcie and Brona ran to Doyen.

"No." Doyen shook her head, holding on to them tightly.

"I will not allow my daughter to remain in these lands to be used by either side," Nemain explained in a calmer voice than Kelcie would've expected. "You know who I am. My seeing always comes to pass. The eye will be found one day. She must not wield it. This is for her own good."

Doyen slowly nodded.

Kelcie saw her little self crumble. "I don't want to go."

"Kelcie can't leave me!" Brona cried.

The two tangled their limbs in an unbreakable hug.

Macha knelt beside Brona. "Don't worry. I will take the pain away."

"Don't touch me!" Brona yelled.

Macha set her palm on Brona's forehead before she could get away. Wind whipped through the room, and Brona passed out in Kelcie's arms. Kelcie burst into tears as Macha picked Brona up.

"I won't ever see her again?"

Nemain scooped Kelcie up. "You will."

"Where are you taking me? Am I going home with you?"

"That's not possible. I cannot be the mother you deserve, Kelcie. For that, I am truly sorry. But I can promise you that you will see your cousin again. That too I have foreseen. Now, get your cloak and shoes. Quickly."

Nemain set Kelcie down. Kelcie looked back at Doyen, waiting for permission.

She nodded, angrily wiping tears. "Go. We must do as they say."

Little Kelcie ran out of the room. Macha gave a last glance at Doyen. "Thank you for being there for Brona. She won't remember you. Tao will only know a past without Kelcie, and to stay away. But don't think I'm not grateful for what you've done for her."

Doyen didn't respond.

Macha took three long strides, and to Kelcie's utter amazement, leaped out the window, carrying little Brona away.

Kelcie couldn't breathe. She felt like part of her flew out the window with Brona.

Nemain turned around as little Kelcie returned. Between her wings, mounted on her back, was the obsidian sword. Kelcie stared at it, understanding. Her mother had brought her something that could destroy the eye. Nemain waved her hand over her loose black hair, turning the ends to soft down that clung to her back and blended seamlessly into her wings.

Little Kelcie didn't see. She was too busy grappling with the metal clasps on her cloak, her small fingers unable to hook them.

"I hate these things."

With a wave of her hand, Nemain did them for her. Kelcie looked up. "Will you teach me to do that?"

Nemain shook her head. "You must accept that this will be the last time you see me. For your own good, move forward. Never look back. Now come to me. We must go before it's too late."

"Doyen." Little Kelcie ran to her grandmother, hugging her, crying. "I don't want to leave you."

"And I don't want you to leave." Doyen pulled her back, sniffling, dabbing her tears with her sleeves. "But in this, we must listen to your mother. I love you." She kissed Kelcie's forehead. "Blessings. All of mine to you."

"We have to go."

Nemain picked Kelcie up before she was ready. She lifted her tiny frame, placing Kelcie's arms around her neck, her legs around her waist. A layer of feathers cocooned and camouflaged her until all that was visible was the top of her head.

"Hold on tight. No matter what happens."

Kelcie wiggled her hand free and touched the feathery tips

above Nemain's shoulders as her mother moved to the window. "Will I have wings like these someday too?"

The question seemed to surprise Nemain. "I don't know. You have your father's eyes, and his beautiful red hair, but I gave you your freckles." She touched the tip of Kelcie's nose. "Hold on. Here we go."

With a single hard flap, Nemain flew out the window.

The bedroom floor quaked. Kelcie's head spun. She grew dizzy. As her eyes settled, she realized she was seeing and feeling through her younger self. She stared up at her mother's face, memorizing everything about it. Her high cheekbones, long black eyelashes, and strong nose. This would be the first and last time Kelcie would ever see her. She took a deep breath, imprinting her mother's scent in her memories too. She wrinkled her nose. She smelled like gunpowder.

Nemain soared higher and higher until they were surrounded by twinkling darkness. Kelcie peeked out of her feathered cocoon to look down, wishing she hadn't. They were so high. She gripped Nemain harder with her legs.

In short order, Nemain descended, sailing over the Academy for the Unbreakable Arts campus. She pulled the obsidian sword from the scabbard on her back and the scroll Kelcie had seen in Scáthach's office from the pouch on her waist.

Nemain held the blade near her mouth. "All the memories my daughter will lose you shall return to her when next she touches you."

The ruby grip lit from within. Then she wrapped the scroll around the blade. Over the Shadow, Nemain let them go. The sword fell straight down, stabbing the earth outside of Scáthach's home.

"For your safekeeping, my old friend."

Then the next thing Kelcie knew they were gliding over Boston Harbor. Nemain pulled a silver chain from her pouch and slipped it over Kelcie's head.

Kelcie held the delicate silver bough in her little hand.

"You will always have the key to come home, and when you're ready, you will find the door. It is your destiny to meet the eye. And you must destroy it. Do you understand?"

In that moment, Kelcie understood everything. "Yes. I will. I promise."

Knowing what was coming, Kelcie shifted. She was going to fall. But for the first time in her life, she wasn't afraid. She could feel her powers racing through her.

The feather cocoon loosened. Sailors on the deck of the USS *Constitution* pointed up at them.

"They will take care of you." Nemain rubbed her cold forehead against Kelcie's. "It is time. You must be brave."

Kelcie nodded.

"You will always be Kelcie. You will always remember your name. The name your father gave you. But that is all you will remember . . ."

Nemain gave Kelcie a final magical kiss. Kelcie felt the warmth of her powers leaving her, shrinking until they were gone.

Panic struck. Was this real? Was she going to wake up and have to relive all those times without her powers, without her memories, without her friends? Without the school she had come to love so much?

"Please . . . don't . . ." Kelcie squirmed. She started to cry. "I don't understand."

"You will one day." Nemain's eyes watered. Kelcie wondered if she was crying too, or if it was the wind in her eyes. Her mother sounded so cold and distant, as if Kelcie didn't matter to her in the least.

Another kiss and Nemain took away her memories until the only thing she knew for sure was that her name was Kelcie.

Kelcie stopped crying and stared up at the stranger carrying her.

Nemain's tears fell on Kelcie's face as she gave her a last squeeze, and whispered in her ear, "I will love you forever."

And then she let go.

32

THE ABYSS

A BELL WENT OFF. Kelcie's brain exploded. Or at least it felt like it did.

Her vision cleared. Kelcie wanted to dwell on everything she had learned. She and Brona were more than friends—they were family. But her fianna was in the fight of their lives, and this madness needed to end once and for all.

Blizzard zoomed at Zephyr, punching and kicking, but the Charger was so strong, he only laughed. "That tickles."

Grimes fired an ice spear. Kelcie jumped over it, her feet somehow finding the ground, amazed that the sword was still in her hand. Her gaze fixed on the eye. She tore off her gloves, throwing them at Grimes, then hurled an airball, sending her barreling into the hall. Niall resorted to stink-bombing the Orange Crush twins, which left them gasping, coughing, and gagging. He kicked one; Brona hit the other in the leg with an arrow.

Only Pethia stood between Kelcie and the eye. The changeling held it up, taunting her.

"Where do you think you will go that Balor won't find you?"

"He doesn't need to find me. I'm going to find him."

Niall waved his hand at the eye. It shot from Pethia into Kelcie's outstretched arm.

She lifted the fabric. Abyss water leaked on her fingers, her arms, her chest, then puddled on the floor. She set the eye down, the fabric already soaking up the waters. Before anyone could get near her, she dove into the Abyss, taking the sword with her.

Kelcie spun out of control through mostly darkness, the only light coming from the eye itself. A rotating spectrum of blue, brown, green, and black. Somewhere in the nothingness, Striker yipped. Relieved, Kelcie splayed her arms, halting her descent.

She felt weightless, her movements in slow motion. The sword in her hand, she started kicking toward Striker's whimpers.

"Striker?"

Dimitri neighed. Out of the murk came Zephyr's horse, galloping toward her. Kelcie grabbed on to her thick brown mane with one hand and held on to the sword with the other. She had never ridden a horse and had no idea what to do other than hold on.

She felt a tap on her shoulder, then a prick.

"Ow!" Kelcie looked back and found the spriggan clinging to her.

Kelcie wiggled as the little guy spider-crawled around the front of her to latch on to her stomach.

You wanted to meet face to face, did you? King Balor cackled.

Pain paralyzed her. A thousand needles stabbed at once.

"You have to drive for me, Dimitri. Go toward the eye." She fell forward, holding on to her neck.

Dimitri neighed in a way that was clearly informing Kelcie she had lost her mind.

I have some friends who want to meet you too.

Vampire bats swarmed like gnats. The spriggan dove for cover under her shirt, pricking her stomach as fangs sank into Kelcie's flailing arms. She swung the sword, making contact with tons, batting them away, but they kept coming back for more. She slid off Dimitri, taking the sword with her, swiping right and left, but the bloodsuckers were relentless. Biting her back, her arms, her legs. There were just too many of them.

Striker came out of nowhere. He leaped over Kelcie's head,

catching a bat's wing in his teeth, only to be bitten on the hind-quarters, and he screeched.

That cú sith never learns, Balor hummed.

Kelcie held her arms painfully wide, crying for help. "Mistral!" Wind whipped, spinning into a cocoon around her, Striker, and Dimitri, batting away the bloodthirsty vermin until they finally gave up.

The aftermath was bleak. Kelcie ached all over from the bites. Beside her, Striker struggled to stand. Dimitri nuzzled her nose against Kelcie's shoulder. Testing his twig arms, the spriggan was in one piece. He glanced at Kelcie's forehead. A drop of blood beaded down her cheek.

"I'm okay. See, they're all over me," Kelcie told him, holding out her arms.

He broke off his branch, dripping the sap on her wound. It healed instantly. He moved over her arms, dabbing a bit into every tiny hole until her skin smoothed over, healed.

"Can I have that for Striker and Dimitri?" Kelcie asked.

He handed it to her.

Kelcie quickly attended to Striker and Dimitri.

A cú sith on a mission, Striker started running. Kelcie helped the spriggan on her back, swam up to mount Dimitri, and rode after Striker. There was no noise, only nerve-racking silence as they headed toward the only light, Balor's eye.

Kelcie waited for him to strike at her again, to fill her body with unbearable pain, but it never came. Perhaps he knew that wouldn't stop her. The mare closed in. Kelcie dismounted wanting her, Striker, and the spriggan to stay at a safe distance. This was her battle to fight.

"Striker."

He came to her.

"You will stay here. Got me? Protect Dimitri and the spriggan."

He whined his disapproval but obeyed.

She hid the sword behind her back as the eye fell on her.

Energy shot out, hitting Kelcie in the chest. It wasn't painful. Quite the opposite. She breathed it in. All consuming, it was the greatest thing she ever felt.

That's it. Stop fighting the inevitable. You know you want this.

Kelcie's grip on the sword loosened.

A thin line shot in another direction. "Kelcie . . ." Draummorc's soft voice flooded Kelcie with relief. He was still alive, still tethered to the eye. Still fighting, this time for her.

Kelcie shook her head, fisting the pommel. "You're wrong. I don't want this! I never did! *Ta Erfin!*"

The last lid lifted.

She pulled the sword out from behind her back.

Balor's pupil dilated until it was consumed by black. A red sunburst erupted. *You dare challenge me?*

Kelcie was thrown with so much force it sent her spinning out of control through time and space. She couldn't tell which way was up.

"Mistral!" She carved the air, slowing her momentum.

Dimitri galloped toward her. She grabbed her mane, and pulled herself on her back. Balor saw the sword. The element of surprise gone, the only thing left to do was fight him head on. Kelcie buried her fear as she kicked Dimitri, spurring her on. They raced back, dodging King Balor's firestorm.

All four lids started to close.

"Dad, you don't want this anymore. Please! Help me!"

Your father's will belongs to me and now always will!

Balor's furious gale knocked her off Dimitri.

"Stay away from her!" she heard Draummorc cry. "*Mistral!*"

Air blasted the bottom of the lids, keeping them from closing.

"Kelcie, now!" her father growled, holding them open.

With the sword firmly in her grasp, Kelcie sprinted toward the eye. Fire consumed her. The blistering heat too much, she fell to her knees. The ruby grip, slick from sweat, slipped from her grasp.

"Don't stop!" Draummorc cried. "Don't give up!"

Kelcie grabbed the pommel with both hands before it could get away. Then the wind came. Pushing against her, trying to keep her from reaching the target. The pupil of the eye. Kelcie put all her strength into holding on to the sword, and pressing forward. But her father's powers waned. The lids dipped.

"Hurry! I can't hold them!" her father growled.

Kelcie's leg muscles burned, but still she pushed on, inch by inch until she was face to face with the eye. Shaking, she hoisted the sword over her head, and with everything she had left, slammed the jagged blade straight into the center. But neither the eye nor King Balor's spirit even flinched.

"You think a sword can stop me? Say goodbye to your daughter, Draummore. I'm going to kill her now!" Balor's powers surged.

Terrified, Kelcie's head told her to run, but her heart refused to let go of the pommel. The obsidian blade glowed, pulsating until it was as bright as the sun. Shock waves rippled through the nothingness, the sword absorbing every last drop of power until, like a star at the end of its life, King Balor's evil eye imploded, and the lights went out.

Kelcie's chest hollowed. "Dad?"

Her call was met with haunting silence.

Abyss water surged. A tsunami wave tore through the nothingness, heading straight for her.

"Uh oh!" Kelcie frantically mounted Dimitri. The spriggan clung to her stomach. "Striker!"

Striker made it to her side just in time for the world to tip sideways, the huge wave carrying them up and over the crest, into Scáthach's office, and the middle of a massive fight.

33

TAKE OUT THE TRASH

DIMITRI REARED, TOSSING Kelcie off, and galloped out of the
office. Scáthach and Regan were no longer statues. Deirdre
Crane and Tad Fagan were there too, in the middle of the fight.
Everyone stopped and stared at Kelcie like she was back from the
dead, then they went right back to fighting.

Pethia pulled her sword, challenging Scáthach. With pred-
atory calm, their preceptor raised a hand. A sword flew off the
wall into her waiting palm, with plenty of time for her to counter
Pethia's strike. At the same time, Brona and Deirdre went after
the Orange Crush twins, who suddenly disappeared. Brona shot
off a quiver of arrows in rapid succession, anticipating their tra-
jectory with precision.

"Ow!" One of the twins turned visible, an arrow sticking out
of her shoulder.

Then the other did too. "I hate being your twin!"

Zephyr grabbed one, while Deirdre kicked the other in the
middle of her wings, which turned out to be a very sensitive spot.
The fairy fell over, her wings paralyzed. Niall returned swiftly
from the hallway with fairy nets, tossing them over both.

Meanwhile, Tad crawled around Kelcie and underneath
Scáthach's desk as the ice fairy came for her. Icicles raining down,
Kelcie whipped the wind, saving herself, but making a mess of
Scáthach's office. Scrolls flew off shelves, parchments scattered

everywhere. Achila Grimes hovered above Kelcie, ice dagger in hand, when Niall came out of nowhere with another fairy net, tossing it over her too. Grimes dropped like a stalled helicopter.

Pethia lunged, and thrust, jabbed, and thrust again, but Scáthach blocked every shot, looking almost bored. She slid her blade up Pethia's until the hilts locked, then jerked the pommel downward, twisting, using a textbook disarming move. The changeling's sword clanked, hitting the floor. Scáthach kicked Pethia, sending her crashing into the bookshelf.

Fagan ran out from beneath the desk and sat on Pethia's back while Deirdre put her in iron cuffs. Then Scáthach beelined for Roswen, cutting her free.

No one noticed Elliott Blizzard until he sprinted at Regan. She lowered her shoulder, jacking him up, tossing him over Scáthach's desk, right where he wanted to be. Completely drained, Kelcie never heard him coming. Blizzard grabbed her from behind.

"You're coming with me!"

Niall narrowed his gaze.

Blizzard grabbed the sides of his head, falling to his knees. "I really hate you Adders!"

Zephyr whacked him with the butt of an axe.

"Nighty-night," Kelcie said as Blizzard fell over on top of the twins.

Niall had a net for him too.

Coach Blackwell and the rest of the Alphas—Killian, Arabel Wasp, Gavin Puce, and Diccon Wilks—ran into the room just in time to clean up the mess. Killian had a fresh scar down his cheek, but otherwise looked okay.

Coach Blackwell's eyes grew impossibly wide at the sight of fairies. "What the bloody hell is going on? I've been locked in the underbelly of the Nether Tower for hours."

"The Haven Hall Dens have all been locked too," Wasp said.

"Seems we were infiltrated by the Winter Queen's forces. They had Balor's eye," Scáthach explained. She padded over the tattered black linen, soaking up the last of the Abyss waters, then used a sword to hurl it into the fireplace. The fabric caught quickly, the fibers turning to ash in seconds. Perhaps it was King Balor's power keeping the ancient threads together. Whatever the reason, Kelcie was glad it was gone.

"Alphas, Coach Blackwell, Roswen"—Scáthach passed Roswen one of her swords—"bind the fairies in the nets and take them to the dungeons beneath the Nether Tower."

"Wait . . ." Kelcie marched to Grimes. She reached beneath the net, and lifted the bough off the fairy's neck. She then did the same with the other three fairies. When she got to Blizzard's, she yanked hers off, making it hurt.

"Ow. You are a wretch, you know that?" Blizzard whimpered. "That's going to leave a mark."

The fairies and changeling were dragged from the room. Scáthach wanted a full report, but Kelcie needed to hug Brona more.

"Do you know?"

"I remember now too." Brona hugged Kelcie back.

"What's going on?" Zephyr asked.

"Cousin," Kelcie said to Brona, laughing through tears.

Brona sniffled in Kelcie's ear. "I'm not crying . . ."

"Me neither," Kelcie snorted. "But don't let go."

"Never," Brona whispered.

"You two are cousins?" Niall asked.

"Wait, you didn't know? How do you know now? What did I miss?" Zephyr scratched his head.

"Later, Chike. Murphy, what happened to the eye?" Scáthach asked.

It took over an hour for Kelcie to recount all that happened. From the overnight, where Zephyr interrupted every few sentences to boast about their teamwork and survival skills, to what happened when she touched the sword her mother left for her, to the part when she stabbed the eye with the obsidian blade and Balor's power imploded.

Kelcie wasn't sure how to feel about her father. There was a time she knew that he loved her. She saw it in the memories her mother infused into the sword, but he was a stranger to her, and more than that, some of what King Balor said was true. He had abandoned her for the power of the eye.

"Could you please check on my father and see if he's okay?"

"Yes. Of course."

Scáthach scribbled a note and sent it off right away.

"I'll have to see to Madame Le Deux as well. A changeling here all year." Scáthach frowned. "She hid the eye well. The ice that made you sick in the Fringe would've been good to mention."

"Yes, ma'am." Kelcie arched a told-you-so brow at Brona, who shrugged if off.

"How well they plotted this." Scáthach sounded envious. "Waiting for you to come of age, getting a teacher into the school, planning lessons so Balor could put you through these trials, and using the overnight and your own boughs to break others into the school. And then to bring out the eye when you weren't here, leaving the school and all of you in the most vulnerable position." She leaned over her desk. "It was flawless, except they missed one very important thing."

"What's that?" Zephyr asked.

"That when you four work together, there is nothing that can stop you from accomplishing your goals."

Kelcie beamed, exchanging cocky nods with her fianna mates.

Roswen brought Zinger and a plate of mallow cookies.

"You all were very brave," she said. "You made me proud. I'm going to the kitchen to make something very special for lunch. There will be dessert with every meal for the next week!"

"Roswen?" Scáthach started to protest, but she was already gone.

Scáthach sighed. Her desk dinged. She pulled out an official-looking gold piece of paper. "Draummorc is exactly where he should be, in his cell, alive and kicking."

"Thank you." Kelcie felt like a huge weight was lifted off her shoulders. But still, she wanted to see him with her own eyes. "We still don't know how Blizzard found me when my mother made everyone forget I existed. How did he know I was the heir?"

"We also don't know how the eye got out of the Abyss in the first place," Niall exclaimed.

"Interrogations are happening as we speak. We'll have answers soon enough," Scáthach explained, but Kelcie wasn't as convinced. "For now, let's be happy it's gone. Thanks to all of you." She stood up. "If there is nothing else, may I suggest we all take the day off and do nothing? I'm exhausted and my home is a mess."

"Nothing?" Brona said, sounding alarmed.

"Yeah!" Zephyr clapped.

"How about we go for a swim in the Saiga Den?" Niall asked.

Scáthach *hmm*ed. "How about you help me clean my office first, and then you swim? And before you ask, yes, Brona, you can sleep in the Saiga Den tonight."

34

A CURTSY FOR THE QUEEN

ELCIE HAD WAITED her entire life to find out who her parents were, and why they left. In her wildest imagination, it never occurred to her that they might be Otherworldly famous. Or rather infamous. When word spread that she was the daughter of a war goddess and Draummorc, reactions were mixed. Her classmates, like Marta Louisa, Gabby, and even Willow, made a point to be overly nice to her, while some of the upperclassmen, like Deirdre Crane, blamed her for the eye being at the school. Kelcie could've cared less. She was having too much fun with the last few weeks of school.

Kelcie and Brona were inseparable. They were hoping to stay that way all break. The only wrinkle was that there had been no word from Brona's father.

"He only writes when he's on shore. He's probably still out at sea," Brona explained after three notes went unanswered.

"Sure."

Kelcie clutched her silver bough. It was a one-way ticket back to Boston. The rest of the Otherworld outside of AUA was locked to her. She wasn't sure her doyen was alive or would remember Kelcie. With her father in prison, her grandmother was the only family besides Brona Kelcie had left. Her mother didn't count. She would never count. Nemain had been very clear that night when she took Kelcie out of the Otherworld. It was the first and last time Kelcie would ever see her.

When the last day of school arrived, Kelcie still didn't know where she was going to spend the break. Dress uniforms were required for the induction ceremony. Kelcie fumbled with the clasps on her cloak. She really wished she had the power to blink it closed the way her mother did, but alas, she was her father's daughter.

Ollie spun into her room. "Killian's already outside. I can't believe he's graduating."

It was cool how tight Killian and Ollie were as brothers. When Ollie thought Deirdre had done something to Killian, it turned out the Madame Le Deux look-alike, Pethia, had kidnapped him and locked him in her classroom in Direwood Keep, making it look like Deirdre did it. All to trick Kelcie into opening the first lid on the eye.

"And he's going on active duty! He just found out. He's really excited." But Ollie didn't look as happy about it. "Any word on you coming home with me to the Woods?" He extrapolated the answer from Kelcie's grim expression. "Oh. Please tell me you'll be back next year!" He held up a yellow piece of parchment. "I hate being alone."

Kelcie opened her drawer. It was empty. "No letter."

Ollie pushed her door. "Ah, Scáthach left you a note."

fianna three, report to the Shadow.

"A bad sign, huh?" Kelcie suddenly felt sick.

"Your mother is an omen. I would say you were born under a bad sign . . ." Ollie grinned, baring teeth.

"Ha. Ha."

"Oh, come on, that was funny," he bellowed as Kelcie walked out.

She wanted to get this over with as fast as possible.

Niall was waiting for her when Kelcie jumped out of Haven

Hall. His green cloak was pressed, his dark hair combed back off his face. He shuffled his feet, staring at the ground, singing to no one in particular. He looked handsome and very nervous.

"All good?"

Niall shook his head. "We've been summoned to the Shadow." He lifted her chin and fixed her clasp. "That's better."

"Thanks." Kelcie cheeks burned. "Did you get your letter?"

"None of us did," Zephyr said, padding over with Brona.

"Maybe the Queen told Scáthach I wasn't allowed to come back," Kelcie admitted. "I'll quit if she lets you three stay."

Zephyr started walking, waving them on. "Kelcie, we saved the school."

"From an evil I unleashed," Kelcie responded, following.

"True." Brona wrapped an arm over her shoulders. "I hope you do it again."

Kelcie laughed, shoving her off. "You're demented."

Roswen had been busy rebuilding, replanting, re-everything that Kelcie and the eye demolished, but she was nowhere near done. Rapshider and his replenished merry band of trolls were on permanent retainer, which Scáthach groaned about every time she saw Kelcie. Maybe it was too expensive to have her back next year.

Niall padded beside Kelcie with a very determined look on his face as they passed through Hawthorn Field where the school assembled for graduation. Three women and two men in brown cloaks and black pants stood at attention on the platform. Another, similarly dressed, spoke to Coach Blackwell. Bald, with a sculpted goatee, his cloak was embroidered on the lapel with gold thread.

"Who are they?" Kelcie asked.

The goatee is the Queen's Head of High Command. The High Guard. His name is Casper Thorn, and he's my stepfather. The others are the Lead Chargers who report to him, one from each of the five regions in the Lands of Summer. The graduating fiannas get their assignments today. They leave right after induction.

"Your stepfather is in charge of High Command," Kelcie exclaimed. "Why didn't you say?"

He shrugged.

"And Regan gets her assignment today?" Kelcie asked.

Niall pursed his lips. "No. Not Regan."

"What do you mean? She's graduating, right?" Brona asked.

Zephyr answered, "Yeah, she is. Why wouldn't she get an assignment?"

"She has an assignment already." Niall bit his bottom lip.

Before Kelcie could ask him what it was, Striker sprinted onto the Bridge of Leaping. He squealed, happy to see Kelcie and Brona. Kelcie was happy to see him too. She rubbed his ears. But Brona ran into the Shadow where she jumped into her father's waiting arms.

Older than in Kelcie's memories, Tao Lee had grown a potbelly and a long scraggly beard, but he still had the same warm smile. He wore a black leather jacket, brown pants, and smelled salty, like the ocean. Scáthach was beside him. She was dressed like the others on the platform, in a brown cloak. Two ceremonial rapier swords with ornate golden grips hung one on each side.

"Ma'am, you asked to see us?" Zephyr asked Scáthach. "Please tell me we're getting asked back. I don't think we can take any more stress this year. My sister took my bed. Seriously. I have no room—"

"Hold that thought, Chike," Scáthach said. "Let me introduce you to Tao Lee, Brona's father."

"Tao Lee, as in The Chameleon?" Niall's jaw dropped.

"The pirate?" Zephyr exclaimed.

"Privateer," Brona corrected.

Tao Lee laughed. "Today, I'm just Brona's Da." He touched Kelcie's cheek. "I was confused at first when I remembered you. And now, well . . ." He swallowed hard. "You've grown up. You look so much like your father. Brona tells me you're a pulse too. All four elements." He smiled at her. "You're on fire duty in the galley."

"Oh no," Zephyr warned. "You don't want her to use any of her powers. Big explosions. Except air. She's good with that one, thanks to Brona."

"Are you saying I can go home with you?" Kelcie asked, beaming at Brona.

Brona squealed.

"Well, there is one other person who needs to grant permission for that," Tao said.

"She's waiting in my office," Scáthach added.

Niall pressed his lips into a thin line. He turned a not-so-subtle shade of green. His eyes darkened to a deep, rich purple. "My mother's here."

Scáthach nodded. "Afraid so."

"Why do you look sick?" Brona asked.

"Oh," Niall took a deep breath. "Because she's the Queen."

"She's what? Who? I mean, all this time . . ." Kelcie fumed. "Talk about keeping secrets!"

"Yeah, O'Shea. That's not something you drop on your Charger after months! What if I said something bad about her?" Zephyr asked.

"I do it all the time." Brona grinned.

Tao shook his head at her.

Kelcie had a few things she'd like to say to the Queen too, like why was her father sitting in prison when she was the one who sent him to find Balor's eye?

"Well, don't right now, Brona, or Kelcie won't be allowed to come home with us over break," her father scolded.

The hallway smelled cloyingly like honeysuckle. Kelcie glared at the back of Niall's head. How could he have kept that a secret all year long? His mother was the Queen? Did he hide that fact because Kelcie was Fomorian? Was he embarrassed to be friends with her?

Kelcie expected a crown and long dress, but Queen Eislyn didn't have either. Her long brown hair was woven into a work of art. Thin braids with tiny flowers buried in the creases. She wore a black unitard and white cape that hid Niall's soon-to-be little brother or sister beneath. The only jewelry was a gold mantle around her neck with a baseball-sized aquamarine. She fussed over Regan, picking lint off her lapel.

"I hate this hair color. Put it back to brown as soon as we get home. You have a fitting tomorrow. Twenty new gowns, and in the afternoon a meeting with the council."

Regan groaned. "My fianna has been assigned to Chawell Woods, Mother. I have a responsibility to them."

The Queen laughed. "You're the Regent, Regan. You'll be saying goodbye to that life as of today. Another Charger will take your place."

"Would you like us to come back, Queen Eislyn?" Scáthach asked.

The Queen started, then drew herself up. When she turned, Kelcie was surprised to see her eyes were the exact same shape and color as Niall's, only different too. Where his were warm, hers were cold—ironic, considering she was the Queen of the Lands of Summer. "I didn't realize we had an audience." Queen Eislyn grimaced at Mr. Lee. "Tao, lovely to see you again. I'm told Brona was the star of the first-year class."

"Scáthach only teaches the best of the best." Mr. Lee bowed slightly with a wry smile. "So, Regan is Regent? And has been here, at AUA?"

"As you well know, my children's identities and their comings and goings are not on public display, for their safety." That explained Niall's secrecy. The Queen's expression dropped into a stern frown. "And I expect any conversations you just heard of the Regent will be kept a secret until Ascension, Tao."

He smiled standing tall. "Of course, Your Majesty."

"Not a single bet placed, Tao."

He chuckled. "Understood, Your Majesty."

Queen Eislyn's frown floated around the room as she instructed, "You all as well. The Regent's identity must always remain a mystery to the Lands of Summer until then. Am I clear?"

Everyone including Kelcie said, "Yes, Your Majesty."

Niall must've seen Kelcie's confusion.

Regan will be queen. She's called Regent.

Kelcie wondered what they called Niall. Prince Niall? Spare Regent? Although from his mother's chilly reception of him so far, maybe she never called Niall anything. Not even his name. She hadn't even acknowledged his presence at all.

Scáthach took over. "Let me introduce fianna three's Charger, Zephyr Chike."

Zephyr bowed awkwardly. "This is so cool. I thought with a couple of demigods our fianna was special."

Why didn't she say anything to Niall?

"Hello, Mother," Niall said.

"Niall." She didn't look at him. The Queen stared at Kelcie like she was seeing a ghost. "You're Draummorc's daughter?"

Kelcie lowered her head.

"I hear we have you to thank for ridding our lands of Balor's eye. But . . ."

"You wish I hadn't done that," Kelcie answered for her.

"Why not?" Niall asked. His concerned stare flipped from Kelcie to his mother.

Queen Eislyn's lips pursed slightly. Her brow lifted in either appreciation or contempt. "Your father was supposed to deliver it to me."

"You sent Draummorc?" Niall interjected.

Kelcie had left that part out when she recounted everything she had seen when she touched the sword on purpose. She didn't want to hurt Niall's feelings, but it seemed his mother didn't care if she hurt him or not.

"She did. I saw it in the memories my mother left for me. You were foolish to think anyone could fight off King Balor's will. It was now and had always been allied with the Lands of Winter."

"Did you just call your queen foolish? And here Scáthach wishes me to unlock your bough so you may remain with Tao."

Queen Eislyn sighed. "I think not. You can return to wherever you came from, wherever that bough takes you."

"Your majesty," Tao said affectionately. "She and Brona are cousins. Please let her stay with me. I'll keep her on my ship at all times and take her to visit her grandmother in Chawell Woods before we sail north."

Kelcie couldn't believe the relief she felt at knowing her doyen was still alive. "I'm sorry. I shouldn't have been so disrespectful."

"My edict stands."

Scáthach let out a disgruntled sigh.

Niall took a bold step forward. "Mother, unlock her bough. Otherwise, the only place she's going to end up is in the Lands of Winter. Think about it. She's been in the human world since the attack on Summer City. Fairies got to her once before and they'll do it again. And the human world has Sidrals to both realms. Do you want a demigod and a pulse elemental Saiga to fall into the Winter Queen's hands?"

Queen Eislyn flared her nostrils at Niall.

"Niall has a point, Mother, not to mention Kelcie saved the school," Regan said.

"From herself," countered the Queen.

"I am extending invitations to this fianna for year two. They are the best in their class, Majesty," Scáthach added.

For several long seconds, Kelcie saw Niall's mother's internal argument play out in a series of bizarre facial expressions. At long last, Queen Eislyn picked up Kelcie's bough and set it against the aquamarine gem on her gaudy necklace. Four new branches grew. "Fine. Sail with Tao, see your grandmother." She crossed her arms, looking down her nose at Brona's father. "I want her kept on a short leash, Lee."

"Yes, Your Majesty."

Kelcie tucked her unlocked bough safely under her shirt before asking, "I'd like to see my father."

Queen Eislyn arched a censoring sculpted brow. "Your father is not allowed visitors."

"But—"

"No. You ask too much. I will allow you to communicate through letters if you wish. Know that they will be read." She set her hands on her extended belly. "Now, shall we get on with the induction ceremony? My feet are killing me."

A s they left the Shadow, Scáthach handed out their invitations to year two. Kelcie never said goodbyes before because she never had anyone she wanted to say goodbye to. But as she stood beside the Sidral, getting ready to return to Tao's ship with Brona, an uncomfortable lump grew in her throat, making it hard to breathe.

Kelcie wouldn't see Niall for eight long weeks, and that bothered her more than she wanted to let on. He apologized for keeping his parents' identities a secret, but made Kelcie, Brona, and Zephyr promise not to tell anyone else. After what Kelcie witnessed, she wasn't mad he kept it from her. She felt so sorry for him. His mother acted like he didn't exist. He told Kelcie when they met that people treated him like that. She saw it with the kids at school, but his own mother? It was worse than hers not being a part of her life at all.

"I wish I didn't have to go home," Niall said.

"Do you think your mother would let you come with us?" Kelcie asked.

It was a nonstarter with her. He pressed his new pair of glasses up his nose. *Will you write to me?*

Kelcie's stomach did backflips. "If you'll write me back."

He smiled shyly, nodding. *I like you, Kelcie.*

"You really get off lucky with that telepathy thing." She pushed his shoulder, looking around to see who was in earshot. "I like you too."

Niall blew out a long, seemingly relieved breath. "Okay. Then you'll write me. Or I'll write you first. Whatever. One of us will go first. No," he argued with himself. "I'll go first."

"Okay," Kelcie smiled, her cheeks burning, an intense blush coming on.

"Niall!" Regan yelled. "Time to go."

"Coming!" Conflicted, Niall clutched Kelcie's hand, then kissed her cheek, and said out loud, "I'll miss you."

He ran off, leaving Kelcie feeling like she could fly to the moon and back.

If this was year one at the Academy for the Unbreakable Arts, Kelcie couldn't wait until year two.

GLOSSARY

INSPIRED FROM LEGEND

CÚ CHULAINN (COO CU-LLEN)

Legendary hero of Ireland, Cú Chulainn was Scáthach's most famous student. His real name was Setanta. When he was a child, he was attacked by a dangerous dog and killed it, but the dog's owner, Culann, was very upset. Setanta took the dog's place as Culann's protector and the name Cú Chulainn. A son of the god of light, Lugh, he jumped the Bridge of Leaping in one leap, so Scáthach agreed to train him. It is said that in battle he could kill eight men with each stroke of his sword.

CÚ SITH (SUE-SITH)

A mythical hound in Scottish folklore. In the Lands of Summer, they are extremely rare and fiercely loyal. Impossibly fast, magical enchantments don't work on them. In order to capture them they must be physically restrained.

FIANNA

Fiannas were small, semi-independent warrior bands in Irish mythology. This name carries on in the Lands of Summer.

FOMORIANS

A magical race noted in Irish legend, said to wield the destructive forces of nature. They lived in Ireland, both before and alongside the people of the goddess Danu.

GOSSAMER QUARTZ

An invasive crystal-weed that grows two shoots when you cut off one.

GRAPPLER EELS

Eels are technically fish but look like snakes. Unlike ordinary eels, grappler eels have been fortunate to dine on enchanted tadpoles in the frigid lake on the far side of the Moaning Mountains in the Lands of Winter in the Otherworld. Those magical frog babies give the grappler eels the power to both elongate to ten times their normal size and multiply when attacked. However, all clones must be swallowed as soon as the fighting is over.

GRINDYLOWS

Originally from English folklore, grindylows live in ponds, waiting for children to come near so they can drag them under the water. In the Lands of Summer, they are frequently added to stew.

HOFFESCUS STONES

Only found at the bottom of Morrow Lake on the grounds of the Academy for the Unbreakable Arts, they are vital components of all glamourie potions.

ISLAND OF ETERNAL YOUTH

A floating island the gods and goddesses of the Tuatha Dé Danann call home in the Otherworld. It is unreachable by Summer or Winterfolk.

KING BALOR (BAY-LOR) AND HIS EVIL EYE

A giant with a cyclopic eye, King Balor once ruled over the Fomorians in Ireland. Dark-hearted, he tried to murder his own grandsons to prevent the prophecy of his demise from coming true. Even severed from his head, his eye wreaks destruction when opened.

MEMORY BEETLES

Found on Mount Echo in the Lands of Summer; heat their bellies and these beetles will mimic sound or speech.

SCÁTHACH (SKAH-HAWK)

Her name translates to "the Shadowy One." In Irish mythology, she was a legendary teacher of warriors to whom many heroes owed their prowess. Her original school was located on the Isle of Skye.

SELKIES

Found in both Celtic and Nordic mythology, these sea people can shift from seal to human form. In the Lands of Winter, selkies inhabit the Gracelan Archipelago. They are inhospitable and feed intruders to their brethren, the sharks.

SPRIGGANS

Woodland creatures in Cornish mythology. Those at the Academy are a unique breed that grow no taller than an action figure, can zap latent supernatural abilities out of their dormant state, and whose sap has healing powers.

SYLPH

A devious, shape-shifting air spirit.

THREE MORRÍGNA

Sister war goddesses in the Tuatha Dé Danann: Macha (MAKH-uh), goddess of strategy; Nemain (NEY-van), goddess of fury; and Badb (BEV), goddess of vengeance.

TROLLS

Trolls are found in many European and Nordic mythologies. In the Lands of Summer, they call the Boline Islands home. They are renowned architects and clothing designers.

TUATHA DÉ DANANN (THOO-A DAY DU-NON)

From Irish mythology, the People of the Goddess Danu were a supernatural race inhabiting Ireland before the arrival of the Milesians, the ancestors of the modern Irish. Legends say they descended to Ireland riding on a cloud of mist. They are thought to have left Ireland for the Otherworld.

WOOD GOBLINS

Goblins are found in many European mythologies. In the Lands of Winter, wood goblins live in trenches beneath the Dauour Forest, eating everything they can catch.

THE OTHERWORLD

ALLTAR

The name of the original united continent that was split in two by war.

SIDRALS

Sidrals are the common Otherworldly name for saplings of the Tree of Life, which grows on the Island of Eternal Youth. Tree travel is the only way to enter the Otherworld from the human world and cannot be done without a silver bough. Within the Lands of Summer, Sidral travel is the most desired and fastest way to get from place to place. In the Lands of Winter, most inhabitants avoid it at all costs. Bouncing around in tree veins has been known to break off fairy wings, and the roots freeze and must be flushed at least once a year.

SILVER BOUGHS

Keys that open the portals to Otherworldly travel. In the Lands of Summer, silver boughs are clipped branches from saplings of the Tree of Life, while in the Lands of Winter, silver boughs are grafted from the roots.

THE ABYSS

How the Abyss happened is still a mystery to Summer and Winterfolk. The only ones who know are the gods and goddesses, who will never willingly divulge the events of the darkest night that turned the waters of the largest river in the Otherworld into an unending jail, a vortex of nothing.

THE NEVER-ENDING WAR

Should you be gifted a silver bough, note that the two realms, the Lands of Winter and the Lands of Summer, are in an unending war. Their continents split by the Abyss, they no longer march massive armies against each other, instead fighting a more devious game of cloak-and-dagger, infiltrating and terrorizing.

ACADEMY FOR THE UNBREAKABLE ARTS
TERMINOLOGY

ALPHA

Each of the five Dens has a designated leader who is both in charge of their Den and tasked with helping new students learn to use their powers.

DEN

During the test, when a prospective student's powers are unlocked by the spriggans' zap, they are designated a Den. It is where they will be lodged during their time at school so that they may interact with others who have similar abilities and learn from their peers.

FIANNA

A fianna is the unit a student is assigned to by Scáthach. Typically, there are four members in AUA fiannas.

THE DENS

Chargers (blue)

Chargers are gifted with incredible strength and a strong connection to horses.

Cats (red)

Cats can shape-shift into any feline form.

Ravens (black)

Ravens can transform into raven familiars. Some can throw their voices, a technique known as bird-braining.

Adders (green)

Adders' abilities vary the most. All are typically telepathic. While some add telekinesis to their arsenals, others turn empathic.

Saigas (yellow)

Fomorians spark one elemental power or another (air, water, fire, or earth) and if fostered, it will grow. If it isn't, the spark dies. A pulse elemental is a Fomorian who can spark all four elements, but those are very rare, generally no more than one in a generation.

A LESSON IN FOMORIAN

A language as old as time in the Otherworld, but rarely spoken anymore in Fomorian families.

Ta Erfin (Ta Er-feen) I am the heir.
Vlast mian (Vlast mee-an) The power is mine.
Vas (vAS) One
Dvan (dv-AN) Two
Trisan (tris-AN) Three
Cheturi (cheh-TUR-ee) Four
Doyen (DO-yen) Grandmother
Doyan (DO-yan) Grandfather
Maya (MY-ya) Mother

ELEMENTAL POWER-SPARKING WORDS
Caenum (CAY-num) Water
Theran (THER-an) Earth
Mistral (MIS-tral) Air
Ignis (IGH-nis) Fire

FAIRY TYPES

CHANGELING
A changeling can transform into anyone they encounter.

CREEPER FAIRY
Creeper fairies are gifted with the power of invisibility. If born with an identical twin, life becomes much more challenging because if one turns invisible, the other will as well, and vice versa.

DECEPTOR FAIRY

Deceptor fairies have the ability to deliver a shocking charge with touch.

ICE FAIRY

The ice coursing through ice fairies' veins is so charged they can freeze their enemies without ever tiring. Their oversized butterfly-shaped wings are strong enough to fly them into high altitudes where oxygen thins.

NIMBLE FAIRY

A nimble fairy can, if in shape, reach the speed of sound. Although they have wings, they are small, and they cannot fly.

SHADOWMELDERS

During daylight hours, Shadowmelder fairies are impossible to see so long as they remain in the shadows.

ACKNOWLEDGMENTS

A T THE ACADEMY for the Unbreakable Arts, you're assigned to one fianna. But to write a book, it takes many. This story is in your hands, readers, because of the unending support given to me by all my fiannas.

First and foremost, my publishing fianna, Tor Teen. They say it takes a village to raise a child. *Kelcie Murphy* was no exception. A big thanks to my editors, Bess McAllister and Elayne Becker. Your creative genius helped transform this book into the best story it could be. Another big thanks to Rachel Bass and Patrick Canfield, who dove in headfirst, managing, juggling, and answering my endless questions about every little detail on the road to publication. Thank you to Saraciea Fennell and the publicity team, to Anthony Parisi and the marketing team, to art, production, sales, and everyone who has worked relentlessly on my and Kelcie's behalf.

A special thanks to Devi Pillai, the esteemed Alpha at Tom Doherty Associates. We've never met in person, but I want you to know that your support during times of change through this journey meant everything to me.

To my early reader fianna, the Thomas family—Aonika, Sean, Lola, and Luc—thank you for reading draft after draft, and always cheering me on. Your insights are invaluable to my process.

To my representation fianna, Sally Wofford-Girand at Union Literary and Lars Theriot at Industry Entertainment. I'm so fortunate to have you both in my corner. Thank you for all that you've done and continue to do on my behalf.

To my two childhood partners-in-crime, Helen Vermillion and Kyra Rogers. It's impossible to put into words what your friendship meant, and still means to me. Thank you for sleepovers, and night swims. Dirt bike riding through Fort Ward, and roller skating in the cul-de-sac. For seeing Star Wars over and over, and over again because I never wanted to watch anything else. But most of all, for being there through thick and thin, especially when life got hard. You were my constants. My friends no matter what. Thank you for teaching me what real friendship means.

And last, but not least, to my family fianna. To those I don't get to see every day, a *humongous* thank you for all that you've done, and continue to do. And to my husband, Timberlake; daughter, Riley; and son, Jack. Thank you. For everything. You are quite simply the best.

ABOUT THE AUTHOR

Erika Lewis grew up in Virginia, where she spent most of her childhood riding her dirt bike through Fort Ward. She resides in the sunshine state of California. When she's not at her laptop, she's usually playing with her big fluffy golden retriever, running, or at one of the bookstores or comic shops by her house. And always drinking coffee. *Kelcie Murphy and the Academy for the Unbreakable Arts* is her middle-grade debut.